THE FAMILY PLOT

TOR BOOKS BY CHERIE PRIEST

THE EDEN MOORE BOOKS
Four and Twenty Blackbirds
Wings to the Kingdom
Not Flesh Nor Feathers

Fathom

THE CLOCKWORK CENTURY NOVELS
Boneshaker
Dreadnought
Ganymede
The Inexplicables
Fiddlehead

THE
FAMILY PLOT

Cherie Priest

TOR

a tom doherty associates book

new york

This is a work of fiction. All of the characters, organizations, and events portrayed in this novel are either products of the author's imagination or are used fictitiously.

THE FAMILY PLOT

Copyright © 2016 by Cherie Priest

A Tor Book
Published by Tom Doherty Associates
175 Fifth Avenue
New York, NY 10010

www.tor-forge.com

Tor® is a registered trademark of Macmillan Publishing Group, LLC.

The Library of Congress Cataloging-in-Publication Data is available upon request.

ISBN 978-0-7653-7824-8 (hardcover)
ISBN 978-1-4668-6065-0 (e-book)

Our books may be purchased in bulk for promotional, educational, or business use. Please contact your local bookseller or the Macmillan Corporate and Premium Sales Department at 1-800-221-7945, extension 5442, or by e-mail at MacmillanSpecialMarkets@macmillan.com.

First Edition: September 2016

Printed in the United States of America

0 9 8 7 6 5 4 3 2 1

This one is for everybody who's ever loved an old house.

ACKNOWLEDGMENTS

In addition to the usual suspects (spouse, agent, editor, etc.) who have seen their names in these paragraphs a dozen or more times . . . I want to thank the folks from Black Dog Salvage in Roanoke, Virginia. I was sitting around with a glass of wine one night, watching a rerun of *Salvage Dawgs* all alone while my husband was out of town, and I happened to catch the "Check out our website/Drop us a line" note at the end of the episode.

I'd had just enough to drink to take them up on it.

So here's to *Salvage Dawgs,* a show that taught me just enough about the business to be dangerous; and in particular, here's to general manager Grant Holmes—who was kind enough to let me talk his ear off on the phone one fine day.

I know I didn't get all my facts perfectly correct, but in my defense (1) Most of what I know about old houses comes from the restoration angle, and (2) Grant really did do his best to straighten me out, I promise, but sometimes the narrative convenience of monsters had to prevail. So again, my thanks for all the help, and my apologies for all the things I screwed up. One of these days, I'll make it out to Roanoke with a U-Haul and shop my face off, I promise.

She buried them under the marble stone,
Then she turned and went on home.

—From the ballad "The Cruel Mother"
(one of many variants)

THE FAMILY PLOT

1

Yeah, send her on back. She has an appointment."

Chuck Dutton set aside the walkie-talkie and made a token effort to tidy his desk, in case Augusta Evelyn Sophia Withrow expected to speak with a goddamn professional. The owner and manager of Music City Salvage was every inch a goddamn professional, but he couldn't prove it by his office, which was littered with rusting light fixtures, crumbling bricks and broken statuary, old books covered in mildew, stray tools that should've been packed away, and a thousand assorted items that he was absolutely going to restore to life or toss one of these days when he got the time. His office was the company lint trap, and it was no one's fault but his own.

He successfully rearranged a stack of old license plates and stuffed all his pens into an I LOVE MY MASTIFF mug, just in time for his visitor to appear. She arrived in a faint cloud of expensive perfume: a tall, thin lady of a certain age and a certain pedigree. Her hair was silver and her dress was blue linen, something with a fancy label at the neck, unless Chuck missed his guess. Her handbag was large, square, and black—more of an attaché case than a purse.

She stood in the doorway, assessing the mess; then she bobbed her head, shrugged, and stepped over a nested stack of vintage oil cans that Chuck kept meaning to relocate.

Chuck darted out from behind his desk, hand extended for a greeting shake. "Kindly ignore the clutter, ma'am—like myself, this office is a work in progress. I'm Charles Dutton. We spoke on the phone, before you met with James."

"Yes, of course. It's a pleasure." She accepted his handshake, and, without giving him a chance to offer her a seat, she drew up the nearest chair—a Naugahyde number that had once sat in a mid-century dentist's lobby. "Thank you for seeing me. I'm sure you're very busy."

Chuck retreated to his original position, sat down, and leaned forward on his elbows. "Anytime, anytime," he said cheerily. "Projects like yours are what *keep* us busy."

"Good. Because one way or another, that old house is coming down. It can't be saved, or at least, I don't plan to save it. But there's plenty on the property worth keeping—as James saw firsthand last week."

"Yeah, he couldn't shut up about it. But this was your family home, wasn't it?" He already knew the answer. He'd looked it up online.

"That's correct. My great-grandfather built the main house in 1882. He gave it to my grandparents as a wedding present."

"And none of the other Withrows are interested in preserving it?"

"There *are* no other Withrows," she informed him. "I'm the last of them, and I don't want it. On the fifteenth of this month, the house will be demolished. By the first of November, all other remaining structures will be razed, and the property will be donated to the battlefield park. The paperwork is already filed."

"Still, it seems like a shame."

"Spoken like a man who never lived there," Ms. Withrow said, not quite under her breath. Then, more directly, "You mustn't cry for the Withrow house, Mr. Dutton. It's a miserable, drafty, oppressive old place with nothing but architectural details to recommend it. James made notes and took photos, but I have a few more, left over from the assessment when I inherited it last spring. If you'd care to take a look at them."

"I'd love to. He said you two talked numbers. I trust his judgment, but my finance guy balked when he heard forty grand, so I'm happy to see more of the details. I hear you've got imported marble fireplace inlays, stained glass, wainscoting . . ."

In fact, Barry the Finance Guy had not balked; he'd put his foot down with a hard-ass *no*. The company was owed a small fortune in outstanding invoices, as least two of which were headed for court. Music City Salvage barely had enough cash on hand to keep the lights running and cover payroll—and if a windfall didn't come along soon, they'd have to pick between the two of them. There was absolutely no stray money for sweetheart deals on old estates.

Period. End of story.

Still, when Augusta Withrow unfastened her bag to withdraw a large folder, Chuck eagerly accepted it. She said, "As for the fireplaces, only two have Carrera inlays. The other five surrounds are tile, but all seven mantels are rosewood, and, as you can see, the grand staircase is chestnut."

"Mm . . . *chestnut* . . ." He opened the folder and ran his finger over the top photo. It showed a staircase that was very grand indeed, with a ninety-degree bend and a platform, plus sweeping rails that terminated in graceful coils. He positively leered. These pictures were a hell of a lot better than the ones James had snapped on his phone.

"I'm told that American chestnut is extinct now."

"It's been that way since the thirties," he agreed. "It's strong as oak at half the weight, and pretty as can be. Woodworkers love that stuff. It's worth . . . well. It's very desirable, to the right kind of craftsman. I don't often see it in stairs, but I'll take it wherever I can get it."

"Then I should mention the barn, too. It's falling down, but I'm fairly certain it's made from the same wood."

"Mm." Chuck's eyes were full of rust lust and dollar signs. He kept them fixed upon the photos so Ms. Withrow couldn't see the greed and raise her asking price even further out of reach.

After the staircase, he found a shot of a large fireplace. It had a double-wide front, with a pair of ladies on either side—their poses mirroring one another in white and gray marble. He spied a few thin cracks, but nothing unexpected. All in all, the condition was better than good. He looked up. "James said something about a carriage house. Is that chestnut, too?"

"Only stone, I'm afraid. It has the original copper roof, but it's all gone green now. You know how it is—the weather gets to everything, eventually."

He glanced up in surprise. "No one's stripped it? No one sold it for scrap?"

"I don't know what kind of neighborhood you think we're talking about, Mr. Dutton, but . . ."

"No, no. I didn't mean it like that." He shook his head and returned his attention to the folder. "I've been to Lookout Mountain before. I know it's a nice place. I wasn't trying to imply it was all et-up with meth heads, or anything like that. It's just something that happens. Over the years the metal goes manky, so people swap it out for cedar or asphalt shingles."

She didn't reply for long enough that he wondered what her silence meant.

Finally, she said, "You won't find any *meth heads,* no. But the house is just barely on the mountain proper. It's down toward the base, and some of the nearby neighborhoods are not as savory today as they were a hundred years ago."

"At the foot . . . you mean down by the Incline station?"

"At the edge of Saint Elmo—that's right."

Chuck frowned. "I know that place; it's a historic district. Do you have the city's permission to bulldoze the property?"

"It's *near* Saint Elmo, not *in* it. I don't need the historic office's permission, and I assure you, all the appropriate legal steps have been taken. Now, did I mention that the floors are heart of pine, over an inch thick? Except in the kitchen, where they were replaced back in the sixties. My uncle was a very *thorough* man, with an unfortunate fondness for linoleum."

"A full inch of pine? Lady, you're speaking my language," he said, and immediately felt silly for it.

She grinned, unperturbed by his informality, and pleased to have redirected his attention. "Then you'll love this part, too: No one's been inside the barn or carriage house since before I was born. My grandfather boarded both of them up, and declared them off-limits. God only knows what you'll find once you get the doors open."

Chuck didn't dare speculate about her age—not out loud— so he asked questions instead. "Not even a groundskeeper's been inside? No maintenance people? Burglars?"

"I won't vouch for the delinquent youths of outer Chattanooga, but barring some unknown vandalism . . . no. The house is isolated, and the property can be tricky to reach. You might need to throw down a gravel drive for heavy equipment or trailers. I assume you'll want to take the colonnades? The portico?"

He sorted through more promising photos.

Four columns held up the side porch . . . he wondered if they were wood, or carved limestone. They weren't pre-war, but if they were stone, they were worth thousands. If they were only wood, they were still worth thousands, but not as many. He said, "I want to take it *all*."

"Then you'll need a forklift, at least."

"Good thing I've got one. Now, in these pictures, the house is still furnished. I assume all that's been cleared out by now?"

"Some of it. Some remains, but I won't kid you about its value. What's left is too cheap or too broken to pique the appraisers' interest. You can have it, if you like. I know your representative said you preferred to work piecemeal on projects like this, but my offer is all-inclusive. I don't have the time or energy to go through the place and put a price tag on every damn thing, if you'll pardon me for saying so. Anything, anywhere, on the four acres that make up the estate is yours for a check and a signature."

Yeah, but she wanted that check made out for forty thousand dollars.

It was the most Chuck had ever paid out for a salvage opportunity, by a long shot—and he was still waiting for Nashville Erections to come collect (and pay for) a haul they'd reserved three months ago. It probably served him right for tying up twenty grand in a company named for somebody's dick, but he knew they were good for it. Eventually. And T&H Construction still owed him for another thirteen grand's worth of room dividers, bay windows, and a turn-of-the-century door with sidelights and surrounds. Chuck had graciously let them take that batch on credit and a handshake, so it wasn't even on the floor anymore.

Because sometimes, Chuck was an idiot.

All right then, fine. Sometimes, Chuck was an idiot. But this was the haul of a lifetime, and it could skyrocket the company back into the black within a couple of months.

Or it could be the nail in its coffin in a couple of weeks.

But what a nail.

Cash was low—*perilously* low—but the stock at Music City Salvage was stagnant. Pickers hadn't brought in anything interesting in months, and a haul like the Withrow estate would be something worth advertising . . . a landmark Southern estate, relatively untouched for generations. He could take out a full page in the paper. They'd have customers out the door, rain or shine; they'd come from hundreds of miles around. It'd happened before, but not lately.

The pictures sprawled across his desk, glossy and bright.

Ms. Withrow's offer wasn't too good to be true, but it *felt* too good to be true, and he couldn't put his finger on why. He was dying to whip out his checkbook and shout, "Shut up and take my money!" But something held him back . . . something besides the fact that he didn't actually have enough dough sitting in the corporate account right that moment. In order to sufficiently fill 'er up, he'd have to take money against a credit card. Or two. Or all of them.

It'd be the biggest gamble of his life.

He looked up from the photos, at the woman who sat with her legs crossed just below the knee. She'd scarcely moved since she sat down. She did not look tense, or sinister, or deceitful. She looked like a fancy old lady with good taste who had one last piece of business to take care of before she retired to Florida or wherever fancy old ladies go when they're finished with Tennessee.

"Do you have any questions?" she gently prompted.

He closed the folder and rested his hands on top of it. "Just one, I guess. Why me? I know at least two salvage crews in Chattanooga who'd be thrilled by a haul this size. Why come all the way out to Nashville?"

"It's only a couple of hours' drive, Mr. Dutton—it's not the Oregon Trail. But since you asked, I visited them both first. Out of pure convenience, let me be clear—I don't mean to imply you're third string, or anything of the sort," she said smoothly, that highbred accent purring. "Scenic Salvage is closing this year; the owner is retiring, and she declined to pursue my offer. As for Antique Excavations . . . well. Let's be honest. They don't have the supplies or the manpower for this job. They were, at least, direct enough to confess it."

"Judy Hanks told you no?"

"She's the one who suggested I try you. I understand you know one another."

They did, but it wasn't entirely friendly. He didn't really like her, and as far as he knew, the feeling was mutual. "Sure. I know her."

"She said you were an ass, but you ran a competent ship—and you'd have the resources to take care of an estate this size."

Ah. That was more like it. "Not a *good* ship?"

Augusta Withrow withdrew another folder from her bag. "You should settle for 'competent.' It's high praise, coming from her. High enough that I've already arranged the paperwork, based on the details James and I discussed—and I've brought it with me. None of this faxing or e-mailing nonsense. I prefer real ink to dry on real paper. I find it reassuring. So, Mr. Dutton?"

"Ms. Withrow," he stalled.

"Going once, going twice—forty thousand dollars, and you

can pick over the remains of my family estate. Do we have a deal?"

He swallowed. He felt the fat stack of pictures beneath his hands. Forty thousand dollars was a lot of money, but the Withrow house was a gold mine. Maybe even a platinum mine, once he got that carriage house open. There was literally no telling what might be inside, if it'd been closed up for what . . . seventy years? Eighty?

But, but, but.

But the company budget was so tight, it squeaked. But the stock was getting stale. But Barry would kill him, if for no other reason than if it didn't work . . . he'd probably be out of a job. For that matter, they'd *all* be out of a job. The business would have to run on fumes until the Withrow estate started to sell. Paychecks might bounce. Lights might dim. Doors might close for good.

But, hell, in another year or two they might close anyway. A family business was a fragile thing, and Music City Salvage was on shaky legs.

But chestnut. But marble. But stained glass and built-ins and heart of pine. But the big locked box of the carriage house, and everything that might be waiting inside. The magical crapshoot of rust lust tugged at him harder than fear, harder than Barry would. Harder than caution, and harder than common sense, perhaps.

But what an *opportunity*. What a Hail Mary pass.

He stood up and reached for his coffee mug full of pens. While he rifled around for one that definitely worked, he declared, "Ms. Withrow, we've got a deal."

"Excellent! Shall we summon your finance fellow, for approval?"

"Nah. He works for me—not the other way around." Until the first paycheck bounced.

She rose to her feet, papers in hand. "You *are* the boss, after all."

"Damn right, I'm the boss." He took her papers and signed where indicated. He produced a checkbook, started writing, then postdated the check by several days. "I'll need to juggle some funds," he explained. "I hope that's all right."

"Juggle away. I'll sit on the check if you like, but you only have until the fifteenth to get the job done. That's when the wrecking ball arrives, and your time is up."

"Two weeks is good. We won't need half of that."

"I'm glad to hear it." Then, for the first time, she hesitated. "And I'm glad that the things which can be saved . . . *will* be saved. I don't know. Maybe you're right, and maybe it's a shame to see the place go. Maybe I should've tried to find a buyer . . . Maybe I should've . . ." She looked at the folder on his desk, and the check in his hand. For a split second, Chuck thought she might tell him to tear it up—but she rallied instead. "No, it's done now. *I'm* done, and the estate ends here. Believe me, it's for the best."

Chuck handed over the check with two fingers.

Augusta Withrow traded it for a set of keys, and thanked him.

"No ma'am, thank *you*! And I promise we'll do our best to treat the old place with the respect it deserves."

Her face darkened, and tightened. "Then you might as well set it on fire."

She left his office without looking back. The sharp echo of her footsteps rang from the concrete floor as she retreated the way she came—between the rows of steel shelving stocked with wood spindles, birdbath pedestals, and window frames without any glass. When she turned the corner beyond the row of splintered old doors, she was gone . . . and only a faint whiff of flowers, tobacco, and Aqua Net remained in her wake.

Chuck took a deep breath and held it, then let it go with a nervous shudder.

Forty grand was a lot of money, but he could swing it, he was pretty sure. He could rig up enough credit and cash to cover expenses for the next few weeks, until the Withrow stuff flew off the shelves and refilled those dusty corporate coffers.

"It's a gold mine," he reassured himself, since nobody else was there to do it. "This is a good idea. We can do this."

"We can do what?"

He looked up with a start. He wasn't alone, after all. His daughter leaned around the doorframe, peering into the office. "The Withrow estate," he told her.

"What's the Withrow estate?" Dahlia Dutton strolled inside and planted her ass in the same seat that Augusta had recently vacated. "Does it have something to do with that old lady who just left?"

"Yup. That's Augusta Withrow."

She gazed across Chuck's desk. "You cleaned up for her. She must be rich. Hey, wait—is this that place James was going on about? The one in Chattanooga?"

"That's the one. You wouldn't believe it—this lady's just walking away from a gingerbread mansion with a carriage house and a barn. James said we could earn back a nickel on every penny."

Dahlia's eyes narrowed. "How *many* pennies, Dad? 'Estate' is usually code for 'expensive.'"

"It was . . . a good number of pennies, yes. But it'll be worth it." He shoved Augusta's folder across the desk.

Dahlia picked it up and opened it. She flipped through the first few pictures, scanning the highlights. She let out a soft whistle. "Many, *many* pennies, I assume. *Please* tell me this is an investment, and not a calamity."

"Life is full of risks."

"And this house is full of furniture," she observed. "Why's that?"

"It's cheap shit, left over from yard sales and estate clearance." He sat back in his chair. It leaned with a hard creak, but didn't drop him. "We can take all that stuff, too—if we feel like it."

"This isn't *all* cheap shit."

"Well, you're the furniture expert, honey, not me."

She nodded down at the images in her lap. "Some of these pieces are good. If the old lady doesn't want them, sure, I'll take them. I could use some furniture right now. I don't care if it's old and dusty. I'll clean it up here, and take it back to my new place."

Dahlia had just sold her house. It was part of the divorce agreement, since Tennessee is a communal property state—and neither she nor the ex could agree on who ought to keep it. Her new apartment was half empty, like it belonged to a bachelor or a college kid. In Chuck's opinion, it was downright pitiful.

She sighed. "Jesus, Dad. Look at this staircase."

"Chestnut."

"Is it? Oh, wow, that's great . . ." But that's not what she was thinking, and he knew it. She was thinking about the staircase in the house she'd lost, and how it had gleamed in the muted, colored light from the stained glass in the front door sidelights.

"Honey, chestnut's a whole lot better than great—and there's a bunch more sitting out back, from the old barn. There's a carriage house, too. Both of them have been locked up since before Ms. Withrow was born."

Her face brightened. "Seriously?"

He'd figured that little tidbit might distract her. "That's what she said."

"And she must be ninety, if she's a day. Let's round it up to a hundred years, then. What did those buildings hold, a century ago?"

"I don't know. I'm going to guess . . . carriages. And barn stuff."

Dahlia tapped her finger on the folder's edge. "We could pry open those doors and turn up anything, or nothing."

"You'll find out when you get there."

"Hell yes, I will. What's our time frame like?"

"Two weeks." He cracked open the top desk drawer, and slipped his checkbook back inside it.

"We won't need that long."

He grinned. A child after his own heart. "I know, but I expect we'll need more time than you think. We're talking four acres, with several outbuildings. The house is some 4,500 square feet. And . . . I hate to mention it, but I can't spare much in the way of manpower or resources right now. I'm counting on you, kid."

"T&H? The dick joint?"

"Neither one of them's paid up. But," he said fast, "Barry's got a lawyer up their asses, and they have until the end of this week, or we're suing them."

"Dad . . ." She sighed.

"I *know*, I know. It'll be tight for a month or so, that's all.

But once you get the Withrow house gutted, I'll fire off a flashy press release, then we can sit back and watch the money roll in. These places don't hit the market every day of the week— you just watch, we'll have designers and construction guys coming out from both coasts, and Canada, too."

"I hope you're right. Because if you're wrong . . ."

"I'm definitely right. We just have to hang on until we get the stock back here, sorted out, and tagged for sale," he promised.

She might've believed him, or she might've just been resigned to her fate. He couldn't tell which when she said, "Then I'd better work fast. Who's coming with me?"

Now for the fun part. He didn't want her to bite his head off, so he started out easy. "You'd better take Brad, for starters."

"Has Brad ever actually *done* a salvage run?"

"Ask him. He might have. You'll want to keep one eye on him when he's using the power tools; but he knows his shit on paper, and he might be useful if you run into permission problems. The place is right outside Saint Elmo, on Lookout Mountain . . . and the historic zoning folks might get ideas about what belongs where. Supposedly this ain't any business of theirs, but that doesn't mean you won't hear from them anyway, when they see you pulling the house apart."

"Fair enough." She slapped the folder back down on his desk. "Who else?"

Next he proposed his great-nephew. "Gabe's done a couple of jobs, now."

"Gabe's just a kid."

"He's a big-ass kid—that boy can swing a sledge like Babe Ruth. Best of all, he adores you, and he'll do whatever you tell him."

"All right, Gabe's in. Who else will I wind up babysitting on this gig?"

Chuck hemmed. He hawed. "Well, James is out picking in Kentucky this week, and Frankie's got to work the floors. I have to hang around and play manager—and that's my least favorite thing, so you know I don't have a choice. Melanie's got the register and phones . . . and that's everyone we have on deck, except Bobby."

Dahlia stopped smiling.

Chuck squeaked, "Baby?"

"Of all the idiots . . ."

"He's not an idiot. You're just mad at him."

"I judge him by the company he keeps. Besides that, he's lazy as hell, and you *know* he won't take orders from me."

"If he won't, he can pack it in. This is a business, not a charity."

"Bullshit. You never could tell your sister no."

Chuck threw up his hands. "All right, fine—it's bullshit, but he's in a bind, and I don't care how well he gets on with Andy. I'll have a talk with him before you go. He'll behave himself, Dolly."

"Don't call me that."

"*Dahlia.* He'll work his ass off, and he'll answer to you—or he'll answer to me. He needs the gig, now that Gracie's gone, and he's got Gabe to think about."

"You say that like she's dead."

"She's dead to him."

She yawned, and didn't try to hide it. "Jail is temporary."

Chuck stared helplessly at his only child. More gently, this time, he tried another approach. "Look, I know Bobby's not your favorite cousin right now, but it's only for a few days. Let's say four days, all in—including me and the Bobcat on the Doolittle. I'll come up for the last day, and help load up the big stuff."

"That sounds about right."

"Five days, and it's a big house. You two will hardly have to see each other, and Gabe will be glad to have you around. You're the responsible adult he's always wanted."

"He's a good kid," she grudgingly granted. "I can work with him. And Brad's not so terrible."

"Brad's not terrible at all, he's just not a handyman—but we can fix that. He's a quick learner. He just needs the guidance of an experienced professional like yourself."

"Flattery will get you nowhere, and Brad's a quick *reader*. That's not the same thing as a quick learner. Now I'm supposed to provide on-the-job training, too? Maybe I need a raise."

"Think of it as an upgrade to a supervising position."

"One of those promotions that doesn't come with any money? Yeah, thanks." Then she warned, "If Brad cuts off a thumb . . ."

"Then our insurance premiums go up, and Brad types his thesis a little slower. Now it's settled," Chuck declared. That didn't make it so—but a man could pretend. "You'll head out tomorrow, and take the two twenty-six-footers; that'll get you started. I'll drive down on Friday with the forklift, and then we can take down the exteriors."

"You think the trucks will hold it all?"

"I hope not. I hope and pray we fill 'em both up to the brim, and when I show up with the one-ton trailer, I hope it barely holds the rest—and then we have to rent another one. Or steal one. This score's on a shoestring, honey."

He shouldn't have emphasized that part. He knew it by the pair of vertical lines that appeared between her eyebrows.

"Daddy, how much money *did* you pay out for this? Tell me the truth."

"Forty." It came out hoarse. He cleared his throat, and said it stronger. "Forty grand, that's all. Drop in the bucket, on a project like this. A nickel for every penny, just like James said."

"Forty . . . ," she echoed the figure. "Do we even *have* that much money right now?"

"Well . . ."

"Christ, Daddy. This'll be the death of us, won't it?"

"Think positive, baby."

"All right, I'm *positive* this'll be the death of us."

"No, no it won't. You have faith in me, and I'll have faith in you. I'll make the money work, and you'll bring home the golden goose."

She sighed hard. "So you'll do the math, if I'll do the heavy lifting. Got it."

"Atta girl." An idea sprang into his head, and he let it fly before he could talk himself out of it—and before Dahlia could second-guess him. "Speaking of heavy lifting, I've got an idea. Since we're hanging by a thread until the Withrow loot starts selling . . . why don't the four of you go camping."

"Beg pardon?"

"You saw the pictures of the big house; it's furnished, sort of. The contract says the power stays on through the fourteenth, so we can run the equipment, no problem. There's no central heat or air, but that's all right. It's cool enough now that you won't need the AC. If it gets too cold at night, there are seven fireplaces in that old behemoth. One of 'em must work."

"Dad . . ."

"*Otherwise,* we're talking four or five nights in a hotel. Three rooms, and that's because I'm willing to bunk with you when I arrive. It adds up, darlin'. It's an unnecessary expense, when you've all got sleeping bags and we're running short." He talked faster as he warmed to the thought. "You can wake up in the morning, make yourself some coffee, and get started. Head on down to Saint Elmo for meals, and charge it all to Barry's AmEx. Minimal interruption, minimal downtime. Just start in the rooms you aren't sleeping in—work from top to bottom, maybe. Better yet, start with the outbuildings, and work your way in."

"Dad," she said more firmly, cutting off his sales pitch. "It's okay. I've done it before, remember?"

"That's right—you stayed at the Bristol joint last year. But that was only an overnight."

"So? Everything was fine. It's no big deal. We can start early, work late, and get the job done fast. We'll turn off the power and bust out the generators when you arrive, then take the windows and fixtures last. It's totally doable."

She gave the photos in her lap another pass, shuffling them around until her eyes caught on this detail, or that fixture. "What a beautiful place," she said softly. "The bones look great, but maybe that's just the pictures. Did that woman even *try* to sell it?"

"I don't know. Maybe it needs too much work. Maybe it's just not worth it, to her, or anybody else."

She shook her head. "I don't believe that."

"Wait until you see it in person," he urged. "You might change your mind. For all we know, the foundation is shot, and the walls are full of termites and rats."

"You want to change my mind about sleeping in this place? Keep talking."

"Oh Dolly-girl, my Snow White child," he teased her, like when she was small. There was a children's book he used to read her about a little girl who got lost in the woods. Even these days, they knew it both by heart. "The rats will give you gifts, and the bugs will give you kisses. The bats will stand guard as you sleep, and the owls will keep watch from their tree."

She tried to muster a smile, and almost succeeded. "So it's always been, and may it always be."

2

B RAD FIDDLED WITH his phone, alternately pleading
with—and bitching at—Siri. "Chatta*noo*ga," he enunci-
ated, trying so hard to rid the word of his Georgia accent that
he formed a newer, more bizarre accent in its place. Siri didn't
recognize that one, either.

"Don't worry about it," Dahlia told him from the driver's
seat. "It's a straight shot on the interstate from here. We won't
need directions until we hit Saint Elmo, and I doubt the phone
will be any good when it comes to finding this house. From
the way Dad talked, its road isn't really paved."

"Then how are we supposed to find it? Did he draw you a
map, or something?"

"Yes," she lied. Chuck had given her directions, but she
wasn't overly confident she could read them. His handwriting
had never been any better than chicken scratch, so her real plan
was to (a) take her best crack at translating them, and then
probably (b) ask around once they hit the historic district.
Somebody, somewhere, was bound to know the spot.

Brad stuffed the phone away in his sweater pocket, put his
feet up on the dash, then pulled them down again. He opened
the glove box, and shut it again. He tapped his knuckle on the
door's built-in cupholder.

"If you're going to fidget like that all the way to Lookout,
you can ride in the back with our gear."

"Sorry. I'm sorry. I'm just nervous. This is . . . this is weird, isn't it?" He turned to her, eyeing her through spectacles that might've been for show. Bless his heart, he wasn't dressed for demo. He was wearing khakis and a pullover, and a pair of Converse sneakers, as a nod toward some latent hipsterism he should've outgrown a decade ago. He was thirty, but he sure as hell seemed younger.

"What do you mean, weird?"

"Sleeping in the house, while we're breaking it down. That's weird, right?"

"I've done it before. It's not that bad, and it saves a lot of money. So it's definitely not weird."

He played with his watch. It was a nice one. Expensive, with a retro design. He had no business wearing it to a salvage site, but whatever—he'd learn the hard way. "We're going to be there, like . . . a *week*. Does it always take a week?"

"No, but this is a big job and we're short-staffed. Try to think of it as a week of on-the-job training." She smiled grimly, and stared straight ahead at the road.

"I can't wait."

"Try not to sound so excited. Dad warned you, this gig isn't indoor work with no heavy lifting, so a little manual labor shouldn't come as a big surprise."

"I'm not surprised. I'm . . ."

When he didn't finish the thought, she flashed him a glance. "Disappointed? Your résumé says academia. So do your hands."

"Is that an insult?"

"No, and don't take it like one. I always wanted a few letters behind my name, myself. But I only survived two years of college before giving up and coming home. I figured out I could learn more from the warehouse than a textbook, and it didn't cost me thousands of dollars a semester. I got paid for my trouble, instead of going into debt."

She didn't get paid enough to go back and finish. She left that part out.

Brad put his feet back up on the dash. His shoes squeaked on the underside of the windshield as he pressed his toes against it. "Yeah," he said sadly. "It's a lot of money. And unlike us credentialed losers, you won't be paying your student loans until social security kicks in."

"True. I ought to have them all killed off before I'm forty. But no one said anything about you being a loser." Because she wondered, she bluntly asked, "Do you *feel* like a loser, working at Music City?"

"No," he insisted quickly. "I'm grateful for the gig. Your dad gave me a chance, and I know I'm not the sort of guy he usually brings on board. But . . . honestly? This job is only tangential to my field—so I feel like I've gone a little . . . offtrack. I thought I was destined for tenure and a foxy grad assistant, not . . . not . . ."

"Power tools and rust. I get it. You don't have to explain yourself."

"I'm not the puss you guys think I am."

"No one said you were a puss, either."

"Not to my face, so thanks for that." He wiggled his toes some more, then realized what he was doing and stopped before Dahlia had to make him. "I know I'm not part of the tribe."

"You're not part of the family. Right now, that's a point in your favor." The last bit came out with a grumble.

"Yeah, what's up with that, anyway? Chuck said you and Bobby grew up close, but you obviously hate each other now."

She took a deep breath that turned into a sigh. "It's not . . . we don't . . . we don't *hate* each other. Exactly."

"Well, you're awful pissed at him." For a guy with a fistful of degrees, he sure sounded corn-fed when he put two syllables in "pissed." Maybe he kept the accent out of pure defiance, a stalwart middle finger to the academic masses who looked down on it. Or maybe he couldn't shake it, not for trying.

"You're right about that. You want the short version?"

"Short, long. Surprise me."

"Okay, then you can have the middle version: I got divorced this year. My ex-husband is Bobby's best friend, and Bobby picked sides. It's the same old bullshit as always. He's always had this . . . *knack* . . . for choosing the wrong company, and being a little too dumb to keep himself out of trouble."

"I know his wife's in jail. Office gossip, you know."

"She went away for identity theft and fraud charges," Dahlia supplied. "Yeah, Gracie's a piece of work. I never liked her, and Bobby finally divorced her about five years ago. He got the car, and she got Gabe, plus a fat stack of IOUs instead of child support. He was unemployed back then."

"Bobby wasn't working here?"

"Nah. He's worked for us before, off and on—summers in high school, a job or two at a time when we needed a warm body and he needed beer money. But he's only been on the payroll for a few months. Dad took pity on him when Gracie went up the creek, so I guess he came on board right before you did."

"Does he do good work?"

"He knows how to do good work."

"A fine distinction."

"Heh." She started to smile, but the other Music City Salvage truck darted into the passing lane. She saw it in the side mirror, and her brewing mirth evaporated. Bobby was talking in an animated fashion as he pressed the gas, pulling up alongside her. Gabe looked bored. She said, "All you need to know about Bobby is this: good work, completed on time, zero bitching. Pick two."

"Gotcha."

Her cell phone rang, vibrating beside the gearshift with a tinny rattle. It was Gabe. He waved at her from the other truck.

She waved back, and answered the call. "You guys need a pit stop?"

"Dad wants coffee. I could use a Coke."

"There's a McDonald's at the next exit; I'll see you there." She hung up and asked Brad, "You want anything?"

"I wouldn't say no to some coffee."

"Me either. I'm not usually up this early."

When the brief detour was accomplished, she took the lead again. Somewhere around Monteagle, Bobby drew up to pass her, but she gunned the engine and wouldn't let him. She could practically hear him swearing back there, undoubtedly deploying one of his favorite expressions, stolen from a T-shirt, something about how if you're not the lead dog, the view never changes. He was probably trying to turn it into a life lesson for his son, who—thank God—was smart enough to recognize bluster and bullshit when he heard it.

She hoped.

The trucks took the Lookout Mountain exit around nine o'clock, and rolled under a railway pass into Saint Elmo a few minutes later.

It was a cute little place, in Dahlia's opinion—a Victorian enclave built around a tiny town center, nestled against the foot of the mountain. The Incline passenger railway launched from the middle, across from restaurants and a coffee shop. At first she didn't see anyplace to pull over and regroup, but then she spied a big, half-empty pay lot beside the Incline tracks. She pulled over there, and waited for Bobby to draw up beside her.

When he did, they rolled down their windows in unison. He asked, "Do you know how to get to this house?"

"Only sort of," she confessed. "You know Dad's handwriting. You want me to try and find it, then come get you? The road's not paved, and we might have trouble turning both trucks around if we get lost."

"Sounds like a plan." Bobby was always happy to sit around with his thumb up his ass while someone else did the work. "Do you think they'll try and make us pay for parking?"

"Not if you're still sitting in the cab. Pretend you pulled over to take a phone call or something, if anybody asks. One way or another, I'll be back in ten."

She rolled up the window and reached over Brad to fish around in the glove box. She pulled out a red spiral-bound notebook that was beat all to hell, and opened it up to a page her dad had dog-eared. "South Broad Street," she translated. "That's the road right there. There ought to be a stoplight around the bend. The road splits, and the highway goes up the mountain. I think."

"You don't really know, do you?"

"Worst-case scenario, I'm wrong, we get lost, and we're eaten by cannibal rednecks."

"Dear *God*."

"Or we could just stop and ask for directions."

"Or that." He gazed out the window at a row of buses. "I don't know. This looks like a little tourist town, or something. Probably not a lot of cannibalism. Only a few banjos."

"That's the spirit."

Dahlia put the truck into gear and pulled back out of the lot, leaving the directions sitting in her lap. She found the stoplight, marked with a historic designation sign, and a couple of stone monuments she didn't have time to read. Then up the mountain she went, on a crooked two-lane road that was steep enough to slide down, and barely wide enough to hold the twenty-six-foot truck's wheels between the lines. One tire skidded on fallen leaves and ground them into a slippery goo on the median. She swore, pulled closer to the middle, and kept on driving through a canopy half changed for autumn, and still falling by the day.

In another month, Lookout would be bald and wearing a ring of frost at its crown. But this was the start of October, and the air was only cool and a little windy. It didn't even shove the truck from side to side, and there was no need for either AC or heat.

She put the window down again, partly to enjoy the weather, and partly to get a better look at any signs she might otherwise miss. "Keep your eyes peeled for 'Wildwood Trail.'"

"Is that it?"

A green city street sign leaned to the south, bent by accident or vandalism. She cocked her head to read it. "Yup. Good call." She took the turn with a smooth pull of the wheel, onto a strip that was blessed with asphalt, but no medians or guiding paint stripes. "Now we're looking for the turnoff to the estate. It should be up here on the right, in another half mile."

"This says it's covered by . . . a bath? Is that what it says? That can't be right . . ."

"Gate," she corrected him without looking. She'd already

decoded that particular bit of script. "Supposedly there's a gate, but it isn't locked. Like, it's barred off to keep cars out, but . . . you know what? I have no idea what it actually looks like. We'll find out when we get there."

On both sides of the allegedly two-way thoroughfare, sheer rock faces came and went, and boulders the size of toolsheds broke up the gullies and pockets of trees. Finally, beneath an arch of ancient dogwood branches, they spotted a long, rusted triangle with one end lying on the ground. "That must be it."

"That's not a gate. That's a knee-high obstacle, and it's about to fall over."

"I can see that, but I'm still not driving over it," she told him. "Get out and move it for me, would you?"

He opened the door and hopped down onto the leaf-littered street, tiptoeing up to the edge of the turnoff. He looked back at the truck, but Dahlia just waved her arms at him and said, "Go on . . . ," loud enough that he probably heard her.

He bent over and pulled, lifting the simple barrier and dragging it over to the ditch. He dumped it alongside one of the dogwoods, and flashed a thumbs-up before scrambling back into the cab. "I hope you're happy. Now I need a tetanus shot."

"You haven't had one recently?"

"Not . . . *super* recently."

"Jesus, Brad. When we get back to Nashville, I'm running you past a doc-in-a-box to get that fixed. Maybe even sooner, depending on what we find here. You need your shots, if you're going to work these sites. Lockjaw ain't pretty."

He held his rust-covered hands aloft, like he didn't want to touch anything—or he was looking for someplace to wipe them. Giving up, he smeared them across the top of his thighs.

"I was going to say to clean your hands on the seat, 'cause Dad'll never know the difference. But I like the decision to run with your pants. It shows promise."

"They're old and ratty. That's why I'm wearing them. I brought jeans, too, I'll have you to know."

She nodded, and patted his shoulder. "Good for you, Sunshine. Now put your seat belt back on. Let's go find this place."

Starting at a crawl, she drew the truck forward. Its top scraped the undersides of the trees with a noise like fingernails on a pie plate. Dahlia cringed, but pushed forward—and on the other side, the way was clearer than expected.

The road was so overgrown you could hardly call it a road, but it was wider than the erstwhile highway behind them, and the truck's axles were high enough to miss the worst of the brambles, shrubbery, and monkey grass that reached up to tickle the undercarriage. They drove on, to the swishing sound of vines and the damp crunch of rotting branches beneath the tires . . . angling the truck up and around on the mountain's eastern face, where the morning light shot sharply between the trees.

"How much farther, do you think?"

"See those pillars?" She pointed at a tall pair of crumbling stone columns, with one corroded iron gate hanging ajar by a single hinge. It'd once been part of a pair that closed together, but the other had long since fallen and been dragged away or scrapped. There was plenty of room to drive between the old sentinels, but she did it slow, in a cautious creep. Beyond those columns there was a stretch, and a bend, and then . . . at long last, the Withrow estate.

The photos hadn't done it justice, but Brad almost did, when he whispered, "Holy *shit* . . ."

The main house was two and a half stories tall. Once it
might've been blue—but over time it'd faded like anything will
if left too long in the rain. Now its columns, wood slat siding,
and jagged remnants of gingerbread were all the color of laun-
dry water. A rickety widow's walk stretched across the roof,
accompanied by a skyline of snaggle-toothed chimneys—
along with a fat, round turret wearing a spiral of weathered
cedar shingles. A wraparound porch sagged out front and
around to the north side, weighed down by a century of Virginia
creeper, English ivy, and a dull green tsunami of kudzu.

" 'Holy shit' is right," Dahlia agreed.

"You really think we can salvage this place in five days?"

"The house? Sure, no big deal. But the house, plus the
barn . . ." she said, pointing at the property's westernmost
corner. "And the carriage house beside it . . . damn. Now I wish
I hadn't made any promises. If we had a full crew, it'd be easy
enough. But with just the four of us . . . Then again, Dad'll be
here on Friday."

She pulled the truck around so it faced the house, perched
with its back to the slope.

"This place was beautiful once," Brad marveled.

"It still is." Dahlia left the engine running, but opened her
door and hopped down onto the yard. There wasn't any driveway, and no one would care if she left a few tire tracks. The
bulldozers would do worse, come the fifteenth. She frowned at
the thought. "Hey, Brad?"

"Yes ma'am?"

"You think you can find your way back to Bobby and Gabe?
And bring them here?"

"I think so. It's only a couple of turns."

"Great. Then the truck's all yours, if you'll go and fetch the boys. I'll open the place up, take a look around, and start pri-oritizing our demo plans."

"Okay. I'll be right back." He scooted over from the passen-ger's seat and slid behind the wheel, then pulled the door shut.

"Take your time." She gave him a parting wave, but didn't look back to watch him go.

Truth was, she wanted a moment alone with the house, with nobody watching or listening. She tried to steal that kind of moment on every job, and she didn't always get it. Sometimes, she had to say her piece in a busy room, buzzing with saws and the thunk of pry bars biting into paneling. Sometimes she had to whisper it like a little prayer from the backyard, while fork-lifts pulled windows from their casings.

The truck rolled away, leaving her alone in front of the massive house.

She took the handrail and, one by one, she scaled the sinking stairs, where the creaking crunch of bug-eaten wood caused the small things under the steps to scatter. At the top, she found a porch cluttered with seasonally abandoned bird nests, brittle veins of creeper vines, and small drifts of fall's first offerings from the nearby oaks and maples.

The boards bowed beneath her feet as she stood before the great carved door, with its leaded glass transom and sidelights, and she tried not to think of the business—of the butchery to come. She tried not to calculate how hard or how easy it would be to remove the whole door in one piece with its transom and sidelights, or consider what Music City might sell it for. Ten grand, that's the price tag her dad would pick. Ten grand, unless they broke something.

She pushed the numbers out of her head, and pushed Augusta

Withrow's old key into the lock. It stuck, but turned, and the door opened with hardly a squeak. It swayed inside like the arm of a butler.

"Hello," she announced herself as she crossed the threshold, into the foyer. The ceilings were high, and the room dividers on either side had curvy white columns atop them. She breathed in the stale old air like it was sweet and fresh. She came farther inside. "My name is Dahlia Dutton, and I'm sorry about what's coming. I want you to know, it isn't up to me. I'd save you if I could, but I can't—so I'll save what pieces I can. In that way, you'll live on someplace else. That's all I can offer. But I promise, I will take you apart with love . . . and I'll never forget you."

Her words hung in the speckled, dusty air. The broad, open space was gold with morning sun, filtered through long curtains in the parlor and sitting room, each drape as frail and light as cheesecloth. Dahlia went to those curtains, window by window, and carefully pulled them open. Their bottom hems dragged patterns in the dust.

Overhead, just inside the front door, a big light fixture stopped short of being a chandelier. Not enough crystals were strung across it, and it didn't have enough glittering bulk. It'd be categorized as a "large pendant" when it hit the warehouse floor.

"Old, but definitely not original," she observed, her voice stuck in that reverent whisper she always used in old places when no one was around to hear her.

She wouldn't feel so bad about taking the pendant, but much of what she saw *was* original to the house, left over from the estate's very beginnings.

The front door behind her and its leaded windows, those

were certainly first run—and now that she was inside looking out, she noticed a rose-like pattern with trailing vines across the arched transom. "Eleven grand," she updated her assessment. It was one of Chuck's rules: If it's Victorian, and it has roses . . . add a thousand to the asking price. People will pay it.

The staircase, oh, that was entirely original. Like everything else, it was coated in a thick gray fluff of cobwebs, dust, and the sawdust of insect damage, but the chestnut bones were amazing, and when Dahlia put her hand on the rail, it held without the slightest wiggle.

The sawdust idly worried her. Termites? Carpenter bees? Ants? Could be anything, but she hoped it was nothing. It didn't matter, anyway, as long as the bugs had left the wainscoting and baseboards alone. Those bits looked solid enough, and they didn't budge when she pushed her fingers or toes against them.

She looked up past the pendant light, and around the ceiling. The whole thing was plaster, cracked with Rorschach lines radiating from both the southern corner and the light's elaborate scrolled medallion. She knew without checking that the trim would be plaster, too. Unfortunately—it was beautifully shaped, but it'd crumble at the first touch of a pry bar. Oh well.

"Can't save it all," she murmured. "Lord knows, I wish it were different."

Dahlia stopped at the foot of the stairs and mentally mapped the place. She stood at the edge of a formal common area. Beyond it was the foyer and front door. To her right was a large parlor with a worn, round rug as its only furnishing; but she spied a set of bay windows that might be sturdy enough to come out in one piece. There was a fireplace in there, certainly.

Probably one with a marble surround, since it was a room where company would wait. She couldn't see it from where she was taking her survey, but it must be on the far wall.

To her left, she noted a formal dining room. It was offset by an opening that held a pair of pocket doors, or so she hoped. It had one pocket door, at least—half extended, partially blocking the thoroughfare. The door had a wood frame, with glass panels and brass inlay details. If the other door was present and intact, and if she could extract them both, along with their rails and wheels, then Dad could probably ask . . .

. . . but no, she was doing it again, assigning price tags before it was time. It felt sacrilegious somehow, almost like auctioning off human organs before the donor has passed. Chuck had once accused her of being morbid when she told him that. He said you couldn't compare a house to a living, breathing person—it wasn't the same thing. In her sentiment, *that* was the sacrilege, right there.

Standing there in the Withrow house, she felt a deep sorrow anyway. It was an acute thing, a sense of grieving that the great old structure surely warranted. And maybe it was only a silly, blasphemous notion, but the mansion was such a *lost* thing. A sad thing, a tragic thing that deserved a better fate than the one it had coming.

An angry thing.

A chill ran from the back of her neck to her knees.

Angry?

Dahlia spent a lot of time angry these days, but the houses themselves were never anything but mournful. Had she called the word to mind, or had she heard it? Now she heard nothing, only that weird, white silence of a place that's been so long closed up and unloved.

Unloved.

The word echoed between her ears, another odd intrusion. She shook her head, but it rang very faintly, a tinnitus-pitched hum that might mean a migraine was coming, or might only mean that her allergies were flaring up. She chose to believe it was the dust, because she didn't have time for a headache. She carried medicine in her satchel for those unexpected just-in-case times of outrageous pain or congestion; but she'd left her bag in the truck.

It'd come back to her soon enough, along with the cooler in the back, stuffed with water, Gatorade, and Monster Energy drinks. Great for refreshment and popping pills alike.

In the meantime, there was plenty of house to see, and nothing she could do about the cotton-candy stuffiness that crept in through her nostrils and clouded her head.

She let go of the staircase rail, swayed, found her feet, and strolled over to the dining room, hoping for pretty built-in cabinetry. Pretty built-in cabinetry could distract her from a ringing in her ears and the uncanny sense that she had heard a voice say things like "angry" and "unloved," because that was ridiculous. In all the years she'd been talking to houses, the houses had never talked back.

Except her own house, maybe—the one she'd lost to Andy being a vindictive dick, taking it away just because he knew she loved it. When *that* house had spoken, it'd said warm things, hopeful things that made her feel like all her decisions had been good ones, and that she was home—right where she was meant to be.

But that meant that houses must be wrong sometimes, because look how *that* had turned out.

Even though she'd done all the work herself, on her own time, at her own expense . . . and even though she'd saved up the whole down payment and gotten the mortgage herself, rather than going back to school for two more years and having something to show for those student loans . . .

It didn't matter. According to the state, Andy had as much right to the house as she did.

Or that's what his lawyer told her. Everybody already knows that lawyers lie—it's part of the job. So maybe it wasn't true, but she couldn't afford to fight it. It was either take half the sale price, or let Andy have the whole house, and walk away.

Dahlia pushed her own house out of her mind. She had work to do. She concentrated on the clean-stamped footprints she'd left in the dust—little trails from the front door, through the foyer, to the staircase, then back across the sitting room to the dining room where, yes, there were pretty built-in cabinets. A whole wall of them, thank God.

She went to the nearest one and leaned her forehead and palm against it, touching it like she'd reached first base, and now she was safe.

"Safe from what?" she muttered. "Jesus, what the hell is wrong with me?"

Deep breath. There you go: pretty built-in cabinets. Push the fog away; it's only dust from plaster and pollen. It's only an antihistamine away from being solved. Concentrate. Ignore it, and you can beat it. Talk through it.

"We can save these. Some of them." She didn't speculate how many, or what they would cost. "That chandelier—oh, God, look at it. Original, I bet. Somebody wired it, somewhere along the way—but whoever he was, he did a nice job. I'll be super careful when I take that out. And this table . . ." Solid and heavy. Quartersawn oak—with too many layers of varnish, but that was easy enough to fix. It was old, but not as old as the house. "Maybe I'll keep this for myself. I'll find some chairs to go with it, and put it in my new place. My home is not as nice as this, but better than letting anybody throw it away."

She went on speaking to the house, instead of to herself.

She found her bearings again, and the strain behind her forehead retreated to a dull nuisance. A good sneeze might banish it altogether, but her nose only rustled up a dull leak. She wiped it away with her sleeve.

Onward, to the kitchen. She found it on the other side of a door—a Dutch door, which was kind of odd for an interior feature, but you couldn't let anything in an old house surprise you. "People love Dutch doors," she said, checking the fastener and seeing that yes, it worked just fine. It would open in one piece, or just the top half alone. "We get asked for them all the time. People want them for back doors, and porches . . . they want to keep pets and kids inside."

The more she spoke, the calmer she sounded, and the calmer she felt. Back on solid ground, even though she was parting out the body before it was dead. It was awful, but it beat a migraine.

She kept talking, and the headache kept going away.

"The kitchen's tiny, but I could've guessed that. It was all redone . . . maybe in the sixties? Seventies? Most of this is garbage, and I don't expect you'll mind if we toss it, now will you?"

She paused, half afraid she might get an answer, since she'd asked the house so directly.

When nothing replied, she continued. "Anyway, I'll check the attic . . . or wherever some of the old appliances might be stashed, if anybody thought to keep them. I'd love to find an iron stove, or an icebox, or that sort of thing. Oh, I ought to check the carriage house," she remembered suddenly. "Fingers crossed that the Withrows never threw anything away."

Outside, she thought she heard the distant crunch of tires on turf. Time was running out. Soon, she'd switch into boss mode, business mode, whatever mode would get the job done. But for just a few more minutes, this wasn't a job. It was a sanctuary.

This sanctuary had a porch, and a pantry, and a door that likely hid a back staircase. Dahlia skipped those for now. She wanted to see the second floor, while she still had a moment of privacy.

Back to the grand entry with its swooping staircase. Each step Dahlia took added new prints in the dust. Up on the landing, there was a hall with a carpet runner that was a sad and total wreck; moths had gotten to it, so its pattern was lost to the fluffy gray mush the little winged devils left behind.

Now, how many bedrooms were up this way? She began to count, but was interrupted by a noise from outside.

Yes, definitely tires. Definitely trucks, coming past the metal bar slung between two poles, which served as a gate. Tick went the clock, and a flare of anger spiked between her eyes—but that wasn't fair. This wasn't her house. This was her job, and their job, too. But God, she wanted them to stay away just a little longer. No. A lot longer.

She hurried through her resentment.

First door, water closet. Added or renovated sometime in the late fifties, if she judged the Mamie pink and the fixtures correctly. Ugly as hell, but some people really liked that stuff.

At least the sink was savable, and so was the tub. If they were careful with the tiles, and if there was time, they could keep those, too. Some hipster someplace would be fucking delighted.

Second door, bedroom. Bed inside—a big four-poster, no mattress. No other furniture, save a rolled-up rug that was almost certainly as tragic and bug-ruined as the runner in the hall. Third door, jammed shut—but she could open it later. Fourth door led to another room, not as large as the others so far; but something about it—some faint odor, or lingering sensibility—suggested a lady's boudoir. Maybe a dressing room, since the house was so big and (if Dahlia understood correctly) the Withrow family was not. If Augusta Withrow was the last, then either their fatality rate was appalling, or there were never very many of them to start with.

A truck door slammed outside. She shrugged it off and kept going.

Yet another bedroom. This last one was the master, unless there was an even bigger, or more nicely appointed one, someplace else. It didn't seem likely, given how grand this space was—and it had a bay window similar to the one in the parlor, but considerably bigger. The fireplace was one of the two with marble on it, and there were original fixtures left around the room. Antiques, too—regardless of what Augusta had told Dahlia's dad. The stuff in here wasn't junk, it wasn't cheap, and it included a king-sized bed, along with a matching wardrobe that looked like walnut. She also saw two lamps with reverse-painted glass shades, and a cedar hope chest that just *might* have saved its contents from the moths.

Only two additions took the edge off the nineteenth-century charm: At some point, someone had installed a ceiling fan, and a rusted-out window AC unit jutted precariously into the room. Knowing good and well what a Tennessee summer felt like, she was prepared to forgive the retrofit.

"Dibs," she declared of the room in general, though there was no one but the house to hear her. The bed didn't have a mattress, but the bay window's double-wide seat was bigger than a twin-sized mattress. It'd suit her sleeping bag just fine.

On the far side of the bed was a door. It wouldn't be a closet, she didn't think, and upon inspection, she was correct. It was a bathroom, added around the same time as the pink horror in the hallway—circa World War II. When she turned the sink's handle, the faucet sputtered and coughed, eventually producing brownish-red water that went clear in a few seconds. She wouldn't want to drink anything from those pipes, but they'd be fine for bathing, hosing things down, or running the wet saw, if they needed it.

"*Definitely* dibs, so I can have my own bathroom. And good on ol' Augusta, for keeping the water and power on. Or for turning it back on, whatever."

Of course they'd have to shut down the power toward the end, and use the generator in the back of her truck for all the equipment. When the real heavy work began, they'd be cutting into walls. Any live electrical system would be a hazard.

Another truck door slammed, harder and louder than was strictly necessary.

Now she heard voices, easily recognized. A window must be open somewhere, for her to catch them so clearly. It sounded like they were just outside the bedroom door.

She poked her head out into the corridor again.

Ah, there it was, down at the end: a window that wasn't

open, but broken. It was a six-pane grid with two panes missing. No wonder the sound carried so easy.

Dahlia left her officially dibbed quarters and peered through the glass, down at the salvage trucks. They were parked so near to the house she might've dropped a penny on the nearest windshield. Beside the trucks, her cousin, his son, and Brad-who-was-no-relation were chattering about the house's exterior. The porch spindles were cool. Some of the gingerbread cutouts weren't rotted out completely. Nice front door.

She turned away. Her time was almost up, and it wouldn't do to waste it.

At the other end of the hall she found a second staircase, this one narrow and dark. She felt around on the wall for a switch, but didn't find one, so she climbed up anyway. She felt a string dangle across her cheek and shoulder. She tugged it, and an overhead bulb crackled to life, revealing dark paneling on one side, and floral paper on the other. A recessed spot on the wall suggested a gas lamp fixture. The fixture was missing, leaving only a shadow and a warm-looking stain.

Out on the front lawn, someone called for her attention. "Dolly? You in there?"

It was Bobby, who damn well knew better than to call her that. She declined to respond. Really, she couldn't possibly hear him, inside that stairwell that was scarcely wide enough for her to walk without rubbing her shoulders on the walls. That was her story, and she was sticking to it.

Her boots were heavy, and so was their echo on the steps, and under them. She paused, kicked gently, and yes—it was hollow under there. Storage? She hoped so. People leave great things behind in storage, when they're done living someplace.

At the top, a trapdoor stopped her.

She pushed her palm against it and it moved easily, letting her up inside a spacious semi-finished attic. It was mostly empty, with no promising crates, trunks, or boxes; but she saw stray books, and the suggestion of toys. Old toys could be worth a mint. She'd take a closer look later on.

She stood on the stairs, her head and shoulders in the naked space—all of it lit by the attic windows (not leaded, not valuable) and as dusty as everything else. It was warmer by a few degrees up there, which made the air feel stuffy. In the exposed rafters overhead, she saw elaborate spiderweb clusters, nets, and balls; and she detected the nibble marks of rats or squirrels (please let it be squirrels) and, along the floor, droppings from the same (probably rats).

"Rats aren't so bad," she told herself, and mostly meant it. "The rats will give you gifts, and the bugs will give you kisses. Right, Dad?" Could be worse. Could be rabid raccoons, or needle-toothed possums. Besides, any rats in the Withrow house wouldn't be the big black plague rats of lore, but little brown wood rats from the mountain. Give 'em fluffy tails, and you'd feed 'em peanuts in the park.

"Dahlia?"

This time it was Gabe calling her name. She dropped the trapdoor back into place and headed down the stairs—then over to the broken window, which opened when she yanked on the latch. She hung her head out, and hollered: "Up here, boys. Come on in, and take a look around."

"We can't." Brad shielded his eyes against the sunny morning glare. "You locked us out."

"I did no such thing . . . ?"

"Then the door locked behind you. Come on down here and let us in," Bobby pleaded.

"Well, shit. Hang on."

Dahlia left the window to stand at the top of the grand staircase and gaze across the first floor. The door was, in fact, closed. Had she shut it? No, she was pretty sure she'd left it ajar . . . but then again, old places, old floors, old frames, old hinges. She hadn't heard it move, but that didn't mean that the wind, the warped wood, or some quirk of gravity hadn't seen fit to shut it anyway.

She took the stairs slower than she could have, stalling the inevitable every step of the way. She didn't want to let them in. She didn't want to start work on the Withrow house. This wasn't some favor she was doing for an old friend; this wasn't a restoration gig to preserve a landmark. This was a vivisection, a slow slaughter of a thing on its last legs. She loved the house, and she loved all its parts, so she hated her job, this time. She didn't want to take anything. She wanted to fix everything, but that wasn't up to her.

The door was indeed locked. Its dead bolt was turned.

Maybe she'd shut the door without thinking. All right, *maybe*—but Dahlia was about 90 percent sure she hadn't done the dead bolt. Ten percent was a hefty margin of error, though, and she'd been lost in her own head, hadn't she?

Lost.

The house was insistent, but its defensive resources were few.

On second thought, Dahlia knew good and well that she must've locked up without thinking about it after all. It was exactly the kind of thing she'd do. She was still dragging her feet. Still barricading forts that had already fallen. Scavenging mementos. Harvesting organs.

But it was like she'd told the house in the first place: It wasn't her decision to make; it was just her job to sift through what was left. Did that make it easier, thinking of herself as more archeologist, less grave robber? It still sucked.

She unlocked the door. "Come on in, guys."

3

I<small>T'S ABOUT TIME</small>," Bobby grumbled. "We've been out there yelling for you for, like, ten minutes."

"No you haven't."

Gabe agreed with Dahlia. "Don't listen to him; we just got here. Man, this place is huge!"

Brad brought up the rear, crowding them all into the foyer. For some reason, no one was in any great hurry to go any farther. "It's almost 4,500 square feet, that's what Chuck said."

"And that's just the house—never mind the outbuildings." A gust of wind took hold of the door, but Dahlia caught it, and closed everyone inside. The wind still pushed, so she reached for the dead bolt. It stuck, and wouldn't move even when she shoved it with her palm.

"Damn . . . ," Gabe said. He strolled forward, into the empty formal room. "Dahlia, you were busy in here."

His father added, "*Really* busy."

She struggled with the lock for a moment more, working it back and forth until it surrendered. "I poked around a little. Tried to get a good sense of the place, so we can get our priorities in order. I figure we start with the barn and carriage house. Once we're done with those, we move inside and take the marble fireplaces."

As if he hadn't heard her, Brad asked, "Would you *look* at that floor . . . ?" He lifted his voice at the end, turning the suggestion into a query.

Dahlia finally turned around to see what the fuss was about.

The floor wasn't just crisscrossed with footprints in the dust—it was scored in a large pattern like a wobbly figure eight, drawn in the drag marks of somebody's feet.

"Oh. That." She shrugged. "With all this dust, every little move you make shows up. Which reminds me: No one gets started on any cutting or removal without a mask. There's probably asbestos, mold, you name it up in here."

"But, seriously," Brad insisted. "What were you doing in here?"

"Sometimes I pace around when I'm thinking." *Or talking to myself, or to houses.* She didn't say that out loud.

"In a figure eight?"

"It's as good a shape as any."

Gabe frowned. "Looks like you've been ballroom dancing."

"Yes. I was ballroom dancing in my work boots." She whapped him gently on the shoulder, and ignored the pathway in the dirt. "Then I did a little tango into the dining room, pirouetted through the kitchen, and sambaed up the stairs. Come on, I'll show you."

She gave her crew the same cursory tour she'd taken alone, and made sure to declare vocal dibs upon the master suite. Brad took one of the other rooms. Bobby wanted to double up with Gabe, but he said no. He wanted the attic.

"But there's bats up there, and Christ knows what else. You'll wake up in the morning with rabies," his father warned.

"I don't care. I don't want to share with nobody."

Dahlia shook her head. "Your dad's right—and that's something I won't say every day, so you may as well listen. Why don't you take that little dressing room—or see what's behind door number three, if you want your own space? The door's stuck, but you're a big boy. You can shove it open. We'll have to get in there eventually, anyhow."

He shot a side-eye toward the attic stairs, then back at the jammed door in the hallway. "I'll check the room out later," he semi-relented. "There's plenty of time."

"True," Dahlia agreed, and she headed back downstairs, the rest of the crew following behind her. "But only *sort of.* We need to get started, if we're going to stay on schedule and budget. Let's open the trucks, pull out the bolt cutters, and check the carriage house. Then we can start making lists, and getting more specific with our task plan."

"Is there any power out there?" Brad asked.

"I'd be shocked to find any," she said. "To the best of my knowledge, we only have power and water for the house."

Then Gabe wanted to know, "Are we going to turn off the water when we get inside the walls? Like we do the electricity?"

She tromped down the last of the stairs, leaving fresh prints across the figure eight and muddying its shape. "Maybe, but I haven't seen any bathroom or kitchen fixtures to get excited about. They're all mid-century, but not in a good way."

Bobby darted around her, heading for the front door. "Some people *like* mid-century. And this family was shitting in high cotton. Even if the fixtures are ugly, I'm sure they're good quality stuff. We ought to take them with us."

"And we might, but only as a last resort—and only if there's room. We're here for last century, not mid-century. Or . . . the century before last, technically. Stupid millennium."

"We'll have plenty of room," he said stubbornly.

"We'd better *not.* We ought to be able to fill the trucks and then some, without ever resorting to that other junk." She pushed past him, reaching the front door first, and grinning like it was some kind of victory. She drew back the bolt and wrenched it open. She paused at the threshold, but didn't look back when she spoke. "Everybody get that? Kitchens and baths are last resort. Don't let Bobby tell you different."

"Fuck you."

Now she turned around. "That's not a nice thing to say to your boss."

"Uncle Chuck's my boss."

"Uncle Chuck isn't here, and you've already had a talking-to about that. Now open your goddamn truck. I think you've got the pry bars and cutters back there. Gabe, lend me a hand, if your dad's gonna be a pain in the ass."

"Yes ma'am."

Bobby glared at Gabe, who ignored him while he unlatched the back of the truck and hoisted the door up overhead.

Bobby reached inside and drew a toolbox out of the back, its metal corners dragging with a screech along the truck bed. "This is what they call a hostile work environment—you know that, don't you?"

"Nobody here gives a good goddamn, Robert."

"If you don't call me Robert, I won't call you Dolly."

"Fine. That's a deal."

Brad looked like he wanted to open his mouth and say something, but he wasn't stupid. He wasn't family.

Dahlia stopped by her own truck for the satchel she used as a purse, because she felt naked running around without it, and she still wanted an antihistamine. Her phone was in there, anyway. Dad wanted pictures, and she needed to take some.

Everyone else picked up something useful but heavy—crowbars, bolt cutters, sledgehammers—and added work gloves and masks to the pile.

This first trip around the property was a survey mission. Over the years, she'd learned the hard way that the best use of her time was to get a plan in order, then get to work. Diving right in was more her dad's style, but she was working on him; one of these days, he was bound to admit the useful glories of a list and an itinerary. Maybe one of these days real soon, if she could break down and cram enough Withrow stuff into the trucks before he got there—but that would all depend on what they found in those two tantalizing structures.

Across the great yard they all traipsed, and when they reached the carriage house, Gabe whistled like he was impressed. "It's even bigger, up close. They must've had some big-ass carriages."

"High cotton," Bobby reminded him. "Nothing but money, these people. This was the four-car garage of its time."

Brad offered the bolt cutters to Gabe, since he'd shown the most interest. "A lot of these old things were converted for vehicles, usually in the twenties and thirties."

Gabe examined the loosely hanging padlock. He positioned the bolt cutters and snipped the thing off with a hearty press. "Uncle Chuck said it'd been closed up for eighty years."

"That's what the Withrow lady told him." Dahlia stepped forward and drew a corroded chain down and away, dropping it into the grass. "Now, let's get all hands on deck for these doors, boys. They're heavy as hell, and the hinges are broke, to boot."

"Hang on a sec," Gabe offered, and took up a position beside her.

Brad reluctantly joined Bobby on the other door. He couldn't figure out where to put his hands for the best leverage, but he made an honest go of it. "On the count of three?" he suggested.

On three, all four people pulled, and the great double doors split open like a wound. They cracked, splintered, and scraped along the ground, just far enough to admit the whole party standing shoulder to shoulder.

Dahlia would've preferred a wider opening for the sake of the light, but that wasn't in the cards just yet. She was fairly confident they'd have to cut out the doors with a Sawzall or just pry them free when they needed more clearance. They weren't chestnut like the barn, and they weren't worth saving.

She stepped forward into the long-closed building, casting a weird, short shadow in front of herself. One by one, her companions did likewise.

Brad pulled a mask out of his back pocket and held it up to his face. Before Bobby could make fun of him, Dahlia said, "Hey, good idea. Masks on, folks."

"Are your allergies acting up?" Bobby asked.

She couldn't tell if he was being an ass, just curious, or even trying to be friendly—which was possible. He could be a kiss-ass when it suited him. "Always, but nobody needs a noseful of paint chips and termite shit. There's nothing manly about a fungal infection, so everybody's going to suck it up and be safe. Now, let's uncover these windows and let a little light in here . . ." She looped her own mask around the back of her head, so the rest came out muffled. "So we can see what we've got to work with."

With nothing but the narrow wedge of sun behind her, she saw only a lumpy jumble of junk and big, dark shapes lined up in rows, with paths running between them. Dahlia thought there might be wheels, table or chair legs, and maybe some doors, but the rest of the details eluded her, no matter how hard she stared.

With feeble optimism, Gabe tried, "You said you'd be shocked if there was any power out here. Oh, wait, I get it: *shocked.*"

"No pun was intended," she said. "But we're definitely out of luck."

His dad confirmed, "Yeah, I didn't see any lines running from the house."

"Me either," Dahlia muttered. "So it's daylight and flash-light, or no light for us."

She took a pry bar to the nearest boarded-up window, and pulled the boards down in under a minute. To her left and right, the guys each picked a spot to do likewise. Soon they had a whole row of east-facing portals sucking up the late-morning sun.

It was enough to get started.

"Good God, what's this over here?" Bobby asked everyone and no one in particular. He pulled a pair of screen doors loose and pushed them aside; their wire mesh collapsing to rusty particles when they hit the dirt floor. "It looks like part of a truck. Or . . . a whole truck? Buried under all this junk?"

Brad hopped to his side. "Something from the early twenties," he assessed with a squint. "Garage gold, if it's intact." While Bobby excavated the vehicle, Brad scoped out another nearby pile. "I think there's an armoire over here. It's under a bunch of windows, and a ladder, and . . . is that a cupola?"

Dahlia raised an eyebrow. "Are you kidding?"

"Probably went on top of this place, or the barn, or some other outbuilding that's no longer standing. It's not very big . . ." He stood beside it, demonstrating that it was only as tall as his shoulders.

"Is there a weather vane?"

"Nope. There's a notch for one up top, but it's missing."

"Maybe we'll find it later." She wandered farther down the line, scanning the ancient tangle of detritus. Broken statuary here, horse tack there. Farming or gardening equipment—it was hard to say precisely what kind. A narrow, curved object standing up on one end—and leaning against a row of crumbling wood shelves.

Gabe came up behind her, and squinted at it. "What's that?"

"Looks like a bridge. The kind you put over a runoff gulley, or in a garden."

"Huh. Well hey, I've found something cool over here. Come check it out."

Back around another corner, almost beyond the sunlight's assistance, Gabe showed off a rowboat filled with doorknobs, a metal fan, and half a dozen cracked slabs of stone. "Here we've got the S.S. . . . something or another. I can't read it. The paint's all come off."

"I can't tell, either." She picked at a flake, and it fell to the ground. The boat was yellow once, with white trim and black letters to tell its name. She thought the wood might be maple or pine, but it was hard to tell in the dark.

"What's with all the doorknobs?" Gabe asked.

"Heaven only knows." She dragged a gloved hand through the little pile, and was pleased to see the glint of brass and scrollwork. "But they're old, and they're lovely. We'll take 'em. I wonder what these . . ." Her voice trailed away as she pushed at the topmost stone slab. It only moved half an inch, but Gabe added his weight to the effort, and it scooted aside.

Their little corner of the carriage house went quiet.

Gabe whispered, "It looks like a tombstone."

She wiped the back of her hand across the freshly exposed surface, but that didn't reveal any clues like scrollwork or letters. "Maybe? I don't see any names or dates. But it's the right kind of stone, and the right shape."

"They're all the same," Gabe noted. "What's that, four or five of them?"

"Yeah. I don't know, they might be something else. Paving stones for a garden? We found that bridge over there, after all. Once upon a time, this place might've been landscaped out the wazoo. Anyway, if they *are* tombstones, they aren't very big."

"Maybe they're for kids."

"Wow, you're morbid." She elbowed him in the ribs, but gently, and with a smile. "Good find, sweetheart. I'm going to make one more pass, and then go get the lanterns. You stay here and pick a few big items we can yank out into the yard so we can clear out some room to work."

She left the shadow of the dark structure and stomped back into the sun.

The day was getting warmer, but it wouldn't top seventy degrees by suppertime, and the sun would have tipped behind the mountain before that. The entire estate sat in Lookout's shadow, where it was cooler and darker than the rest of the city, even in summer.

The steep grade did something funny to the light, Dahlia thought. It spilled between the half-naked trees in a warm yellow glow, but vanished too soon, leaving a dry grayness in its wake. Or maybe it was just the season—the smell of fall coming in fast, and winter sneaking up behind it—that made everything feel so sharp and loud: the distant sound of a train calling out as it crossed the overpass, and the sound of the Withrow house itself, neglected and angry and unloved.

The grass was high enough to slap against Dahlia's knees when she trudged through it, back across the yard to the trucks parked side by side on what should've been the front lawn, but was now just a derelict space where the only things that grew were overgrown. But that's what happened when you stopped working against the weather in Tennessee. It all got away from you, and the land went back to seed faster than you'd ever think. You leave it alone for a few years, and this is what you get.

It was a wonder that things weren't worse. It was nothing short of a miracle that any paths remained at all, and the creeping vines hadn't yanked the siding loose from every wall.

She rolled up the truck's back door and pulled out three or four LED lanterns, bright enough to bring daylight to the carriage house, even in its farthest corners. She slung a couple of head lamps onto her wrist, too, in case anybody wanted one, then closed the truck again. She wasn't sure why—they hadn't seen another living soul, but it was habit. She was always more cautious than she really needed to be, or that's what Andy would've said, back when he was still her husband.

Boring and stuck in her ways. Control freak. Totally OCD. That's what he did say, after the papers were signed. But, seriously, fuck *him*.

It was a beautiful day, and this part of the job was nothing but fun. She might as well enjoy it. She might as well enjoy something.

Arms full and heart almost light, she headed back to the carriage house. It was right across the yard, but she didn't take the straight path because she saw a trail worn into the grass. It could've been a leftover walkway—or, more likely, where deer came and went often enough to leave a notch.

Taking the trail was easier than lugging all that stuff through the thick grass, and it only took her ten yards out of her way. It was a nice opportunity to see more of the grounds. They were beautiful and mostly quiet, except for the distant hum of traffic every now and again, when someone hit the brakes or the horn over on Ochs Highway. The trees rustled in the wind, and the ground was dry enough that there wasn't any mud to hang onto her heels.

Might as well take the long way around.

The mountain was just beginning to turn a sharp red all around her, with undercurrents of orange and yellow burning through the forest foliage. In another month it'd all be brown. In another month, those little flashes of color would fall, and rot to mulch.

Except.

Dahlia knew in a blink that something else was on the mountain, moving with the breeze. There was a flash of a different yellow. Butter yellow. It flowed; it didn't flutter.

She froze, and the lanterns clanked together in her arms.

She'd glimpsed it, but she couldn't have said what it was. It was only there for an instant: an impression of someone at the edge of her vision, off to the left. Almost behind her, but not quite. She looked back that way, harder, watching the scenery for another hint of fabric. Yes, *that's* what it was. A dress or a skirt. A scarf. Something cotton and light, for summer—not darker, and thick for autumn.

She didn't see it again, but she spied something else: a suggestion of shapes in the underbrush, something solid and straight-edged beneath a winding, twisted rose tree that'd grown to the size of a car. Her forehead furrowed, making those sharp "elevens" between her eyebrows that she'd always had, and always hated.

Andy used to tell her she ought to Botox it, just to see what it was like. It might be pretty. She'd replied that he ought to wax his balls. By the same rationale, that could look nice.

Goddammit, there he was again, worming into her thoughts unwanted.

Goddam him, in particular.

She set the lanterns down in the grass and gravel near the rose tree, letting the head lamps slide from her wrist. Grateful for her work gloves, she pushed the lowest thorny branches aside, and brushed a smattering of twigs and leaves away from a large, oval tombstone.

She could've pretended it was something else, but why bother?

It'd fallen, and it'd been chewed up by the seasons, but she could still read the face: PFC REAGAN H. FOSTER, 1897–1915. The military logo was worn, but still visible. He'd been eighteen years old, and in the army. He'd likely died in World War I.

"Aw." She scooted over to its side. Call it superstition or politeness, but she didn't want to stand on anybody's grave, if she could help it. "Poor kid. Barely any younger than Gabe."

Dahlia's knees cracked when she stood up straight again. With her hands on her hips, she surveyed the rest of the area. It was a level corner of the lot, with several more roses and a lilac or two planted haphazardly . . . or, no, not haphazardly. They were planted deliberately, on an incomplete grid.

She tiptoed through the site, and found another stone. This one was facedown, so she couldn't read it. When she tried to turn it over, she disturbed some worms, then swiftly lost her grip. The marker collapsed back into the earth with a thud, but beside it, a broken nub was hidden by the grass. She didn't see the top of the stone, but the bottom bit read, "his everlasting arms."

She squeezed herself between two small trees, and three more tombstones revealed themselves—all with military insignias, all with dates in 1917. And over by the trunk of an oak tree that must've been a hundred years old when it fell . . . there were two others, both belonging to women, Mary Joanne Alber and Christina Fay Wright. If they were related, there was no indication.

Pieces of at least four other stones littered the remains of a paving stone path. Dahlia was just starting to hunt for more when Brad said her name. He only spoke it, not called it, but she jumped. She hadn't heard him approach.

"What are you doing?" he asked.

Flustered, she replied, "I found a cemetery. I didn't know . . . well, it wasn't in the paperwork."

He perked right up. "What? Where? I don't see . . . ," he began, but his eyes landed on the rose tree, and the things beneath it.

"I counted about a dozen graves, but I only just started looking."

"And your dad didn't mention it?"

"Maybe he didn't know about it. Some of the stones are from the First World War, but others seem to belong to random people. I don't see the Withrow name on any of them. But . . ." She used her hand to shade her eyes, and scanned the area. "There could be more. I can't tell how far back the plot goes."

"Yeah, this is pretty overgrown. How'd you find it?"

She thought again of that flicker, a billowing flap of light fabric. It might have had flowers on it. Or was she only making up details after the fact? "I . . . um . . . I thought I saw something. Out of the corner of my eye, you know. Figured I'd go take a look."

"A hidden cemetery is pretty cool, but it's no good to us, is it? We can't take the stones back to Nashville."

"Of course we can't. It's just strange, that's all. I wonder what the demo crew will do about it when they tear everything down."

Brad shrugged and picked up the LED lanterns where Dahlia had dropped them into the grass. "Probably the same thing the Withrows have done for the last hundred years: Ignore it, and forget about it. Let the woods have it."

"They can't, if it's an open cemetery. They have to cordon it off, preserve it, something like that. There are laws about that kind of thing—and, besides, if we need to make a path for Dad and the big trailer . . . it'll cut right across this part of the property. I'd better call home, or maybe Ms. Withrow herself. We might have a problem."

The lanterns jangled in his hand. "Why would we put the pathway here?"

"Where else would it go? The Dooley probably won't fit through the main pass, so it'll have to come around that bend, instead. Even if by some miracle it *did* squeak through the squeeze—the demo crew will need a wider route to bring in the bulldozers when they come for the teardown later this month." The idea of a cemetery holding up the demolition was almost a little ray of sunshine. "Ms. Withrow's timeline for destruction might require some adjustment."

"Ours doesn't. Not yet."

"I know." She joined him on his walk back to the carriage

house. "I'll drop Dad a line tonight or tomorrow, and we'll figure it out from there. Anyway, I guess my smoke break's over—it's back to work for me."

"You don't smoke. Wait, does anybody here smoke?"

"No, but a smoke break sounds better than a cemetery break, doesn't it?"

"No way. I'd rather take a cemetery break any day of the week."

She nodded approvingly. "And that's why we like you, Brad."

Together Dahlia and the guys passed the next few hours in the carriage house, dragging piece after piece of promising loot and outright junk into the relative brightness of the lawn. Once there, it was easier to check the condition and potential of everything, unencumbered by the lamps and lanterns and masks—though they needed the extra lights less and less, as the first floor grew emptier and the light from the windows had more room to sprawl.

At some point, Bobby went back to his truck and pulled out a dolly, then a jack and a wheeled platform, which was more useful to their cause than Dahlia cared to admit. With the extra tools and a little group effort, they removed the rowboat, the front half of the truck (the rear had rusted into a lump, and could stay where it was), two armoires, one desk, several cabinets, the skeletal remains of an Indian motorcycle, a couple of tables, half a dozen wooden wheels, a proper old sleigh with some of its decorative paint intact, some children's sleds, and one stove that wasn't original, but was close enough to make Dahlia happy.

By noon, the crew members had stripped off sweaters and flannels, and were down to T-shirts and gloves. Bobby wiped his forehead with the back of his hand and announced, "I'm starving. Let's see about lunch."

Gabe looked at Dahlia like he was half afraid she'd argue, just because his dad had been the one who proposed it.

But she didn't. "I'm getting there, myself. All right, let's wrap it up here and drive into town—or walk into town, whatever."

"I'm driving," her cousin declared. "Out past the railroad overpass, they've got a whole string of fast food places. I hear the Taco Bell calling my name."

Dahlia mumbled something about Taco Bell being gross, and Gabe halfheartedly agreed. She knew that he loved Taco Bell, but he was tired of taking his dad's jabs about how he was getting big and soft, instead of just big. He suggested Subway instead.

Dahlia liked that idea better. "No reason you can't do both. Pick me up a sandwich, would you? I'll write down what I want, and while you're out making a food run, I can start unloading our camping gear."

"I could give you a hand," Gabe suggested. "I'll write down my order, too."

Brad considered his options. Apparently he'd rather ride with Bobby than unload gear. "All right," he said. "It's me and you, man—and tacos are fine with me."

"See? Even the bookworm likes tacos, Gabe. Nothing wrong with tacos."

"I know. I just don't want any right now," the kid protested. Dahlia suspected that he'd jump in front of a bus for a taco, so it was either sweet or sad how he chose to stick with her instead. Avoiding even the appearance of evil. Or temptation. Whichever.

"Bookworm?"

Bobby smacked Brad on the back, a little harder than he needed to. "Don't take it the wrong way."

"It's not much of an insult."

"Then I'll have to come up with something better on the way."

Brad shrugged, and Dahlia realized that a lazy shrug was his submissive response to almost everything. "Whatever makes you happy, man."

"Tacos make me happy."

They wandered back to Bobby's truck together, while Gabe and Dahlia went to hers. "Thanks for staying," she told him. "These coolers are heavy."

"I've spent enough time in a truck with Dad today." He whipped the vehicle's back door open with a jerk of his elbow. "I like Brad all right, and I wasn't trying to throw him under the bus . . . but it's someone else's turn to hear Dad rattle on about Marlene."

"Brad made his own damn choice. And who's Marlene?"

"Some girl he met on the Internet. She's not, like, a kid, I mean. She's your age, or something. He found her on a dating site."

Dahlia looked away to hide a smirk. "I'm sure she's lovely."

"That's what you always say about people when you think they're probably awful."

"Well, all I said out loud is, 'I'm sure she's lovely.' You can't prove anything else." She drew one of the coolers out from the truck, and only barely kept its back end from crashing to the ground. She caught it with her foot, and a grunt. "Besides, you shouldn't listen too hard to anything I say. That's what your dad would tell you."

"He ain't never said that." Gabe picked up the end of the cooler on Dahlia's foot, then got a grip on the other side, too. "Not out loud."

She let it slide. "Honey, you don't have to carry the whole thing."

"Yeah, but I *can*. You get the bags. Those are easier. Let me get these."

"You're a sweet one."

He nodded, and set off for the house. "That's what they tell me."

She watched him leave, and looked over her shoulder toward the graveyard. It wasn't much of a yard. It was barely a field anymore—if you didn't know what you were looking for, you'd assume it was another derelict corner of the property, with nothing of note worth mentioning. But she'd seen something there, hadn't she? Something had called her attention to the irregular square, this patch of grass that was left to go wild like the rest of the place.

A yellow dress. Flowers.

The sense of something billowing in the early October breeze. That didn't make sense though, not really. Yellow cotton and flowers are for April, or maybe May. Yellow flowers were for months with a girl's name, not for Halloween.

She stared hard. Whatever she'd seen, it didn't reappear.

The bags in the back of the truck held canned groceries and sodas, batteries, toiletries, towels, soap, and all manner of things you'd either bring camping or expect to find in a hotel. Everyone had at least an individual duffel bag and a sleeping bag, but the rest was expected to be communal. She decided that the boys could drag their own personal items inside, and she'd go ahead and get set up the rest.

Back in the house, she found Gabe standing in the great common area, or living room, or whatever you'd call it—the open place just past the foyer. He was staring up at the grand staircase, specifically at the platform where the staircase turned. A cooler sat in the dust by his feet.

"Everything all right?" she asked.

He looked startled, like he hadn't heard her clomp up the porch stairs lugging duffels and grocery bags. He pulled off his old brown trucker hat and tweaked the visor in a weak, nervous gesture, then put it back on. "It's all good," he drawled. "I was just wondering . . . I don't know. Dahl, you didn't see Brad or my dad leave the carriage house, did you? Before they left for lunch, you know."

"Except for hauling things outside, no."

"Then it's . . . I mean, look at them footprints."

"Gabe, we've gone over this already. Those are *my* footprints, from when I first came inside to look around."

He shook his head. "Yeah, you said that about the ones in the floor, in that weird figure eight. But you didn't bring high heels, I bet."

"Sure I did. I need the added height for pulling down corner blocks."

"Don't bullshit me, Dahl. See over there, and tell me it don't look like someone's been running around in high heels."

"Fine." She set the bags down on the floor beside Gabe's cooler, and followed his gaze to the stairs. It did indeed look like a small army had marched up and down them, but four people's footprints could do that. It wasn't a mystery. "I don't see anything weird."

"Look closer. Look *higher*, up at the landing. I can see it from here."

"You and your tall-ass self," she mumbled. "All right, I'll go see."

She climbed to the landing and stopped, looking down at the dusty, dark wood.

"You see them, don't you?"

Dahlia didn't like the soft urgency in his voice. He was unhappy about something, and he wasn't really saying what. "I see . . . all right, it looks like footprints up here. But it's just some of ours, making a funny pattern. There's a couple of smudges, but . . ." Like a person had been standing there, looking over the rail. A person wearing chunky high heels, maybe the old-fashioned kind. That must've been what he was talking about. "One of us must've dropped something, or tripped. All kinds of things could leave a mark like that."

She didn't mention that she saw other prints, too—the ones on the rail. Not the marks of shoes, but hands. Squeezed right into the filth. They were so clear she might've lifted fingerprints from them, if she knew how.

So maybe when she'd agreed not to bullshit him, that was bullshit, too.

She cocked her head down at Gabe, who was big and soft, but not so big that he could've possibly seen the footprints (or the handprints) on the landing above him. He wasn't a goddamn giraffe.

Slowly, she asked, "Do you think . . . are you trying to tell me you think someone else has been in here?"

"I don't know, but it could be. We just got here." He fiddled with his hat, put it back on again, and put his hands up. "We haven't even seen half the estate. Maybe we should search the

place, and make sure we're alone. There could be squatters, or
meth heads looking for scrap."

"That's not the worst idea I've ever heard." After all, she'd
seen that dress. Someone must've been wearing it.

Except that wasn't true, and she knew it as soon as the
thought bubbled up in her head.

"Sometimes I have a good one."

She was willing to play along if it made him feel better.
"We might also be infested with kids who like to take pictures
in old houses." She tried not to look at the handprints on the
rail right in front of her. They could be hers. They could be
Brad's, maybe. "All right, I'm on board. Let's get the trucks
unloaded, then me and you can make a sweep of the place. Let's
see how much space we can cover before the guys get back
with lunch."

Maybe it'd make him feel better. Maybe it'd make *her* feel
better, except she wasn't worried. Not exactly. She wasn't even
afraid. She *was* curious as all hell, but she wasn't quite ready to
talk about seeing ghosts.

With another two trips, the pair of them had unloaded all the
daily necessities. Together they wore yet another smudged
path in the floorboard dust, this one from the porch to the
kitchen.

Dahlia opened the butt-ugly harvest gold fridge and stacked
the energy drinks inside. It smelled like an old man's closet in
there, but it was running, and it was cooler than the rest of the
house.

Gabe stopped her before she made it to the bottled water. "Don't worry about the food yet. We were going to look around, remember?"

The more she thought about it, the less she saw the point. She didn't honestly believe they'd find anyone—much less anyone in a yellow dress and high heels, or anyone who left perfectly clear handprints on the rail at the staircase landing. But he was giving her the puppy-dog eyes, so what if they found nothing?

For that matter, so what if they found ghosts? If he stuck with this job long enough, he was bound to see one eventually.

She said, "Right. The rest of this will be fine without the fridge. You want to take the first floor, or the second one? I already looked around a little, but it won't kill us to look again."

"No, let's stick together. This ain't *Scooby-Doo*."

"All right, but I've got a great Daphne costume."

"Really?"

She laughed. "Naw. I was always more of the Velma type."

"Brown hair, yeah. But no glasses. No orange turtleneck dress. You're *way* more Daphne. And Andy . . ." He balked, then went ahead and finished the thought, since he'd already started it, and now they were both thinking it. "Looks a lot like Fred."

It was just a habit, talking about Andy. He'd been part of everyone's life for as long as Gabe had been alive. It'd take more time, more life without Andy in it . . . maybe a *long* time . . . before Dahlia and her family could talk about anything on earth without bringing him up.

She tried to be okay with that. She tried not to flush, and she tried to sweep it away fast, before Gabe started apologizing.

"Andy's a towheaded blockhead—you've got him there. So where do we begin?"

Relieved, and still tense, Gabe decided. "We'll start here. We can do it fast, and cover most of the place before Dad gets back. You know him—he'll drag his feet. He's never ordered off a menu in his life."

"Or we could wait for him and Brad, if you'd rather take the place inch by inch."

He shuffled his shoulders and opened the pantry door—poking his head inside, and withdrawing again. "Let's do it without them. Dad'll give me shit. He says I'm paranoid."

"You're cautious, and there's nothing wrong with that—or, if there is, I'm screwed up, too. Just ask your Uncle Chuck." For show, she opened the nearest, largest cabinets, confirming that they were empty. "He gripes about it all the time, about how I'm too slow at salvaging."

"You *are* a little slow."

"Hey now, I thought we were on the same side." She spied no one inside the dumbwaiter, but she'd check it out more carefully later on. Once those things stopped working, they sometimes turned into trash pits—and one man's trash was another woman's payday.

Gabe smiled, and nudged her gently as he passed. "Come on, slowpoke easy. We can do a little dash."

But they'd taken too long unloading her truck, and now they both heard the second truck scraping under the dogwood branches at the front gate. "Sorry, toots. The dining car has arrived after all. I'll call for a search once we're settled in for the night. That way your dad won't give you any shit. He can just add an extra measure to the shit he's giving me."

"He hasn't been real bad. Not so far."

"No, but we've barely started."

Deflated, and still weirdly twitchy, Gabe relented. "Yeah, I know. But this afternoon, we should lock up the house when there's nobody inside. How many keys did Uncle Chuck give you?"

"Only the one. There's an Ace on the way into the neighborhood. Maybe I'll make copies, if that'll make you happy."

She'd do it, if it'd set his mind at ease. She didn't figure it'd make the property more secure, not when there were broken windows and (almost certainly) unknown entrances and exits, but if a touch of security theater let Gabe sleep through the night, it was worth trying.

"Okay," he said. "That'd be cool."

Bobby pushed the front door open with his hip, declaring, "All we need is a tablecloth, and we can get this show on the road!" as he hauled the lunch offerings inside. "Dahlia, did you pack one?"

"Check the Bi-Lo bag by the mantel."

Brad came in behind him, pulling the door shut. "You really *do* think of everything."

"Do we have any chairs?" Bobby asked.

Gabe volunteered, "I saw two stacked in the pantry."

"Dibs on one of them," Dahlia called.

"No way," Bobby started to argue, but she cut him off. "Ladies first."

"This ain't a sinking ship," Bobby protested as he rooted around for the tablecloth. He found it, flapped it open, and dropped it over the big dining room table. "But since you're the boss, you can have one, and I won't fight you for it."

She returned a moment later with a vinyl dining chair that had seen better days with more stuffing. Its metal frame was more rust than steel, but it didn't wiggle when she set it down, and it held her weight when she plopped onto the seat. She made grabby hands toward the Subway bag, and Brad passed it her way.

For thirty seconds, the room was loud with the crinkling of plastic wrappers, then it was quiet except for the sound of Brad bogarting the other creaking chair, and the happy chewing of people who've worked their asses off all morning.

In between massive bites of greasy tacos, Bobby said what Dahlia was thinking: "This isn't so bad. Maybe it won't suck after all."

And she couldn't even argue.

4

THE AFTERNOON WAS dedicated to excavating the first
floor of the carriage house. When it was entirely emptied,
the tally of salvageable items had risen by a pie safe, two
sugar chests, a tangled stash of nineteenth-century birdcages,
half a dozen oil lanterns with different colored glass lenses, two
embossed metal fire extinguishers, a stick-style rocking chair,
and some dented body parts for the vehicle downstairs.

As the last of the new items were sorted in the yard, Brad
gestured up to the loft windows. "I want to see what's up there."

Gabe agreed. "Me too. I'll go get the ten-footer from the
truck."

"Wait. Let's hold off on that for now." Dahlia shaded her eyes
with her hand, and stared up at the horizon behind the tree
tops. It was after six o'clock, and a thin film of gray clouds
spilled over Lookout's crest, seeping across the sky. "Let's load
up the truck instead, and get this stuff someplace secure. We
might get some rain before nightfall."

"You think the carriage house roof's all right?" Bobby asked.

Dahlia pulled out her phone. "No, but one more night won't
make any difference. Don't forget, when we're finished with
everything inside, we're taking that roof with us. The copper
will be worth a mint. We can probably just roll it up, stomp it
down, and shove it in last, like a cherry on top of whatever else
goes in the trucks."

"It *does* smell like rain," Gabe said, almost dreamily. "I like it."

His father grumbled, "You won't like it if it catches us while we're working. Snap out of poetry mode, and bring the truck around. Keys are in the ignition."

Dahlia checked the weather on her phone and saw nothing predicted for another couple of hours . . . but she decided to trust the lift in the breeze, the damp smell of leaves, and the roll of the cloud bank instead.

Upon closing the app, she realized she'd missed a call.

Gabe was almost to the truck when she called out, "Y'all get started without me. Dad called, but I didn't hear the phone, so I'm going to ring him back and see what he wanted."

Three grunts acknowledged her, and nobody argued or complained, so she hit "call back" and strolled toward the house. It was quieter up on the porch—nothing but the trees swaying and the old house creaking in the wind.

She leaned forward on the rail, ignoring the flecks of damp paint that brushed off on her sleeves.

Chuck picked up on the third ring. "Sweetheart, there you are."

"Sorry I missed you, but we've been climbing around in that carriage house. Things have been noisy."

"I bet. Did you find anything good?"

She gave him a rundown of the highlights, and added, "The guys are loading Bobby's truck before we get started on the second story. I think we're in for some rain."

"And everything you just listed . . . that came from *just* the first level?"

"Correct. Maybe we'll poke our heads around in the loft after we eat, but we'll have to save the real work for tomorrow. So what'd you call me for, anyway?"

"Oh, I was just checking in," he told her. "Wanted to make sure you got there okay, and everything at the estate was as-advertised."

"Mostly."

"Mostly?"

She watched as Gabe awkwardly, but carefully, backed the truck past the little cemetery and up to the carriage house. "The mansion is a real piece of work. It's gorgeous, and Augusta Withrow is a liar if she says it can't be saved."

"Now, honey . . . you're not there to save the house. You're there to save our family business." He said it like he was joking, but they both knew better.

"No pressure." She waved away the seeds of his lecture, even though he couldn't see her. "And we've had that talk before. I won't bore you with how badly I'd like to keep it. But I do think there's something funny about it."

"Funny like what?"

"Funny like a bunch of resident dead people. Did Augusta say anything to you about a cemetery?"

The way he replied, "A cemetery?" was answer enough. "No, why? Did you find one?"

"Uh-huh. It looks like a little family plot, maybe, except . . . the whole thing is weird, Dad. The house, the offer . . ." Her voice trailed away.

"How big is the cemetery?"

"I counted about a dozen stones, but I wasn't looking hard—and there might be twice that many, buried in the overgrowth. I didn't want to burn too much daylight on it, not when we just got here. It's not like we're salvaging the headstones."

"But it's really overgrown?" he pressed. "Nobody's been buried there recently?"

"Doesn't look like it. I didn't see any dates later than World War I."

She heard a note of relief in his voice when he said, "That's a good sign. If it's just a small, private plot, it's probably closed. It shouldn't pose any problem to your demo."

"No, I'm not worried about that. It's not in the way, or anything. Not in *our* way," she specified. "But it might be a problem when you come with the Bobcat. That thing's trailer won't make it through the gate; it's too wide, too long. You'll have to come around to the side, and the cemetery's in the way."

"You know that for a fact?"

"Well, I eyeballed it. I might be wrong about the trailer, but I won't be wrong about the teardown crew coming on the fifteenth. It'll hold up *their* work, even if it doesn't hold up ours."

Chuck was quiet for a minute. "You're grasping at straws. They won't stop the demolition because of an old cemetery."

"Jesus, Dad. I'm not an idiot. I'm just throwing it out there. If the plot can be saved, the park service might be interested in it. Augusta's donating the land, isn't that what you said?"

"It's all going to the battlefield. But Lookout's a Civil War hot spot, with nothing related to World War I. I don't know if the Lookout Mountain people will give a shit. They may keep it, or they may relocate it. They may pretend it doesn't exist."

"The people buried there must have relatives. I doubt they'd find that kind of solution very satisfactory, and they might object to everyone being relocated. So do you have a number for Ms. Withrow? Maybe I'll give her a call."

He relented with a sigh. "I don't have one right in front of me. Give me a few minutes, and I'll text it to you when I find it. I don't know what you expect her to tell you, but if it'll make you happy . . ."

"It'll make me happy."

"Will do, then. Love you, baby."

"Love you too, Daddy. I'll let you know if we run into trouble, or find anything particularly cool."

They said their good-byes and she closed the call, staring down at the small screen as if she could will it into producing that phone number on the spot. But her father wasn't a wizard, and the digits failed to magically appear. She'd have to give him time.

A drop of water landed with a splat on the porch's handrail.

And now she had to give the guys a hand, as they loaded the truck. Between the four of them, it shouldn't take long—and it was either put it all away now, or cover it with tarps, so she hustled down the steps and went to go help.

By the time the rain fell in earnest, everything was packed away, secure and dry.

With Dahlia directing, the entire haul was jammed into about a third of one truck's available space—a task made easier when the small boat fell apart, and the pie safe collapsed into dust. Two big items were therefore checked off the list and left behind. It was unfortunate, but not a catastrophe.

A few of the other promising items were abandoned too, or returned to the carriage house for further evaluation later on. If the trucks were going to fill up this fast, they might have to prioritize, or wait to see how much would fit on Chuck's trailer when he finally got there. But it'd wait. It'd have to, for the weather and the late hour conspired to cast the whole estate in grim, gray darkness that would settle into a pitch-black cover in another thirty minutes.

"Come on, let's call it," Brad begged. They all stood inside the truck's remaining cargo room, where the rain echoed nicely, but it was starting to get chilly. Everyone's words, coughs, and footsteps echoed in the metal container. "Please? I'm *beat*."

"I'm hungry," Gabe added.

Dahlia rolled her eyes. "Big babies, the lot of you."

"Hey, don't lump me in with those two kids," Bobby protested. "I could go another hour."

Dahlia rolled her eyes. "You're only saying that because you know it's too dark to follow through. But you know what? I don't really care. We can go inside for sandwiches and Cokes—no more fast food today, we can't do that all week. After supper, we can drag out the ladder, maybe . . . if that offer of another hour's work still stands, and any of you want to take a peek at that second story."

Gabe asked, "Sounds good to me; I want to see what's up there. Hey, is the house unlocked?"

Forgetting about her earlier promise to keep the place secured, Dahlia said, "It ought to be. Last one off the truck has to close the door and lock it. Mad dash in three . . . two . . . one!"

She leaped off the back bumper and landed square on her feet, at the very moment a text message hit her phone with a tinny chime. Her dad must've come through with Augusta Withrow's number.

She heard the truck's door rolling shut, but didn't look back to see who'd drawn the short straw. It wasn't raining so badly as it sounded from within the metal interior; and she wasn't so wet that she was in a real hurry. She ran anyway, back to the safety of the porch, and then into the house. She left the door open, and went to stand in the open living area with the double-wide fireplace and all their gear piled up where they'd left it.

She sighed.

The house sighed in return. The front door swayed back and forth, and closed on its own with a heavy clack.

Dahlia jumped. She didn't know why. It was only the wind—there was *plenty* of wind—and the boys were coming, so she ought to open the door. They'd complain if she closed them outside again, even though it wasn't her doing.

The knob turned in her hands and she pulled the door back just in time to keep Brad from knocking.

"Why'd you—?"

"A draft took it. Get in here."

"I need a towel," he declared with a shiver.

"Your bag's over there. If you packed one, you've got one."

He was barely any wetter than she was, but if he wanted to be fussy about it, that was up to him. When Bobby and Gabe arrived together, moments later, they were more damp by far—so damp, you'd have to call them soaked.

A clap of thunder on the far side of the mountain said they'd just barely beaten the worst of the storm, so Dahlia felt better about cutting the day short. Well, tomorrow, they could run from breakfast to sunset proper, like it or not. They'd finish the carriage house and start on the barn . . . they might even *finish* the barn, if there wasn't much of value inside. Taking down the exterior chestnut boards would be hard work, but it wouldn't take all day.

Assuming the rain broke, at some point.

But on this first night inside the house, she could relax and explore, help herself to snack food, or make phone calls, while the others divvied up the bread and deli meat. From the kitchen, she heard the pop and hiss of soda tabs and the crinkle of trash bags. The guys were already busy, tearing through the supplies. Even if they heard her on the phone, they wouldn't pay any attention. They wouldn't ask why she was dialing up the woman who'd sold the house to be butchered.

The number Chuck gave her rang, and rang, and then stopped with a click.

"You've reached Augusta Withrow. I'm not home right now, so please leave your name and a message, and a number where I can reach you. I'll return your call when I'm able. Thank you."

Holy shit. Dahlia had reached a landline with an answering machine. It surprised her so much she almost forgot to say anything after the beep.

She found her voice and fumbled with it. "Hello, Ms. Withrow? My name is Dahlia Dutton—I'm Chuck's daughter, and I'm at your old house, leading the salvage operation. I've encountered something strange, and I was wondering if I could speak with you. Perhaps you could swing by, if you're in the area? Or . . . or you could call me back, if you prefer. It's pretty important, I think." She paused, uncertain as to how she ought to wrap up. "I'd really appreciate a minute of your time." She left her cell number, and hung up. Then she joined the guys in the kitchen and made herself a meal stacked with slices of turkey and ham.

The rain came and went, mostly letting up by the time the sandwiches were reduced to crumbs and greasy fingerprints.

Dahlia checked her phone enough times to decide it was stupid to keep looking, and that no self-respecting old Southern lady would return a call after eight o'clock. She stuffed the phone in her back pocket, collected her belongings from the foyer where everything was still piled up, and left them in the master bedroom. Then she returned downstairs and announced her intention to climb up into the carriage house loft before showering and settling in for the night.

"The rain's tapered off," she noted, "and it's too early to crash. I'm kind of restless, anyway."

Gabe leaped to his feet. "Me too!" Because of *course* he was. They'd never gotten around to that safety survey. He probably wanted to check the rest of the place for stowaways and creeps.

Brad was already half asleep on top of the remaining sleeping bags. He didn't open his eyes when he flapped his hand in their direction and said, "I can't move. Go on without me."

Bobby tapped him with his foot. "Come on, now. Get up."

"Leave me behind," Brad pushed back. "My arms are killing me. My legs are killing me. My back is killing me."

"Uncle Chuck will kill you if I tell him you were useless."

Dahlia frowned. "Knock it off, Bobby. Today was his first full day on this kind of job, and he did good. Give him a break."

"Nobody ever gives *me* a break."

"You take plenty without asking. Now shut up and either help me and Gabe, or don't. This is an after-hours project for funsies. If you're not going to be any fun, then stay here with Brad." She strolled to the door, trusting Gabe to follow her.

Bobby hesitated beside Brad's prostrate form, sprawled across his improvised chaise. Dahlia assumed that her cousin's laziness would beat out his curiosity—after all, he wasn't working for Music City because of any particular passion, he was only in it for the steady paycheck, and maybe to prove something to his kid about holding down a real job. Unless that was giving him too much credit.

Either way, he surprised her by asking, "Is it still wet out there?"

"If a little damp is all the difference between you being useful or not, then don't waste our time. You and Brad can stay here and have a little slumber party."

"Go . . . ," Brad urged. "Let me nap in peace."

"All right, I'm going."

It surprised Gabe, too. "Really, Dad? You want to come?"

"Yeah, really. Hold the door, I'm right behind you."

Dahlia grabbed an LED lantern as she left. She turned it on, and turned it up. It flared bright white, throwing hard black shadows all over the porch. They moved like puppets, jerky and bouncing, and when she skipped down the stairs into the yard, they only grew taller behind her. They multiplied when Gabe and Bobby joined her in the wet grass, each one holding a lantern of his own.

She didn't like the look of it, these projections of stretch-limbed monsters. She especially didn't like the way they moved when she moved, waving the lantern to light up the guys, the yard, and the scenery as far as the lamp would reach.

She held it high and looked back and forth between the carriage house and the trucks, but a fine mist of drizzle fogged the space between her and the buildings. She saw nothing but their vague and angular shapes, hulking in the muted dark.

"I'll get the ladder," Gabe offered. He made for the truck.

"So it's me and you, then?" Bobby gave Dahlia an elbow to the arm, almost friendly. "Just like the old days?"

She could've pushed back, but it was late, and her heart wasn't in it. He didn't want to fight, and she didn't, either. "Yeah, finding this place . . . it would've really been something, when we were kids." She stomped down toward the carriage house, its lawn dotted with leftover piles of things they'd planned to keep, before they changed their minds.

The growing scrap heap by the door was covered by one of the flapping blue tarps. As Dahlia passed it, she checked to make sure it was tied down all right, secure enough against the rain.

Encouraged by her idle nostalgia, Bobby said, "We could've spent a week, poking around the grounds."

"We're *going* to spend a week, poking around the grounds."

"But now it's a job. Back then, it would've been an adventure—a real one. Not like that cave on Aunt Edna's farm. Not like the empty dry-goods store, before they tore it down. And it's *way* cooler than that duplex on Vine Street."

"Way bigger, too. Best of all, there are no dead mummy cats. So far."

He fell into step beside her, and helped with the sagging wood door they'd shut before leaving. "Bigger, older. It even smells better; never mind the rat shit. You remember the magazines? They'd all turned into sticky bricks, from the floor to the ceiling. You remember?"

"Yeah, Bobby. I remember."

The old man on Vine Street had been a hoarder. When he died, the fire department had to cut a hole through the side of the house and pull out debris with a bulldozer in order to reach his body. All the neighborhood kids had sat on the curb, enraptured, as the scene unfolded. Some of them came back later.

She and Bobby had snuck out of their respective houses after the body was gone, and climbed inside through the hole the bulldozer had left. They'd brought dinky plastic flashlights, and a disposable film camera. None of the pictures ever came out. Even with the flash turned on, there was nothing to see but dirty junk and the occasional white orb reflected off a mirror or a window, bleaching even the junk away.

Dahlia nodded. "I remember the garbage. The Tupperware

containers Mr. Hunt had labeled with masking tape and a marker . . . all of them full of mold and black slime."

"You remember the plants?"

She finished pushing the door far enough open to let Gabe inside with the ladder. She could hear him closing up the truck, so he'd be along shortly. "They'd been dead for so long, they looked like statues made out of sticks."

"You wouldn't let us steal anything, you goody two-shoes."

"There was nothing worth stealing, you thug. I still have trouble breathing, just thinking about that place." The mold. The mildew. The dander of animals long since rendered as ghostly as the potted plants.

Gabe announced himself with the jostle and clank of the aluminum ladder knocking against the scrap heap, the doorframe, and then the edge of the door itself. He strolled past his father and Dahlia, and set it up firmly beneath the big square hole in the ceiling. "Wow—I left you alone for two whole minutes, and you didn't bite each other's heads off."

"Dahlia's not your mother," Bobby shot back. "She gives me a fighting chance."

Dahlia coughed to mask a laugh. She followed Gabe, and pressed on the ladder's braces to double-check that they were set, and set firmly. Everything looked good. "All right, kid. You toted the equipment, so you get first gander, if you want it."

He was halfway up the ladder before the last word was out of her mouth. It made her smile. Bobby was in it for the money, such as it was . . . but Gabe had been well and truly bitten by the bug. His head and shoulders disappeared through the hole, followed by his arm, holding a light aloft.

"What do you see?" his father asked.

"Y'all hang on. It's dark up here."

"I know. That's what the light's for."

Gabe sighed, and took another step up on the ladder. "Thanks for the tip. There's a lot of space, all right? It's all cluttered. It's hard to see anything." He pulled one knee up onto the landing. "It's just walls and walls of stuff, like, closing in on you, almost."

Dahlia winced to hear a timber groan beneath his weight. "Gabe, baby—be careful."

"I *am*."

The other knee came up too, and the beam moaned, but did not crack. He bounced gently. "I think it'll hold me."

"You *think*?" his father demanded.

"It looks more solid over here. This part, it's rotted out. There's . . ." He huffed, and puffed, and pulled himself off the ladder altogether, bringing his whole body onto the second floor. "There's a hole in the ceiling. Water's gotten inside, but only right here. Right over the hatch."

"So that's why there's no ladder left behind," Dahlia observed. "It must've rotted out." But a glance around the floor didn't reveal any hints of an old ladder, wooden or otherwise. Whoever had last used the place for storage must've taken it with him.

It was a small detail, but it bothered her all the same. She couldn't shake the idea that someone had thought they shouldn't look up there, like there was something they shouldn't see, or something that wasn't safe.

She should've gone first. She shouldn't have let the biggest member of her crew climb up in an uncertain space. She regretted it with every noisy footfall overhead. "Gabe, I'm coming up behind you."

"And I'll be right behind *her*," Bobby declared.

But she stopped him. "Wait," she begged. "Just wait a minute. Listen, you heard the floor, didn't you? It's no good up there. Let me check it out first. If one of us falls through or gets stuck, we'll need you to help us out."

"You're trying to hog my kid again."

"What?"

"You heard me. You like him better than you like me."

Her eyes narrowed. "I've known you twice as long; but between the two of you, he's the most loyal." Any idle goodwill Bobby'd mustered with his trip down memory lane fizzled right out. "I'm trying to look out for him, that's all."

"That's *my* job."

"It's also your job to do what I tell you, at least while we're here." Before he could wind up to a dying duck fit, she held up a finger and lowered her voice. "You outweigh me by fifty pounds. Let me test the floor up there. If it's safe, I'll holler, and you can come on up. Your kid is happy we haven't killed each other yet. Throw us all a curveball for once, and don't let him down."

Without waiting for a retort, she slipped the lantern's hanging loop down around her wrist and started to climb. "Gabe?" she called out. "You're being awful quiet. Did you find something?"

At the top of the ladder, she was greeted with a drop of water to the eyeball. It wasn't raining again, but Gabe was right: The roof had a hole in it. On the other side, she could see lacy black clouds just a half-shade lighter than the sky itself—pierced here and there by only the most determined stars, and a smudged gray shadow that showed where the moon ought to be.

She wiped her eye and cheek with the back of one arm, and took the lantern by its handle again.

The second floor, or the loft, or the attic, or whatever it was . . . it wasn't packed to the rafters like the first floor used to be, but it was plenty cluttered. At a hasty glance she saw furniture, paneled doors, milk crates—or maybe peach crates, or some other kind of crates—and more horse tack. She picked out a set of oars that maybe went with the rowboat that had fallen apart downstairs.

She didn't see Gabe.

"Gabe? Where'd you go?" Dahlia climbed off the ladder, testing the floor with every step to see if it would hold. It squeaked, creaked, and once she got past the loft entrance, it held just fine—even when she rocked back and forth on her feet, and stomped a couple of times. "Gabe?"

"Over here." He breathed it in a whisper so soft, she barely heard it over the faint patter of drizzle on the copper roof.

She followed the whisper around a pair of French doors with the glass all shattered out. Her feet crunched across the broken pieces, and her footsteps were far too loud in her own ears.

Why hadn't she heard Gabe moving around up there? He was twice her size, easy, and none too light on his feet at the best of times. Why wasn't there a ladder under the loft entrance until they brought one? Why was her cousin whispering? Who was wearing yellow cotton, all out of season?

Ahead she saw the glow of his lantern, reassuring in the cave-like loft.

He was on the far side of a set of fin de siècle screens, moth-eaten and ravaged by rats, mold, and anything else that will ruin fine silk on a balsa frame. A scene was painted upon them, or embroidered onto them, Dahlia couldn't tell. She saw the ragged outlines of trees, mountains, and water. The rest was too badly damaged to make out.

Gabe's body showed through the holes. His shadow was large against the rest of it. He was hunkered over something, or crouching down.

Dahlia rounded the screens with her light and saw him, knees bent, his hands clasping the edges of an open trunk. He was pale, even when she considered the vivid, stark white produced by the lanterns. He clutched the trunk like it was a toilet and he needed to vomit.

Slowly, she set her own light down and crouched beside him. "What have you got there?"

"Just an old trunk," he whispered.

"That's . . . that's what it looks like." Inside she saw folded items, discolored fabric. Scattered dominos that were yellowed and cracked, and a single shoe that was sized for a baby, or a large doll. "So . . . what's wrong?"

With a rasp, he said, "Nothing."

"You're a liar—and a shitty one, at that. What'd you find?" She leaned past him and put her hands in the trunk, sifting through its contents with her fingers. The other shoe turned up, as well as some vintage children's books, their cardboard backs gone soft from the years of damp. "It's just a bunch of kid's stuff."

The temperature had fallen ten degrees in the last hour, but Gabe was sweating. "No creepy dolls, or anything." He sniffled and rubbed at his nose to keep from sneezing. "I don't know what's in here. I don't know what he . . ."

"He?"

Gabe looked over his shoulder, and held still long enough to listen for footsteps—on the ladder, or across the rickety attic floor. "The kid. This is his stuff, I guess. He wanted to show me something."

"There was a kid up here? No, don't you tell me that; I won't believe it for a second, and whoever this trunk belonged to . . ." Her fingers crawled through the blankets, the nightshirts, the toys as fragile as bird bones. "He's been dead since before you were born."

She was rambling, and she knew it. She was rambling because she already knew what Gabe meant, before he could say it outright. Her hand knocked against something solid, something that crackled between her fingers. She lifted it up into the light: a book with tattered black pages, loosely bound. The pages were flaking, shedding like leaves.

Gabe nodded earnestly, but said nothing. Now they heard feet on the ladder, and a way-too-loud voice rising up into the eerie space.

"Where the hell *are* you two? Hey! Is it . . . is it safe up there? Is it . . ." Bobby gave up on an answer and threw himself over the lip anyway. Dahlia heard him land with a thud, hard enough to send splinters raining down below, tinkling as light as confetti and ash. "I see your light. I'm coming your way."

"We're over here, Dad," Gabe called out, but his eyes were still locked to Dahlia's. His pupils were the size of the acorns that were scattered all over the porch, clogging up the gutters.

She wanted to ask him what he'd seen. No, she *didn't* want to ask him what he'd seen.

Nothing felt like the right thing to do, so she looked down at the book she'd found instead. Its covers were leather, and the metal rings that held its pages together had rusted away to powder. Down in the trunk, a lacy baptism dress had red, round stains left behind by the book. Another crumpled wad of fabric was stashed beneath it. She began to unfold it, smooth it, touch the long lines of lace that were stitched down the front, but Bobby crashed the scene—moving heavy and hard, like the climb up the ladder had winded him.

"What the hell, Gabe? I expect *her* to ignore me, but you?"

"I didn't ignore you. I told you I was over here."

"Not until I was already up the ladder. Jesus Christ," he swore. He put his hands on his hips and glared down at them both.

Dahlia dusted off the book with the back of her hand. She muttered, "No, he said something before that. So did I. Must be a trick with the acoustics in here. I couldn't hear him either, not at first."

"Really? You want to blame the acoustics?"

"See? You heard me fine, this time. It's something weird about all the junk, and the metal roof, and the rain. Don't make a mountain out of it. Hey, look at this, huh? Looks like something we would've found on Vine Street."

He was on the verge of toppling into a full-on grown-man sulk, but he held it at bay long enough to ask, "What is it?"

"A family album. Photos, and . . ." She flipped it open. It fell open to a page with a birth certificate so faded that the lantern blanched it beyond all reading. "Papers, and the like."

"Nothing we can sell," he said, still teetering on that edge. "Nothing valuable."

"Not to us, no. But Augusta Withrow might want it. And it's . . . interesting, don't you think? I bet there's pictures of the house in here, before it looked like . . . like it does now. Pictures of the family, and all that. Gabe found it," she said, trying to pull him back around again. For his son's sake. Sometimes if you could just get him talking, or listening, and you did it fast enough—he'd forget whatever had pissed him off. "He found this trunk. Some of these toys might be worth something, and the dominos . . . the dominos are a nice set. Maybe we'll find the tin they came in. They might even be real ivory."

"But we can't sell real ivory," he argued without conviction.

"There are laws about it, but there are exceptions for antiques. I don't know all the ins and outs. Brad probably does. Dad *definitely* does."

Bobby took a deep breath, and let out a sigh that deflated the worst of his irritation. He put his hands on his hips, letting the LED lantern dangle against his thigh, so the light hit both Dahlia and Gabe square in the face. They squinted hard at him when he said, "Ivory's good, then. That's something."

Behind him, beyond the pattering pings of small droplets hitting the roof, a low grumble of thunder rolled over the mountain. No one saw the lightning that preceded it, but another faint, brief, violent glow was followed by a rumble some five or six seconds later.

Dahlia said, "Might get worse out there, before it gets better."

"Good thing we're all set up for camping," Gabe said.

"And it's mostly dry in here," his dad added.

"Yeah, but . . . I don't want to stay." The kid stood up and dusted his hands on his sweater, then his pants. He closed the trunk lid. "We ought to come back tomorrow, when the sun's up. Even if it's still storming, it'll be easier to see. It's hard, with just these stupid lanterns."

"We'll still need the lanterns tomorrow."

"I know, Dad. But you know what I mean."

"What's the matter with you, all of a sudden? You were all gung ho to come kicking around up here, and now you're itching to leave? When did you get so chickenshit about working in the dark?"

Dahlia jumped in again, hoping it wasn't too late. "He's right. It's hard to see anything up here with just the LEDs. Everything's either too bright or too dark. Makes the whole place look . . ." She almost didn't say it. ". . . haunted."

Bobby waved his hands like Bela Lugosi. "*Oooh.* There it is. You two are scared of ghosts."

Dahlia shrugged, stuffed the photo album under her arm, and started walking back to the ladder. "Put away the jazz hands, dumbass. I'm not too scared of ghosts, but I have a healthy respect for them. That's just common sense, right there. If you see dead people running around and you're all, 'Whatever,' then there is something *seriously* wrong with you."

Gabe scrambled to his feet, and fell into step behind her. "Who said anything about ghosts?"

His father brought up the rear. "I seen a ghost once."

Dahlia reached the ladder, turned around, and descended, one echoing metal rung at a time. "Oh God, don't tell him that story about the Walmart."

"I *will* tell him the story about the Walmart, if I damn well please."

"Can it wait until we're back in the house?" Gabe paused until Dahlia reached the floor, then climbed down behind her.

She laughed so faintly that it came out her nose like a sigh. "Don't worry, kid. You won't need all the lights on. It's a dumb story, and it's not scary."

"Unless you believe it," Bobby insisted from the loft.

"You won't believe it," she assured Gabe.

But the look on his face said maybe she was wrong. Maybe he was in the mood to believe all kinds of dumb stories, bless his heart. She guessed that made two of them.

5

T HEY CLOSED UP the carriage house and sprinted back to the big house, arriving at the porch damp, but none the worse for wear. Brad had fallen asleep, as promised, but he awakened with a start when they tumbled inside and shut the door against the weather. The big chandelier (no, it was a pendant) was lit above him, and the dusty bulbs cast a warm yellow light that wasn't as bright as the lanterns, but was much more comforting. Dahlia liked the old-fashioned feel of it, how it was almost as flattering as candlelight . . . to people and derelict houses, and everything else.

It was also nearly as hot as candlelight.

"What's that smell?" Gabe asked with a wrinkled nose.

"The lights," she told him. "The bulbs got hot, and now they're burning off the dust." And dead bugs, and termite shit, and everything else. It was a sour smell, with a top note of old ashes and scorched feathers.

"Will it start a fire?"

"I doubt it. Hey, Brad?"

He saluted from his nest of sleeping bags. "Yes ma'am?"

"You all right?"

"I'm even more sore than I was an hour ago, but I'll survive. Did y'all find anything cool?" He rose to a seated position, and rested his forearms atop his knees.

Gabe said, "Not really," and went to the kitchen. They heard the fridge open and shut, and the peeling pop of a soda being opened.

But Bobby did a full 180 and valiantly corrected him. "The kid found a trunk of old baby stuff, full of toys and books. Dahl thinks the domino set is ivory, so that's a good score. Otherwise it's kind of a wreck up there. We'll get a better look in the morning, when there's more light to go around. For now, you can stick a fork in me, because I'm *done*."

Dahlia resisted the urge to roll her eyes. "Wait until morning. Sounds like a good idea; I wonder whose it was."

"Who cares? We found some good shit at the end of the day, and now we can call it. Hey, what time is it?" he asked.

"Late enough to relax."

"Late?" her cousin laughed. "The bars have barely opened. What is it, maybe nine o'clock?"

"We aren't here to barhop, Bobby. Let's get settled in, take our showers, and get familiar with the house."

"Why?" He shook himself out of his wet jacket and went digging around in his duffel for something dry. "Like you said, we're done for the day. You don't need me anymore, and I need a drink. And some alone time."

"Don't do it," Dahlia warned him.

"Or what? You'll fire me? I'm off the clock."

"No one's off the clock until the job is finished. *You* won't be off the clock until Friday."

He found a thick plaid flannel and shoved his arms inside it. "I've been up since dawn, driving and digging around in vintage garbage ever since. I deserve a beer."

"Then go buy a six-pack and bring it back," Gabe suggested anxiously from the dining area.

"Naw, I've had just about enough social time with you people tonight." Straightening his collar, he felt around in his pocket for the keys to the truck. "Nothing personal."

Brad watched them, his head bobbing back and forth like a cat's at a tennis match.

"But you were going to tell me your ghost story . . ." Gabe prompted.

"Later," Bobby said on his way out. "Or just ask Dahlia. She tells it better, anyway."

The door clapped shut behind him, and Gabe looked helpless, standing there with a cherry 7Up fizzing in his hand. He looked to Dahlia like she ought to say something, or do something—like *somebody* ought to, and she was the nearest adult.

"You're going to let him take the truck? Uncle Chuck'll kill him if he wrecks it, and it's wet out there . . . and dark . . . and he's going drinking."

"You'd rather I wrestle him to the ground and take the keys?"

"I could do it. Maybe I should've tried."

She shook her head and sighed. "Baby, that's not your job." She muttered the rest, knowing they could hear her. "He's an accomplished drunk, and he knows what he's doing. Oh well. I should've guessed he'd take off first chance he got."

Brad finally cleared his throat and raised his hand. He raised a couple of fingers, anyway. "Are you sure? The truck has all today's stuff in it . . ."

"Goddammit, I should've told him to take mine. Mine's still empty, so we wouldn't be out a day's work and all that loot if he trashed it." Before Brad could add anything else, she said, "But he's not going far. There are half a dozen bars between here and the interstate, and that's not three miles, as the crow flies. I know neither one of you likes it, and I don't like it either—but it was either let him leave, or fire him and let him hitchhike home."

"You *are* the boss," Brad reminded her.

"And these are family politics," she snapped back. "If I fire him on the first night, he'll go crying to my daddy, and it'll be my word against his. Dad will believe me, but he's soft, and it won't matter—he'll give Bobby his job back, and act like nothing happened. From then on out, Bob'll be fucking insufferable, because he'll know for a fact that I can't touch him." She ran her hands through her hair, and leaned against the arched entryway that separated the foyer from the living area. "So long as we all pretend, he might behave himself and get a little work done during daylight hours. If he doesn't, and he blows our timeline, then Dad might see reason and cut him loose for real. It's as close to a win-win as we're gonna get."

Carefully, Gabe asked, "Is that what you want? For Uncle Chuck to cut him loose?"

Shit. "Yes. No. Sometimes. Honestly, it might be good for him, in the long run. It might be the kick in the pants he needs. But you shouldn't worry about it, one way or the other," she assured Gabe quickly. "You're a good worker, and you've always got a job with us. You won't go homeless or hungry. We'll see to that."

So long as the family business kept its head above water. Christ, she hoped she wasn't lying to him.

Gabe gave up, and went to sit on the edge of the fireplace. "That's good to hear, I guess. Dad talks like this thing at Uncle Chuck's is a fresh start, but he talks about a lot of things that don't turn out worth a damn." He swigged deeply from his soda, and belched hard. "So to hell with him, for tonight. Tell me his ghost story, Dahlia."

Brad perked up. "Bobby has a ghost story?"

"Everybody's got one, right?" Dahlia dragged a sleeping bag out of Brad's pile. "Everybody who breaks down old buildings for a living ought to have a handful on deck, I swear. Some of the shit I've seen . . ." She reached for one of the communal duffels, one she'd packed herself with first-aid supplies, extra batteries, and booze. She pulled out a bottle of Maker's Mark and a sleeve of clear plastic cups.

"Whoa . . . sweet! You brought Maker's!" Brad exclaimed. "Why didn't you just tell Bobby and keep him here so we could . . . um . . . ?" The question died under the force of Dahlia's pursed lips and lifted eyebrow. "Got it. I didn't realize he was *that* kind of drinker."

"It's not that he drinks a lot, exactly," she said as she undid the twist tie that held the cups in the bag. She pulled out three, kept one, and tossed the other two at her remaining crew members. "It's that he's bored and greedy, and if you've got some of anything, he wants it all for himself."

Gabe nodded, half a smile on his face. "That's a good way to put it. And, um . . . you don't care if I . . . ?"

"You're a working man now," she told him. "A couple of years on your driver license don't make a difference to me, so long as you won't go blabbing about it. I'm not an idiot. I know your dad's hooked you up before."

"But *you* haven't. So . . . fill 'er up? And what's this ghost story that no one will tell me? Is it about a salvage job?"

She picked at the bottle's seal with her thumbnail. The bright red wax collected on her fingers and under her nails. "No, your Daddy's story didn't come from working salvage. To tell you the truth, it's hardly a story—and he was wrong. He tells it better than I do." Wriggling the stopper free, she poured herself a slug, then passed the bottle to Brad. He was closer. When he'd poured all he wanted, he forwarded the bottle along to Gabe, who was modest with his own serving—like a girl on a date who doesn't want to order the lobster.

"Thanks," he said as he sent the bottle back. "I've never had anything this posh."

"Maker's isn't posh. It's just good. Bottoms up . . ." She lifted the glass.

"No, we need a toast," the kid insisted.

"All right, 'To the Withrow Estate. That I should look so good when I'm 140 years old.'" With a hoisted cup and a swallow, she made it official. "And to ghost stories, too. Bobby's is short and sweet."

Dahlia took another swig and leaned back into the rolled-up bag pressed against the side of the staircase. She half thought about lighting a fire before launching into the tale, but, like she said—it was short and sweet, and it wasn't that cold yet. Only wet. She didn't know if the fireplace was any good, anyway.

"So Bobby had a part-time gig working as a stock boy at Walmart, on the overnight shift. It was one of those big twenty-four-hour stores, the kind that never closes; but in the wee hours of the morning, there aren't really any customers. That's when they restock all the shelves, and check all the inventory.

"They had Bobby driving this mini-forklift thing, pulling pallets out of the stockroom and bringing them out into the aisles. He'd set them down and go get more, and whoever else was stuck overnight would have to restock the shelves with whatever he brought them. His manager liked to go smoke weed out behind the service entrance, so it wasn't like Bobby had a whole lot of oversight. He ended up spending a lot of time doing wheelies and playing forklift bumper cars with his buddy Drew, who got him the job.

"Anyhow, one night he was absolutely *positive* he heard somebody crying. At first he thought it was coming from the break room, but every time he checked, it was empty. Then he thought maybe someone was hiding back there, messing with him.

"Drew said he'd heard the crying, too—but he didn't know where it was coming from. He'd tried to follow it back to the source, but every time he thought he was getting close . . . every time he called out, asking if anybody was there . . . the crying would stop.

"So your dad and Drew got the bright idea that they were going to track down the crier together, and figure out what was going on. The next night, Bobby swore he heard it clear as day—so clear, that this time he was sure it was a woman crying, probably an older woman. Once he realized that, it kind of worried him . . . like some old lady was trapped inside the store, wandering around all confused. He remembered seeing something on the local news about an Alzheimer patient who went missing after she'd walked out of her nursing home. What if this was that lady? What if she had family looking for her? What if she needed help?

"I think he liked the idea of being a hero as much as he liked the idea of solving that little mystery. Who wouldn't?"

She took another sip, sniffed against the background stink of dust trying to catch fire overhead, and continued. "Now, Bobby didn't have any idea why some senile old lady would wind up roaming a stockroom at a Walmart, much less how she could've hid back there for a couple of days without anyone seeing her, but that was his theory, so he ran with it. The next time he heard the crying, he got off his little forklift and started sneaking around, real quiet. He tagged Drew on the shoulder, held his finger up to his lips, and cocked his head toward the noise.

"Drew nodded at him, because he heard it too, and then they crept around together—up and down the aisles of those big stock shelves that went all the way to the ceiling. According to Bobby, the closer they got, the more the fluorescent lights flickered, like they were about to go out . . . and then, finally, they turned a corner back by the drinking fountains, and they saw the crying lady.

"Bobby said she had white hair, and she was wearing a housecoat. She had her face to the wall and her shoulders were shaking. Drew froze, but not Bobby—or that's how he tells it. He went up to the lady and touched her on the shoulder. He asked if she was okay, and if he could help her."

She paused.

Brad said, "And then?" He and Gabe were both looking at her, big-eyed and unblinking.

"And *then,* she turned to look at him . . . real slow . . ."

Gabe breathed, "And . . . ?"

"She screamed in his face, and vanished into thin air. She was right there, solid enough that he could touch her, and then she wasn't. There was nothing back in the stockroom but everything Walmart sells, a break room, a couple of drinking fountains, and your daddy and Drew—who fainted dead away."

"But what'd Drew say? Did you ever ask him?"

"I asked him once." Another sip and another pour, to top herself off before she ran empty. "He said your dad was full of shit. All he remembered was hearing some funny noise, and going to check it out. Then he hit his head or something, and the paramedics came to give him stitches. He said he never saw any old lady. But I'll tell you this: He didn't want to talk about it, and I find that strange. Drew would talk the ears off a wooden Indian, and he clammed right up when I bugged him for details. That's what makes me think there might be a grain of truth to it."

Brad's clear plastic cup was still mostly full. He held it like he'd forgotten about it. "Did they ever find the old lady? The one from the nursing home?"

"I have no idea. Let's say yes, so the story makes sense. Let's say they found her frozen to death in a ditch beside the Walmart parking lot."

"Why would you say that? That's awful." Gabe frowned and took a ladylike sip of his bourbon.

"So what? It's probably not true. She probably turned up overnight, while accidentally shoplifting a Snickers from a gas station. Your dad and Drew had probably been drinking before their shift, or their manager shared his stash."

She climbed to her feet too quickly, then steadied herself and her drink.

The photo album she'd found in the trunk was on the floor by her feet. She picked it up and tucked it under her arm. "On that note," she said, "I need a shower. Desperately. My stuff's already upstairs in that master bedroom, so I'm going to go ahead and clean myself up now."

"Let me know how it works out," Brad asked. He caught himself. "Wait, that sounded weird. Just . . . what I meant was, tell me if there's hot water. And tell me if it's clean, or if it looks more like bourbon than Mr. Bubble."

She flashed him a thumbs-up, turned around, and grabbed the staircase railing. "I'll be back down in a bit. Don't finish the bottle without me."

"Wouldn't dream of it," Brad promised.

Up the stairs she climbed, past the handprints that remained on the rail at the landing because no one had wiped them off, not even her; and she proceeded up to the second-floor hallway. She flipped a switch, and the hall light failed her. The bulb was dead, or the fixture. Either way, it didn't work.

She went to the room she'd claimed for her own and tried the switch there, just inside the doorway. With a click and a fuzzy pop, the ceiling fan's bulbs flickered and brightened, and the blades began to turn.

"Ugh. No," she told it. She reached up for the chain pull and, after a few tries, stopped the spinning blades. It wasn't warm enough for that, and it'd only spread the dust around. Her eyes and nose were already itching again, and maybe there was another headache on deck. Maybe she should pop a couple of Benadryl on top of the booze. She'd sleep like the dead. That'd be nice.

Her bags were sitting on the oversized window seat. She unpacked them enough to takeout what she wanted, and left the rest tidily stored—with the Withrow photo album resting on top of her work pants.

She retrieved a set of fleece pajamas and a black tank top, some socks and underwear, a bottle of all-in-one shampoo and soap, and a bath towel. Carrying it all in one stack, she mentally crossed her fingers that the lights in the bathroom would work—because showering in the dark was no damn fun, and she didn't want to hike back downstairs to grab a lantern.

She should've brought one up, but the Maker's had her half mellow, half petulant. Or it might not have been the Maker's. It might have been a yellow dress, or an album full of faded pictures on brittle black paper. Or Bobby. Or Andy, who wasn't even there to be mad at, but somehow always hovered at the edge of her thoughts. Jesus, it'd been months since the divorce was filed. One of these days, he'd *have* to go away for good. Wouldn't he? God knew *he'd* moved on.

Fuck it.

She needed a shower, that was all. A little hot water and soap would make everything better. After that, a nightcap, if the boys had left her anything.

(They would. Of course they would. But she should get the bottle before Bobby came back. Bobby could buy his own hooch, and leave hers alone.)

The light switch in the bathroom was a discolored plastic push button. She hit it with her thumb, and the vanity lights flared. One bulb coughed and blew out, leaving a dark cloud of soot inside where the glow ought to be. The other two wobbled, but stayed lit. They gave off an ugly light, neither warm nor cool, just shrouded with grime.

Eh. It beat showering in the dark.

She dropped her bundle of nighttime supplies on the closed toilet lid, leaned inside the tub, and wrenched the hot water knob until the spout provided a rusty liquid that cleared by the count of twenty.

There wasn't any shower curtain. She should've brought one, and she kicked herself for not thinking of it. She'd add it to her list of not-exactly-camping supplies for the next time a job like this came around. Yes, she had a list. It was a shitty, incomplete list, but it was better than nothing at all—and, hey, Bobby'd been impressed when she'd produced a tablecloth.

But the list was a work in progress.

Steam rose up from the spout. When Dahlia ran her hand under the water's flow, she was glad to feel that it was properly hot and the water pressure was good, even if it smelled like old metal and mildew. She held her head out of the way and tugged the tiny lever that would switch the faucet to "shower" mode, and the spray fluttered, coughed, and then gushed out nicely.

She tweaked the cold knob, just a hair.

The evening was looking up, even if she was going to soak the floor because she hadn't thought to bring a shower curtain. Or an extra towel to use for a mat. Extra towels were never a bad idea, anyway.

The porcelain tile floor grew slick with damp, as the drop-lets scattered and the room filled with warm mist and fog. That same funny smell of burning crept into the bathroom as the soft stench of lightbulbs warmed up and toasted the dust that'd gathered there.

The dry corpse of a spider toppled into the sink, and rolled down the drain.

Dahlia leaned her butt on the edge of the vanity and stripped off her clothes, starting with her socks and work boots. When she was naked, she went in toe first—one foot over the edge and into the tub, for the sides were tall and slippery. She bent over, held on, stepped up, and swung her other foot inside—into the stream of scalding water, shooting out hard enough to blast the paint off a car.

"Perfect . . . ," she breathed. She stood up straight, smoothed her hair back, closed her eyes, and plunged her face into the cascade.

The bathroom shook. It flickered and buckled, as if it'd been struck by lightning.

Dahlia staggered and slipped. She caught herself, grasping the showerhead pipe for balance.

She opened her eyes—then closed them again until she

could escape from the water, and haul herself out of the tub. Standing knock-kneed on the slippery wet tiles, she wiped at her face with her hands.

The old lightbulbs were still ugly and dim, and the room was more dark than bright, more damp than dry. The water gushed behind her. The bathroom didn't shake.

"The hell was that?" Her question bounced off the Mamie pink walls.

The house didn't answer.

Dahlia's heart pounded. She closed her eyes again, and opened them, and nothing was different. Nothing had happened, but her whole body was in fight-or-flight mode. Shaking, dripping, and listening for all she was worth for the sound of a storm outside, or the pop of an electrical fuse, or anything else that might have rocked the house . . . she waited.

She heard nothing, felt nothing.

"This is stupid," she told herself, and the bathroom, too. "Just some . . . trick of the electrical system. Or something."

She put one foot back inside the tub and looked over her shoulder, out into the bedroom. From the doorway, she could see the edge of the big four-poster bed, the AC unit jutting into the room, one end of the bay window seat where she'd left her bags. She saw only the ordinary shadows and lines of an old house without curtains, and the moon coming and going behind the clouds.

Her heart slowed. She was alone.

She was wasting hot water, and she had no idea how long she could expect that precious commodity to last. The air in the bathroom was thick with steam; it felt good in her chest, and everything was fine. She braced one hand on the tub's edge once more, and climbed back into the jet spray of the showerhead.

This time she didn't close her eyes.

This time, she saw the flash—an instant of whiteness so bright that there were no details, no fixtures, no bathroom. Nothing but white, and the sense of the whole house shuddering.

It was over as soon as it'd happened, but she was already off her feet. She fell sliding into the tub, landing on her back under the full force of the water. She scrambled and stumbled, and pulled herself out of the tub—over the side and onto all fours on a floor that was so wet she could see her own reflection when she stared down, panting, at the space between her hands.

Behind her reflection in that thin sheen of puddle, a shape darted, loomed, and disappeared.

She sat up so fast that she cracked her shoulder against the tub. Ignoring the pain and using the lip for support, she climbed to her feet. She clung to the tub's edge, for it was heavy and sturdy and old, and she trusted old things, even though the floor was uneven and the cast-iron tub rocked slightly from foot to foot when she clutched it.

The steam was so thick, it was like breathing soup. It was hard to catch her breath while inhaling it, puff after puff after puff.

But the bathroom wasn't so large. The mist was not actually soup, and she could see just fine. There was no one there, and no room for anyone to hide. No shadows but the ordinary kind. Nothing looming or lurking—not behind her, not beside her, not over her head, where the ceiling was stained with rust-colored water and a gray-green shadow of mold.

She half considered turning off the water so she could listen. Maybe if she listened real hard, without the water running, she'd hear Brad and Gabe downstairs. Then she'd know that everything was fine, and nothing was wrong.

None of this calmed her heart. It slammed around in her chest, insisting there was something else to hear, and it was important. It was deadly. It was close.

She stood up straight, concentrating on keeping her bare feet flat on the wet floor, and taking careful footsteps through the doorway and into the bedroom. Nothing moved except the ceiling fan, which limped one last half turn and came to a stop. No wind, no storm, no chatter downstairs. No curtains, she remembered—as she stood in full view of . . . well, in full view of no one, really.

If she was mistaken and some pervert was hanging out halfway up the mountain with a pair of binoculars, let him look. He'd gone to a lot of trouble.

She prowled the bedroom, leaving a trail of watery footprints in her wake and collecting dust on her wet feet. The bedroom was bigger than the bathroom by far, and it came with a few more hiding places. But the wardrobe was empty, as was the nook between the door and the wall.

She closed the bedroom door all the way. The knob was original to the house, and it locked, if you had a key. Dahlia didn't have a key. She looked around for something else to secure it, and spied the awkward old end table that served as a nightstand. The little table wouldn't really keep anyone out, but it'd make a fuck-ton of noise if someone tried to shove past it. She'd settle for an early warning system.

She half carried, half dragged it to the door, and kicked it up against the frame.

"This is stupid," she reiterated to herself, or the house, or whoever. She left the table there anyway.

Back in the bathroom, satisfied that she was alone, she took another crack at the tub. With one eye on the doorway and the rest of her attention devoted to not falling . . . she climbed back inside with her bottle of soap.

She barely blinked. She sudsed up everything with a little plastic wash poof, careful to keep the soap out of her eyes, because she couldn't stand the thought of closing them again, even when she washed her face. All the while, her heart kept a steady, terrified beat. She told it not to. She told it how stupid this was. Her heart didn't care. It must've known something she didn't.

"I'm going crazy," she admitted to the bathroom, for she couldn't look stop looking for the shadow. It might flicker again, and next time, she needed to see it. If it came back, she needed to know what to call it.

She finished up fast. She turned off the water. It slowed, dribbled, dripped, and then stopped.

Dahlia's towel was moist with the hot fog that filled the washroom and spilled out past the bed frame and the AC unit. It was scarcely dry enough to serve its purpose, but when she was as water-free as she was going to get, she used it to turban up her hair.

Underwear, socks, and a tank top.

She wore nothing else yet, as she glowered around the room. She was calmer now. Without the water running white noise, without being naked, without being penned up in that tiny pink room . . . things felt quieter, and she felt stronger.

"This was stupid," she concluded.

She refused to think about the blind horror, the trigger-light sense of hysteria. There was more to it than that. She didn't want to wonder why she'd been so certain, so bet-your-life positive that there was someone in the bathroom with her, waiting to do her some terrible harm.

What kind of harm? She didn't know. And why bother imagining it? Don't borrow trouble, that's what her dad would've suggested. Nobody was waiting to ax-murder her, strangle her, beat her to death, or drag her to hell.

Goosebumps reminded her that she had fleece pajamas waiting to be worn, so she added those to her attire, pulled on a pair of slippers from her bag, and felt more human. Less vulnerable.

Still, she jumped out of her skin when Gabe knocked on the door.

"Hey, Dahlia? You okay in there?"

"*YesIamokay*," she said, entirely too fast. "I'm almost finished. I'll be back downstairs in a second."

"All right. We just . . . we were starting to wonder. We could hear you, downstairs—were you moving furniture around?"

"Yes. There was a rat. I freaked out, sorry."

"Rats?" His voice came through the door with a high-pitched note of dismay.

She shoved the end table away. It scraped and scooted loudly, and the ordinary sound helped bolster her bullshit. She turned the knob and opened the door far enough to display her bathed and unharmed condition. "Rat. Singular. Just the one, so far. I didn't mean to worry anyone."

"Naw, it's cool. God, Dahl . . . how hot do you take your showers?"

She looked back and saw steam congealing on the windows; small droplets of water were starting to slide and streak. Her hands were lobster pink, and the rest of her probably was, too. "Hot enough to boil pasta. The plumbing here may be old, but I give it my seal of approval. So, did you guys leave me any bourbon, or what?"

He smiled at her, looking relieved for no good reason whatsoever. Nothing had tried to jump *him* in the bathtub. (Nothing had tried to jump her, either. It was all in her head. All in the house. All in someplace, or another.)

"Half the bottle's got your name on it."

"There's that much left? So I take it your father hasn't reappeared."

She shouldn't have said that. His grin faded. "Not yet, but I figure he won't be back before midnight."

"Yeah, you're right. That's fine, though. With him out of the way, you can take the attic, if you want. Leave him a note, and let him sleep alone someplace where he can snore his head off and not keep anyone awake."

"But you said rats . . . and now you've *seen* a rat . . ."

"Pretend they're squirrels with naked tails. Or take down that door in the hallway, and see what's behind it. All I'm saying is, your dad will come back when he comes back, and you might as well be asleep by then—someplace where he isn't likely to bother you. Settle in, get comfortable. Don't worry about him, or me either." She shook her head, and the towel unspooled into her hands. "I'm going to comb out my hair, pop a couple of allergy pills, and head downstairs to work on that bottle."

"Yes ma'am." He gave her weak smile and disappeared down the hall. His feet were heavy on the stairs, pausing at the landing, then stomping down the rest of the way to rejoin Brad.

Dahlia let out a long, hard sigh, and went to go find a comb.

She settled for a plastic hair pick dredged from the bottom of her messenger bag, and tackled her unconditioned mane as she strolled downstairs. The guys were talking quietly. She heard the tone of the conversation before she could make out any words. They weren't whispering, but there was an undercurrent of secrecy to it. She waffled back and forth between sneaking up on them to listen in, and announcing herself like a civilized person—but the blue plastic pick slipped from her hands and clattered down the steps, making the decision for her.

"Dahlia?" Gabe called.

"Who else?" she said back. She hoped it came out light and friendly, and not as strained as it felt. "Someone pour me up another slug, would you?"

"Brad can do it. I'm not old enough to serve alcohol."

"Very funny." She thanked Brad, who handed over the same plastic cup she'd had before, now refreshed. "And if you two want any more, you'd better pour it now. I'm turning in, and I'm taking the bottle with me."

"Already?"

"It's not that late, but I'm old and tired. Tomorrow will be another long, hard day, so you might want to think about doing likewise. Find someplace comfy and make yourselves at home."

"We already have," Brad insisted. He did in fact look comfy, arms and legs cushioned by the sleeping bags and backpacks.

"Fine, then. Stay put, and when Bobby gets back he'll yank his stuff out from under your ass, trip over you, and generally make you wish you'd gotten a hotel for the night."

Everyone agreed she had a point, so with a final round of Maker's they went their separate ways—Brad to the bedroom nearest the hall bath, and Gabe to the attic. Whether or not he'd stay there, Dahlia didn't know; but he wanted to give it a try, rats and bats and all. There was still something of a little-kid-adventurer in him, and she loved that. She hoped he'd be safe and happy, and sleep well despite the bugs and the threat of rodents.

Or anything else.

When she got back to "her" room, she made a request of the house while she unwrapped her sleeping bag and set up her bedding. "Look out for him, okay? If there's any good spirit left in this place, and I believe there *must* be, then I'm asking you: Watch over him, and keep him safe."

She didn't do much praying, and wasn't sure there was any God on the other side of the ceiling who might be listening, but she believed in ghosts, both good and bad. Besides, the house was listening. She believed that with something steadier than her heart.

By the time she killed the lights and fell into bed, she'd almost forgotten about the photo album. She remembered it just in time to wish she'd opened it before she fell asleep.

6

DAHLIA AWOKE AROUND one in the morning.

She squeezed her phone's side buttons to light it up, then let it go again, considering a tap of the flashlight app. The master bedroom was utterly dark; not even the moon flared in through the windows, and the soft patter of rain smacking on the glass told her why. Groggily, she recalled her earlier terror in the bathroom, but she didn't feel anything like that now. She didn't think she'd heard anyone or anything moving in her room, rodent or otherwise. She couldn't figure out what had disturbed her.

She wriggled out of her sleeping bag and went in sock-soft feet to the door. She hadn't braced it before bed, and the end table was still where she'd pushed it when she'd greeted Gabe. She poked her head out into the hall and realized that there was a little light downstairs. The foyer's chandelier, probably—not the big pendant in the main living area, or else she'd have seen the glow peeking around the door.

Voices drifted up, along with the faint illumination from a floor away.

A door closed, loud as a gunshot.

No, not really. Dahlia wasn't sure why she thought of it that way, or why it made her jump. She knew the voices: Gabe and Bobby. Bobby's surprised her. The bars didn't close until 3:00, so he really had his big-boy pants on tonight. He'd probably expect some praise for this admirable level of responsibility, come morning.

He'd better not get his hopes up.

Whatever her cousins were talking about, it didn't sound heated; it sounded like Gabe trying to parent up. She wished he didn't have to do that, but the pattern was locked in place—wrapped around his DNA, practically—and there wasn't much changing it now.

She sighed and closed the door, then used the light of her phone to stumble back to the windowsill and cocoon up in the bag. The light rain sent her back to sleep, and she stayed that way until half an hour after dawn.

Morning came gray and muggy. The rain had mostly petered out, but all the leaves left on the scraggly trees were damp and heavy, and branches drooped all around the house. Even the remaining ivy looked lank and sticky, like Dahlia's hair felt—for it hadn't entirely dried overnight.

She sat up, yawned, and put her feet down on the floor. Sometime in the night, one of her socks had been eaten by the sleeping bag, leaving one foot bare. The other sock sagged down around her ankle. She used the naked toes on the free foot to pry it off and kick it aside.

When she set both feet flat again, the wood floor was cool, but not cold.

She leaned back to unlatch the window behind her make-shift bed, and pushed it open enough to stick her hand outside. The temperature was about the same as the day before. She could live with it.

She dressed herself in jeans and a tee, with a soft flannel pulled over it. She fished a thick pair of socks from her duffel bag and tied her work boots on over them, not too tight, but not so loose that they'd flop around.

Then to the bathroom, for the usual morning routine.

She hesitated at the doorway.

No. She had nothing to be worried about, especially not in the light of morning. Did she?

She crossed the threshold and turned on the bathroom sink, hard and fast, before she could talk herself out of it, or look too hard for shadows hunkering in the corners. Concentrate on the task at hand. Let the water do its job; let the water drown out the dark thoughts.

Or did the water bring them?

She looked back at the tub, still glistening from last night's moisture. Christ, there wasn't a bit of ventilation in that little room, was there? No fan, either.

She wiped the mirror with the back of her hand, then immediately felt the need to wash both hands, repeatedly. Her all-in-one soap was still by the tub, and it'd work on her hands as well as everything else. That was kind of the point.

Finally, teeth were brushed, face was scrubbed, toilet had flushed, and there were no weird cracks of light or darting shapes at the corner of her vision. She turned off the water and knew (or at least insisted to herself and to the house) that she'd been right the night before: Nothing had happened.

Opening the bedroom door again, she heard exactly nothing. Not even any snoring, much less the sound of someone rummaging for coffee in the kitchen. Had she brought any coffee with the communal supplies? Only the instant stuff, if she remembered right.

Instant coffee was not worth getting dressed for. But there was a coffee shop down in Saint Elmo, not even a mile away. It was easy walking distance, and she could use a walk. Something restless twitched under her skin. She wanted out, away from that nasty bathroom with its wet and dirty walls.

She could grab a cup and a breakfast sandwich, and maybe even be a hero of the revolution if she called Brad before heading back. She could bring coffee for everyone. Wait. Did everyone like coffee? Come to think of it, Bobby didn't always care for it—and she didn't feel like doing him any favors. Gabe didn't like it, either. If he wanted caffeine, he reached for a Coke, and they had plenty of those in the fridge and cooler.

She went for her messenger bag and remembered the photo album. She tossed that in, before slinging the bag across her chest and tiptoeing downstairs. On her way out, she left a note in the kitchen saying to call her if they needed anything, and she'd be back soon.

Then she headed to town, on foot.

Outside, a breeze rustled through the trees, the porch spindles, and the lank, half-naked ivy that hung along the house. She buttoned her flannel at the belly, and it was warm enough to keep her comfortable—especially once she got walking.

The woods were crawling with paths, trails, and rutted roads, and Saint Elmo was a straight shot down the hill. A straight shot that meant jumping a gully or two and climbing over some vintage military earthworks, then navigating around a couple of boulders. She imagined there must be easier routes, but a touch of minor, solitary adventure wouldn't be the end of her. If anything, it was a pleasant distraction.

The canopy above shook cast-off rain as the wind picked through it. Last night's water and wind had pulled down much of the flame-colored foliage and left it glistening damply on the forest floor.

Before long, she found the asphalt road without any lines painted on it and followed it down to an intersection where the tiny street pinched down to one lane . . . then went slinking beneath the Incline's tracks. The tracks themselves disappeared into a layer of cloud cover that squatted across the mountaintop, spilling over and dripping down, but not quite reaching the little valley below.

On the main drag nearby, morning traffic crept in from Georgia. It was stop-and-go up through the blinking light at the pedestrian crosswalk, and then sluggish as hell out of the neighborhood and into the city. It was just as well that Dahlia hadn't taken one of the trucks.

She strolled past a wee strip mall that looked a hundred years old, a burrito joint, the Incline station, a restaurant, and a flower shop—everything still locked up for the morning.

Dahlia's phone said it was barely seven thirty. Only the coffee shop was open, and it hadn't been for long.

Inside, the atmosphere was warm and noisy. Someone was grinding beans, and someone else was steaming milk. Two or three customers waited ahead of her, so she took the time to check her e-mail, catch up with a couple of messages from her dad, and start a game of solitaire on her phone before a girl with thick glasses and a nose ring took her order.

"Tall coffee, black, please. One of those egg and cheese croissants, too, and do me a favor and throw in a cookie, while you're at it."

She could grab something for Brad before she headed back, but first she wanted to hang out for a few minutes—eat her breakfast and wake up good. The hike down the hill had gotten her blood flowing, and coffee would get her brain in gear.

Between the exercise and the caffeine, she might actually be ready to tackle another workday with Bobby underfoot.

She struggled to keep from thinking about how mornings used to be, when Bobby would come over to her house on the weekends. She'd let him and Andy cook breakfast, and she'd clean up. They'd empty the Netflix queue. She'd smoke her one weekly cigarette. Be lazy as hell, just that one day—because nobody was ever game for church.

None of it was real anymore, not the house and not the husband, and not the amicable family atmosphere. Could be, she was rose-tinting it in retrospect. Maybe it was never really that idly pleasant, and it wasn't worth mourning.

She shook off the memory of scrambled eggs bubbling and Marlboros sizzling.

The high-pitched squeal of the milk steamer rang in her ears again, and the cash register pinged. Chairs squeaked on the tile floors. The bell on the door rang, and rang again. She let the new noises wash away the old ones. It worked a little better than the water at the Withrow house.

Dahlia sat down at a corner table and put her phone away. She took a sip of coffee, pushed her plate aside, and withdrew the photo album from her bag. She ran her hand over the cover, partly thinking that this was none of her business—and partly feeling like everything in the house was her business, because her father had paid for it and this was her job, to recover all the things worth recovering.

She flipped the cover open, and was greeted with the musty smell of old paper. It wasn't entirely unpleasant, but she wrinkled her nose and slipped her fingers inside the cover. Someone had put a bookplate there, declaring *ex libris* but not naming anyone in particular. She mumbled, "Someone didn't care too much about their *libris*."

She was too far away to be talking to the house, but no one was sitting close enough to accuse her of talking to herself. Dahlia took a bite of her sandwich, and another swig of coffee.

The black paper was as light and flaky as a butterfly wing. There weren't any photos attached to the first page, to the right of the open cover with its blank bookplate. She turned to the next one. A photo fell out, shedding the tiny black corners that had kept it in place. She caught it, and put it back where it belonged, though it wouldn't stay there. All the glue was shot, and all the small corner pieces rustled around like so much confetti.

Gingerly, she straightened the images so she could see them in order.

At the top left was a very old shot, from the early 1880s—or so she guessed from the clothes. A man and a woman sat in a studio, straight backed and wearing neutral expressions. They were youngish, maybe thirty years old. The woman held a baby wrapped in such a profusion of lacy clothes that only its round little face was visible. Along the bottom, right across their knees in ink that'd faded to a rusty brown, someone had written, "Francis and Mary, with baby Judson."

Two more photos followed at five-year intervals, both of them missing Francis. Perhaps he'd taken the pictures himself, or he'd died somewhere offscreen. There wasn't much evidence either way, for he never appeared again.

On the next page, Dahlia found a wedding photo. Baby Judson was all grown up, gone tall and lanky. His bride wore cascades of lace and a veil that draped across her shoulders, pooling in the chair. It must've cost a fortune.

"Judson and Eleanor, 1899."

Beneath it, another picture—taken no more than a handful of years later. Eleanor appeared much the same, but now she stood with two small children beside her, a boy and a girl. They were posing stiffly in a patch of grass, perhaps on the lawn of the house itself. Nothing was written on the picture or beneath it, but a third image showed three children together: the boy, the girl, and a toddler, sitting in a line on the steps of what looked like the Withrow front porch. They were identified in different handwriting, using a pencil that was scarcely legible against the black paper. "Abigail, Buddy, and Hazel."

A long black shadow stretched toward them, a man with his legs slightly apart, his arms bent. "Oh. The photographer." It was probably Judson. He was backlit by the sun, so he'd joined the picture by accident.

Dahlia took another bite of sandwich, chewed it, and chased it with more coffee. The next few pictures featured mostly the same five individuals, aging with every turn of the page. A few stray cousins were introduced, but never more than once. Judson and Eleanor became older and heavier, and their children grew taller.

As the next ten years went by, the photos became less formal, less precisely composed. Personalities cracked through the sepia.

Dahlia decided that Judson was formal and stern, fair but stubborn. In one washed-out image, he wore a military uniform, but the image was in such a poor state, it was hard to say what kind. He held himself like a man with money—a man who expected his family to uphold certain standards of decorum. Eleanor may or may not have agreed, but she was dressed beautifully in every image. "Quite the fashion plate," Dahlia breathed into her beverage.

Eleanor smiled softly, showing no teeth. She always looked at the camera, never her children.

The farther Dahlia browsed, the more confident she became that something had been wrong with Buddy. Something about his blank face and permanent squint . . . was he blind? Mentally delayed, somehow? He often stood apart from the rest of the family, though his little sister Hazel sometimes held his hand, as if she was trying to keep him close, or draw him in to the circle.

By her preteen years, the oldest girl, Abigail had developed a classic case of resting bitch face. She'd turned out pretty, but her mouth aimed down at the corners. Her eyebrows had a permanent arch that suggested that whatever you were saying, she didn't believe it.

Hazel was more of a mystery. The youngest and smallest, she came off as the quiet, bookish type. Or was Dahlia making up details, in the absence of information? Maybe . . . But if she looked hard at this picture, or that one, she could see a curious gleam in the girl's eye. She was almost a fey little thing, with her braided hair and tiny bow mouth. Was she a trickster? A flirt?

The croissant sandwich was almost gone. Dahlia popped the last chunk into her mouth, and turned the page with the two fingers that had the least amount of breakfast grease on them. She stopped chewing and almost choked, but caught herself; then swallowed too hard, too soon.

She coughed into her hand.

Abigail, 1915.

She would've been about fifteen or sixteen years old, in that awkward space between being a girl and a woman, and her clothes showed it. She was wearing a long, light dress that was not exactly a child's, but not from her mother's wardrobe, either.

Dahlia had seen that dress before. She would've sworn it on her own mother's grave.

In just a flash, yes—just a pattern of fabric billowing in the breeze, out of season. Was it yellow? Everything was yellow in a photo that old. She ran her thumb over the image, smudging away a dusting of black paper. The dress's fabric had a pattern to it, something small. She couldn't suss out the details, but she knew it must be covered in flowers.

The dress fit Abigail funny. Either she wasn't wearing it correctly, or it wasn't the right size, or . . . something.

Dahlia leaned down closer, wishing for a magnifying glass—and nearly fell out of her chair when her phone rang. The ringtone brought her back to the present, to the coffee shop, to the foot of Lookout Mountain. She fished out her phone and checked the display.

Her throat hurt from the bite she'd gagged on, and her voice was thick when she answered, "Hey, Brad."

"Hey, yourself. Got your note. Any chance you could grab me some coffee?"

"I was already planning on it. Are Bobby and Gabe up and around yet?"

"Gabe's up. He's still in the bathroom. Don't know about Bobby."

"You have my full permission to find him and kick him awake. I'd love to see everyone up and dressed by the time I get back. We've got a lot of work to do, and the sooner we get started, the sooner we can knock off for lunch. "

"How far away are you?" he asked.

"Just down the hill. I'm almost finished here, so I'll head back in a few minutes." She asked if he needed any food, sorted out a few particulars, and closed out the call—then gathered up the photo album and stuffed it back into her bag. Since the line had cleared out and no one else was waiting, she went directly to the register to grab something for Brad, as promised.

She put in her order, and pulled out her wallet.

The cashier with the nose ring looked down at Dahlia's chest. "Music City Salvage," she read.

Dahlia looked down and realized the company T-shirt was peeking out from the top of her flannel. "Yup, that's us."

"You're here about the Withrow place, right?"

"Uh-huh." The register chimed and offered up a price. Dahlia picked out a few bills and handed them over. "You ever been there?"

"Not . . . officially," she said conspicuously. "Not by invitation, or anything."

"You like poking around in old places?"

Nose ring girl nodded. "Hell yeah. I don't bother anything," she added quickly. "Or steal anything. But I like to look around, take pictures. You know."

"Actually, I *do* know."

The barista pulled out a to-go cup with a recycled cardboard sleeve around it. "I got some really weird shots out there a couple of years ago. Me and some friends had the bright idea of checking it out on Halloween. A place that old, it's got to be haunted, right?"

Dahlia didn't answer that one. She just handed over the money in trade for the cup, then dropped her change into the tip jar. "Where are the . . . ? Oh, I see them." The airpots were on the other end of the counter.

"We got some recordings, too. Voices, that kind of thing. My boyfriend caught this sound on his phone—it sounds like a baby crying. *So* creepy."

"Well, me and my crew are staying in the house for now, so don't scare me too bad. We've got to sleep in that place."

The girl shuddered. "How long will you be there?"

"A few days. My dad's bringing a trailer on Friday, so we'll head back to Nashville when everything's wrapped up. The real demo starts after we leave. We're just taking out the good stuff—the things people want, if they've got an old house of their own."

"Like the tubs, windows, that kind of thing?"

"Yeah. That kind of thing. Anyway, thanks for the coffee, and stuff."

Even the secondhand rain had quit altogether, and a thin vein of blue sky showed through the clouds. Dahlia hiked back through the neighborhood and up the hill again, balancing the coffee and her messenger bag, watching her step over fallen logs and along damp-slicked roads that weren't half so well paved as they ought to be.

She made it back in twenty minutes.

Brad greeted her at the door. He was wearing a bathrobe over his clothes. She handed him the coffee and didn't say anything about the bathrobe, but her stare made him defensive. "It's cold in here."

"It's not *that* cold. And it'll be warmer in an hour—or whenever we get started."

"I'll swap this out for a sweater before we get to work. I

packed a hoodie. And see?" He did a little two-step, showing off a pair of jeans. "Work pants."

"I'm very proud of you," she said, strolling past him into the kitchen—where Gabe was assembling breakfast from the bags they'd left out or stashed in the fridge. No one really wanted to open the fridge, which smelled like ass. But that's where the sodas were, so he braved it anyway, fishing around until he found the right color and flavor of energy drink to kick-start the day. He pulled out two, and left one on the counter.

"Welcome back, Dahl. Dad's up, too," he said before she could ask. "He's in the shower, and he'll be down soon. He said he'd be ready to get to work before you got back, but you know him."

Brad took a manly swig from the mostly-still-hot coffee. "So, what's the plan for today?"

"Today." She took a deep breath. "We finish the second floor of the carriage house, and move on to the barn. There's not much in there, I don't think; we're mostly parting it out. We'll stash that stuff in my truck—all the surplus building parts, the wood and windows and whatnot. We'll save Bobby's truck for the antiques and fixtures, unless the balance tips too hard in one direction or another." She leaned on the counter, recoiling when her elbow landed in something sticky. "After all that, if we still have daylight to burn, we'll start on the inside of the house. It'll take us forever to pull these fireplace mantels. It'd be nice to get a lead on them."

Heavy, uneven footsteps on the stairs heralded Bobby, freshly showered. His hair was wet and his eyes were red. What bits of him weren't blotchy from the hot water were pale as a fish. "I'm up," he announced, like he didn't quite believe it himself.

"What do you want, a cookie?" Dahlia asked.

Gabe grabbed a spare energy drink, and chucked it his way.

Bobby caught it with one hand. He popped the tab, and tossed his son a nod that was supposed to stand in for a thank-you. "I don't know if we brought any cookies or not, but I'll settle for this. So what's the plan today?"

Gabe threw himself on that grenade before Dahl could snipe about him being late to the party. "I'll fill you in over break-fast." He frowned at his dad, not for being slow and wet, but out of concern. He asked, "Hey, Dad, are you okay?"

"Me? What? Okay? Yes, okay. Very okay."

"You don't *look* okay. You've still got some soap on you . . ." Gabe gestured at his neck.

"It's just soap. It's still okay. I just took a fast bath, because I didn't want to hear about it from the boss-lady over there."

Dahlia didn't quite believe him. She knew that weird, frozen look on his face. It meant he was lying, and he was upset. "Bobby," she asked, "did you use the shower down the hall?"

"Yeah, of course I did. The Pepto-Bismol suite, with all the ugly tile. By the way, it's wet in there. We forgot to bring a shower curtain."

"I know. I've put it on my list. But you didn't . . . you didn't go through my room? You didn't use *my* bathroom?"

"Jesus, Dahl. We're not twelve years old. I'm not trying to sneak around and read your diary. *No,* I didn't use your bath-room."

"I didn't mean it like that," she protested. Then she wasn't sure how far she should push, so she backtracked, and picked another path. "I was only thinking, I might hike down to the Walgreens over lunch and get a curtain for myself. I'll get one for your bathroom, too, while I'm at it."

Bobby belched. "Or you could drive. I know you're a puss about the trucks, but it's not a big deal. They get in and out of here just fine."

"The weather's nice. It's not raining anymore, and it's not very far. I could be there and back in less than an hour."

"Or *I* could drive, and pick up whatever else we forgot to grab before we came. The whole trip would take fifteen minutes."

She waved her hand, shooing the offer away for now. "Forget it. We can talk about it later. Me and Brad are going to gear up and hit that carriage house again. Let Gabe bring you up to speed, grab some food if you want, and come join us. Sooner rather than later, please."

Before heading out, she left her bag with the photo album back in her room, and poked her head into the hallway bath. It was a sauna in there, but it wasn't weird or dark. She didn't see anything in the mirror, not even her own reflection.

"Come on, Brad. You ready for day two?"

"I took a fistful of ibuprofen. Once it kicks in, I'll loosen up just fine."

Most of the gear was still in the carriage house, piled on the first floor behind those oversized doors that neither opened nor shut correctly. "We probably shouldn't leave the place unsecured," Dahlia observed feebly, remembering yesterday's promise to Gabe. She dragged the nearest door all the way open to let in the light.

Brad shrugged stiffly. "Why not? Who would come after any of this stuff? I haven't seen another soul since we got here."

She grunted, and set the door down hard—narrowly missing her foot. "Gabe saw someone, or he *thought* he did. He brought it up yesterday, and I told him . . ." She went to the pile of useful work things, and retrieved her gloves. She slipped them on, using her teeth to drag the right one into place. She wiggled her fingers to settle them in. "I told him he was right, and we should lock the place up better when we're not around. I've been lazy about it, though. I guess I feel a little bad about slacking off on the security issue, because it seemed real important to him. He was a bit shaken up; wanted to search the premises and everything, but . . ."

"But you think he's being overly cautious?"

The ladder was right where they'd left it, with the top step barely a foot below the entrance to the loft. Dahlia put one foot on the bottom rung, and gripped the sides. "Not exactly."

"Then . . . what? You think he saw a ghost?"

She stopped, half on the ladder, and half off it, ready to climb. "Why would you say that?"

"I saw Bobby's face when he came down the stairs. You know how people say, 'You look like you've seen a ghost'?"

"Yeah."

"He looked like that. I'm just curious, since you guys do these teardowns all the time, and demo is supposed to stir up the spirits. Or that's what I've heard."

"Have you seen anything creeping around?"

He took a breath, looked behind him at the open doors, and let it out, all in one sentence. "Okay, this might sound nuts but I thought I saw a guy over by the graveyard you found yesterday."

She pulled her foot down off the rung and turned to face him. "A guy? Are you sure?"

Brad fidgeted under her stare. He shook his head, stuffing his hands into the pockets of his hoodie. "If I was sure, I would've said something sooner."

"What did this mystery guy look like?"

"Young. Clean-cut. He was wearing a uniform."

"A uniform? Like an army uniform?"

He nodded. "How'd you guess? Oh, wait, never mind. The tombstones, they were from World War I."

"Right. So . . . you think the ghost is a soldier, maybe?"

He pulled his hands out of his pockets and tugged his sleeves down until he could ball them up in his fists. "You know what? Forget I said anything. It was just my imagination. I was looking outside, from that window in the parlor—I was thinking about the fireplace mantel in there, and wondering if you'd want to save the tiles on the floor around it, even though half of them are broken. I was staring off into space, you know . . . but staring toward the cemetery. The whole thing was daydreamy bullshit; let's write it off to that."

"If you'd rather."

"Yeah, I'd rather."

Dahlia took the lead up the ladder. "All right. But for what it's worth, and in case it makes you feel better . . . ," she said over her shoulder as she climbed.

"If *what* makes me feel better?" He started up behind her.

"I *do* think Gabe saw a ghost. I think he's seen a couple, since he's been here: a woman, and a little boy." She stepped off the ladder carefully, across the water-softened wood and onto a steadier patch of boards. "That's why I think it's pointless to lock up: Even if we searched the property, we wouldn't find any flesh-and-blood intruders."

Brad started climbing behind her. "Seriously? You're not making fun?"

"Seriously. It's like you said, I've done a lot of old houses. I've seen stuff, and heard stuff that made me wonder if my eyes and ears were playing tricks. Once or twice, I've even seen people—or leftovers of people, who couldn't have possibly been there, you know? Shadows, and shapes. Voices. Whatever stays behind. I had an old house once, myself . . . it might've been a little haunted, I don't know."

"You did?"

"The one I lost," she said. She waited a moment for the usual lump to rise in her throat, but it didn't, so she kept talking, daring it to make an appearance. "In the divorce. Andy basically forced me to sell it. Watch your step there, sweetheart—rain's been coming in, and the floor's not safe until you get over to this section."

Brad stretched his leg over the rotted patch and joined her on the safe side. "Oh, right. The divorce."

"Most days, I'm more mad about losing the house than losing Andy. The house was a lot of work, but it was never an asshole. It's funny, though," she said. "As soon as I bought the place, everyone in the family wanted to know about the ghosts. That was the first thing—not how much it cost, or where it was, or how big it was. They heard it was built in the 1890s, so somebody must be haunting it. Then they'd sit around and share stories about their own ghosts through the years. They all took it all for granted that someone was hanging around."

"You think they were right?"

She dusted her hands on her jeans and looked for the trunk Gabe had opened last night. "Probably. I never saw much of anything, but sometimes I felt like I wasn't alone, and somebody was watching me. Sometimes I'd lose things, little things—never anything big—and they'd turn up in strange places. Eventually, I got used to it. So if I *did* have a ghost, it wasn't a very interesting one. It never scared me, or anyone else."

"I've never had a ghost before," Brad said quietly. His eyes ran from stack to stack, taking it all in. "But this is as good a place as any for my first one. Would you *look* at all this?"

"I know, right? It's not as much stuff as we found downstairs, but there's plenty to sort through all the same. Too bad a lot of it's gone soft with rot, and we'll have to throw it out. We're lucky, really. Another ten years, and the floor here"—she tapped her foot on the plank below her—"would've fallen right through, on top of everything we scored yesterday."

"Timing is everything. Some of this looks pretty heavy. How do we get it down the ladder?"

"We don't. When Bobby and Gabe arrive, we'll pass the smaller things through the hatch; but for the bigger stuff we'll chainsaw a hole . . . over there, maybe—" She pointed at the far end of the room. "Then throw a pulley from one of these cross joints, and send it down that way. But let's make a wish list first, and then move on to the engineering particulars."

"Okay. I'll go right. You go left."

"Works for me," she agreed. "Holler if you see anything worth drooling over."

They set off in different directions. Dahlia found the children's trunk again, without even trying. It was still on the floor, lid closed (Had she closed it? Had Gabe?), and when she opened it, the contents appeared undisturbed. She left it where it was, filing it away for future reference.

Before long, Gabe and Bobby arrived, gingerly stepping across the rotted places and getting to work. There wasn't as much to take as she'd hoped, since water had come farther inside than their cursory nighttime inspection suggested. But they still found loot worth saving.

Nothing was big enough to require the chainsaw and a whole

new window after all, so everything went down the ladder—even the trunk. The trunk came down last.

"What all's in this thing, again?" Bobby asked, setting it down on the ground. He nudged it with his foot. "Clothes and toys, I remember. Is that all?"

"Open it and see." Dahlia climbed down the aluminum ladder and started breaking it down behind her.

He was way ahead of her, already knocking back the lid. "I'll give you a pass on the toys, but do we really need clothes? Can Uncle Chuck sell them?"

"Some of them are nice. Vintage baby wear, and what looks like a wedding dress." The last bit fell out of her mouth before she had time to consider it. Was there a wedding dress? Had she seen one, last night? Well, she couldn't see much of anything by the LED light. She'd check it again in the daylight. Maybe there was a wedding dress, and maybe there wasn't. Maybe there was a yellow cotton dress with tiny flowers on it, circa 1915. Wouldn't that be a kick?

"Hello?" The word was accompanied by a soft knock on the edge of the carriage house door.

Everyone turned around.

"Hello," the woman said again, this time without the question mark.

Dahlia half recognized her, and half guessed at her identity. She'd only seen her once, in passing. "Ms. Withrow?"

"Yes, and are you Dahlia Dutton?"

Dahlia pulled off her gloves and crammed them into her back pocket, far enough to stay there and wave at anyone who came up behind her. She held out her hand, saw how dirty it was, and wiped it on the top of her jeans. "That's me. Thanks for coming—I didn't know if you'd be able to make it or not.

But I'm glad you're here." She put her hand away with a sheepish smile.

"Never mind that," Ms. Withrow said pleasantly, with regards to the truncated handshake. She was wearing a cream-colored turtleneck and slacks, with pleats as crisp as the leaves around her, plus tasteful gold jewelry that was probably worth more than at least one of the salvage trucks. She was one part somebody's great grandmother, one part 1960s *Vogue* cover girl. "Getting dirty is part of the job, I understand. You've gotten quite a lot of work done, haven't you?"

"Oh, we're barely started." Dahlia turned back to the rest of the crew and said, with a wave of her arm, "Guys, this is Augusta Withrow. This is her family estate we're disassembling."

Bobby fired off a little salute. "So I gathered."

"Nice to meet you, ma'am," Gabe offered, and Brad said something similar.

"Likewise, of course. And it's . . . the four of you, is that all?" she asked.

Dahlia said, "My dad is joining us on Friday, bringing a Bobcat on a Doolittle. We're saving the heavy equipment for last."

"Ah." She peered curiously into the carriage house, which was more empty than full by now. Anything even remotely promising had been drawn out into the yard.

"Would you like to . . . um . . . can I show you around?" Dahlia asked. She felt stupid for asking, so she amended, "This was your place, and all, but you said nobody'd been inside the carriage house for years, and I thought you might like a look at some of the things we've found. In case there were any family items you'd like to keep."

The woman's eyes landed on the trunk, lingered there a moment, and flickered back to Dahlia. "That's quite all right. I don't mean to interrupt, and the things you find here . . . they all belonged to people who died before I was born. If you can find some use for them, that's wonderful. But I came because you said there was something important . . . ?"

"Yes!" she said, too fast and too eager. "Boys, why don't you finish up without me, or . . . or get set up over at the barn, since it looks like we're just about done here."

"Will do . . . ," Bobby murmured. He shouldered the collapsed ladder. "See you in a bit."

They filed past her, headed for the barn nearby.

"Thank you so much for coming," Dahlia said again, ushering her guest toward the lawn. "You didn't have to, I know. But I thought I ought to call you, and see what—if anything—you want us to do about the little cemetery."

Augusta's face went blank. "The cemetery? Good God, dear . . . what are you talking about?"

"It's right here, between the garage and the house's front lawn. You didn't mention it in the paperwork, and I thought it was just an old family plot or something; but when I went digging around, I didn't see any Withrows anywhere, so . . ." She indicated the patch with the rosebushes, the fallen logs, and the broken stones.

"Over there, you say?"

"That's right." Dahlia looked at Augusta's low navy pumps, and wondered how they'd fare across the grass. Should she offer to help? Maybe it would offend her. "If you look close, you'll see . . . I found a whole bunch of stones. Most of them are broken, or they've fallen over. Some of them, you can't hardly read what's carved on the front anymore, but most of the ones you can belong to World War I veterans."

"Wait, now . . . hang on just a cotton-picking minute . . ."

Augusta Withrow ignored the terrain, approached the nearest stones, and crouched down. Despite the dirt and moss, she held herself steady with one hand on the nearest marker. With her free fingers, she traced what remained of the letters there. "Oh my. Oh dear, oh . . ." She let out a small, raspy laugh that said none of this was funny, but it ought to be. "God*dammit,* Grandpa."

"I beg your pardon?"

Augusta stood up straight and clapped her hands together to dust them off. "My grandfather. This is . . . oh, darling. This isn't a cemetery; it's a poorly conceived joke. But how awfully sweet of you to be so concerned," she added, seeing the baffled look on Dahlia's face. "I *assure* you, no one is buried here. My grandfather had a peculiar sense of humor, and a fondness for Halloween. These monuments came from his company. That's why the names are all random, and none of them suggest any long-gone Withrows. They were all unclaimed, you see . . . and one year, he set them up like this. He covered them with pretend spiderwebs, and scarecrows, and stuffed blackbirds, or that's how my father remembered it. Good heavens, I haven't thought about it in years. I expect no one has."

Dahlia's throat was dry. She swallowed. It didn't help. "He brought the stones from his company?"

"The Withrow Monument Company. Grandpa married Grandma's money, but he had his own skills, and in time, his own business. He made tombstones, mostly. Sometimes he did plaques, or other monuments. I think, upon occasion, he could be persuaded to craft a birdbath or a fountain, for the right client and the right price. But all of this . . ." She laughed again, less raspy. Less ironic. "I'll tell you the truth: I thought Daddy made it all up."

"You never noticed it? But didn't you live here?"

Augusta's mood darkened, and there was smoke in her voice when she replied. "I didn't live here very long. I left as soon as I was able, just like everyone who ever had a lick of sense. And when I *did* come back, after my parents died . . . I didn't do much exploring. Besides, that was decades after this . . . this *farce* was installed. It was already overgrown by then."

"I'm sorry, I didn't mean to pry."

"Why not? You're prying apart everything else."

Dahlia was confused. "I'm sorry?"

Augusta sighed and shook her head. "No, I'm the one who's sorry. You're only doing your job, and a very thoughtful one, at that. You seem like a nice girl. You seem like you care."

"It's a job, yes. But I want you to know, I *do* love old houses. Desperately, I admit. I hate to see them come down, even though I understand that sometimes, they have to go."

"This one can't go soon enough."

"So you said. Or so my dad tells me you said." Dahlia was getting tangled, feeling strange. If there were no bodies, and no ghosts, and no yellow dresses flashing pale in the early fall forest, no soldiers come home from the front in a box, then who . . . ? "In any case, I apologize—because I didn't mean to waste your time. But there *is* one more thing, if I could bother you for just another minute."

"Now that I'm here, you might as well."

"There's a family album. I found it in a trunk, with some clothes. The photos are quite old, and not all of them are labeled. Would you . . . would you like to have it? It's not really worth anything for salvage purposes, but it must be important to you, or your family." She made the offer hoping that the answer was "no."

Augusta considered it longer than Dahlia had expected. "I . . . I don't want it, no. But I think I'd like to see it, if you don't mind."

"Of course. It's yours, after all."

"No, dear. It's *yours,* like everything else on this land. Your company bought it. I am now a tourist, passing through. And that's how I prefer it."

Dahlia nodded, almost like she understood. "Right, okay. Well, it's inside the house, if you'd like to—"

"No," she barked. "I don't want to go inside. I'll wait on the porch. You can fetch it, and bring it down. I'd like to see it, but I'd rather not follow you."

"All right, ma'am, I'll go get it. Give me one second, and I'll see you on the porch."

She darted back to the house, trusting that Augusta Withrow would arrive at her leisure, but half suspecting she might disappear the moment her back was turned.

She entered through the front door (which wasn't locked) and left it open behind her, barely glancing at the handprints on the rail at the landing (they were still there, and that was odd, wasn't it?). She hardly noticed the smell of soap and wet plaster coming from the hall bath with its Pepto-pink tiles.

The album was where she'd left it, so the Withrow estate wasn't like her old house—a place where things moved around. But her house had never moved anything so big as the album, with its black pages and heavy cardboard covers, overlaid with brown fabric that had frayed at the corners.

She retrieved it and hurried back downstairs, noticing with

only half her attention that an extra door was open in the hallway—the one door that was always stuck was unstuck, now, and hanging ajar. Gabe must've opened it; he must've decided he didn't like the attic. But she had other things to think about now, and other questions to ask—and she had no idea how long she could expect Augusta's patience to hold out.

Dahlia was huffing and puffing by the time she'd made it to the bottom of the steps, through the living area, down the foyer, and out the door (still open, not shut and locked in her wake).

As promised, the old woman was waiting for her.

She was seated in a rocking chair covered in peeling paint, which didn't bother her any, despite her fancy clothes. She picked at it with her fingertips, picking it away in little patches and dropping them on the floor.

"Here it is," Dahlia said. A wicker ottoman rested nearby, its seat covered with leaves and half of a bird's nest. She brushed the ottoman clear and drew it up beside Augusta Withrow. "It was in a trunk with a bunch of children's things, and a wedding dress." (She was confident that she remembered a wedding dress, whether she'd seen one or not.)

"A wedding dress? I wonder whose."

Ms. Withrow accepted the album and laid it across the top of her knees, flattening the pleats in her pants. Her legs were so thin with age that the book's edges hung off either side of her lap when she opened it. The front cover leaned against the arm of the rocker, and stayed there while she perused the pictures, one by one.

"The first few photos are labeled, sort of. The handwriting is hard to read against the black paper. I think it's just pencil."

"My word, these old photos. Judson—oh look, that's him

as a boy—that's the fellow who set up the cemetery you found. That would've been shortly after the First World War, I think. Right around the end, at any rate."

"I wonder why he left it standing, for all those years afterward."

Augusta shrugged, and turned the page. "Tombstones are heavy. I suppose he didn't feel like going to the trouble. He wasn't so young anymore, not by then."

"He'd have been in his forties, if I read the dates right. That's not so old. *I'm* almost forty."

"And you're a mere babe," she murmured in return, keeping her eyes on the pages before her. "Judson didn't build this house, you know. His father, Francis—he's the one who built it. But he and Mary both died, not too long afterward. Judson was still a boy."

"Poor kid."

"It happens. It happens more often than it should, around this house." Another page, and another mumble—a softly spoken name or two, and flecks of black paper falling onto her lap like pepper.

"Does it? It's such a beautiful place."

"Beauty lies, dear." She looked up, meeting Dahlia's eyes in a hard, serious gaze. "So do houses."

"I don't know what you mean."

"Oh, I think you do. You're a hopeless romantic; it's written all over your face."

Dahlia grunted a laugh. "You've got the hopeless part right, but the romantic's been burned right out of me."

"Then there's hope for you yet. Don't get too attached, Miss Dutton. This place, this family . . . I'm the last of them, you know."

"That's what my dad said. I'm sorry," she added lamely.

"Why?"

"It must be lonely."

Augusta shook her head, and returned her attention to the album. "It's a relief. The Withrows have had their time, and they spent it poorly. Oh, it's Aunt Hazel." She pointed at a photo of a woman holding a carnival mask and grinning broadly. "Speaking of spinsters . . . or, not speaking, but I was thinking about them—spinsterhood was the only way a woman might get out alive, so you can see why we're finally dying out." She tapped a fingernail on the photo of Hazel. "This picture must've been taken in New Orleans, around 1930. Aunt Hazel had . . . interests."

"In New Orleans?"

"In the dark things taught there. She went to Lily Dale, too, and Cassadaga in Florida. She wanted answers, and never got them—though she hunted all her life. Maybe she found them after the fact. I'd like to think so."

"She was a spiritualist?" Dahlia guessed. "Interesting hobby."

"It's a religion, you know. Don't be condescending."

"I didn't mean to be. I'm sorry."

"You apologize too much. It makes you look weak, not polite."

Dahlia fought the urge to apologize again. "Yes ma'am, you have a point. But let me ask you, did something happen to Abigail? There aren't any pictures of her, not after that last one in the yellow dress."

The old woman blinked slowly, and the corners of her mouth tightened into something like a smile, but not a smile. Not quite. "That dress . . . it *was* yellow, wasn't it? Not that you can see from the picture," she murmured. "But I'll tell you what happened: She died, sometime in the early twenties, I'm not sure exactly when. It was her death that prompted Aunt Hazel's interest in the far side of the veil, you might say. I think Hazel was trying to protect herself. And my father, Buddy. She wanted to protect him, too."

"From what?"

"From whatever Abigail became." She closed the book, then closed her eyes for a moment. When she opened them again, she said, "It's an old story, the kind they used to write songs about: Abigail fell in love, and she tried to elope—but her fiancé vanished. She cried her eyes out, like you do; but being young and resilient, she fell in love again a year or two later. I never heard too many of the details, but I think the second betrothed was a better match, so far as the family's opinion went."

"You mean, he had more money."

"Undoubtedly. But, fortune or none, it wasn't meant to be. The wedding never occurred, and in my opinion, the young man dodged a bullet."

Dahlia frowned and crossed her arms. Across the yard, she heard the sounds of pry bars and splitting wood, and the guys chatting back and forth. She ought to get back to work, but not while she held Augusta's attention on a thin string that could break at any moment. The wrong question would do it. The end of the album would do it, if nothing else. "So it didn't work out."

The woman nibbled at her lip, and let it go. "The night before the wedding, Grandpa threw a party. I wasn't there," she noted. "I wasn't born yet—not for another handful of years. According to family lore, my father went up to the bride-to-be and asked her, quite frankly, if her baby would be in the wedding."

"Her *baby*?"

"That was everyone's reaction. Well, Abigail swore she had no idea what her brother was talking about, but he insisted. He told everyone she'd had a baby, and buried it under a tree."

"You mean, she had a child with the first fiancé?"

"One must assume. You should understand, my father . . . he was always a bit funny, and he got funnier with age. These days, I think you'd call it autism, or something like that; I'm sure there's a term for it, but we didn't have a polite one, not back then. Daddy often said inappropriate things, but he never meant any harm. Likewise, my mother was very patient, and more than a little odd herself. They were a peculiar match, but a good one."

"And they're gone now? You said they died, and you came here . . ."

"Oh yes. They've been gone for quite some time—I lost them to a car crash when I was fifteen years old. I see you on the verge of offering sympathies, but I wish you wouldn't," she said, heading Dahlia off at the pass.

"As you like."

"Thank you. At any rate, Daddy's little question at the engagement party was a public accusation, and that was unfortunate. Abigail frantically denied it. But she was a terrible liar: For all she cried about how my daddy'd made it up, and he was weak in the head, and he didn't know what he was saying, it was all nonsense, every bit of it. Daddy was funny, but he wasn't stupid."

Dahlia was both rapt and appalled. "So . . . what happened?"

Augusta returned the album and rose to her feet. She dusted a smattering of black paper flecks off her designer pants, and held the rail as she took the porch steps slowly and carefully, her shiny pumps crushing leaves and pine needles as she went. She paused at the bottom of those stairs, and looked back up at the house. "As I've heard it told, Abigail swore to God there was never any baby—and the devil could carry her off if she was lying. She vanished that night, and no one ever saw her alive again. Some say the devil took her up on the offer."

A great silver Lexus was parked by the house. Dahlia wondered why she hadn't heard it arrive, except that she'd been working in the carriage house, and talking with the boys. There wasn't any driver waiting. Apparently, Augusta Withrow preferred to handle such things herself.

She walked away from Dahlia, heading for the car without looking back. "It was a pleasure to meet you, Miss Dutton. Thank you for your attention to detail, and I wish you and your crew the best. But goddamn this house, and this land, and everything left upon it. When you're finished here, the devil can take that, too."

7

DAHLIA CLUTCHED THE photo album to her chest and watched Augusta Withrow drive away.

The book crackled and crumbled, shedding yet more black paper flakes across the porch as the sleek silver car did a perfect three-point turnaround and squeezed back through the old stone piles where the gate used to be.

It hadn't been gone for fifteen seconds when Bobby hollered from the barn. "Fucking *Christ,* Dahlia—are you ever coming back? Come on, we have work to do!"

"And we need leadership!" Brad called out. They all three cackled.

She couldn't see them from where she was standing, and didn't know if they could see her—but she flipped the bird in their general direction and went inside to stash the album. It was hers now, free and clear, and for keeps. Back into her messenger bag it went, up on the oversized bay window seat that made an adequate bed if you spread a sleeping bag there. She pulled off her flannel and tossed it on top of the bag. It was getting too warm to wear it.

Out in the hallway, where the broken window let in sunlight, rain, and sound, she heard the guys talking. Their words were so clear they might've been standing beside her, or having a sleepover in the room next to hers. They'd found something odd, and couldn't decide what it was.

Gabe made a guess: "Part of a wagon, I think?"

Brad didn't quite agree. "Farm equipment. Maybe a plow, or some kind of . . ."

"This wasn't a farm." Well, Bobby wasn't wrong about that. "So either it belonged to somebody else, or it was something else. Who cares, anyway? It's fallen apart now, and that wood it's made of . . . that ain't chestnut."

Dahlia went to the window and planted her hands on the sill, leaning forward to look outside as she eavesdropped.

Gabe wasn't ready to fight him on it. "Whatever it was, it must've been big. Like, the size of a truck."

"But older than that," Brad added. "Look at this, it's part of a wood wheel."

A breeze kicked up, the kind of breeze that sounds like radio static, and is thick with falling leaves. Someone said something next, but Dahlia didn't catch it. Her ears were full of the fluttering, flapping, raspy sound of foliage and fabric. There were leaves, red and orange. There was a dress, yellow cotton.

On the other side of the yard, the cemetery plot was barely visible from her second-floor vantage point. She could only glimpse the northern edge, where it bumped against the path that scrolled past the carriage house.

At that intersection between yard and plot, a figure stood, staring up at the mansion.

No, it was looking at the window.

No, it was looking at Dahlia. It met her eyes.

Not a woman in a dress, but a man in a suit. No, not a suit. A uniform, just like Brad had somewhat reluctantly told her. This soldier was scarcely more than a teenager, but broad-shouldered and fair-haired. He looked like a fellow who'd worked hard for a long time already, before he took up the military. He could've been any football player Dahlia had ever gone to high school with, as if the whole breed just fell out of a mold.

Maybe it did.

Her breath caught in her throat, then climbed back out again. This wasn't a ghost. It was a flesh-and-blood thing, solid as the tombstones behind him. Ghosts were not so sharp. Ghosts did not shift their shoulders, adjusting their rifles. They did not lean from foot to foot, like they'd been standing for too long, waiting for something or someone who was taking her own sweet time.

She pointed down at him. She whispered, *"Don't move."*

Did he hear her? Did he give a damn?

She flung herself down the stairs, through the living area still cluttered with bags and work gear, along the foyer, past the formal parlor on one side and the dining room on the other, and out through the front door, where she could stare squarely at the family plot that wasn't a family plot at all—seeing it from end to end, all the way back to the tree line where the saplings and pokeweed nibbled it away to just another crabgrass-covered corner of the family land.

There was nothing to see. There was no one there.

She dashed to the spot where the soldier had waited, and she stood in the place where his boots had been planted. She caught her breath one mouthful at a time—and with the air came the smell of something else, something rotten. Gunpowder and blood, and graveyard dirt. Burned wool. Shoe polish. Sulfur.

She drew it all down into her lungs and held it there, investigating every molecule.

The soldier had been there, on this very patch of turf. No,

there weren't any footprints, and no, there was no sign that anyone had hiked through the brush, the weeds, the monkey grass
and gravel and unwanted stuff from the carriage house that
the crew had left on the front lawn. Nothing had disturbed all
those things too broken to save, too heavy or rotten to keep.

"Nobody's buried here," she assured herself, and the tombstones around her. She did it quietly, in case the guys were
within earshot. Pretty much everything was within earshot at
the Withrow estate; every soft sound bounced off the side of
the mountain and lingered, half echo and half memory. Every
footstep, every gasp. It all stayed longer than it ought to.

"Nobody's buried here. There are no soldiers. No girls in yellow dresses."

And there was no reason to stay there, standing in a not-a-
cemetery like a fool. She shivered, wrapped her arms around
herself, and wished she'd kept the flannel—but didn't go back
inside to retrieve it.

For October, the weather was positively warm.

It was good weather for hard work, and for camping in
old houses that were more drafty than cozy. It was good
weather for ghosts, except there weren't any. Not on the Withrow grounds.

Surely, the devil had taken them all.

She left the crooked, shattered stones and the roses, brambles, and flaky dead hydrangeas as brown and muddled as old
coffee filters. She trudged thoughtfully back toward the barn.
The non-cemetery begged a question: If the Withrows weren't
buried there . . . and no one else was buried there, either . . .
then where *did* the dearly departed Withrows actually rest?

Later on, maybe she'd spend some time on her phone, kick-

156

ing around on the Internet. She might get lucky and find some of those dusty dead listed online. If they were interred locally, she might even be able to visit their final resting places and pay her respects, or grab phone pictures of their tombstones.

Not that it would accomplish anything. It wouldn't explain any ghosts. It wouldn't save the house, which the devil would take soon enough.

"*There* you are," Bobby groused, when she finally reached the barn.

"Here I am. Did you guys make this mess, or was it like this when you got here?"

They'd pried open the barn doors without her, a process that involved pulling one of them right off its hinges—and breaking the other one into pieces. Now both doors lay flat on the grass, their rusted metal fixings jutting up from frayed, twisted beams spiked with bent nails.

Gabe confessed, "We did most of it. We couldn't get the doors open, not to save our lives. Brad said we should just pull out the hinges, that'd be the easy way. We're going to take the wood, anyhow, and it doesn't matter if we leave it open."

Brad nodded. "But everything was rusted to everything else. Honestly, we could've opened the thing faster with a chainsaw."

Dahlia shrugged. "Oh well. We'll have to drag the power tools out eventually, because we'll never get these bigger beams free with just crowbars and sledges. Gabe, you want to bring my truck around?" She fished keys out of her pocket and tossed them to him. "The generator's in the back, along with some gas to run it. We'll fire it up and go to town. The wood . . ." She poked the toe of her work boot against the nearest door. "Yeah, it's chestnut."

"As advertised," Gabe called cheerfully, as he strolled toward the truck. "Uncle Chuck is gonna be so psyched!"

"Damn right, he will." Dahlia stepped past the fallen doors and let herself inside the barn. "Is there anything but the wood worth saving in here? Or have you had time to look?"

"We've had plenty of time, what with you chatting up the old lady." Bobby adjusted his cap, and wiped his forehead with the back of his hand. "What was that about, anyway? What did she want?"

She told the truth. "She didn't want anything. She didn't even want to see the place. Good God, look at this hulk." She turned sideways to sidle past the enormous pile of wood and wheels, which was surely what the guys had been arguing about when she'd heard them from inside the house . . . before there was a soldier who fidgeted in the cemetery, back and forth, foot to foot.

Brad crouched beside the hulk in question. He used a scrap of lumber to poke at the side of the pile. "Mostly there's just a bunch of rotten crap in here, but this is pretty cool. It was some kind of wagon, or cart. It looks old, but I don't think we can save it."

"No, this is beyond hope," she said. She picked up a long piece of splintered wood, and used it to push the debris around. She spotted what looked like curtain fringe, and bits of broken glass. "But I bet I know what it was."

"Really?" Bobby raised an eyebrow.

Gabe returned with Dahlia's truck. The driver's door slammed, and the big kid hopped down off the running board, into the grass. "Hey, Dad. I'll need a hand dragging this thing out. It's hella heavy."

"In a minute. Your cousin thinks she knows what this thing used to be."

The boy trotted into the barn to join everyone else. "Cool. What was it?"

"I bet it was a hearse. The horse-drawn kind, from way back in the day." Dahlia lifted the edge of fringe, and let it fall. She jabbed a padded seat that had long ago been pillaged by rats in search of nesting material, and knocked on something hard and heavy. She paused to put her work gloves back on, then stepped into the collapsed pile carefully, to feel around. She withdrew a metal handle. "See?"

"See *what*?" Bobby demanded.

"It's a casket handle." She turned it over, and used her gloves to rub off some of the tarnish. "And it's silver. See, funeral companies used to make these kits for people who couldn't afford a nice casket. They'd stick the nice hardware on for the service, just for show. When all the prayers were said, someone would yank everything off before the box went into the ground—then use it again later."

"That's . . ." Brad looked like he wanted to say "gross," but he settled for "strange."

"Nope. It was logical. If you weren't rich, why would you pay a fortune for silver or gold casket trimmings, just to bury them? The dead didn't care, and the living needed the money." Dahlia thought she'd found another one, but it turned out to be the corner of an empty box, rusted and crushed into a lump of scrap. "So bring out the lights and get yourselves some shovels or something. Dad will go apeshit for Victorian casket bling, even if it's not solid sterling."

Brad used a pry bar, Dahlia took a shovel, and Bobby dove

in with his hands and feet, lifting and shoving the bigger pieces with Gabe's help.

Gabe took a door panel that was partly intact, and turned it around. There was artwork on it, something painted but terribly faded. She could almost make out the words "funerary services." He pointed at the letters and asked, "How did you know, Dahl?"

"Know what?"

"How'd you know this was a hearse?"

She tagged something heavy with the shovel's edge, and squatted down to dig it out by hand. "You know those tombstones we found in the carriage house?"

"Yeah?"

"The Withrow family used to make them. They had their own business: the Withrow Monument Company." She extracted another handle from the rubble. "Got another one. Y'all need to catch up."

"What if there *aren't* any more?" Bobby fussed.

"There should be four, at least, more likely six. Assuming the set's intact. So keep looking." She dropped the handle with a clank beside the other one. "Anyway, I figured if the Withrows were making tombstones, they might have branched out in the death business. I saw the curtains, and the glass . . . it was an educated hunch."

Bobby grunted, signaling that he was about to argue, or accuse her of making a lucky guess—but the grunt turned into an exclamation. "Hey, I got one over here." He picked it up and rubbed it on his jeans. "This fucker's heavy. I bet it's solid." He tossed it to her.

She added it to the pile. "Solid *something.* We'll let Dad decide what it's made of."

Gabe stumbled forward, catching himself on his hands and turning one of the hearse's back panels into sawdust. It crumbled beneath his weight, and beneath years of termites and rodents and rot, all doing their worst. "One more," he chirped. "Bruised the shit out of my hand, but if it's silver, I'm not complaining!" He passed this one Dahlia's way. "So did Mrs. Withrow tell you about the family business?"

"Yep, just now. I showed her that photo album we found, and she told me about some of the people in it."

Brad paused, and rolled up his sleeves a little higher. He pushed them past his elbows. "Is that why she was here? You called her about a photo album?"

"I called her about the cemetery. She said we shouldn't worry about it. I showed her the album as an afterthought."

Brad's eyes were full of dubious concern. "She said . . . not to worry about the cemetery?"

Dahlia wondered if he'd told anyone else about the spectral soldier. "According to her, it's not a real cemetery, and nobody's buried there. It's an old Halloween prank, using unclaimed tombstones from the shop."

"So you're saying there aren't any bodies," Brad stated flatly.

"No bodies, no coffins. That's what she told me."

He shook his head and paid an awful lot of attention to the task of digging in the remains of the collapsed hearse. "Bullshit. I call bullshit."

Gabe had his back. "I don't buy it, either."

Bobby stopped what he was doing and watched Dahlia with interest.

She stood up straight, and leaned on the handle of the shovel. "Why not? Because all of y'all think the place is haunted?"

The barn went quiet. Everyone stopped scrabbling around

in the dirt, the crumbled timbers or wheels, and the ashy dust left behind by the hearse as it'd rotted through the decades. Nobody said anything in reply.

She sniffed. "At least nobody's arguing with me."

Brad put his hands up in that half-shrug, half-surrender he did so well. "You said it yesterday—we were talking about ghosts and old houses. Why shouldn't the Withrow house have a haint or two hiding in the woodwork?"

She adjusted her grip on the shovel. Its metal head scraped on the unfinished floor. "I never said it wasn't haunted," she said carefully. "This is an old house, an old estate. Lots of people came and went. Some of them probably died, and if you believe in ghosts, there's no good reason to think there aren't any here."

"You saw something?" Bobby asked. It was barely a question.

She wanted to pitch it right back at him, and ask if he'd seen anything himself. She didn't. "It's . . . not exactly like that."

But Gabe pushed the matter. "Well, *did* you, or not?" And in his eyes she saw something very close to desperation.

"I've felt things," she said, still playing it cool. It wouldn't do any good to scare the whole crew half to death. They were jumpy enough as it was. "Like someone's watching me, or like maybe I saw something out of the corner of my eye. None of it was worth getting too excited about, and there's nothing to worry about, that's for damn sure. Let me make myself clear: I *never said* there aren't any ghosts on the grounds. I only said there wasn't anyone buried in the cemetery—because it's not a cemetery. That's what Augusta Withrow said."

Brad didn't buy it. "She might be lying."

"She might be, yeah. But I went looking through that photo

album, and I didn't see any of those family names on any of the tombstones over there. There's not a single Withrow stone, and that doesn't make any sense if it was a private cemetery on their land. The names are just . . . they're all random. So can we let it go?" Dahlia lifted the shovel, jabbed it into the rubble, and resumed her search for the silver casket handles. "Ghosts or no ghosts, we're burning daylight. We can't salvage ghosts. They don't sell for shit."

One by one, the guys resumed digging, but they did it in silence—until Brad scored the final two handles, hiding side by side under one of the back wheels.

"That makes six," he declared. "I'll go lock them in the truck."

"Why?" Dahlia asked.

"Because . . . they're valuable? Maybe?"

Bobby grunted. "Everything's maybe valuable. Nobody's here to take it. Don't be paranoid."

Gabe shot Dahlia a dark look, but he didn't say anything.

She didn't sigh, but she wanted to. "I don't know, Brad's probably right. They're shiny and easily portable. If anybody comes up around here, scrapping or scavenging, these would look like an easy score. It's no more effort to lock them in the cab than to stack them in the rear. Gabe, you still got my keys?"

"Yes ma'am." He tossed them back to her.

"I'll go ahead and put them away. You and Bobby, get the generator out and running. Brad, get the Sawzalls ready to go. Check the blades and unroll the extension cords."

"Why don't we use the cordless models? This generator business is a pain in the ass," he complained.

"You need electricity to charge batteries—so on a long job

with no power, you'll need the generator anyway. Just . . . go get everything. We'll need it all, before the day's out."

The crew spent the rest of the morning disassembling the biggest pieces of the barn; and when lunch rolled around they were nearly finished—so they worked through until two o'clock, then called it. Several large piles of lumber were loosely organized by size, shape, and condition, to be loaded into the truck after a meal break.

"Then what?" Gabe asked. He was wrapping up an orange extension cord, folding it in loops between his elbow and thumb. It coiled tighter and tighter, thicker and thicker.

Dahlia didn't have anything hard and fast in mind, so she guessed. "By the time we get all that lumber loaded, and all the nonscrap items into the other truck, it ought to be getting dark."

"Then we could always get started on the house's interior," Brad suggested.

Bobby disagreed. "*Or* we could have a drink and take a fucking rest. I could use a beer. Or two, or three. Hell, we're ahead of schedule, so we might as well relax. You think it'll take us all day tomorrow and Thursday to break the house down? You're crazy."

"Like you'd know anything about how long it takes," Dahlia grumbled.

"Hey, I might not have done a million of these, but I'm no idiot. The house is mostly empty, except for the stuff we plan to pry loose and make off with. It shouldn't take a whole day."

"I *have* done a million of these, and I can tell you those mantels will take for-fucking-ever to get out." Dahlia took another long snake of extension cord and started winding it, somewhat more fiercely than Gabe. "You have to reinforce the marble where it's cracked, or else the whole thing will crumble, and then what? Then the mantels and surrounds aren't worth shit, that's what."

"Only two of them are marble."

"Either one could wind up taking us all afternoon to secure—and they're valuable enough to spend the time doing it right. Who's the boss, Bobby?"

"Go to hell."

"*Who's the boss?* Tell me now, or pack your shit and go back to Nashville." She flung the rolled cord onto the ground, and started picking up the power saws. "You've been getting too comfortable here, Bobby—thinking you can jerk off like usual, and all you have to do is be a little nice once in a while. Well that ain't the case, and you can't just squeak by on the bare minimum. So I'll ask you again: Who's in charge?"

He spit on the floor and turned on his heel. "You are, bitch."

She told him, "Go get some lunch, asshole." But he was already out of the barn and halfway back to the truck he called his own. She kept twisting the cords, squeezing them like she'd prefer to squeeze somebody's neck.

Gabe rolled his eyes. "Cute. Real cute." He collected the rolls of cord like oversized bangles on his forearm. "You two are *real* mature."

She did her best not to snap, to be a grown-up and the boss instead. "I love you, Gabe, but you've gotta leave it alone. He can call me a bitch if he wants, so long as he does what I tell him."

"You didn't have to ride him so hard. He's done all right, so far," he protested.

She carried the Sawzalls out of the barn and to the back of her truck, which was parked much closer. "You mean except for now? And last night, when he ran off drinking?"

"He was here working this morning, while you were hanging out with that old lady."

"He was here arguing with you all about what you found. I could hear you, you know, the whole time. Inside that house, with that window broken on the second floor . . . you can hear everything, all over the property. He wasn't even breaking a sweat."

"He was working before that. We all were, except you."

"Gabe, *seriously*."

"I'm just saying, you should cut him some slack," he said, stubbornly. He followed behind her with the cords, and loaded them up.

She left him there, and went back for the rest of the equipment. Over her shoulder, she said, "He's had nothing *but* slack, his entire life. Always needing a break, always needing money, always needing another chance, and this time, things will be different. Now, at his age . . ." She seized the last of the power-tool cases; they knocked together in her arms as she walked back to the truck yet again. "He doesn't know how to behave like a goddamn adult, because nobody's ever made him."

"When did it become *your* job to make him?"

"When Daddy hired him, and put me in charge—*that's* when." She flung the cases into the truck and yanked the rolling door down. She locked it in accordance with Gabe's preference, even though she was starting to get a little pissed with him, too. "Now, aren't you hungry? Go get yourself some lunch."

Out by the front entrance, she heard the sound of Bobby's tires peeling out through the grass and gravel. Well, at least he hadn't started drinking yet. Maybe he wouldn't have half a dozen beers at lunch, and he'd make it back in one piece.

Unless two days of decent behavior in a row was too much to hope for. "He'd better drive careful in that thing. Every time he takes it out, it's carrying more loot, and we can't afford for him to crash it or get it stolen. Now, where the hell did Brad go?"

Gabe paused and looked around. "I don't see him. He could've left with Dad . . . ? They get along okay."

"I admit, it kind of surprises me."

"Why? Because Dad doesn't have any friends?"

"He doesn't have any friends like Brad. Gabe, honey, come on. You know what I was trying to say."

The boy relented. "Brad *is* kind of fancy for this line of work. But he's doing all right, too. Maybe he went back inside. There's plenty of sandwich stuff, if you don't want to walk or drive all the way to Saint Elmo."

"Do you want a sandwich?" she asked him.

"Not the kind we got in here. I want something hot. There's a barbecue place down the hill, isn't there?"

"Yeah, I saw that." It was a good excuse to cool down. She didn't need Gabe thinking she was angry with him, because he wasn't the problem. "Hop into the cab, kid. Let's go find some real food. We'll bill it to your Uncle Chuck."

"Will he be okay with that?"

"As long as we don't expense any booze, I doubt he'll care." She paused, and said, "Let me look in the house. We'll see if Brad wants to come, if we can find him."

But when she rounded the truck, she spied him right away. He wasn't in the house; he was standing in the cemetery that wasn't a cemetery. "Brad!" she called. If he heard her, he ignored her. Maybe he was listening for the rustle of fabric, or the whispering rush of nonexistent ghosts clamoring for his attention.

They could get in line. She wanted his attention first.

She tagged him on the shoulder. He didn't jump like he was surprised when she asked, "Dude, are you all right?"

"It's bullshit . . . ," he whispered, looking down at the graves that weren't graves. "I *know* there's something buried here."

"Honey, I wish you were right—believe me. I halfway thought, maybe, if there was a cemetery here, then we'd get lucky. I thought there was a chance the demo crew wouldn't be able to take down the house if this was in the way. I thought it might buy the place some time."

He looked at her, confused. "You want to save the house?"

"I *always* want to save the house." She sighed. "Except for the one time when I bought the place myself, it's never worked out. But this one, this Withrow house . . . it's a hot mess, but I really love it. It speaks to me."

"Yeah? What does it say?"

Because he sounded honestly interested, she answered him. "It's unhappy. It's angry."

"The house, or you?"

"Can't it be both of us? Look, I'm sorry, but I don't know what to tell you except . . . I'm going to look up the Withrow graves—the *real* ones—and if I find where they're buried, I'll let you know. I'll . . . I'll call the county, too. If there was ever a cemetery opened on this property, even if it was just a family plot, there'd be some record. I might be able to buy the place a stay of execution."

Brad nodded, and kicked gently at the nearest stone. "Okay. But I know what I saw, Dahlia. There's somebody here, trying to tell us something. And it isn't the house."

From the other side of the truck, Gabe cried out, "Dahlia? Brad? Where the hell are you?"

"Over here!" she shouted back. "We're coming."

Brad frowned. "We are?"

"Yeah. Aren't you hungry?"

He shook off whatever spell had held him there, and said, "You know what? I *am*. What's on the menu?"

8

Lunch went as planned, and so did the afternoon's truck loading—even though Bobby came back to work smelling like beer. He didn't act any drunker than usual, and at least he was on time. He also kept his mouth shut, and he did his part to hoist the lumber up, over, and into the back of the truck right alongside Gabe, while Dahlia and Brad stayed inside the truck.

The trucks always held more than it looked like they ought to.

The day had warmed up to seventy-five degrees, and it was downright hot inside that truck; but the sun went behind the mountain around six, right about the time the last of the timbers were jammed into place.

It was as good a stopping point as any.

They packed up their equipment and locked the trucks, then headed inside for a cold supper—as penance for the money they'd spent on lunch. While the guys made sandwiches and cracked open cans of Chef Boyardee, Dahlia checked her messages and plugged in her phone at an outlet in the dining room. She set it on one of the built-in cabinet shelves and checked its display. The signal was good, but her battery was dying, and she didn't want to drag her laptop all the way back down to the coffeehouse for Internet . . . but she *did* want to look around online, to see if she could find those Withrow graves. But first, a bite to eat.

She turned around to join the kitchen crew, and Bobby was there. Right behind her, like he'd snuck up and was about ready to yell, "Boo!" . . . only he looked just as surprised as she felt. He held up his hands and took a step back.

"What are you doing?" she demanded.

"I said your name about a dozen times and you didn't answer." He cocked his head. "I wasn't trying to scare you."

She exhaled. She was jumpy, and while plenty of things might be described as Entirely Bobby's Fault, this wasn't one of them. "I was . . . distracted. What's up?"

He scrunched up the side of his mouth like he used to when they were kids, when he had a question he didn't want answered—but one he needed to ask. He checked back over his shoulder and either saw Gabe in the kitchen, or heard him chatting with Brad. "I wanted to say something, about this house. About ghosts. I want to ask you real serious-like, if you've seen anything weird."

"Bobby, you're just . . . you're talking up nothing."

"You haven't seen anything? For real?"

She leaned back against the cabinet—half sitting on it, beside her phone. "No."

"You're a liar, Dahl. But I don't know who you're lying to: yourself, or just me. This whole place is weird as hell, and it isn't empty. Maybe the cemetery is empty, I don't know; but there's something dead hanging around this place all the same, and it don't want us here. It doesn't want the house torn down."

"That makes two of us."

"Oh, for fuck's sake, *stop it.* You can't fall in love with every place you scrap. It's not healthy."

He was half a head taller than she was, but she glared him down. "You think you know something about me?"

"You're practically my sister."

"But I'm *not,* because that kind of blood would be thicker than water, wouldn't it?"

"Oh, for Christ's sake, Dolly . . ."

"We had a deal, Robert."

"Okay, then I want to make another deal, a new one: No bullshit. Not between us grown-ups." Fast on the heels of that, he clarified, "Not between you and me."

There was a fight to be picked, and she wrestled with the juvenile itch to run with it. But it wouldn't do her any good. It wouldn't do anyone any good, and it'd give him ammo if he went back to Chuck and complained about her management skills.

She relented, more or less. "All right, fine. But you tell me first: What's got you so spooked?"

He stunned her by answering honestly and quickly. With details, like he'd been taking notes. "I saw a girl. She was eighteen, twenty years old, and she had blood and dirt all over her." He checked the kitchen again, with one eye and one ear. He lowered his voice. "She did something bad, Dahl. I don't know what, and I don't know who she did it to—but she wants to keep doing bad things, and she can't. Not once the house is gone."

Dahlia couldn't think of a good response, so she just said, "Jesus, Bobby."

"You ain't seen nothing like that?"

She whispered, "No! Nothing like *that.* If it makes you feel any better, I thought I saw a girl, but she didn't look dead, or messed up. She was wearing a yellow dress." Suddenly she remembered the wedding dress in the trunk, and she was seized with a desire to find and inspect it, even though she knew that it wasn't the dress in question. Where had the trunk gone? Was it packed into one of the trucks? Had they brought it inside?

"You still have that old photo album, right?"

"Right."

"Can I see it?" he asked, with a plaintive note at the end that was almost as good as a "please." "I want to see if she's in there."

"Sure," she nodded. "Yeah, I'll go get it for you in a bit. But let's eat first, okay? You're getting all wound up."

"I've *been* wound up, since this morning. The only thing that *un*wound me was a beer at lunch."

She remembered seeing him on the stairs that morning, wet and still soapy in his clothes. "What did all the winding?" Then, before he could answer, she blurted another question: "Was it something in the bathroom?"

His eyes widened, and he might've responded with something more concrete than a shocked expression—but Gabe picked that moment to lean around the corner and ask, "What are you two gossiping about?"

"You," Dahlia said fast, and with a smile. Bobby was crowding her. She nudged him away: one step. Two steps. Until it didn't look like a conspiracy.

"Aw, come on . . ."

"I'm just yanking your chain," she promised. "We're talking business, hon. What's gonna go in which truck tomorrow, that kind of thing. So did you leave us any turkey, or are we stuck with the salami and cheese?"

Bobby wasn't quite so slick, but he gave it a shaky try. "You'd *best* have left me a can of SpaghettiOs."

"I counted four of them, still in the bag. You want me to warm one up?"

"Nah, I'll eat it cold. I like it that way."

"Yuck," Gabe declared, and returned to the kitchen.

Dahlia took Bobby's arm. "We can talk about it later," she told him. "There's no need to scare him, or Brad either. Brad's already worked up in his own weird way."

"Weird how?" he asked, but she was already drawing him into the kitchen.

"Later."

Later came, and darkness settled across the mountain.

Dahlia picked at the red, green, and cream swirled tiles on the dining room fireplace. It wasn't an impressive piece, not like the ones with the marble surrounds, but it had a nice splash of arts-and-crafts tiles to recommend it. One or two were missing. Three or four were loose, and twice that many were broken beyond saving—crushed by a cast-iron summer cover that'd fallen down one time too many.

"Whatcha doing?" Gabe asked.

Without looking up, she said, "I'm wondering how big a pain in the ass it'll be, pulling these little bastards off. We'll probably break a few in the process, but someone, somewhere, will be happy to have the rest."

He crouched down beside her. His breath smelled like PBR and baloney on white bread. "Are they worth a lot?"

"Maybe a few hundred bucks. It depends. Most likely, we'll sell them by weight. Scrap them out, you know—to people with old houses, looking to match broken pieces for repairs and restoration."

"So . . . this style, these colors . . . they were pretty common?"

"Eh." She settled back on her ass, crossing her legs beneath herself. It wasn't late, but she was bourbon warm and happy to talk about something safe, something easy. "Most of the time, for projects like this, there was somebody on site who whipped up a batch for each fireplace while it was being built. Or, I'm guessing by the style . . . these were probably added later. They aren't as old as the house itself, so there might've been a fire, or some kind of accident that destroyed the original setup. Maybe we'll find something older underneath—stone, or fired pottery tiles, or something like that. These are good colors, though. Somebody with a turn-of-the-century Craftsman will decide they're close enough, and feather them in for patch work."

"That's cool."

"Uh-huh. It's a hell of a lot cheaper than finding someone to manufacture a perfect match. Art is fucking expensive," she concluded.

"Tell me about it. Hey, Dahl?"

"Yeah?"

"Can I see that photo album? The one we found in the trunk?"

"Man, that thing's popular, all of a sudden."

"Huh?" he asked.

"Nothing. Sure, you can see it. It's upstairs, in my room. What do you want with it?"

He turned his head and belched, almost discreetly. "I told you . . . I saw a boy, up in the carriage-house loft. I want to see if he's in the album."

She climbed to her feet, and he stretched back to a standing position. "What did he look like? This boy?"

Gabe rolled his shoulders and retrieved a can of beer he'd left on the mantel. Before she could tell him to wipe off the damp ring it left behind, he took care of it with his sleeve. "Well, if he's in that book, I'll show you."

"All right, have it your way. Hey, speaking of your dad, where's he at?" she asked abruptly.

"Upstairs. He was poking around that extra bedroom, like maybe he wanted to take a pry bar to the door that's all closed up."

A memory flared in the back of her head, cutting through the bourbon. There'd been a soldier downstairs. She'd been running to catch him. Out of the corner of her eye, she'd seen an open door that used to be shut. "It's still locked up?"

"I guess, if nobody opened it."

She shivered. "Well then, I guess Bobby's welcome to knock it down if he likes. We have to get in there one of these days."

"Why'd you ask? About my dad?"

"Because he wanted to see the album, too. I figured I'd just give it to the pair of you, and let you traipse down someone else's memory lane together." That wasn't what she meant, but the alcohol was running interference between her brain and her mouth. It shouldn't have left her so foggy. She hadn't had very much. They hadn't even cracked the second bottle yet, and she'd even let Bobby have some of the Maker's before it was gone. Was she getting another headache? The cotton-candy feeling in her skull might be the start of one of her odder migraines, but she was too tipsy to panic about it. She barely had the concentration skills to even *hope* it was something else.

She strolled through the arched entryway into the main living area, kicked a mostly empty duffel bag out of the way, and hollered, "Bobby? Where'd you go?"

A muffled response suggested someplace on the second floor, as reported, so she went toward the sound of his voice, with

Gabe following behind her like a big duckling. "Hey Bobby, remember you wanted a look at that photo album?" she shouted in his general direction. "Your boy does, too. It's in my room, if you care to join us."

Up the stairs, past the ninety-degree turn at the landing, at the rail where the handprints and footprints had finally been smudged away by traffic coming and going . . . and onto the second floor, where there was almost a mezzanine, now that she thought about it, before you got to the hallway with the bedrooms—and the one door that was stuck, unless it was open.

The door was still firmly shut, but not for Bobby's lack of trying.

He'd pried the right side of the frame clean off, and it lay on the floor in pieces. He'd left the doorknob untouched, thank God. It was a beauty—oxidized metal with scrollwork and a tidy little spot for a key. Not an ounce of rust. Positively pristine, and likely original to the house. It would've pissed her off to no end if he'd broken it.

The man himself appeared with a Sawzall in hand, attached to an orange extension cord that disappeared around the corner, into the bedroom he'd chosen to squat in. "Sorry, come again?"

"The photo album. You wanted to . . . and Gabe wants to . . . wait. Were you going to cut the knob out of the door? That's a solid wood door, Bobby. It's in good shape."

"I know, but it's either the door or the hardware, *boss*. That fucker is stuck but good." He pointed at the frame. "I'm doing my best to keep from hurting it."

Grudgingly, she agreed. "Okay, I get it. Between the two . . ." The door might go for more money, but she liked the hardware better. There were a dozen other doors. They could sacrifice this one. "You're making the right call, but don't tell Dad I said so. If he were here, he'd tell you to take the wood instead."

Bobby grinned like he'd finally done something right, then the grin turned into a wrinkle of his lips. "Right on. I'll cut it down in a minute. You said something about the photo album?"

"Yup."

Gabe stood behind her, doing a sheepish shift from foot to foot. "I want to look at it."

"Why for?"

Gabe stood up straighter, and traded his sheepishness for defiance. "Because I saw a ghost, and I want to know who it was."

Bobby didn't blink; just stood there holding the saw, staring at the both of them until he got his shit together enough to stammer, "You saw . . . you saw a what now? Where? Here?"

The kid bobbed his head. "Out in the carriage house, on the second floor. It's how I found the trunk. Some little boy *wanted* me to find it."

"What'd the little boy look like?" Bobby demanded.

Gabe sighed with great drama. "Like I told Dahl, if I find him in the pictures, I'll point him out." He turned around and headed toward her room, still talking, his voice trailing along behind him. "If I don't find him, well, he was a kid, all right? Maybe seven or eight. Dark hair. Wearing old-fashioned clothes."

Dahlia and Bobby looked at each other, then at Gabe's retreating back. They fell into his wake.

"Can you be more specific?" Dahlia asked him. She jogged to catch up. "Old-fashioned . . . that can mean anything. If you can remember some details, it might help date him. I'm good with old clothes."

"I don't remember." Gabe had spotted the album on the window seat where Dahlia'd been sleeping. He sat down on the edge of her bedding and opened the cover with great care, but that didn't stop a small cloud of black paper dust from rising up like smoke, and falling down like ashes. "But let me look, let me see . . ."

Bobby plopped down beside him. "Let *me* see."

"Why?"

"Because I saw a ghost, too."

Gabe paused, holding one sheet aloft, mid-turn. "You saw the boy?"

"No, I saw a girl. A teenager."

Gabe stared at his dad instead of the photos. "For real?"

Bobby kept his eyes on the book. "For real. So . . . keep flipping. I'll stop you if I see her. Dolly, did you find *your* ghost in here?" He lifted his eyes, winging her with a fast glance.

"I did. Turns out, her name's Abigail."

"Great, just great," Gabe said under his breath. "Everyone's seen something, and nobody's said anything, all this time."

She rolled her eyes. "We've only been here a couple of days. We're saying something now."

"You knew this place was haunted all along. You knew it was bullshit about the cemetery," he answered, turning one sheet more. He collected a photo that'd slipped free, and placed it carefully upon its rightful page. It dropped down into the seam, and stuck there.

"No, that's not it at all. I believe Augusta Withrow. She was telling the truth, or she *thought* she was."

Dahlia might've gone on being defensive, but Gabe smacked a finger down on the family photo with all three siblings together. "That's him. *That's* the kid I saw. That's what he was wearing, even." He pressed a big fingerprint on Buddy's chest, and tapped it again for emphasis. "Or something like that. It's definitely him."

"But, Gabe . . . ," she objected.

Bobby deciphered the pencil notes and declared, " 'Buddy,' that was his name. That's what it says."

Dahlia shook her head. "Buddy was Augusta's father. He didn't die as a child; he grew up, got married, and was killed in a car crash when Augusta was fifteen," she insisted. "You must've seen somebody else."

"Maybe he was just messing with me. Or it could be that he didn't want to scare me. I was scared anyway," Gabe admitted. His pupils were as big as drain stoppers even now. "But it would've been worse, if it'd been some old dead dude, instead of an old dead kid. Old dead kids are sad, more than scary, when you stop to think about it."

Bobby didn't really agree. "If that's what you think, you should watch more horror movies. Turn the page."

"Was the ghost you saw a scary one?" Gabe asked him, letting go of Buddy. The next page fell.

"She was scary as shit."

"Why?"

"Old dead teenage girls are just as bad as old dead kids, that's why," he informed his son, but he didn't say the rest, about her being covered with mud and blood and the miasma of having done something terrible.

Gabe went past the childhood photos and got to the one of Abigail in the yellow dress. He paused there, and asked, "Is that her?"

Bobby nodded slowly, then faster. "She's about the right age, and the right everything. That's her, but she looked . . . different."

"Different how?"

"Dead. Really, really dead."

But Dahlia wasn't sold. "No, you guys . . . I told you, I saw this girl, looking just like she was alive. *This* Abigail." She tapped the photo. "She was even wearing this same dress, and it gave me a heart attack when I opened the album and saw the picture. This is who I saw in the cemetery."

"I thought it wasn't a cemetery," Gabe said, half teasing and half wondering, like they all were.

It was Dahlia's turn to sigh. "I never said there weren't any ghosts. I only said there weren't any bodies . . ." Something faint and sharp pinged at the edge of her hearing. She stopped what she was saying and listened.

"What?" Bobby wanted to know. "What's the matter?"

"Do you hear that?"

"Hear *what*?" he asked again.

Ping. Ping. Ping.

"That . . . it's like a chime, sort of. Not like a phone, not like a computer. Like hail on a metal roof—or, like . . . it sounds like . . ." She jerked up straight. She hadn't even realized she'd been hovering, bent-backed and too close while the guys were going through the album, but her neck cracked now, and she held up her index finger, signaling for their attention. "You guys, where's Brad?"

"Don't know." Gabe shrugged.

Bobby added, "Haven't seen him in a while. He said he was taking a shower and settling in early."

"Yeah, well. I think he lied."

She darted to the hallway, to the broken window at the end where you could hear everything on the mountain, if you listened hard enough—and yes, it was louder there: the sound of metal on rocks. It was a shovel, and there was a light down in the cemetery that wasn't a cemetery.

One of the LED lanterns cast a brilliant white bubble against the shadowed side of the mountain, the clouds, and the faint haze of drizzle that had started up fresh and might get worse. A cool breeze spit past the broken pane and into Dahlia's eyes. She wiped them and leaned forward carefully, so she didn't cut herself on any silk-fine shards that might be left behind.

At the top of her lungs, she called out, "Goddammit, Brad—what the hell are you doing?"

He didn't answer. He didn't stop digging. Scoop by scoop he added to the pile he'd made, beside the tombstone of a veteran who surely wasn't buried there.

"What's going on?" Gabe asked from the bedroom.

She dashed down the stairs, stumbling a little, despite the fact that the bourbon had almost burned itself out of her blood by now, and she was thinking she could seriously use another drink, the sooner the better . . . maybe even before she went outside, except the bottle wasn't on the way and this was not the time. Unless it was the perfect time.

Were there new handprints on the railing? She didn't look.

Was that a yellow dress, at the very far edge of the living area? Did it flutter in wet gusts that filled the whole house, but shouldn't have? It was only one broken window. It was only that second-floor hallway. It was warm in there, a few minutes ago.

But Dahlia was running too fast to wonder too hard.

She skidded under the oversized pendant light and looked back in time to see the guys leaving her bedroom. She blinked, and they were on the upstairs landing, and there was a door open in the hallway to their left—one that needed to be cut open, but no one had cut it open yet.

But Brad was in the cemetery, so she ran to him, across wet grass that slapped around her ankles and left the hems of her jeans damp and sticky against her calves. She slipped in mud that'd been earth just an hour before, but now some maniac had scooped it up and flung it out, certain there must be a grave underneath it.

It only *looked* like a grave, that's what she told herself. Brad only *looked* like a grave digger, and the flash of pale motion behind him only looked like a yellow dress.

None of it was true or real, and none of it deserved this muddy imposition—not from Brad, not from the salvage company, not from the bulldozers that were coming next week. She felt it keenly, the ache of an old injury that had never healed right. She felt it along her forearms, the sharp burn of a blade and the heat of warm blood pooling and falling.

She looked down. She was wearing her gray flannel again, and the sleeves were soaked.

They were red. They were hot.

She looked up, and Brad was covered in reddish-brown earth that was full of clay. It spattered him from head to toe, gumming up his hair and giving him a slippery grip on the shovel's handle.

"What . . . ?" she started to ask, but who was she asking?

Brad wasn't paying attention, and Bobby and Gabe weren't yet on the scene. But there was someone behind Brad, anyway, and she wasn't wearing a yellow dress, not this time. She was only a shadow, something as ragged and wet and filthy as the mud she stood in.

Dahlia pushed up her sleeves and found slash marks, long and red. "What . . . ?" she tried again, this time imploring Brad with her eyes, with her arms held out, reaching for him to notice her. She'd bleed to death in another minute if nobody did anything. "What's *happening*?" she asked, showing him the blood.

"It's bullshit," he said. The same thing he always said. He swung the shovel down again, stepping on it to force it farther. "It's bullshit."

"Brad, help me . . ."

"No, you help *me*!" He swung the shovel harder, with anger, and when it pierced the lot again, the metal didn't ping with that oddball chime. It stuck in place. He used his shoe to hold something down, and yank the shovel out.

"Brad, something's wrong . . ."

"It's bullshit, Dahlia. Holy God. It's bullshit, and I knew it. Look at this . . . I found him."

Huffing and puffing, Bobby staggered into the sphere of light. "Found who?"

Brad smacked the head of the shovel against the broken tombstone. "Private First Class Reagan H. Foster, *that's* who."

Gabe staggered a little farther into the light, up to the edge of the ragged hole. "Holy shit! Dahlia, holy shit!"

"Boys . . . ," she said, feeling faint. Of course she felt faint; she was *going* to faint, or throw up. Any moment now, she'd lose consciousness or lose her lunch, and it'd be the last thing she ever did.

Gabe was distracted by the hole, and what was in it.

It was Bobby who asked after her first. "Dahl, what's wrong?"

"Bobby . . . ," she whispered. She held out her arms to show him the flannel sleeves shoved up around her elbows, and the wet, white skin that was bright as marble in the lantern light. "Bobby, my arms . . . there's . . ."

There were goose bumps.

Bobby took her wrists, and examined them one after the other. "They look all right to me. What'd you get, snakebit or something? Did a spider catch you?"

She sucked down a gasp and jerked away from him, forcing the cuffs back down around her wrists. She couldn't breathe. She couldn't think straight. "Nothing. It's nothing, it's nothing . . . it's bullshit," she stammered, stealing Brad's line. "Never mind. I'm sorry. I didn't mean to . . . to freak out." She stepped around Bobby, to stand near where Gabe was standing slack-jawed and glassy-eyed, staring into the hole. She slipped in the mud, caught herself on Gabe's arm, and gasped Brad's name.

Down in the ground, there was a smattering of rotted fabric. Inside that fabric was a coat.

Rain was falling now, so the droplets washed mud from the buttons in specks, letting a little light of brass shine through. They were sewn onto fabric that could've been any color once, but now it was the shade of clay and dirt, and beneath it was a scaffolding of ribs. The ribs were gray and white with streaks of rust-colored earth. They jutted from the shallow grave like teeth, like stones, like fingers.

"I found him . . . ," Brad breathed. All the air had been let out of him. He dropped to his knees. For a second Dahlia thought he might pass out on the spot, but he only panted and jabbed the shovel into the earth beside the mess he'd made. He looked up and let the rain hit his face. "Oh my God, I found a body. You guys, we have to call the police."

Dahlia wanted to protest. It was almost a knee-jerk response, like she was the same dumb kid who'd been caught lifting beer from a 7-Eleven—because no, you don't call the police. Not unless you have to. The police only make things worse—that's what she almost said, but she didn't.

Bobby was the one who pumped the brakes.

"Hang on, hang on," he urged, gazing down at the exposed corpse. Everyone was looking at it. No one could resist it. He pointed down at the ragged coat, the brass buttons. The jagged ribs. "This old soldier . . . the stone says . . . what's it say?" He tore his eyes away to scan the marker's inscription by the lantern light. "He's been here since 1915. So you were right, man: This *was* a cemetery. But you can't just call the cops and tell them you dug up a dead soldier!"

Dahlia choked on a horrified gargle. "Jesus, Brad . . . what the hell have you *done*?"

Frantic, he shrieked back, "I only dug him up because you said there was nobody here!"

"That's the craziest thing I've ever heard!" she yelled in return. She had no patience left, no calmness. There was no more room for reasonableness. "You can't blame this on me!"

"Then blame it on . . . on the Withrow lady! She's the one who lied to us!"

Gabe paced around the edge of the hole, wringing his hands together and wiping the rain off his forehead. "Maybe she didn't know. Maybe she was just wrong."

"It doesn't matter," Dahlia said, wet and rattled to the core, but determined to get a grip on the situation. "*You* did this, and you can blame whoever you want—but when you call the cops, they'll smell bourbon and think *you* got drunk and went grave robbing. Because that's pretty much what happened. You understand me?"

He shook harder, and the rain kept coming down. There

wasn't any thunder or lightning, only the persistent thud and splatter of the bottom dropping out. He didn't quite whimper when he said, "None of you have my back?"

She took him by the shirt and pulled him away from the grave, and up close to her face. They both looked cadaverous in the lantern light. "I *do* have your back, and that's why we're not calling the cops."

"You're not?"

"*No one* is going to call them, not yet. Not me, and not them, either." She indicated her cousins. "Not until we've had some time to think. Because even if the cops don't arrest you for grave robbing, they'll almost certainly tell us to pack it up and head home."

"But . . . it's only a gig," he mumbled, wriggling backward, trying to get away.

She held on tight, and yanked him closer. "If the Withrow estate doesn't pan out, it's our *last* gig, okay? Dad sank every penny we've got into the salvage rights. If we don't pick it clean and sell it fast, Music City will fold up shop. Is that what you want?"

"What? I . . . no, of course not, I . . ."

Gabe froze. His forehead crumpled, and his fingers tied themselves into knots. "Dahl? Is that true?"

She let go of Brad. He staggered backward.

"Yes," she admitted. "But it won't come to that, I swear. We'll salvage the house, and we'll make a killing back in Nashville. Everything will be fine. My dad won't stop smiling for a month."

"So we're *not* calling the police . . . ?" Brad pulled his hoodie tighter, drawing the hood up over his head and tugging the strings until his face was all that showed.

Bobby took a crack at being a reassuring adult. He gently pulled Brad's shovel out of his fingers, and slung an arm around his shoulder. He led him away from the hole. "That's right, man. No cops, no trouble."

"Not until I've had some time to think," Dahlia specified.

Brad stumbled, and almost resisted. "But . . . we can't just leave him like that."

Bobby paused. "We should do *something*."

Gabe raised his voice to cover the white-noise drumming of the rain. "We could cover him back up?"

"I'll take care of it. Y'all get back inside." Bobby hoisted the shovel and used it to wave toward the house. The grave was already filling with water, and the disturbed earth around it was so wet it was almost runny. He grabbed a scoop anyway, and tossed it into the hole.

Dahlia didn't argue with him. She was exhausted, frightened, and relieved to have the help for once. "Brad. Gabe. Come on, now. Leave him to it. Thanks, Bobby."

He grunted his "you're welcome" and struggled to load another shovelful.

Everyone else trudged back up to the house.

Shoes came off, and rested on the porch to dry out later. Flannels came off and flopped together in a sodden pile by the door. Dahlia said "to hell with it"—and unhooked her bra inside her shirt, then pulled it out through one sleeve. It came out limp and slimy with rain. She pretended to slingshot it up the stairs, but it landed on the rail and dangled sadly over the side.

Bobby caught up sooner than expected, dashing up the porch steps as Gabe was shuffling around in sock-feet, looking for the bourbon.

"You're back in a hurry," Dahlia noted.

"Fuck it. Rain started coming down like crazy, and there's nothing but mud to work with. I threw a tarp over him, and put a couple of rocks on the corners. Tomorrow or the next day, whenever it dries out . . . I'll finish the job."

"No, I'll do it." Brad sat forlorn on the edge of the fireplace step. "This is my fault. I'm sorry. I was just so goddamn sure there was a ghost, and if there's a ghost, there's a body, someplace . . ." His voice petered out. He put his head in his hands.

"All you did was make a mess." She ran her fingers through her hair, where they snagged in the dripping tangles. She untwined them, and dried her hands on the one unsoaked corner of her shirt. "As long as we all keep our mouths shut, we can undo the mess later, and pretend it never happened. Now. Who wants to take a shower first?"

No one responded. No one made a move toward the stairs, or toward the agreed-upon bedrooms with all the towels and toiletries.

She tried again. "Nobody? No one wants to hole up in a pink bathroom, turn on the water, and try to take a shower without shitting yourself from fright?"

No one answered that, either. The guys stared at the floor, or their hands, or their socks.

"Got it," she said. "Everybody knows there's something bad in the bathrooms. Fine, I'll go first. We'll do this in shifts: one person washes up, one person stands guard outside. I don't know if it'll help or not, but it'll make *me* feel better. Any objections?"

The guys shook their heads.

"All right, then. There's a fresh bottle of bourbon in the kitchen, in the cabinet next to the dumbwaiter. It ain't Maker's, because I ain't made of money. Everyone, help yourself."

Bobby lifted an eyebrow. "You don't want a couple of fingers before you hit the shower?"

"I've already had a couple, but they're worn off now, and that's all right. I want to pay attention. I want to see if I can . . . see anything." But even after that speech, Dahlia didn't move; so they stayed there in that grand living area, listening to the rain knock leaves from the trees, and puddle in the clogged gutters. She hugged her arms, and let them think it must be for warmth.

She was stalling.

"Gabe, do me a favor, hon? Give me a minute to get my clothes together, and then come camp out in my room to keep watch for me."

He agreed, and up the stairs they went.

At the top, Dahlia looked left, at the broken window. Through the window, the air was mist and autumn—just like it'd become inside. Beyond the window, there was no soft pinging of a shovel, no lantern light, and no soldier, either.

She knew it without going over to look, or listen. If she put her head past the broken pane and leaned out into the night, she'd see something worse, something bad and covered in blood, despite the hearty rain. She knew it as sure as she knew she wasn't alone in that pink bathroom.

She just didn't know why.

9

DAHLIA DUTTON BRUSHED her teeth, watching her own reflection the whole time. She examined her face like she'd have to describe it to a police sketch artist, pore by pore, line by line. It was better to count frown lines, better to watch the toothpaste foam collect in the corners of her mouth, than to let her eyes wander to the mirror's edges—and maybe catch a glimpse of something she didn't want to see.

The bathroom was pretty big, so far as old bathrooms went. There was plenty of room for someone or something to stand behind her. Several someones. Several somethings.

"Gabe?" she called out.

He answered from the other side of the door. "Right here. Not touching anything. Still covered in mud, so hurry up."

"I'm going to open the door a little bit, then start my shower, okay? I'm trusting you."

"I won't peek."

"You better swear it."

"Dahl, don't be gross. It'd be like seeing my mom naked."

"Thanks . . . ?" She tried to shine the word up with a joking smile, so he didn't hear her shaking when she said it. "Okay, here goes."

She opened the door, far enough that she could slide out sideways without touching it, if she wanted. It gave her a little privacy, but left her an escape route. With that in mind, she stripped down to nothing and leaned over the side of the tub, turning the porcelain knobs to start the water. It came out brown again at first, then cleared up as it warmed.

Looking around the bathroom, she was halfway glad it would all get torn down in a week. It was a mess—covered in muddy fingerprints, footprints, and a floor full of wet, dirty clothes. It'd be easier to total it than scrub it down.

She looked over her shoulder, checking the mirror without meaning to. Thank God, she didn't see anything but her own bare back in a pink tiled room, slowly filling up with steam.

Deep breath.

She was only naked. It was only a ghost. Ghosts can't actually hurt you, can they? "Let's say no," she whispered to herself, and stepped over the cold, smooth lip of the tub. One foot at a time, she climbed inside until she stood mid-thigh in the stream. She reached up to adjust the shower head. She closed her eyes. Water hit her face.

And the other thing hit her, too—the Taser-sharp, heaven-bright flash of light and electricity.

Blinded, even with her eyes open now—they *were* open, weren't they? And stinging—she staggered, slipped, and caught herself. She put one hand out for balance, hoping to find the wall, with its slick tiles that felt like a salamander looks. But the wall wasn't there, not where she thought it should be. She'd turned herself around and wiped at her eyes, willing the vivid static to pass. It faded, then flared again.

"Oh God," she gulped. Her feet made squeaky noises on the enamel as she shuffled this way and that, hunting for the wall, or the showerhead pipe, or the tub's edge. If she could find the edge, she could get out, and the light could go away and her heart could stop trying to hammer its way up and out of her mouth, and how *big* was this goddamn tub, anyway?

She spun around and slipped. Floundering, she almost called out for Gabe, but bit down on her tongue as her hand flew out.

It caught something, or something caught it. Another grasp. Another hand.

Not a big one.

It wasn't the hand of a heavyset kid a few inches over six feet tall in his bare feet—not her cousin, keeping his word on the other side of the bathroom door. No, this was a small hand, with bird-light bones and fingers as narrow as sticks of chalk. Dahlia recoiled, but the hand came with her, squeezing hard as she pulled away, as she scrambled to escape the bathtub and its scorching jets of water that brought the electric lightning and the shocking water terror.

That's right.

"What? What are you, what did you, what's right?" she blubbered quietly, not wanting Gabe yet—she didn't want to scare him, and didn't want him to see her like this, and anyway, this was only a child. A dead one, maybe, but Gabe had said it himself—a dead child is more sad than scary. Unless it isn't, and it's reaching for you, holding your fingers with its own and squeezing so tight you think your bones might break.

The tiny hand let go.

Without its resistance, Dahlia toppled out of the tub face-first onto the floor—and when she tried to push herself up, her palm slipped out from under her. She finished falling all the way, bouncing her forehead against the tiles.

"Dahl?" Gabe's voice was at the door, staying obediently and modestly behind it. But there was fear in his voice. "You okay?"

"Yes," she wheezed. It wasn't true, but she said it again, regardless. "Yes, I'm fine. I slipped, baby. I'm fine. It's wet in here, and I still . . . I forgot to go fetch a shower curtain. Is everything okay out there?"

"Yes ma'am."

"All right, then give me another minute, just another minute or two. I'm almost finished."

She climbed to her feet and planted her hands on the sides of the sink. She shook her head. It hurt, but she hadn't broken anything. A check of the mirror told her nothing was bleeding, and she wouldn't even get a goose egg for her troubles. It wasn't so bad at all. There wasn't anyone else in the room. No spectral little boys, no mud-and-blood-covered girls, and no soldiers.

She mouthed the words, "Fuck this, and fuck you," into the glass and to the room at large—silently, and angrily. She grabbed her soap and climbed back in on the far end of the tub, where the jet of water hit below her crotch and the terrifying water hadn't flashed her yet, because she wasn't all the way in it and—

That's right, something said again. *The water.*

She froze. It wasn't the voice of the house, the one she'd heard on her first day at the estate. Not a girl's voice, or a boy's either. Was it a woman? Another thing entirely? She refused to close her eyes. She needed to see, if there was anything to be seen.

"*What's* right?" she breathed, so soft the water would cover the sound of it.

It's in the water. She's trying to tell you.

"I have no idea what you're—"

Something moved in the steam—the impression of something. Not even a real, solid something at all, except that it had arms and legs and a head, and then it wasn't there. It ducked into the mist and was gone. It appeared in a corner, and vanished again. It slithered behind the sink, crouched beside the toilet, and melted away when the steam rolled past it in a frothy cloud.

Dahlia tracked it, squinting to make out any detail.

Whatever it was, it was too big to be a child. Too fast and smooth and ephemeral to be flesh and blood, much less alive. But it kept its distance so long as she kept her face out of the water. That was the trick, wasn't it? It was something about the water on her face, on her head.

That's how they hurt her. That's how she hurt him.

Trembling, she lathered up and sloughed off as much of the mud as she could. Her legs shook and her eyes stung with the tap water spray, but she blinked them clear and monitored the steam. In it, she spied a glimpse of arm. The back of a leg. A flicker of hair. She knew it was not her imagination—not some trick of that fuzzy place where the brain seeks a pattern, and in the absence of one, creates its own.

"*Got you . . . ,*" she said, still so very, very hushed—in order to keep Gabe from knowing.

She was lying. She didn't have anything, except the certainty that she wasn't alone. But the thing in the fog was leaving her be, so long as she didn't duck under that stream from the shower head.

The temperature of the bathroom had hit sauna level, and that was fine. It was nice.

She closed her eyes in an act of faith. Shaking and covered in goose bumps, even in the tropical bathroom, she soaped up her face and ran the lather up behind her ears, into her hair. The soap bubbled up brown from the mud.

Gabe pressed himself against the door, trying to keep from closing it—or opening it, either. She heard him shuffle back and forth, and hold it steady by the knob. "Everything still okay in there?"

"Everything's still okay," she assured him. She sounded like she was telling the truth, this time. "Is everything cool out there?"

"Yes ma'am. Everything's still good."

She held out her hands, cupped together, and filled them with water. She splashed it on her face, then repeated the process a dozen times more to rinse off her head.

No shocks. No zapping buzz of current on each temple. Only the anxious bracing that was almost worse, every time the water hit her. It was self-torture, at that point. No one was hurting her; this was only the lingering terror of being touched.

She climbed out of the tub to turn off the water, feeling something akin to victory when the flow ceased and she was still standing—and standing alone, with nothing in the mirror to threaten or warn her.

"Gabe? I'm finished in here, and I'll be fine now. Go ahead and take off, and shut the bedroom door behind you. I forgot to bring any clean clothes in here with me."

"Are you sure?"

"I'm damn sure, honey. Thank you for waiting around and keeping watch. I appreciated it."

"No worries, so long as you'll do the same for me."

"You got it," she promised. "Give me five minutes to throw on something clean, and the water closet's all yours."

The bedroom door shut and the old knob squeaked, clinked, and fastened into place behind Gabe. When Dahlia was certain that he was gone, she flung the bathroom door open wide—letting all the steam loose, and banishing whatever had been inside there with her. At least that's what she wanted to think, as she stood there wearing a towel and a thin layer of soap, because hard water never rinses everything away, no matter how long you stand there and let it hit you.

Her feet left moist spots on the wood, and picked up old dust when she walked to her bags. She pulled out a pair of fleece pajamas and pulled them on, then sat on the window seat to add some socks and sneakers. She wasn't going to bed right away, and the floors were covered in splinters, dirt, and everything else that falls when there's no one to clean up for years and years. She didn't care how silly it looked.

From her spot at the window, she had a direct line of sight into the bathroom. She watched that wet pink room, still suspicious . . . and with a dawning sense of confusion, she saw that steam was still billowing forth.

It shouldn't be. Not anymore, since the water was off and the room was so chilly . . . and that wasn't normal, was it?

She didn't realize she'd stopped tying her laces, or that she was barely breathing while she watched that bathroom doorway that should've been empty, but gusted clouds like a fog machine was running full force in there; she knew because she'd used a fog machine once, when she and Bobby and Andy had worked a haunted cave just before Halloween. Right about this time of year, a whole decade ago.

What a crazy thing to think about, sitting on the window seat, watching the bathroom fill with white mist as thick as cotton. What a stupid moment to wish Andy was there to flip the switch and turn it off, or even just hang out beside her so she could tell him what was going on. He probably wouldn't believe her, but he'd lie all the same if that's what she wanted. He'd always lie to make her feel better. He'd always lied to hide things, good or bad. It had been all the same to him.

She stood up, trying to step away from the spiral of confusion and fog in her own head, never mind the one in the bathroom. She had to do something. She had to *open the bathroom window* first, and let it all spill down the side of the house and roll off into the woods.

Something moved. In the bathroom, behind the fog.

Something shaped like a woman—she saw it clearly enough, this time. It was shaped like a woman, yes, but it didn't move like one. It moved like a spider, something with a fiddle or a bowtie on its back. But not an hourglass. An hourglass shows time moving, one direction or another. Whatever this was, it was stuck in time, if not in place. It was venomous. It was coming.

The thing darted, corner to corner, just like in the bathroom. Only now it was here—in the bedroom where there wasn't any water, and the rules weren't very clear anymore, were they? The pattern wasn't much of a pattern.

She might've screamed, but the shadow charged her and she ducked out of the way.

It backed up, and gathered itself. It took the shape of a girl wearing a smock that had been rent into rags. The girl was covered in mud, in blood, and in the stink of death. Only for a moment. She barely took shape long enough to say she'd been there at all. Half a blink, and Dahlia would've missed her.

The girl dissolved into the white smoke again, so that meant she was coming again—hiding before revealing herself in these violent fits and spurts. "Abigail?" Dahlia gasped. "Is that you?"

The wet-haired, mud-faced, bloody-handed dead girl hardened. Step by step, she came forward. There was nowhere for Dahlia to run. She was cornered, and the exit was on the other side of this phantom with murder in its eyes.

No.

That voice again. A woman's, yes. But not *this* woman, with the boneless hands and the body made of mist.

No, the other voice said again. *Leave her alone.*

Out in the room—no, in the bathroom behind her—she heard a scraping noise, and then the soft crack of glass that wasn't ready to move. It was the light, popping noise of a windowpane splitting, but not shattering. Then she heard the scrape of a frame that's been nearly painted shut, and doesn't want to give way.

It did anyway. It opened.

The dragging, yanking sound echoed on the pink tiles, and the steam, or fog, or whatever it was . . . it withdrew, as if someone had pulled the plug on a drain—and it all sucked back into the bathroom.

The suite was filled with the sharp, high howl of a tea kettle ready to pop, or wind cutting through a cave. The noise left through that bathroom window, and the shadow of a woman who moved like a spider left with it, drawn backward, drawn away (if not out).

Dahlia leaned against the wall. It was either that, or fall flat on her ass.

She clutched her chest. It was rising and falling too hard, with leftover panic, but that was a comfort to her. The sound of her own breath gasping in and out of her lungs, the rumble of her heart in her ears, the patter of the rain outside . . . there was a rhythm to these things, and they calmed her, until the voice came again, from everywhere and nowhere.

She doesn't listen.

"Who?" Dahlia asked, blurting out the word before the speaker had finished. "Who are you? Who was that? Was that Abigail?" She looked around, and the room was still empty and shut, sealed up except for the open window in the bathroom.

But from the bay window, a reflection watched. It wasn't Dahlia's own, or Abigail's, either—not the young woman in the dress, nor the poltergeist in mud and blood, if they were one and the same in some warped recollection of death.

This was a woman, to be sure. A calm woman, old enough to be Dahlia's mother. Her hair was salt and pepper, curled into a halo; she wore pants and a fitted jacket with 1970s lapels.

Dahlia whispered, "If I turn around, you won't be there, will you?"

I'm not behind you.

She checked anyway. She saw nothing, so she watched the reflection instead. "Should I be afraid?"

You are *afraid.*

"Of Abigail? Was that her? The devil took her, that's what Augusta said."

The devil did take her, but it took him awhile. She was sent away, first.

Dahlia felt a flash of memory that belonged to someone else. It flickered across the glass, lit up by the light she'd left on the nightstand. She saw walls covered in tile, but not pink tile. There were showers and sponges, and straps. Tubs full of water and ice.

"She was sent to a sanitarium?" she guessed.

She's taken a liking to you. She thinks you understand.

"This is how she treats the people she *likes*?"

A loud knock on the door. Too loud.

So much louder than the woman with the vintage jacket.

Dahlia jumped. Her heart leaped into her throat again, and trembled there. She looked back at the door, and then back to the window—but the older woman was gone. The steam was gone. The creature was gone. And Bobby was at the door, hollering for her to answer him.

"What's going on in there? Who are you talking to? Dolly, you okay? Open the door, would you?"

"It's open," she barked. Her voice was raw. Her throat grated every word into dust.

"Nope." He wiggled the knob back and forth. "You locked yourself inside."

She stepped away from the wall, swayed, and steadied herself. Deep breath. Another one. More of them. They seemed to help. She went to the door and turned the knob herself. It spun the ordinary way and the door swung open on hinges that weren't happy about it, squeaking to let her know.

She poked her face around the side, and hoped she didn't look too crazy. "I don't think it *does* lock. This thing's been broken longer than I've been alive." She drew the door back all the way, so he could see for himself.

He eyed her, up and down—wild wet hair, pajamas, sneakers half untied. He looked past her, into the room that looked like it'd always looked. "What's going on in here?"

She leaned against the door, but it was shit for balance, so she changed her mind and leaned against the frame instead. Exhausted from fear, but still afraid, she told him, "Goddamn, Bobby. I don't even know. I saw something, and it didn't like me. And I fell . . . ," she oversimplified.

"Is that what happened to your forehead?"

She gently touched the place where she'd struck the bathroom floor. "Bathrooms are slippery when wet. It's not bleeding. It's not even swelling. Hardly," she amended, feeling the start of a lump.

He shook his head, then gave the wall an openhanded smack that was heavy nonetheless. "This place is *fucked up*, Dolly. We should pack up what we've got, and leave tonight."

"You know we can't do that, and you know *why*." She walked away from him, and didn't chase him out when he followed her into the bedroom.

Bobby sat down on the window seat, next to Dahlia's sleeping bag. He rubbed his eyes. He'd been drinking again, but that was all right. Dahlia was the one who'd told him where the bottle was. "I stand by my assessment. You swear you're not really hurt?"

"I swear I'm not really hurt. Ghosts can't hurt you; everybody knows that. All they can do is scare you, and we only need to hold out for another couple of days." She sat down over by her stuff, on the window seat. "We can suck it up for a couple of days. Tomorrow, though . . . if it stops raining, we really *do* have to get that body squared away before anybody wanders by and sees it. We'll look like crooks, and Dad will go broke, and we'll all be out on the streets."

Bobby sat down on the ledge beside her. His voice got quiet. "Tomorrow, yeah. We'll cover him back up again, don't worry. But listen, I've got an idea."

"God help us," she said, but she didn't stop him.

"Yeah, yeah. I know, but hear me out before you shut me down." Then he got all earnest on her, which almost worried her. Bobby didn't do "earnest" very often. "While I was out there, I got a look at the stones—and I believe what Withrow told you. None of them matched, and none of them were for any family members. But we found somebody *anyway* . . . so what do you think that means? What if he's not the only one buried there?"

She thought of the bathroom, the fog, and the ghost who climbed walls. She considered the woman in the seventies lapels, reflected in the glass but never standing behind her.

Bobby continued. "I'm saying: What a great place to hide bodies—in a cemetery that everyone knows is just pretend. What if someone's been stashing murder victims there for years and years? Could be, Grandpa Withrow had a secret and a long game."

"Or," she stopped him right there, "it could've been an honest mistake. He could've been put there by someone who believed it was a real cemetery."

"That's just crazy talk."

"I *do* feel pretty crazy right now . . ."

Bobby patted her on the knee. "It's been a crazy night. But maybe, on our way out the door come Friday, we should mention to someone that we *accidentally* found a body in that fake cemetery—maybe say we ran over it. Truck got stuck in the mud, spun a wheel, and we saw something poking out of the dirt. I don't know. Something like that."

"Plausible deniability. One of my favorite kinds of denial." She turned to him with something like optimism. "Hey, you think if they find more bodies, they won't tear down the house for a while?"

"No idea," he said with a shake of his head. "But all I'm saying is, if we've just tripped over a hundred-year-old murder conspiracy, that'd be cool as shit. We might make the papers. Free advertising!"

She laughed in spite of herself, and in spite of him, too. "Sure, Bobby. Free advertising. Way to polish this turd of a week."

"I'm here to help!"

For a minute, they sat there in silence—staring straight ahead instead of at each other, like they used to do on their grandmother's porch swing, come holidays when the cousins were all together. The kids always ran around outside, while the adults drank and smoked inside, and someone had to keep an eye on the little ones. Dahlia and Bobby were oldest of the seven, so that was their job when all the grown-ups were lit.

For old time's sake, or maybe just because there wasn't anybody else to tell it to, she confessed to Bobby: "I don't know what to do. It's not safe here, and I couldn't live with myself if something happened to . . . to Gabe, or Brad."

"And me?"

"You? I've worried about you for so long, I haven't got the energy for it anymore."

He took it in stride, or at least had the decency to pretend he did. "I don't need anyone worrying after me. Anyhow, salvage is a risky gig for everybody, especially new guys like them two downstairs. Every job is different, right? Every job is dangerous in its own way, that's what Uncle Chuck says. So this one has ghosts."

"Don't act like you're some kind of expert; you're new here, too. Kind of."

"And you're only half my size—so all God's children got problems, when it comes to power tools and crowbars. I won't lie to you," he said—and that might've been a lie itself, but she didn't interrupt him. "I hate this place. It scares the shit out of me, and that's not something you'll hear me say twice. I'll deny it with my last breath, if you tell a living soul."

"Then I'll keep it to myself."

With that assured, he told her, "I don't want to stay here. In the daytime it's not so bad; but at night, I'd rather sleep in a doghouse by the interstate than close my eyes up here and act like everything's all right. If you asked Brad and Gabe, they'd say the same—I promise you."

"At first I thought Augusta was crazy, when I heard she wasn't even *trying* to save it. Now it makes more sense. Did you know that poor woman used to live here?"

"When?"

"After her parents died, she said. And not for very long, but she hung around long enough to hate the place."

"What about Uncle Chuck? Have you talked to him yet? Did you tell him about . . . ?"

"About the body? No. He's got enough to worry about back in Nashville, running the shop on money fumes. He thinks I've got all this under control; and is counting on us to put the business back in the black this year." She leaned forward and put her face in her hands, on top of her knees. "Fuck, Bobby. We can't leave yet, just for being scared."

"Okay, okay. Fine, nobody's leaving. We're just none too happy about staying. Let's get this gig wrapped, packed, and shipped—fast as we can swing it. And then let's get the hell out of here."

Her voice was muffled, because she spoke into her closed-up fingers. "Deal."

10

DAHLIA AND BOBBY headed downstairs together. Dahlia stopped at the landing turn; Bobby kept going, all the way down to the big living area where Brad was sprawled out on the bags, lacquered in dry mud and holding a drink. Gabe emerged from the kitchen with a stray piece of sandwich turkey rolled up like a cigar. He took a big bite out of one end and played with the rest of it, trying to hide how badly his hands were shaking.

Dahlia planted her hands on the rail, right where the prints used to be. "All right, everybody. Family meeting time. Or . . . company meeting, Brad. You're in on this, too."

"Because everything's all my fault?" he asked. Every square inch of him was still covered in graveyard muck. He looked like a fugitive from a hillbilly zombie flick.

"No, only *some* of this is your fault. Me and Bobby have been talking—"

"Seriously?" Gabe interjected.

His father got cranky on him. "Yes, *seriously*. Now shut up and hear her out." He went for the bourbon and helped himself. Brad held up his drink. Bobby gave him a long-distance clink for a toast. "You want one, Dahl?"

"Yes, for the love of God. Now, I want to make sure we're all in agreement: Nobody's calling the cops about that body in the cemetery, at least not while we're still working the job."

Brad and Gabe offered mumbles of assent, while Bobby called back like he was in church. "Preach it."

"Because if we do, we're likely to get shut down, and Brad might go to jail."

"What about after the job?" Brad asked, warily sensing some odd loophole.

"After the job, or at the very end, we should give a heads-up to Augusta Withrow, so she can warn the contractors about the dead soldier. We can rebury him, but it'll still be obvious that someone went digging there. Someone's going to notice," she said, making up some details as she went along—but feeling pretty good about her logic. "We can claim we turned him up by accident . . . a truck slid in the mud, or whatever. But obviously we're salvage artists, not archeologists. It's none of our business, and not our problem."

Brad's jaw fell open, and the wrist holding up his glass went a little slack. "Do you think we'll get away with it?"

"Why not? Augusta knows we found the cemetery, and she told us there was nobody there to disturb. We took her at her word, and we drove right through it. Our bad."

"You think she'll vouch for us?" Gabe wondered.

"I don't see why not."

Brad wasn't sold yet. "So I have to lie to the police?"

Dahlia rolled her eyes. "Oh, for fuck's sake. No one's asking you to lie to the police. I'm telling you that *I'll* lie to the woman who sold us the estate, and she can tell them whatever she wants. The dead guy's on her family's land, isn't he?" She tossed her hands up, almost spilling her drink. "Or, you can go ahead and open yourself up to grave-robbing charges, if you're that hell-bent for honesty. I don't give a damn. But until we're done, we keep that corpse to ourselves. Or . . ." She took a swallow too big to call a sip. "We're all out of a job."

"No pressure . . ." Brad stared anxiously down into his glass.

Bobby refilled it, and put the bottle back on the fireplace mantel.

"And now for item of business number *two*," Dahlia continued. "First, we keep our mouths shut about the soldier in the cemetery until we're halfway back to Nashville. Second, we quit pretending this house isn't haunted as *fuck*."

Brad and Gabe lowered their eyes, and generally acted like guilty children.

"We've all seen things, and some of those things have been pretty freaky. But we only have two more days on this gig before Daddy shows up, and we're going to make the best of that time like sane, reasonable people who don't want to go bankrupt because we ran away from a job. This may be a shitty work environment, but OSHA doesn't have any guidelines when it comes to ghosts. We'll have to make up our own as we go."

Brad gulped his drink like he was mad at it. "Are you even *listening* to yourself?"

"Says the grave robber who saw the dead soldier's ghost before anyone *else* did," she accused, not specifying that she'd seen him too. "The soldier is spooky, but I don't think that he's dangerous. His friend, on the other hand . . . she's a real bitch . . ." She slowed. A possibility occurred to her, but she filed it away. "So we need to talk about tonight, and tomorrow night."

"What's the plan, boss?" Bobby asked gamely.

"Tonight we're all sleeping down in this central living room, and if everything goes all right with that arrangement, then great, we'll do it tomorrow night, too. If things get scary or out-right dangerous, then I'll tell my dad we ran into trouble and I'll get us a couple of hotel rooms on the company card."

Brad frowned. "That's an option? Why don't we do that *now?*"

"Because we are *trying* to keep him from knowing that things *aren't okay!*"

She didn't mean to shout. She didn't want to let things get even further out of control than they already were, but she was still shaken up from the corpse, and the shower; and she was getting tired, and the bourbon didn't take the edge off any-thing. Or it didn't do enough. One more gulp from her glass, in case the next one would.

Calmer by liquor or by force of will, she said, "I'm trying to keep us on schedule, and keep this gig together. We need every useful scrap we can pry off this wreck, and we'll need every hour of daylight to get it. What Daddy doesn't know won't hurt him. And it won't hurt us, either. Not if we keep our heads on straight, and stay cool. We can do this—just give it one more night. If it sucks, we take a vote tomorrow, and I'll find us a Motel 6."

Brad wouldn't look up at her. He stared down past his glass, at his knees or at the floor. But Gabe nodded like he under-stood, and Bobby flashed a thumbs-up.

She exhaled, and finished her drink. She smacked the glass on the rail for emphasis, and let it balance there. "So that's the plan. Those are the items of business. Oh, and one more thing," she added. "When it comes to taking your showers . . ."

Then she told them about letting the steam out, and keep-ing the water away from your face and head. It hadn't worked perfectly, but it might be better than nothing. "I know it sounds weird, but it kept me from having a freak-out. Whatever's hanging around in there . . ." She said the name, in case names had power after all. ". . . I think it's what's left of Abigail Withrow—she leaves you alone if you don't get your head wet."

"That is completely insane," Brad marveled. There was a slur around the edge of his wonder.

"Yeah, but it works. Give it a try, unless you want to freak out, fall, and bust your head open. I don't want to explain 'murdered by a ghost' to Daddy's insurance company." She said that last bit with finality.

The moment hung in the air, until Brad officially gave in. "Well, all right. I'll try it, and see if it helps. But it's . . . it's awful in there. I don't even want to close the door."

"That's why we're teaming up, and keeping watch for each other. It's a little weird, but two's company."

"And three's a séance," Bobby said, with a wry little laugh that didn't suit him.

Gabe chucked a shoe at him. "Ugh. Seriously. *Don't.*"

Bobby picked it up and tossed it back. "All right, I won't. Gabe, I'll keep watch outside your shower, if you want. Dolly, you and Brad can haul all your stuff down here, and we can have ourselves a slumber party."

"Stop calling me that," she said, without any real push behind it. "You've been doing it all night, and it's making me crazy."

"Sorry."

"I still need a shower, too," Brad noted.

Bobby corrected him. "No, *I* still need a shower. *You* need a fire hose and a gallon of bleach."

Dahlia smiled in spite of herself. "We're short on fire hoses, I'm afraid, and the bathrooms have worse things in 'em than ugly tile. So to recap: Open the bathroom window to let out the steam, and leave the door open so your shower buddy can keep an ear out. Don't get your head wet until you have to— and don't dunk it, just splash it. You ought to be all right."

"This job has the weirdest rules of anyplace I ever worked." Brad picked himself up off the lumpy place where he'd been sprawled, having flattened a few rolls of paper towels, some rags, extension cords, and folded tarps. "Weirdest coworkers, too."

"And on-the-job hazards," Gabe added, stomping back down the stairs with an armload of sleeping bags and pillows. "But you get some cool scars out of it. Ladies dig scars."

"What the hell would you know about ladies, kid?" Dahlia teased as he passed her on the stairs.

"About as much as the next guy. So . . . basically nothing."

"Ladies *do* like honesty," she said helpfully. "Scars are a distant second."

When everyone was cleaned up from the day's work, and no further unsettling incidents had occurred, Bobby headed out for the bar. It annoyed Dahlia, but didn't surprise her, and she didn't have it in her to yell at him when he announced his plan and jangled his keys to say good-bye. Mostly, she was just tired of being mad at him.

"And to think," she groused weakly. "For an hour there, I almost didn't want to kick your ass."

"I won't be gone all night."

"You swear to God?"

He shrugged. "Sure. God, and whoever else. This is where all the action is. It's just . . . not where all the alcohol is."

"There's still . . ." She checked the bottle. "Almost no bourbon at all. Goddammit, Bobby."

"The one you hid in the empty cooler is mostly full. I hardly touched that one."

"Goddammit again," she repeated. "Tomorrow, you're going on a field trip to the liquor store on your own fucking dime."

"Yes ma'am," he agreed, the door clapping shut behind him with a bang.

Gabe appeared in the kitchen doorway. "Was that my dad? Did he *seriously* just leave again?" He took an angry bite of whatever new pre-midnight snack he'd made. "I thought you were the boss, Dahl. You should've made him stay."

She closed her eyes and leaned back against the fireplace. "Baby, it's after hours, and I'm too wiped out to give a shit. I hope he doesn't get himself killed. I pray he doesn't wreck the truck, or hit somebody with it and get Daddy sued. He'll be back soon, up early, and ready to go in the morning."

"You think?"

"I think he'd better be, since there's nothing left to tackle but the house. Not even your father can sleep through a Sawzall."

Gabe chewed on, unconvinced. Around a mouthful of food, he declared, "Sometimes he really *is* an asshole."

"Oh, honey . . . I am begging you, do *not* make me defend him. He'll be all right. We'll all be fine. He'll just be *drunk* and fine. And I have to tell you, I envy him for it: He didn't leave us hardly anything behind. Maybe me and him should go to meetings or something. It'd be cheaper than blowing all this money on booze."

Gabe wasn't sure what to say to that, which was fine by Dahlia. She only said it out loud because it wasn't the first time she'd thought it since the divorce.

But she didn't go to any meetings, mostly because she told herself she was living in a post-divorce window, and it was fair game to fall apart for a while. A friend of hers had said there was a formula to it: You were allowed to mourn a relationship for half its length—but that sounded excessive. Dahlia and Andy had been friends for twenty years. They'd dated for two, and were married for six. Did that mean she could take ten years to drink herself stupid? Four years? Or only three?

She'd go broke, trying to drink like this for three whole years.

Either that, or she'd die of liver trouble—that's what her dad would say if he knew about the formula. So it was just as well that he didn't.

Dahlia was about to ask Gabe what was left in the way of sandwich stuffings, but a clatter upstairs stopped her cold.

A door banged open, then slammed again, and after a series of loudly stumbling steps, Brad stomped to the top of the stairs holding a toothbrush and waving a washcloth. "Fuck *that!*" he shouted, to her and Gabe and the house at large. "Fuck that *sideways.*" He grabbed the rail like an aging movie star in a turban, and clutched it as he descended. "You called her Abigail? That thing in the bathrooms?"

"What'd she do this time?" Dahlia asked, only kind of caring.

"Same thing as last time, that crazy bitch—all I did was try to wash my face, and she grabs me, and pulls me, and she . . . she shocks me, and it gets all bright, and there's somebody there in the room with me—someone who will murder me the second I close my eyes. I can't work like this!"

"Brad. Brad. *Brad.* It's happened to all of us, okay? I understand exactly how you feel, you have to believe me. Finish up and come on down, have a drink. We can commiserate."

"There isn't enough booze in the whole world. Literally. Like, not if I stood here and drank myself to death on the spot," he complained at top volume, barefoot and pissed, clomping down the remaining steps.

He stormed past her into the kitchen. Gabe ducked in after him, saying, "I'll clear off some stuff. Got to get all the food away from your corpse-enriched hair products."

"Shut up."

Dahlia left them to it, took the last of the bourbon—Bobby'd only left a couple of fingers in the bottom—and dropped herself onto her sleeping bag and extra blanket. She arranged the pillows she'd brought. One was filled with buckwheat, and it rustled like a beanbag; the other was an ordinary feather jobbie. She fluffed them both, positioned them where she wanted them, and lounged against the marble mantel.

There was no point in bothering with a glass. She didn't intend to share the rest, and the boys could have the cheaper bottle that her cousin had hardly touched. She swigged from her own with her eyes shut.

Gabe came back from the kitchen. His footsteps were heavy, and his pace was familiar; Dahlia knew it instantly, and it didn't worry her. He came and sat down beside her.

"Hey Dahl?"

She still didn't open her eyes. "Yes, baby?"

"Who do you think the soldier was?"

She opened one eye, then the other. "He might be . . . private Reagan somebody or another. Whatever it said on the stone."

"Dad said he didn't think so. Dad thinks maybe he was murdered, and someone hid him there."

"That's what he told me, too, and I bet he's right. No casket, shallow grave. Brad's no lumberjack, and he didn't dig very deep. Someone buried the poor kid fast and cheap."

"But if he's not the soldier on the tombstone, then who is he?"

"I don't know for sure, but I can make a guess. He's connected to this place. To that family." She sat up straighter, leaned forward, and put down the bottle. It was easier to talk when she could use her hands for emphasis. "See, there were three children: Abigail, Hazel, and Buddy. Buddy, like I told you, was Augusta Withrow's father—so that ought to give you some idea about how long ago this was. Supposedly Abigail tried to elope with a boy, but it all went to hell. Augusta acted like her grandfather just forbade the whole thing, but what if he went further than that? What if he murdered the kid to keep him away from his daughter? Then he buried him in the last place anyone would ever look: a cemetery that was all for show. Everyone knew nobody was buried there. No one would've ever thought to look."

"I like that theory." Very, very casually, he picked up the bottle. "It's way cooler than just . . . everyone forgetting where some soldiers are buried."

Dahlia thought about reclaiming the bottle, but she wasn't really feeling it anymore. Another mouthful and she'd regret it in the morning. Such was the privilege and despair of being thirty-seven: she'd learned her limits, and they weren't what they used to be.

He removed the lid, wiped off the bottle's mouth, and downed half of what remained in a single swallow.

Brad emerged before the bottle was entirely empty. He wore long plaid sleeping pants and a Hanes T-shirt that used to be black, paired with flip-flops, so he wasn't running around bare-foot, collecting splinters and spiderwebs.

"Do you feel better now?" Dahlia asked him.

He scratched at the back of his neck, then started folding his towel. "Yeah. I'm sorry about that. I'm sorry about *everything*. I didn't mean to yell at everyone. I didn't mean to . . . dig."

Gabe swallowed the rest of the bourbon fast, lest he be asked to share it. "It's this place, man. It gets to you."

"I still feel stupid for losing my shit. What if it's all in our heads?"

"Oh, honey," Dahlia said with honest sympathy. "If it's all in our heads, then at least we're going crazy together."

11

THEY SETTLED IN for the night, leaving lights on in the foyer and in the kitchen. No one wanted to sleep in the full mountain dark, with all the lamps off and not a single streetlight for half a mile. Besides, when eleven o'clock came around, Bobby still hadn't returned from the bar—so they might as well make things easier for him, and themselves. If he came back drunk and couldn't see where he was going, he'd turn on every damn switch and wake them all up without even trying. If the rooms were dim, but navigable, perhaps he'd spare them.

Gabe and Brad dropped off to sleep almost immediately. Dahlia had a little more trouble.

She hated sleeping in unfamiliar places. Even the fanciest five-star hotel would've driven her crazy. For that matter, her new apartment still felt too new to be home yet.

Here in the Withrow house, she stared at the ceiling and the chandelier in the foyer, or the pendant above, or the cracks around it that radiated from the medallion and the corners of the room. It felt very *Phantom of the Opera,* very vulnerable staring up at that feeble ceiling and the heavy things that hung from it on ancient chains, held by vintage bolts. She wished she'd picked someplace else to put her sleeping bag. She wished she'd pressed her dad for a set of hotel rooms instead of this house with all its anger and unhappiness, though she would've felt bad for spending extra money.

Outside, the rain picked up. It smacked against the windows, whereas before it'd only spattered them in a friendly, easygoing spray. Upstairs, drops flew in through the broken panes in the master bedroom, and in the hall. They flew inside like bullets.

Upstairs, a door opened.

Dahlia's eyes opened, too.

She listened hard, but heard only the vicious rain, and Brad and Gabe snoring in tandem, then the rustling shuffle of Gabe turning over inside his sleeping bag—which was almost too small for him. There were no footsteps on the hallway runner. No high-heeled shoes stepping down the stairs. No sound at all that wasn't entirely expected, given the state of the house and the drive of the storm.

But a door had opened. A key had clicked, a knob had turned, and old hinges had squeaked softly.

Dahlia dug down deeper into her sleeping bag. "Nope," she whispered.

If this was an invitation, she had zero problem ignoring it. If the door wanted to lock itself back up again before morning, that was fine. She'd cut it open with a power saw, just like Bobby had planned. But if the house, or Abigail, or whoever, thought she was dumb enough to accept that summons, those things or people were *beyond* wrong.

The warmth of the bag worked together with her bone-deep weariness to almost send her to sleep despite her fear and discomfort. She was almost there, almost out cold—drifting at the edge where it's calm and dark, and a smattering of half-lucid dreams would kick up in another few minutes—when she heard Bobby's truck pull up in front of the house.

The tires strained against the mud even as he parked it, and the slap-slap-slap of the windshield wipers said they were running full speed until he turned them off, cut the engine, and opened the driver's door. She heard it all so clearly she didn't need to sit up and see it. Sound traveled so strangely in that house, and around it, even with the rain running white-noise interference. Either you heard everything, everywhere, or you couldn't even hear your cousin standing behind you, calling your name.

It must be something about the high ceilings, the plaster, and the wood. It was something about the dead.

If she were honest with herself, she'd admit to being relieved that Bobby was back, even though it meant she was wide awake again. She pretended she wasn't when he came inside, got himself a glass of water in the kitchen, and crashed into his own set of sleeping bags and pillows—which had been left out and carefully arranged by his son, who was entirely too good to him.

In Dahlia's opinion.

Soon Bobby's snores joined the rest of them, and Dahlia wished she'd thought to bring headphones or earplugs. Once more, she did her best to relax, not listen to the guys around her, and drift off without thinking about the door upstairs or wondering if it was still open.

Bobby hadn't turned off any of the low-set lights. She could get out of her bag and look. She could probably see it from the steps, if she went halfway up them and stopped.

"Nope," she whispered again. "Fuck a whole bunch of *that*."

And then she must have slept, because she was jolted awake by the sound of a toilet flushing on the second floor. But of course it'd be flushing on the second floor; there wasn't so much as a powder room on the first floor, now, was there? With a groan, she cursed the Victorians and their lack of foresight regarding a future of indoor plumbing. She'd been so close to sleeping until dawn, and now there was no hope of it.

She roused herself up onto one arm and looked around. Gabe's sleeping bag was vacant, so he was the one taking the midnight piss run. It was frankly impressive, how he'd gotten all the way up there without awakening her. It was somewhat unsurprising, how the ringing, throbbing rattle and clank of century-old plumbing had done the job for him.

She sighed and dropped her head back down, then changed her mind and refluffed her pillows before trying it again.

The bathroom door creaked open.

Any minute, Gabe would come back down. He'd crawl back into his nest and start snoring, with that infuriating ability men seem to have to fall right back asleep the moment they drop horizontal. Any minute now.

She listened. She didn't really mean to, but now that she'd heard him, she wouldn't sleep through his return, so she might as well wait up for him. Or wait down. She looked at the stairs, wondering who had been standing there the other day, if it was a woman and she was wearing heels, holding the rail. Was it the older woman Dahlia had seen in the window's reflection? She'd seemed harmless enough, or benevolent enough, if those two things are different when you're talking about dead people.

Any minute now.

Except he wasn't coming back. He was walking slow and quiet, but not toward the stairs. Not down them. He was walking down the hall—creeping down the hall, really. He was a big boy, but he sure was light on his feet when he wanted to be sneaky.

Dahlia sat up straight. "Oh, God, the door."

She hadn't heard it close, so it might still be open. He might have seen it. He might be on the verge of investigating, and what if he did? What would he find? Her chest tightened, stomped upon by the wild, unreasonable thought that the room might consume him, and refuse to give him back.

Writhing out from her bag, she scrambled to her feet. She couldn't remember where she'd left her shoes, but she was wearing thick socks, so at least she wasn't barefoot. "Gabe!" she loud-whispered, in case the magical acoustics of the house carried his name all the way up there without rousing anybody else. "Gabe!" she said a little louder, as it crossed her mind that there was no good reason to let Bobby and Brad sleep—and they were snoring so hard, she might've beat a snare drum without either of them noticing.

She was up the stairs fast, slipping only once on the mostly smooth wood, in her mostly soft socks that had owls on them— because she liked owls, that's why.

At the top of the steps, she looked both ways and didn't see Gabe. She didn't see much of anything—not even the locked room, with its door that only opened when no one was watching. Was it open now? She squinted. The shadows didn't tell her much. She couldn't bring herself to let go of the stair rail.

"Gabe?" she tried, in an almost normal voice.

No response. It was dark up there. No one had left a light on in the second story, since no one was expected to go there—except for the restroom, and that was immediately next to the staircase landing.

But Dahlia had left a lamp or two behind in the master bed- room before she'd abandoned it for the communal area below. In fact, if she remembered correctly, one of the big lanterns ought to be right beside the window seat. And there weren't any curtains, so maybe there'd be a little light in there, even with the rain clouds hiding the moon.

Except that there wasn't. She found the lantern by fumbling around in the dark, tripping loudly over everything in her path, and clicking it on as if it'd save her. It only gave her light, and something to carry. But the plastic housing was cool and solid in her hands, and the broad beam was enough to illuminate the entire room.

It brightened up the hall, too, and it showed quite nicely that—just as she'd feared—the locked door was not locked anymore. It was open.

"Gabe," she said, not calling him so much as declaring that he must be there, somewhere, and informing him that she was on her way.

But she did not run to the door, not even in her concern. She tiptoed to it, lantern brandished like a weapon. She hoped it was a weapon. Dark things hated the light, didn't they? No, that was nonsense. She'd seen dark things in broad daylight. They all had.

When she reached the room, she pushed the door open a little farther—then all the way, until it knocked back against the wall. No surprises. Nothing hiding behind it.

She swung the light into the room, sweeping for any sign of her young cousin. He wasn't there. "Gabe? Where the hell did you go?" Did the room eat him after all? No, that was a stupid thing to think. He was only someplace else. That's what she told herself over and over again, until she could pretend that she believed it.

She didn't retreat. She didn't close the door, or head back into the hall to check the other rooms, but she didn't hear him out there, either. Why didn't she hear some sign of him, somewhere else in the house? She hadn't heard a peep, not since the bathroom door had groaned open, letting him out.

But *this* door was open. No saws required. For a limited time only, or so she strongly suspected.

She hesitated. She looked around and saw a bed, a dresser, an old lamp, and some old fixtures, old rugs. An old vanity. Old wardrobes—two of them, against the far wall on either side of an old window. Everything was old, but not the Victorian kind of old, like the rest of the house. Everything in the locked-up room was covered in dust that glimmered through the lantern beam, disturbed by this midnight intrusion. Except for that dust, it looked like someone had lived here just a few minutes ago. A time capsule, that's what it was.

Near Dahlia's feet, beside the door, she spied a trunk. A soldier's trunk?

No, it was never used for military duty. It was more for decorative storage than rough-and-tumble transport, with a pretty paper design peeling from the sides, and a brittle latches that wouldn't withstand even the gentlest prying.

One foot still in the hallway, Dahlia leaned forward and opened the trunk. Inside, she found a stash of books. Good. Books were heavy. She wanted something to stick inside the doorway so it couldn't close up again behind her.

She grabbed the nearest handle and pulled the trunk across the floor until it rested between the door and the frame.

Logically, Dahlia knew that anything strong enough to slam a door (and climb around a room like a spider) was strong enough to move a trunk of books (and light enough to wear a cotton dress), but logic was well out the window by now. It'd flown out into the wet, windy night when she opened the bathroom window and the steam spilled out onto the mountain.

"What are you doing?"

"Jesus Christ!" Dahlia shrieked, in a whisper that was hardly any softer than a scream. Her light caught Gabe square in the face. Hitting him from below because she was short, it made his eyes look sunken and his chin look craggy. He was a funhouse version of himself, and it horrified her.

"It's only me!" he pleaded quietly, holding up his hands like she might shoot him.

"I know it's only you!" she hissed back. "I've been looking for you!"

"Why?"

"Because you didn't come down from the bathroom, and I heard the door open . . . I heard *this* door open . . ." Her breath pumped in and out of her chest so hard, she was mere seconds from hyperventilating. She clutched her own throat with her free hand, closed her eyes, and opened them again—counting backward from five. A therapist had told her that counting and breathing could be calming, and he was wrong about almost everything, including that particular tidbit of information. But it gave her something to do until she could pat Gabe down, and make sure that he was alive, warm, and very much present. "Are you all right?"

He looked past her, into the room. "I'm fine."

"Where *were* you?"

He looked back at her again. "In the attic."

"What? *Why?*"

Between clenched teeth, still trying to keep his voice down despite Dahlia's climbing volume, he said, "I thought I saw that boy again. I tried to follow him, but I lost him on the attic stairs. I feel like . . . like he wants to tell me something. But he doesn't talk. He never talks. Do the ghosts ever talk to you, Dahlia?"

"One of them did," she admitted. She immediately changed the subject. "But check it out—this door is open, now. It's amazing. No one's been in or out in ages."

"Why did you drag this trunk over here?"

"To hold the door open. It opens and shuts on its own. I didn't want it to close me in here so one of y'all had to cut me out." She shrugged off his skeptical expression. "Well, it sounded like a good idea at the time."

He nudged past her, stepping over the trunk and into the room. "You're right, this feels like it's been boarded up forever. Or . . . not *forever*-forever."

"Why would you say that?"

He picked up something from the nightstand, and answered her with a question. "How long has Victoria Holt been writing books?"

"Um . . . I don't know. I think she died back in the nineties."

"You ever read this stuff? Ladies in fluffy dresses . . . I bet there's *romance* in here."

She took the paperback away from him. It was covered in dust so thick, she had to wipe it away to read the title. "*The Legend of the Seventh Virgin*," she announced. "I've read some of these. I was a teenage girl once, and gothic romances are kind of awesome, so you can shut right up. This one was published in . . ." She checked the inside cover. "1965." She thought about it as she shined her light around. The beam's reflection caught a mirror, and she winced against the glare. "Which Withrows were still living here in 1965?"

"You tell me."

"I would if I could." She ran through her sketchy knowledge of the Withrow family tree, but drew a blank. "Augusta lived here when she was a girl, but that would've been . . . well before the sixties. Someone else, then. A woman. This is obviously a woman's room."

"Because of the book?"

"Because of the curtains, the bedding . . ." Dahlia opened the nearest wardrobe and found a row of hangers. Some were still loaded with long, wispy dresses. The rest had disintegrated with moisture, moths, and time. They rested on the floor in wrinkled little piles. "And the clothes. It's a shame these are mostly gone."

"Why would a ghost want to keep this door closed?"

"For that matter, why would a ghost open it again?" she asked. "Why do ghosts do anything?"

"Good point. Why would that boy try to send me up to the attic?"

She shined the light at him. "Did you bring a flashlight up there?" A look at his empty hands answered her question. "Right. So if the boy *did* want to show you something, you might not have been able to see it."

"Can we go check?"

"After I poke around in here for a minute . . . ," she told him. "Or, go ahead and get a lantern from downstairs, and then I'll come with you."

"Are you okay in here all by yourself?"

"Sure," she said. She even meant it. Something about the relative normalcy of the place reassured her. This was a comfortable room, a refuge for a reasonable woman. Dahlia might be angry and unhappy and insomniac on top of everything, but she was still reasonable. "I'll be all right. If for some reason the door shuts and locks me in, your daddy's Sawzall's lying on the floor just outside the door. I'm trusting you to bust me out."

He disappeared into the hall and headed down the stairs.

She sat down at the vanity and started opening drawers.

In the top right drawer there was another gothic romance, plus a couple of antique Harlequin paperbacks that might actually be worth money to the right reader, somewhere. In the next drawer down, she found several pairs of gloves and a couple of small hats—fascinators, really—with their accompanying pins. "Nice," she said, pulling one out and letting it sparkle in the light.

Thank you.

Dahlia jumped, and this time her heart nearly stopped. It couldn't take two shocks that bad in such a short span of time. She dropped the hat pins and lifted the light, blinding herself in the mirror again, and leaving blobs of yellow, green, and purple swimming in her vision.

She pulled the light down into her lap, away from the mirror. "Hello?"

The only reply was the sound of Gabe stomping gently back up the stairs again. Out in the hall she saw the harsh white glow from another LED lantern. Then she saw a hand in the mirror behind her. A raised finger, and a pair of lips behind it.

Gabe stuck his face around the corner. "Still good?"

"Uh-huh," she nodded. She didn't look away from the mirror. She couldn't do it if she'd wanted to. "Go on, I'm right behind you."

When Gabe was gone, she swallowed, and counted, and breathed. She looked into the mirror, then quickly away. It was shadowed by weird gleams and angles thrown by the flashlight in her lap. She felt a breath on her neck, a cotton-soft gust that wouldn't blow out a candle—and she threw up her hands without even meaning to. She closed her eyes. It was easier that way. "Who are you?"

Open the left-hand drawer.

With quivering hands, she did what she was told, looking away from the glass. She blinked down into the drawer and saw a metal pendulum on a string and a series of cards. One card had a circle with numbers around its edge, like a clock. One had letters. Below the cards, she turned up a dog-eared paperback on astrology, and another one regarding communication with the dead.

"Are you . . . are you Augusta's aunt, Hazel?" Dahlia guessed. Suddenly, she didn't want the lady to leave. "Was this your room?"

Down in the drawer, a scratching noise—like a large bug, or a small mouse. The pendulum wiggled. Dahlia picked it up; it vibrated in her palm. "Hazel?"

No one answered, and Gabe was on his way back. He was on the attic steps, descending swiftly toward the hallway, and toward the door that shouldn't have been open—but was all the same. "Dahlia? Dahlia, I found something. Come on. Come and see."

She tucked the pendulum and the cards into her pocket. Rising to her feet, she checked the mirror one last time. She saw nothing and no one except herself, her image bleached out by the yellow-white circles cast from her lantern.

"Coming, Gabe. I'm coming."

She climbed over the trunk and into the hall, slipping in her sock-feet and catching herself on the carpet runner—which disintegrated as she tripped through it, yanking it from whatever tacks had held it into place. It came apart in decaying rags. "Ew," she complained, shaking the gray fluffy dust off her toes and smacking at her sock to clean it further.

"*Ew* what?"

"Moths and old fabric. What'd you find upstairs?"

"Come on, I'll show you."

She fell in line behind him. "Why didn't you just bring it down?"

"Because I can't," he said, holding the lantern up and forward to illuminate the entrance to the narrow set of attic stairs.

"What is it?" she pressed. "Give me a hint."

"It's a message. It wasn't there yesterday, or the day before."

The walls were close around them as they scaled the creaking steps single file. Wallpaper hung in strips, dangling over the holes where fixtures used to brighten the cramped nook. Dahlia and Gabe's two bouncing lights made the space look and feel like a funhouse that was no damn fun at all.

Dahlia was relieved when they reached the top of the stairs and Gabe lifted the hatch. He climbed through it ahead of her. For an awkward moment, his ass was fully in her face; but she crawled behind him. She was about to ask what she was looking for when she saw the message carved into the floor. You couldn't miss it: The letters were a foot long each. They were roughly scrawled like they'd been cut with a huge fingernail, or a carving knife.

YOUR FAULT

"My fault?" She crooked her neck and stepped closer. "Somebody else's fault? For what?"

"Who do you think wrote it?"

"Abigail," she replied, with an unsettling degree of confidence. The devil had taken her, Augusta'd said, but he'd taken his own sweet time, and maybe he didn't take her very far. "But I don't know why she'd accuse *us* of anything. We just got here."

In one of the dark corners where the roof sloped low toward the floor, something moved. Dahlia chased it with her light, but caught only the impression of someone small, and then no one. Nothing. Not even a rat or a bat. But there was a scrambling noise in its wake, and the image reappeared—flickering swiftly in another corner, beneath another web of batshit-covered support beams. It looked away. It vanished.

"Gabe . . ."

"It's him. You saw him."

"I saw something."

She could still see something, but just an outline of darkness—a cutout silhouette, snipped from the same paper as the photo album. It moved, but it did not breathe. It hunkered. She pointed her light, trying to pin the shade into place so she could see it better, but the specter only absorbed the beam, swallowing it up. It drank the light down, and snuffed it out.

Dahlia crouched down. Her knees popped, so she stood again—not straight, not certain. She kept her back bowed so she could leave the center where the ceiling was high and the way was clear and go towards the lower corners where the walls met the roof. She ducked slowly, dodging the supports as she pushed onward, a small, terrified step at a time, toward the little shadow that curled up tight with its arms around its knees and its head tucked down against its chest.

"Buddy?" The word came out cracked. She said it again. "Buddy? Is that you?"

The huddled shape gave no response, only the impression

that as she approached it . . . it grew smaller before her eyes. When Dahlia reached it, leaning the light around a support post covered in nails, she saw nothing there at all.

No child-shaped ghost of a man long dead gazed up at her. No phantom with charred-out holes for eyes. No sad-faced soldier giving a longing or threatening salute, and no poltergeist girl in a yellow dress or covered in mud and blood offering screams or warnings or threats.

There was no one. Nothing.

"What is it? Do you see it?" Gabe asked. The white gleam from his lantern went wobbly as he passed it to his other hand and wrestled with the idea of joining Dahlia.

"He's gone. But there's something else back here. Not a ghost," she was quick to clarify. "It's a box. Maybe a suitcase. Or a briefcase. Something like that."

She wished she'd found her sneakers before embarking on this adventure; there was rat shit, bat shit, and probably possum shit and snake shit up there, never mind all the nails and splinters. She stuck the lantern's handle between her teeth and braced herself anyway, hanging on to a nail-free spot on the support post with one hand while she reached for the object with her other one.

Her fingers brushed against dry, brittle leather. She found a handle, and pulled. The container came free. She teetered on the balls of her feet, but held steady, adjusting her balance.

She let go of the wood and retrieved the lantern from her mouth.

There wasn't any clean space to sit, but she sat down with the case anyway, fiddling with the latches on top. The briefcase, or satchel, or whatever it was had had a combination lock years ago. Now it'd rusted to the point of being useless, and the elements had shrunk the leather back away from the hinges. With a twist of her hand, the contraption broke and the bag opened wide.

Gabe sat down cross-legged beside her. "What's in it?" he asked before she had a chance to see for herself. "Just dump it all out."

"No way. There could be rats. Spiders."

"Oh yeah," he said. "But hurry up."

Gingerly, all the while wishing she had her work gloves handy, she withdrew the contents in clumps and spread them out in the light of their lanterns. "Gabe . . . these are . . . they look like medical records."

"Whose?"

She read a few lines, turned the page, and scanned a bit further. "Oh, God . . ."

"Dahl?"

"The water," she said, which didn't really answer him. "I knew it had something to do with the water. This is a report on patient care from a sanitarium in Michigan."

"Was Abigail there?"

"Looks like it. I wonder if they sent her away to have the baby? No, that can't be right—if no one but Buddy knew about it. Maybe she left it somewhere, or gave it away. Maybe it died."

"Maybe she killed it."

Dahlia didn't know how to respond. She didn't want to think it, and she hadn't planned to say it out loud. "If it died, one way or another, I wonder if anyone ever found its remains. You'd think Buddy would've known where to look."

Gabe frowned, and poked at the nearest folder with his finger. "Why didn't he show them?"

"Maybe he kept his mouth shut so he wouldn't make things

any worse. He was only a kid," she reminded him. "The message might be for him. Everything after that wedding party . . . everything that happened to Abigail was his fault. These records here . . ." She scanned them quickly. "At this sanitarium, they were treating Abigail for hysteria—like it was still the nineteenth century, or something. They used hydrotherapy on her."

"That's what she blames him for? Water? Come on. It could've been worse." He wiggled his fingers like he was trying to zap her. "It could've been shock treatments."

"I don't think they used shock treatments back then, but water therapy wasn't exactly a walk in the park. It involved a lot of unwanted baths. Ice water, high-pressure hoses, that kind of thing. No wonder the poor ghost has a hate-on for plumbing." She pushed some of the pages around, ignoring the things that looked redundant and discarding the paper that was too deteriorated to read. "It looks like she was discharged in 1924. They sent her home, and . . . and then what? There are no more pictures of her, no further mention of her anyplace in the family record, as far as I know."

"What did Miss Withrow tell you?"

"Not everything, apparently. She said Abigail disappeared after the wedding fell through, but it's more like she was banished."

Gabe eyed the attic with a wary expression. "Maybe they locked her in the attic. I bet she went crazy up here and died."

Dahlia whapped him with her light. "And you gave *me* crap about the gothic romances."

"She must've died somewhere!"

"Yeah, but not up here. This attic was never finished out—there's no Sheetrock or plaster, no insulation. Just subflooring and exposed beadboard. This was never a living space. I can't imagine why you wanted to stay here the other night."

"It's kind of cool, until the ghosts show up."

She sat back and fiddled with the light, aiming it from page to page. "Whatever, man. Tomorrow," she said suddenly, pointing the light at Gabe—then away from his face. "Sorry. But tomorrow . . . or this morning—God. I don't know what time it is, but it must be so late that it's early. When the sun comes up, at any rate, I'll start looking for the real Withrow plot, and see if she's buried there. I bet it's close by, and if we find her grave, we'll know when she died. Maybe even *how* she died. Sometimes they would put that stuff right there on the tombstone."

"Good idea."

"I'm full of them. Now, what else is in here?" she asked herself. The rest was mostly receipts, church bulletins, and two old issues of *National Geographic*. The folders with Abigail's sanitarium records were the only thing of interest. She pushed everything back inside the weather-ruined satchel, then picked it up. "Let's put this downstairs in Hazel's room. That seems like a safe place."

"Who's Hazel?"

"Augusta Withrow's aunt. I found her name in a book, after you left," she lied. It was easier than telling the truth. "After that, you and me, kid—we're going to get some more sleep."

"I don't know, Dahl. I'm pretty worked up. I don't know if I can go back to sleep now."

She stepped around the thin sheets of subflooring and tried not to look at the accusation carved there. It wasn't meant for her. "Me either, but we've got a lot of work to do over the next couple of days. We need all the rest we can get."

He fussed along behind her. "I don't know how anyone's supposed to sleep with that storm going on out there. And in here, we've got more ghosts than rats."

"There's nothing to be done about the ghosts, but storms are great for sleeping through."

"Not when the house is full of holes." He descended the stairs, letting the trapdoor fall down quietly behind him. Now that they were headed for the main part of the house, he lowered his voice. "The wind makes all these whistling noises, and the house sounds like it's going to fall apart."

"This house has been here for a century and a half. What are the odds it'll fall down now, the week before it's torn down? You worry too much, kid. Leave that to me."

At the hallway landing, they saw that Hazel's room was still propped open by the trunk full of books. Dahlia added the satchel and paperwork to the stash of romances and travelogues, and closed the lid. She pushed it inside, but didn't shut the door. "If Hazel wants it shut, she can do it herself. I don't want to accidentally lock us out. Now, go on downstairs, and try to get some sleep."

"Aren't you coming, too?"

"Yes, but now I need to pee. And I'm leaving the door open, so I want you to go down ahead of me. Give a girl some privacy. And, hey . . ." She stopped him with a hand on his arm. "Your daddy and Brad . . . they don't need to hear about that message in the attic. It'll only spook them."

He half shrugged, half nodded. "You're probably right."

"I usually am. So go on, and settle in. Let me piss in peace."

When she was done, she flushed, and the pipes rattled from floor to floor; but by the time Dahlia was back inside her own sleeping bag, Gabe was snoring again anyway. She was happy for him and his dudelike gift for tumbling back into his dreams. She was jealous of him, too.

She wriggled down into her bag, this time propping herself up on her pillows against the fireplace surround. The stone was cold through the feathers and foam, and she didn't care. It was cold everywhere, and everything felt damp because of the broken windows upstairs and the water drumming down hard on the roof, on the gutters, and on the porch. By the sound of it, the wind was blowing in every direction at once. It must be some drafty trick of the mountain behind them, twisting the air around as it blustered over the ridge. That must be why the house felt like the center of something, a storm's eye that wasn't calm now, and probably never would be.

Dahlia wasn't getting any more sleep, not anytime soon.

She briefly considered going upstairs and rummaging in Hazel's trunk some more, then discarded the idea. She didn't want to go back and see the door shut, or get another glimpse of a dead boy who used to be a man. She didn't even want to talk to Hazel, who seemed to mean no harm—and might even want to help. And she definitely did not want to catch Abigail, full of rage, with razor-blade fingernails or the strength to wield and carve with a knife. If she could do that to the exposed subflooring, what would she do to flesh and blood?

No more upstairs investigation. Certainly not in the middle of the night.

She pulled out her phone. It offered the only Internet available, and what else was she going to do while everyone else slept? With a flick of her thumb, she turned off the sound, then called up the Web.

She started with a couple of searches on the Withrow family in general, then narrowed it down. There was plenty about the

Withrow Monument Company and Judson himself, and a few local history stories about his wife's philanthropy. Dahlia found the birth announcements for all three children, a marriage announcement for Buddy, and even the announcement for Abigail's wedding that never happened. "Tate Arthur Hurley," she read softly. "So that's who you almost married, the second time around."

It *must've* been the second time around, given the date. There was no mention of the first engagement to be found, so Augusta was probably right about the attempted elopement. If it had ever happened at all, there was no official commentary. Just family gossip.

On an image search, she found black-and-white photos of the Withrow house in brighter days—including a bit about the annual Halloween parties. Apparently the whole neighborhood came out for them, with small trick-or-treaters climbing all the way up to the mansion to collect treats, drink apple cider, and play ghostly games in the pretend cemetery.

She found only one mention of the cemetery specifically, only a brief note in a self-published book regarding the neighborhood's enthusiasm for holiday fun.

It wasn't terribly useful, except that it verified Augusta's version of the cemetery story, which was . . . neither here, nor there. That's what Dahlia decided. Augusta had every reason to believe she'd told the truth; but there was at least one body there now, and he'd been there for quite some time. Even if he *was* a murder victim, it made no difference to the Music City Salvage plan.

The police report could wait. Besides, what if the cops came out in the rain and tried to investigate? It'd be one big mess for everybody, all they'd find was a ninety-year-old corpse. Who gave a damn about a murder that old, anyway? Everyone who'd ever cared was dead.

She glanced over at the other sleeping bags. Gabe was hanging half out of his. Bobby was flat on his back, snoring at the ceiling. Brad was balled up inside of his, breathing slowly, and snorting.

Maybe she ought to call her dad.

Not right that moment, but tomorrow, in the morning, whenever. She could give him a progress report, and tell him everything was all right. He'd like that.

Her mind was wandering. Maybe another hour or two of sleep wasn't completely out of the question after all. The phone's screen darkened like a hint, but she tapped it again and tried one more round of queries.

It took less than thirty seconds to learn that the Withrow family members of yesteryear were all buried at the Forest Hills Cemetery, barely a mile away. The rest was good news/bad news.

The cemetery was active and open, with over a hundred thousand people buried there—many of which were unmarked and unknown. That was the bad news. But the Withrows were rich, well connected, and they'd had their own monument company. Their graves were listed right alongside those of the city founders, Civil War officers, and noted politicians of the previous century or two. That was the good news.

Dahlia checked the search records and found the plot numbers for the Withrow clan, but there were no handy-dandy photos of tombstones to click on, so the information didn't do her much good from where she was sitting. She could wander over there tomorrow at lunchtime. According to the map, it was a two-minute walk from "downtown" Saint Elmo. She might not

THE FAMILY PLOT

even need to excavate the trucks from the mud; she could hike down there, if the weather let up.

The thought of the trucks gave her pause.

If the weather *didn't* let up, they might have problems. The trucks were heavy even when they weren't loaded down. The roads weren't paved around the house, and all the turf was slick, soaked grass interspersed with gravel.

A distant grumble of thunder sounded on the far side of the mountain—the first she'd heard so far. It might be a good sign. If the storm was that close, it might pass overnight. If the rain stopped by morning, they might be able to rebury the soldier and strip the copper roof off the carriage house. Dad would be delighted if that was squared away before he arrived.

The phone's screen went dark again, and this time she let it stay that way. She pulled her pillows over her head and closed her eyes, just in case sleep might take her despite her doubts.

The last thing she remembered was the creak of a door somewhere on the second story, then a soft squeak, and a click. There was rain on the windows, broken and whole alike. Thunder, spilling over the mountain. The whispering scratches of nails on wood.

12

TWO MORE HOURS of sleep were better than no more hours of sleep, but not by much, in Dahlia's opinion. She was awake at dawn, goddammit all, and she knew if she tried to wring out another hour, she'd only be more miserable for the effort.

She dragged herself out of the bag and carried her stuff upstairs. She needed to pee again, and brush her teeth, and she didn't want to get dressed with the boys slumbering right beside her. Bobby and Gabe didn't matter so much—hell, she'd been forced to take baths with Bobby until she was old enough to remember it. But Brad didn't get a free show.

She set her overnight bag down in the bathroom, and leaned her head around the corner to take a look inside the master bedroom. Apparently a tree branch had broken the bay window sometime during the night. The window seat was soaked, and there was a dark patch of wet wood for a yard or two around it. Everything else looked okay: The wardrobes, the bed frame, and the fixtures remained unmolested by water, and stray ghosts.

A fine, spitting spray still flicked inside through the missing windowpane, but last night's deluge was over for now. If she was lucky, it'd be completely finished before the day was out. If not, maybe Dad knew somebody with good towing equipment.

It was too early to call him. He wouldn't be up and moving until eight o'clock at the earliest.

So she did what she set out to do—washed her face, brushed her teeth, and got dressed—successfully killing about twenty minutes. After that, her cell said it was only 7:21, which was still too early to rouse the troops or phone home.

She reconsidered getting the boys up, despite the hour. The sun was creeping across the sky, gray and watery such as it was. They could get to work. The house was huge, and they needed to start on those mantels and surrounds. Seven twenty-one wasn't such a crazy time to begin. If Andy were there, he'd have had half the first pink bathroom stripped down already. He always liked being up before everyone else, and he had god-awful taste. He would've been on Bobby's side about the tiles.

She pushed his name out of his head, and out of her morning thoughts. There was no good reason for him to be there. He'd almost never worked with her and Daddy—only once in a blue moon, when they were desperate and he was between jobs. No. There wasn't any room for him here.

She laced up her work boots and chased down an umbrella, then left the house quietly—closing the front door behind herself and not really caring if the boys slept in. It'd be easier to work late into the night than to start this early. Or maybe they'd knock off and go drinking, or find a hotel.

It wasn't that she didn't care; it was that she didn't know. The house might throw a new monkey wrench in their direction, and they'd have to recalibrate their plans. Safer to stay flexible, and rested, and ready.

Two out of three ain't bad.

She drew her coat tight. It was colder out there, on the porch. Colder than inside, and colder than the day before. It actually felt like autumn for the first time since she'd arrived in Chattanooga.

The umbrella flapped open and she latched it into place. It was blue and white, and enormous—a golf umbrella she'd snagged from her dad's office ages before. It was almost overkill.

The hike downtown went faster since she'd made it before. She knew where to dodge the rivulets that had turned into rushing streams overnight; and she'd figured out which little roads connected with which bigger, paved roads.

She made it back to the coffeehouse in about fifteen minutes. The girl with opinions on ghosts wasn't working, which was just as well. Dahlia wasn't awake enough for idle chatter with strangers. She was barely awake enough to idly surf the Net while she munched slowly on an egg-and-cheese croissant—dodging the baleful, begging eyes of a chubby beagle who'd been leashed by his owner to the next table over.

When she was nearly done, she palmed the last bite of croissant and slipped it to the dog. He smacked his floppy lips and wagged discreetly. His person never looked up from her book.

Up by the front counter, there was a plastic tub on a tray. Dahlia bussed her own table, tossing her trash and putting the plate in the tub, then she turned to the barista, who was checking his e-mail on a phone that looked a lot like hers. She asked, "Hey, there's a cemetery around here, right?"

He nodded. "Right over there."

"Over where?"

He led her to the window and pointed. You could see the cemetery's entrance from the front door.

She thanked him, and composed a text message to the boys back at the house.

> Getting breakfast. Back soon. Be ready to go at
> 9:00. We start with the marble fireplaces.

She hit "send" and set off for the cemetery. It was only a block or two away as the crow flies. She paused when she saw that the grounds didn't officially open until 8:30; but the gates were wide open regardless, so she sauntered on in, passing an office with all its lights still off. This office was a square stone building so small that you could've parked it in the Withrows' foyer. If it'd been open, she could've gone inside and asked for help finding the Withrow plot, but it wasn't.

On the upside, there *was* a large bulletin board to the left of the front door—complete with a map. It wasn't a great map—it'd been blown up from a smaller line-work illustration, and it was difficult to read.

But it was better than nothing.

She stood there in the rain, the umbrella casting a huge, tinted shadow around her. The map was tricky, but if she read it correctly, the Withrows were down toward the front. She checked the general direction over her shoulder and saw a number of expensive-looking, oversized tombstones, and even a handful of vaults. When she looked down another path, she saw more modest graves. According to the Web site, if she went beyond the next few hills, she'd find vast lots of paupers, slaves, orphans, and flu victims. Some had stones, some went without.

She did a quick spot comparison between big names and lot numbers, and, armed with the information she'd swiped from the Web, she set off down a rough-paved road to the east.

"Withrow, Withrow, Withrow," she muttered, like she could summon them on command.

Simple legwork found them in five minutes, no magic required.

They had a large family monument, classic and tasteful, and

no doubt pricey if you weren't the folks who owned the company. It said, simply, WITHROW, and it was surrounded by smaller stones with more information about who was lying underneath them. Some of the older graves went back to the 1800s. Among the more recent ones was Hazel Withrow, who'd made it all the way to 1969. The lack of a nearby spouse or an additional surname implied she'd never married. Augusta's parents were right behind her, having died together on the same day, in that car wreck.

"Hello, Buddy," she said. "And Hazel. And um . . . everybody else."

Except Abigail. There was no sign of her. Now Dahlia had the photo, Augusta's lore, and the briefcase with the sanitarium records. It still amounted to family legend, instead of proof.

"Where *are* you, Abigail?" she asked the plot at large, but it wasn't like thinking out loud inside the mansion, where you might expect a reply. Her gut said she knew the answer anyway, but her gut was a big fat liar. Her gut had told her if she married Andy, he'd settle down. Her gut had told her—

Never mind.

She threw up her hands, and the umbrella dumped extra spray onto the nearest stones. "I guess it's just a fucking mystery," she announced to no one in particular, then turned and headed back out of the cemetery, past the hogback ridge, up the side of Lookout Mountain, and back to the Withrow house.

By the time she trudged past the stone gateposts, it was almost eight thirty. The guys ought to be up and dressed, if not entirely ready to engage with power tools, but when she arrived inside, they were still staggering around like zombies. Gabe was upstairs taking a quick morning shower with the door open, steam spilling out into the hallway. Brad was groggily eating cereal in the kitchen, and Bobby was starting on the day's first beer.

He must've brought it back last night, because there hadn't been any in the fridge, that Dahlia knew of. She couldn't bring herself to get too worked up about it. Let him have a beer. God knew she wanted one. She thought about asking, but restrained herself—beer and coffee for breakfast, she'd be peeing all damn day.

"Good morning, boys."

She got a low grumble of acknowledgment from both, followed by a belch from Bobby. "You didn't bring any coffee?"

"I took a detour on the way back. It would've gotten cold. And you never drink it, so what do you care?"

"Where'd you go?" he asked, exactly as apathetic about the oversight as he ought to be.

She pulled a seat up to the kitchen bar near Brad. "I went to the cemetery across the ridge. I found the Withrow plot."

Brad brightened, and swallowed a mouthful of cornflakes. "And?"

"And . . . everybody's there except for Abigail. I think she's the big bad ghost who's been bothering everyone in the bathroom, so I've been trying to piece together what happened to her between the time she came back here and the time she vanished from the family record."

Bobby burped again, and the room smelled sour. "Obviously, she must've died."

"Yeah, but when? And how? Your son," she pointed at her cousin, "thinks they might've locked her in the attic."

"A madwoman in the attic," Brad mumbled. "Isn't anybody tired of that one, yet?"

"Anyway, that's not what happened to her." Dahlia told them

about finding the satchel with the sanitarium records. She concluded, "They sent her away, but she was discharged, and she came back here, and must have died here. So why isn't she buried with the rest of the family?"

Bobby wasn't so sure. "You're hopping around a lot, making a bunch of assumptions."

"Eh." She waved her hand in his directions. "I have circumstantial evidence on my side. The only question is how she died."

"And *why*. And where she is now," Brad insisted. "Those are also questions."

They all went quiet. They were probably all thinking the same thing, but it was Brad who said it out loud: "She might be buried in that little cemetery."

Dahlia scooted her chair back, and pushed it out of the way. She refused to indulge the idea, no matter what her gut said. "Too bad we'll never know."

"We could . . . ," Brad began.

"No. We *couldn't*. We have an epic shit-ton of work to do today, so there won't be any time for any further grave robbing, thank God. We still have to rebury the soldier, for heaven's sake. Besides, I don't think the weather's going to hold. Except for some quality shovel time for you, Brad, the rest of the work stays indoors."

Bobby glanced out the kitchen window. "It's not raining half so bad as it was last night."

She checked the weather app on her phone, and turned the screen around to show him. "The radar says we're in for a beating over the next couple of days."

Gabe appeared in the kitchen entryway, rubbing his head with a towel. "What about Uncle Chuck?"

"What about him?" Bobby asked, finishing off the beer and tossing the bottle into the trash. "He can't control the weather."

"But he's still coming tomorrow, right?"

"No, not until Friday, unless . . ." She scrolled around on her phone, and saw that the forecast was even worse for Friday. "Hm. I don't know. We can get most of the house done before bedtime today, between us. If we can get Daddy to come down tomorrow, I bet he can help us wrap up a day early."

Brad leaned back to take a peek at her phone. "How bad does it look?"

"There's a storm front headed right for us. Tell you what, I'll give him a call and see how he wants to play it. The rest of y'all, get your asses in gear. I won't be a minute. Knowing him, he probably won't pick up."

She left the kitchen for the communal living area, then climbed the stairs, as if she needed some privacy. She didn't, but she took it anyway. As predicted, Chuck didn't answer. No great shock. Half the time he didn't hear his phone, and half the time he forgot to carry it. She left him a message.

"Hey Daddy, it's me. I know you planned to show up on Friday, but I was wondering if you couldn't drive down tomorrow instead. The weather is going to get bad tonight, and worse tomorrow. We may have to skip some of the house's exterior stuff, but we'll still have a hell of a haul, I promise. This was a good buy, and it'll pay off—even without the bay windows and whatnot, so don't worry about that. Anyway, call me, would you? We should talk. You should come out tomorrow." She paused, and then said quickly, "We're all tired of camping here at this crazy-ass house, and we want to come home."

She ended the call, and put the phone in her back pocket.

A dull drone in the background turned out to be the rain

kicking up again. She strolled to the broken hallway window and stood in the spray of water and chilly air that splattered through the jagged pane of glass. There was no dead soldier standing in the cemetery below; just a tarp weighted down by rocks, covering the spot where he'd been laid to rest in a shallow grave under someone else's headstone.

"Were you Abigail's first lover? What happened to you?"

The house didn't answer, and neither did any helpful ghost.

With that thought, she turned around—and saw that Hazel's door was closed again. The trunk that'd held it propped open was now sitting outside, in the hall. Dahlia approached it, and nudged it aside with her foot. It was heavy, but it moved. The lovely doorknob wiggled, but didn't turn. Hazel had locked her out again.

"I've got to get in there someday, Aunt Hazel," Dahlia said to the closed room. "Please don't make me destroy this door to do it. I'd rather not ruin anything I don't have to," she said under her breath. But when she thought about it, and tested the sound of the words again, she wasn't so certain. "I wish we could save this house . . ." didn't taste right anymore. She tried again. "Fine, the house can go to hell. But you seem all right, Aunt Hazel. I apologize to you for everything that's coming. I've already apologized to the house, but if you're hanging around, and if you still care for the place, then you get an apology, too. That's literally all I can do for you, now. If Daddy were here, he'd say it's more than I *ought* to do."

She looked down at the trunk, pushed out into the hall where it clogged the thoroughfare. One heavy corner had shoved up against the rotted carpet runner, and torn a great hole in it—leaving a drag mark in the old boards beneath.

She bent down to open it again and examine the contents

in daylight. The flimsy old latch hadn't mysteriously locked since last night, so that was something. Not everything closed for good when you looked away.

This time, she saw the same paperbacks as before. And something else.

Atop the jumbled pile of romances, gothic and otherwise, rested an overstuffed envelope. Dahlia picked it up. It smelled like mildew and dried flower petals. Inside, the folded papers were as fragile as tissue, brittle and brown with age.

My dearest Gregory, I want you to know that I'm yours, every inch of me—but my father's starting to wonder, and I fear he will give you grief when you come to get me...

The handwriting was slender and tidy, and very precise. The words were composed in pen, but the letters had faded to the off-brown color so very common to old missives, courtesy of all the iron in the ink.

Dahlia closed the trunk lid and sat down on top of it.

...not our type, as Mother puts it, but how would she know? She does not see the best parts of you, as I do. If father were not in the way, I think she might come around, in time. But you know she'll never stand against him. No one ever does, not even Hazel—who is quite fond of you, and thinks that you and I would make a very nice match. That's how she put it, when I pressed her on the matter. She's concerned for me. For both of us, I'm sure.

But this is not the time to dally. Time is running short, and in this case, we must risk asking forgiveness, instead of permission. You know as well as I do, that we must risk it soon. Come another few weeks, and people will be counting the months since our honeymoon, and raising their eyebrows high.

"Dahl? What are you doing?"

Gabe. She hadn't heard him come up the stairs, nor down the hall, nor to the spot where he was now standing over her shoulder, but he hadn't startled her, not exactly.

She looked up and gently waved the old paper. "Aunt Hazel locked us out again, but she left a little present." She pointed to the signature at the bottom on the back side. "Abigail's love letters to Gregory."

"Gregory who?"

"I have no idea. Lovers don't generally use their full given names when they write back and forth."

"Not in e-mail, but this was, like, the olden days, right?"

"Not even in the olden days. She didn't date these, either. I don't know if she mailed them, or snuck them out of the house through a friend, or a servant, or something. But Gregory . . . that's the name of our soldier downstairs, I'd bet money on it. I'd also bet money . . ." She closed the trunk and sat back on the lid, still scanning the narrow lines of penmanship. "They both knew she was pregnant. There's a bit in here about counting the months after the honeymoon."

Gabe crooked his neck to see the letter better. He began to

sit down beside her on the trunk lid, then changed his mind. It was old, and it might not hold them both. He leaned against the wall and folded his arms. "What else do the letters say?"

She flipped through them, skimming quickly. "Oh, the usual. Lots of 'my darling,' 'my dearest,' and promises of eternal love. She was worried about how the family would take it, so maybe her dad really did fly off the handle and do something rash. But I wonder why . . ." Dahlia carefully checked each page. "I wonder why only Abigail's letters are collected here. You'd think she would've saved his letters in return, wouldn't you?"

"Could be there weren't any. Or maybe he gave these back to her," Gabe proposed. "Because the feeling wasn't mutual. Dads have killed boyfriends for less than knocking up their daughters. Since the beginning of history, I'm pretty sure. Maybe that's how he died."

Dahlia stood and put the letters back into the trunk, closing it up and fastening the latches without locking them. "True, but if he knew she was pregnant, you'd think he'd whip out the shotgun and force them to make it legal. Regardless . . . could you do me a favor and go stuff this trunk up in the attic, out of the way?"

"Why me?"

"Because you are big and strong, and I am small and super tired from last night. Please? I just don't want to trip over it all day as we start the breakdown."

Her phone picked that moment to ring, so she asked him "Please?" one more time and answered it. "Hey Daddy, there you are."

"Here I am. What's this about closing up shop a day early?"

She shooed Gabe away. "Right. About that . . ." She gave him the breakdown on the weather. She wandered back to the broken window while she talked. "And in case you don't believe me, can you hear that?"

"Hear what?"

"Rain, Dad. Lots and lots of rain. I'm afraid you won't be able to bring in the trailer if it gets too much soggier, and things will only get worse through tomorrow night. If we weren't on a time limit, that'd be one thing."

"Technically we have until the fifteenth."

She shook her head, like he could hear it rattle. Down across the grounds she stared, picking at the broken glass with her fingernail. "I know, but nobody wants to stay another night. That's the truth of it, okay? This place isn't . . ." She struggled with how much to tell him, and how much to keep to herself. "Let's just say it's not healthy, and now that I've spent some time here, I totally understand why Augusta wants to see it leveled."

"Seriously? You? Ms. Savior of the Old Houses?"

"Yes. Seriously. Me. Next time we're all sitting around drinking, I'll tell you about the ghosts. I'll take rats and bugs and bats any day of the week."

"Since when are you afraid of ghosts?" he asked, half joking and half wondering in earnest. "In our line of work, I'd think you'd get used to them."

"I've been afraid of ghosts since I met the ones here in the Withrow house. There's one in particular, this awful girl . . . it's weird and bad, and . . . Let's just get the house into pieces and hit the road as soon as possible. Please?"

He was quiet, and then he asked: "How much have you sorted out already?"

"The carriage house and the barn are all done, except for that metal roof, but we've barely started on the house. We'll get everything but the last of the fixtures by tonight. The last thing we want to do is sleep here without power."

"It's that bad, huh?"

"And then some. But nothing tried to murder us or scare us half to death last night, so we can swing another one—if we all stick together."

"What do you mean, stick together?"

"I mean, we're all sleeping in the living room, with the lights on."

"No shit?" He sounded completely baffled.

"No shit, Daddy."

"All right, if it's that important to you . . . I'll pack up and see what I can do. I'll get one of the guys to watch the shop, and head down first thing in the morning. Will that make you happy?"

"Yes. Oh God, yes, it totally will. The boys will be thrilled. Thank you, Daddy."

"No problem, baby. But what about that cemetery? Will I be able to get the trailer up to the house? You said it might be a problem."

"Fuck the cemetery. Drive a tank over it, for all I care."

"Wait, what? Did you talk to Old Lady Withrow about it?"

She stared out the window, down at the place where an open grave was covered by a tarp, collecting a puddle. "I talked to her, and she said it wasn't a real cemetery. Her grandpa owned a monument company, and had a funny sense of humor. Apparently it was all part of some neighborhood-wide Halloween party, back around World War I."

"That's . . . that's the craziest thing I've ever heard."

"Well, that's what she said. She swore on a stack of Bibles, ain't nobody buried there."

"Do you believe her?"

To lie to Dad, or not to lie to Dad? Dahlia hedged her bets, and told half the truth. "I don't know. It sounds crazy, but it's within the bounds of Tennessee crazy. I looked it up online"—that was a fib, but not quite a lie—"and it's not an open cemetery so far as the county is concerned. If anybody's buried there, you couldn't prove it without a shovel."

"That's a lovely image. Thank you, dear."

"I'm here for you, Pops. Just get down here, would you? We'll figure everything out when you arrive."

"I'll drag out a shorter trailer for the Bobcat, if you think we can do without the extra storage in the one-ton. You pack your trucks so tight they squeak. Do you think we can make it work?"

She mentally mapped the remaining space in the two trucks she had on hand. "I think so, yeah. Bring straps and we might be able to roll up the copper roof and tie it up. We still need to grab the stained glass, and there's a lot of it . . . but we'll have room. The rose transom can ride shotgun between me and Brad if it has to."

"All right, then that's what I'll do. If worse comes to worst, I can always drive back down before the fifteenth for one more go."

With a plan in place, they said their good-byes. Dahlia hung up, relieved that he was coming, and wondering what the hell she was going to tell him about the tarp outside, if they didn't have the time or weather to finish covering up poor Gregory.

She was doing her dad a favor, really. He was happier not knowing, she was sure of it. He could find out after the fact, when Bobby or Gabe inevitably spilled the beans; but by then it'd all be over, and he could freak out all he liked.

A prickly feeling tickled the back of her neck.

She turned around and saw nothing and no one, so it must've been the atmosphere. The broken window would let in anything, even those curly little drafts of cold, wet air. Just standing there beside it, she could almost see her breath.

"Temperature's dropping," she muttered to herself. "I ought to throw some plastic up here before some birds or bats find their way inside. Or more bugs."

As far as she knew, there hadn't been a good freeze yet. She'd been smacking mosquitos left and right outside, which implied the thermostat hadn't fallen that far yet. What if it froze overnight? Would they get some snow, or would all the mud freeze?

She shuddered at the thought of throwing blocks of frozen mud on top of the old soldier, but if it came to that. "Ugh."

Back downstairs, the guys were ready to get moving. "I talked to Dad," she informed them. "He's coming first thing in the morning, so let's cross our fingers and hope it stays too warm for ice."

"Preach it," Bobby muttered. "So let's quit burning daylight, huh? We've got a shit-ton of work to do if we're going to have the house ready before Uncle Chuck gets here."

Dahlia laughed. "Who are you, and what have you done with the real Bobby Dutton?"

"I am a man who's had just about enough of this bullshit house and its bullshit ghosts who like to jump you in the bathroom and give you bullshit dreams."

She almost asked about his dreams, but didn't. "Once again, we are on the same page. If I'm not careful, I might forget you're a lazy douchebag."

"And if I'm not careful, I might forget *you're* a controlling bitch."

"We'll have to be on our guard, then." She put her hands on her hips. "All right, fellas. Let's spread out and wreak some havoc. Leave the electrical fixtures for now, and leave the plumbing in the bathrooms alone—they don't have anything we want. But tonight, before bedtime, we're turning off the water, okay? Nobody gets a shower, because we're safer without them."

Brad frowned. "What about the toilet?"

"If it's yellow, let it mellow. We'll fill up a few buckets to flush, and leave them in the tub. But once that's done, I want the water *off*."

"Where's the main?" Bobby asked.

"I haven't the foggiest. Check around outside—it can't be far off. But there's no rush for now. As long as you get it done before dark, I'll be happy." Dog tired and desperately wanting a nap, she tried not to sound exhausted when she continued, "So here's where we're at: I want Gabe and Bobby on the stone mantels and surrounds, because those things are fucking heavy. Brad, me and you will start tackling the smaller things, like some of the stained glass and the gothic windows above the kitchen—"

"Are you calling me a puss?" he objected.

"No, I'm saying more than two people on those stone surrounds will be too many cooks in the kitchen. Bobby and Gabe, if you need help, you holler for us."

"Yes ma'am," Gabe promised.

"When we're all done—hopefully before lunch, but afterwards, if it comes to that—we'll pool our elbow grease and start grabbing whatever's upstairs, then work our way down-stairs, and then to the floors."

"Give me your keys, and I'll pull both trucks up as close as I can get them," Bobby offered. "Some of that old shit won't stand for getting wet, and the marble won't travel across the yard too well."

"I like it." She fished her keys out of her pocket and chucked them into his open palm. "Bring those bad boys around, and haul in what's left of the tools. Let's make this happen."

Gabe took his father's keys and made for the other truck. Brad turned to Dahlia and asked, "Got anything in particular in mind for me? I kind of . . . I don't know where to start."

"You could start in the kitchen if you want. We've eaten through most of our food, and the rest will fit in the coolers. The cabinets and appliances look like shit, but double-check and make sure all the cabinets are sad mid-century particle-board. If some of the original stuff is there, and it's solid, let me know. Check the dumbwaiter and find out what's at the bottom. Go exploring along those back stairs, and see if there's anything worth grabbing, and look under the house, while you're at it. Gas fixtures are fair game, so grab them if they're good—because the gas has been off for years. Everything in this house has been electric since the sixties. If the fixtures are newer, or they're rewired for electricity, don't touch them until we've closed down the breakers."

His chin was up and down, following along with her off-the-cuff instructions and getting the idea. "And if I run across anything, but I'm not sure—I'll set it aside and ask you later."

"Good man. Yes. Do that."

"Where are you starting?"

"Upstairs," she said firmly. "I'm working top to bottom. But first, I'm going to do something about the hole in the hallway window."

"Why?" he asked. "If we're just going to tear it out anyway?"

She went past him to one of the bags of tools and assorted useful items. A roll of duct tape was right on top. "The windows will be among the last things we yank, along with the electrics. There's no need to let the floors up there get soaked, on the off chance we can salvage what's underneath that god-awful runner. Honestly, I should've done something about it sooner." She collected the tape and a cheap painter's tarp, then took a box cutter and carved off a large square. "But once I get that patched up, I'll make sure there's nothing worth taking from the attic, then start working my way through the second floor. When you're done in the kitchen, you can help me with the furniture. I want to take some of the things in the master bedroom, and we'll need to get inside Hazel's room—which may or may not require the Sawzall."

"Hazel's room?" He gave her a funny look.

"Oh, the locked one up there. It was open last night and me and Gabe took a look around. But it's locked now, so unless she sees fit to open it up again, we'll have to cut the door. I'd rather not, but I guess it's up to her." She said that last part loudly, in case Hazel was listening.

"You are so weird."

"*I'm* weird? Should I bring up your speculative grave robbing again?"

His face went sour. "I wish you wouldn't."

She stopped. "All right, then I won't. But we need to do something about that tarp and that body before my dad gets here, and you offered to fill the grave back in. Pack it down good, and throw some rocks over it—if you can find any gravel, that'd be perfect. Daddy might need to drive over it when he gets here."

"That sounds awful."

"Then pitch me something else," she commanded. "You're the one who made this mess."

"Do . . . do you think Chuck will fire me, if he finds out about it?"

No, she didn't. Her dad was the softest touch this side of the river, but she was annoyed with Brad, and she didn't feel like reassuring him. "I don't know, man. Either he'll laugh it off, or he'll call the cops and pretend he's never heard of you. So if I were you, I'd bury the poor guy again, and keep my mouth shut."

She left him and went to see about the upstairs window, stopping by the bathroom to grab a towel someone had left behind on a hook.

Carefully she swabbed the damp glass, losing another few shards in the process. They toppled out into the rain, breaking on the ground below, but she didn't hear them. The rain drowned everything out, leaving the sky too gray for morning. Even though the painter's tarp was light and opaque, once it was taped into place, the hallway felt unnaturally dark.

She stood with her back to the window and listened to the sounds of the trucks barely rumbling over the rain.

Downstairs, the clatter of cabinetry suggested Brad had started his tasks; and if the sound of truck engines straining against the wet grass and mud meant anything, Bobby and Gabe were moving, as well. It was time for Dahlia to get started, too.

A gust of wind rattled hard against the plastic patch, but didn't strain the tape too much.

"The attic it is," Dahlia concluded, and returned the now-damp towel to the main bathroom down the hall. Before leaving, she paused and looked around the violent pink bathroom. There was nothing in particular she wanted to keep, and she sure as hell didn't want to waste time pulling pink subway tiles down from the walls. Maybe if there was literally nothing left to do, and she couldn't sleep.

She stared into the mirror, daring it to show her something other than her own damn face. "I'm on to you, Abigail," she told her reflection. "You can't slow me down. You can't stop me, either, and that means you're going to have to leave soon. You don't have to like it, but there it is. Whatever's on the other side of . . . of wherever you are these days . . . you have to go find it."

Out in the hall, a click and a creak echoed off the paneling.

She popped her head around the bathroom door. It looked like Hazel had decided to cooperate, because her bedroom was open once more. "Thanks," she said to anyone who might be listening. "You're saving me a lot of trouble, and saving your door a date with a power saw."

"Dahlia?" Bobby called loudly from downstairs. "You talking to someone up there?"

"No one but myself," she replied in kind.

Dahlia's phone said it was barely breakfast time, but the dull gray light indoors felt like the far edge of dusk—and inside the narrow stairwell leading to the attic, she was climbing almost blind. But she knew the way by now, and didn't even hit her head when she reached the trapdoor. She pushed it up with her elbow and climbed into the angled space of wide, exposed rafters and bat shit.

And rat shit, she remembered as she scattered some with the toe of her work boot.

YOUR FAULT

The message was carved deep and wide, but that didn't make it true. She didn't know what had really happened to Abigail, and everyone who did was dead, or disinclined to talk about it. Maybe the girl'd had her reasons. Maybe she'd been off her rocker.

But the lovingly penned notes from the trunk nagged at her: all of them from Abigail, none of them from Gregory in return.

A crack of thunder shook the house, rattling the attic windows in their rot-softened frames. Wind whistled through the chips and past the rotted, splintered fascia beams, and the drafty, unsealed room felt even draftier.

Dahlia hugged herself, and thought about a hoodie. No— the flannel ought to be enough, once she got moving. It was only wet and gusty, and that made everything feel colder than it really was, and she wasn't moving yet. She was standing in an empty attic, peering into corners. She already knew there was nothing worth salvaging up there, but she couldn't admit to herself that she was looking for something else. Hints, or more hidden compartments.

She didn't see any such thing. She saw her breath, coiling and white. She saw a boy-shaped shadow flicker behind a support column.

Dahlia froze. If she was patient, he might . . .

. . . yes. A round head, or the suggestion of one. The

impression of eyes, sunken and dark, in a face that was no more substantial than a shadow.

"Buddy?" she breathed. "Is that you?"

She took a step toward the hiding spirit, but the boylike wisp shuddered and threatened to vanish.

"No, please, don't go. I won't hurt you. I couldn't if I wanted to. Just so we're clear, though . . . you know . . . don't you?" She shoved her hands up under her armpits, and shivered. "You're dead. You've been dead a long time, but you weren't . . . you didn't . . ."

You were a grown-ass man when you died, she wanted to say. For whatever reason, she didn't. It was easier to think of this faint, cowering thing as a child. It might've been deliberate—dead children aren't as scary as dead men, isn't that what she'd told Gabe? Or had Gabe told her that? Her head felt uncomfortably full again, all that spun cotton crammed between her ears. She opened her mouth, yawned, and popped them.

Buddy didn't acknowledge anything she said. He only stared, and when she made any motion toward him, he wobbled in distress. But he was letting her see him. He was hiding, but he wasn't running away.

"Is this—" She bobbed her head toward the message on the floor. "—directed at you? Did Abigail blame you for what happened?"

The boy's head shot up, but he wasn't looking at Dahlia anymore. He was looking at the far wall. The rumbling sky was throwing lightning now, and it was flashing so bright in the dim space that she could see a vague black mist over there. It swirled and congealed. In the middle, there were two dark places that might have stood for eyes.

"Buddy?"

She looked back to the support where the little thing had stashed itself, but he was gone. She was alone with this new thing, and it didn't look happy. It grew before her eyes, until it was much larger than a person. Much darker, much more hateful, much less solid. A roaring hum vibrated between her ears, and in that hum she heard words—but not clearly. She heard them the way you think you hear words when the radio is stuck between two stations and only white noise comes through.

She began to back away, but changed her mind. She needed to get back to the hatch. There was nothing here for Music City, no good wood to pull from the floors, and the windows were all broken and splintered. There was nothing to be saved, not a tiny ghost boy, and not this swirling beast that fixed her in its sights—if it even had eyes at all.

It did not feel like daytime.

It did not feel like just-past-breakfast, when the power was on, and the house was full of people who were awake, and working hard, working fast. This thing in front of her—it should've come at night, but it had come after dawn, when everyone else was downstairs. It had come with a cold, stale smell like frozen pond water, thick with mud. It spread with a viscous rolling, billowing sprawl as slow and thick as oil in winter.

Dahlia could not freeze. The hatch was only a few yards away.

Something buzzed in her jeans pocket. She tagged it, wondering what it could possibly be. This was too small to be her phone. It fit in the almost decorative slot below her right hip.

Harder and harder it shook, until its presence was painful against her hip bone. She jammed two fingers in there and yanked out the small metal pendulum she'd found in Hazel's room. Once exposed, it lunged toward the hatch. Dahlia barely caught it by the bauble at the other end of its chain—but she *did* catch it, and she let it draw her to that hatch, within mere feet of the angry thing with claws that could carve wood like a holiday turkey.

She flung herself down the stairs and dropped the trapdoor behind her, but it flew open again, and that chilled, weird stink blasted down into the corridor.

The pendulum said to keep moving, and Dahlia couldn't argue with it. She followed it into the hall, a couple of doors down, and into Hazel's room—where the door slammed shut and locked itself behind her.

The door shook and rattled.

Clutching the pendulum like it could protect her, Dahlia stood before the dresser and stared back at that locked door, panting even though she hadn't run far, and she wasn't really tired. She was scared for her life, because whatever Abigail was, she could haunt by day and slice up floors, so why not skin and bone?

A series of hard blows rained against Hazel's door, echoing through the whole house. Dahlia was sure of this, and someone must have known that there were bad things afoot. Her voice shook when she said, "Fuck this!" but the door held despite her lack of faith, and she squeezed that little steel pendulum she'd taken from Hazel's drawer.

She looked down at that drawer, and then up at the mirror.

Whatever was beating on the door gave it another half-dozen blows; Dahlia was positive that the force would push it off the frame and send it crashing inside.

But she was wrong. The door stayed where it was.

Dahlia was standing before the mirror. In the mirror, she

looked ragged and wild. In the mirror, Hazel Withrow looked calm and barely dead at all.

Hazel wore a sharp suit of salmon polyester. Her hair was streaked with silver, and her glasses were the shaped like cat eyes. Her fingers were long, and they sported several expensive rings; her bones were thin, and the pleats in her pants were as crisp as the last day she pressed them.

She can't come in.

"That's why you keep it locked," Dahlia stated. No question of it, though it sounded raspy coming from her fright-stiffened throat.

Anyone would go mad in this house without a refuge.

"Sister, I *hear* you."

She's weaker in the day. Not weak, but weaker. You've worn her out, for now.

"Hazel," she said. "What do I do?"

Do your job. But don't stay here tonight. Find a hotel, and return in the morning. You won't be safe when the sun goes down.

"Aunt Hazel, please tell me," she tried . . . but there was no one in the mirror. Dahlia was alone. Brad and Bobby were beating on the door, calling her name.

"I'm in here . . . ," she said; then, again, louder and stronger. "I'm in here!"

"Open the door!" Brad sounded as frantic as she'd felt ninety seconds ago.

"I'm trying!" She grabbed the knob and yanked it. It rolled over, easy as pie. She drew back the door and stared wildly at all three of them—Gabe had just joined the party, having run up the stairs sweating and covered with rain. "Dahl?" he asked, toppling toward her, pushing Brad and his father aside.

"The door slammed shut behind me! But . . . I'm fine. I'm shook up, is all."

Bobby rubbed his hands on his pants. They were red and rough, and the knuckles were chapped from where he'd been banging on the door—as hard as Abigail had, almost. "What the hell just happened? We heard you running downstairs, and something banging around . . ."

She looked out into the hall, both ways. Seeing nothing, she waved them all inside Hazel's room.

The guys filed in anxiously behind her. She closed the door and leaned her back against it, pretending she was only tired and winded.

"We're all safe in here," she said to herself, but she let them hear it. Her voice was normal again. She forced it to be. "Safer than we are out there. Hazel did something to the room—she made it a sanctuary, and Abigail can't come inside. She can't touch us."

"Abigail was in the attic?" asked Bobby.

"She chased me out. Hazel opened the door, and let me come in here. Abigail tried to follow . . ." She rubbed her hands together, then on her jeans. When she did that, she could pretend they weren't shaking. "But she didn't. She couldn't."

"You sure you're all right?" Brad asked.

She might've asked it in return. He looked as frazzled as she felt—or worse. God, she *hoped* she didn't look that frayed around the edges. Somebody had to hold it together, because the job wasn't done yet, and she couldn't walk away. She couldn't even run.

"I've been better," she told him, in case there was any solidarity in suffering. Anything else would've looked like a lie. "But whatever's in the house—whoever's in this house . . . I've been calling her Abigail, but she's only a shadow, only some weird leftover—she hasn't hurt any of you, has she?"

"She about scared the shit out of me," Bobby complained. "Does that count?"

"But she didn't touch you? She didn't chase you, or try to harm you? Any of you?"

As she asked the question, she was already sure of it—Abigail didn't want their attention, not like she wanted Dahlia's. The realization didn't make her feel special, so much as targeted. When the boys all shook their heads, admitting with manly grunts that no, Abigail was only scary as fuck, Dahlia tried to take some comfort in that. If Abigail wanted to pick on somebody, better it was her than one of the boys. Dahlia could take it. She had to. She was the boss.

The resolution made her calmer. It gave her direction.

"All right, so all she's done is . . . be creepy as shit."

Gabe read her better than she thought. "What about you, Dahl? Has she ever hurt you?"

"No, just scared me half to death. Well, I hit my head, once, when she scared me out of the tub and I fell," she added, so it sounded like full disclosure. "But that's the worst of it."

She didn't mention that Abigail had tried to do worse, and she didn't say anything about the carved-up message in the attic, or how she'd wondered if the ghost could carve up bones the same way. She didn't see any reason to.

Instead, Dahlia concluded, "She's only scary. We can work around that. So here's what we're doing now, boys: First of all, scratch the attic. There's nothing good up there, I checked." The look Gabe shot her said he wouldn't tell anyone about the carving if she didn't. Bobby and Brad didn't need to know. "Second, plan to wrap up before dark. Fuck this place, and Abigail right along with it. We're getting a couple of hotel rooms. Bobby, you and Gabe can share, and Brad, you and me can bunk together, unless you want to front something with your own money. We'll get something with two beds."

Brad was not bothered by the sleeping suggestions; if anything, it came as a relief. But the time frame worried him. "Do you think we can get the place cleared out by then?" His eyebrows were all knotted up—and Dahlia wanted to think it was all about the job, but it probably wasn't.

"No, but I don't give a damn." She was surprised to hear herself say it, and even more surprised to know it wasn't bravado and bullshit. "We'll get enough of it done, and that's what matters. We'll buckle down, get organized, and do what we can. The rest can wait for Daddy in the morning, and we can spend all day tomorrow tying up loose ends."

"He's going to think we're crazy," Gabe said.

Dahlia didn't give a damn about that, either. "Only if we're lucky. If he comes to town and the house stays quiet, yeah, he'll think we're crazy. But if he meets the resident poltergeist, he'll understand why I'm with Augusta Withrow—why, if it were up to me, I'd burn this place to the ground and run."

Bobby's gaze swayed from side to side, like he was looking for someplace to spit for emphasis. "Let the whole world think we're crazy, I don't care. Actually . . ." He sat down on the side of the bed. "That gives me an idea. We've all got phones, right? And those phones have all got cameras. I say we keep them close at hand, and whip 'em out if shit goes south."

"So you can . . . what? Sell the footage?" Dahlia flipped her palms up in the universal gesture of "What the fuck?"

"So we can *have* the footage. So if Uncle Chuck thinks we're idiots, we can point to it and say, 'See? Weird shit happened, and it was bad, and we weren't jumping at shadows.'"

Brad sat on the edge of the dresser. It groaned, but held him. "That's not a terrible idea."

"See? Even the nerd thinks it's a plan."

"Yeah, I do. Because you know why every damn cable station has its own damn ghost-hunting show?"

"Wait. Not *every* channel . . . ?" Gabe sort of asked.

"Yes, every last one of them," Brad confirmed. "Not just the science fiction channel, but travel channels, true crime channels—shit, probably C-SPAN has one. I know for a fact the animal channel does. And . . . and it's a riot, you know? Because nobody ever catches anything on camera except for shadows and little lights that could come from anywhere. So what are the odds," he asked, half earnest and half tap-dancing on the edge of hysteria, "that any of us would actually *catch* anything?"

Bobby snorted. "Son, you ever see *The Blair Witch Project*?"

"Don't call me 'son.' And that was *fiction,* you idiot. In real life, real people—real cameras . . . they don't catch *shit*. It's like . . . it's like the cameras are some kind of talisman, keeping the supernatural at bay. If we all keep our cameras, or our camera phones running—"

Dahlia cut him off: "—then we'll all be out of battery life in a couple of hours."

He gave her a look like he wanted to kill her. "I have a regular camera."

"Fine, then use that. If there's any chance that a camera will scare her off, it's worth trying. We have regular old digital cameras in the equipment stash. All right, everybody: Use your phones, use the cameras in the stash, and keep your things charged up if you can. If I'm going to get chased away by a ghost, I want some proof that I'm not a goddamn crybaby. So either we stay ghost-free, or we walk away with proof of the afterlife. It's not exactly a win-win, but I'll take it."

"We can put them around the house, swap them out, change the batteries," Brad pressed. "One on the mantel, one looking at the stairs, one in the bathrooms . . ."

"I think we only have two. But between those and the phones, we can get the place covered. Either Abigail will show herself, or we'll have a nice, peaceful day of hard-ass manual labor," she declared. She opened the bedroom door without any resistance from Aunt Hazel, stepped into the hall, pulled out her phone, and took a deep breath.

13

DAHLIA STOOD ON the front porch surveying the rain, the carriage house, the disassembled barn, the blue tarp with rocks on top and a corpse underneath. "Open up the trucks, and let's start tearing this place down."

Gabe was usually the first to get moving, but this time, he hesitated. "I don't know, Dahl. The trucks are heavy, and it was hell to pay bringing them up so far into the yard. Me and Dad were talking, and maybe we should suck it up and drive them back to solid ground. We ain't made of sugar. We won't melt in the rain."

"Both of those things are true, baby . . . but not everything we want to save can stand getting wet. And what solid ground would you recommend? The mountain is turning to swamp, right in front of us."

"We could go out to the asphalt road and leave the trucks there," Bobby proposed. "Pull 'em off to the side, so they won't block traffic."

Brad leaned on the railing and gestured out at the vast expanse of lawn. "That's half a mile away! How are we supposed to load them with the real heavy items? The furniture, the flooring, the windows? The dollies won't be any use to us, not across all that mud and monkey grass."

"Then we don't load them at all, not yet," Dahlia declared. She was back on firmer footing, and it felt good—even as the memory of a black smoke thing with knife-sharp nails lingered behind her eyes. "We take the heavy stuff down to the sitting room and stack it up there. If we fill that up, we'll start cramming it into the parlor across the foyer. We'll leave it that way for now, and load the trucks when the weather permits. Boys, I know you just went to a lot of trouble to bring them up close, but you're probably right. Take them back out to the road so they don't get stuck in the Withrow swamp, and we don't wind up stranded here. Come sundown, we'll lock up the house, grab some umbrellas, and make for the trucks. Tomorrow's gonna suck, but it won't suck as bad as another overnight in this hellhole."

She half expected Bobby to make some obnoxious joke about how she'd seen too many of Brad's ghost-hunting shows, but he didn't say a word. All he did was nod, pull his keys out of his damp hoodie pocket, and tell his son, "Dahl left that big blue and white umbrella down in the foyer to dry. Why don't you grab it?"

Brad took his phone out and fiddled with the camera's settings. "I'll get my charging cord, and I'll prop this thing up wherever I'm working. I'm just going to let it record, and record, and record."

"You do that, sweetheart. I'll get mine ready, too. In case you're right." Any port in a storm—that's what Daddy would say if he were here, and if he believed her.

"Oh, I'm right. You'll see. Cameras are practically magic. They'll keep this polterbitch away."

She ratcheted a smile into place, and held it there. "If you catch her on camera, you can sell the footage and pay off your student loans ahead of schedule."

When he was gone, Dahlia lingered. But Hazel didn't reappear, so she went back to the master bedroom. This time, she didn't brace the door behind her. Hazel was helpful. Hazel would open her room, if it needed opening. She relied on this thought, and propped herself up on it.

The little crew wasn't alone in this, strangers in a house full of teeth, and not everything that lurked was murderous.

Blessings: counted.

In the bedroom where Dahlia had spent the first two nights on the job, the bay window seat was ruined. Rain had come in through the busted pane, and water had soaked it down to the supports. It wasn't a shame, she didn't think. They would've never gotten that whole thing out in one piece. Even if her dad were bringing the big lift, and the big trailer, it was too high up to cut it down safely. One way or another, it was doomed to ruin.

In the end, water was just as dignified as a wrecking ball.

For some reason, that thought prompted her to try her dad again. He might answer, and she wanted to hear his voice.

He did answer. On the second ring.

"Dolly? Everything all right?"

"Yes and no," she answered, almost unreasonably relieved to hear him. "The job is going all right, and we're on track to have . . . well, almost everything wrapped up by the time you get here in the morning, but we can't stay here anymore. We have to get a couple of hotel rooms tonight. Bobby and Gabe can bunk together, and I'll get something with a pair of beds for me and Brad. I'll find someplace cheap."

She might have rambled further, but he asked, "Did something happen?"

"Lots of somethings have happened. I told you, it's not safe here."

He was quiet for a few seconds. "I don't understand . . . it's not safe *how*? Is it the electrics, or mold, or . . . ?"

"If it was that easy, I would've said so. Daddy, I told you already: We're not alone."

"You want me to spend a few hundred bucks on hotels because you're afraid of ghosts?"

"This is more than a ghost; it's something else. And between you and me . . ." She checked over each shoulder, but the guys were off working their respective jobs. "I'm afraid it's going to hurt somebody."

"Why?"

"It's been messing with us. I don't know how strong it is, and I don't want to find out. If it's just the money you're worried about, then fuck it—I've got a credit card, and I'll pay for it myself."

His silence suggested she'd hit a nerve.

"Daddy? It's only a couple hundred bucks—if that much. This ain't Manhattan. I can take care of it."

"You shouldn't have to. And one way or another, if you pay for it—I'm paying for it. Now, tell me the truth, Dahl. Is the house a score or a bust?"

"From a money standpoint? It's golden. We already have enough in the trucks to break you even, I bet. And we haven't done hardly anything on the house itself. That's just the chestnut and the goodies from the carriage house."

"Jesus, I hope you're right. This place has to keep us afloat. We need to bleed it dry, and take home every scrap, you understand?"

All too well. "When you get here, we'll scrape this baby clean. It'll probably take us from dawn to dusk, but we'll get every last thing, dump it all at the shop, and sleep in our own beds.

Once we get it all parted out and cataloged . . . we might not get a nickel for every penny, but we ought to double our money, easy."

"I love the sound of it. And I appreciate all the hard work you've done on this one. It sounds like . . . I guess it hasn't been easy."

"Worst . . . job . . . *ever*."

"Yeah, and it sounds like you're saving some for me. How far behind schedule are you, really?"

She sighed, and thought about it. "Honestly, we could use another two days besides this one. We haven't been able to yank all the boards off the barn, and we can't pull the floors yet, because we're moving the trucks out to the main road."

"Why the hell would you do that?"

"It's been raining for days. The Withrow property is a swamp. If we don't move the trucks now, we'll never get them out of here without a tow. If it dries out tomorrow, we'll bring them back. If it doesn't, you can use the forklift to tote stuff between the house and the road."

"So it's not the ghosts what slowed you down?"

"The ghosts are only a problem at night. Um . . . mostly. During the day, we've kept busy as planned. We've been working around the weather, trying to prioritize, but there's only so much we can do while the bottom's falling out. I'm sorry, but the worst of it will be waiting for you."

"When I get there, you really think we can catch up?"

She hesitated. "Probably? I think, in a perfect world, yes. If not, we'll return on Friday to bat cleanup on the details. It all depends on the weather, and whether or not you want to drive back down, or help me pay for another night in the hotel."

"Rock and a hard place."

"Maybe we'll get lucky, and from here on out, everything will go smoother than whale shit through an ice floe."

"Here's hoping."

The line went quiet. It was time to wrap up, and they both knew it.

Dahlia took the lead. "Anyway, Daddy . . . we're getting a hotel tonight, but don't worry about the money. The house is a treasure chest, and we're going to raid the shit out of it. Even if we don't grab every board and tile on the way out the door, Barry won't have to kill you or anything."

"He'll think about it."

"I'll protect you," she promised. "Just get here good and early, and we'll do our best. You're going to love this place. Except for the poltergeists."

"I liked it better when you called them ghosts."

"To be fair, I think it's just the one poltergeist. But one is too many, so . . ."

"So . . . I'll be there in the morning."

They hung up. Dahlia felt both better—because there was an end in sight, and worse—because the stakes were so very high, and there was still so much to be done.

Forty thousand dollars, that's what Chuck had paid for the rights—almost twice what she made in a year. She could've laughed. Well, if it all went tits up, she could always ditch her new apartment and move back home. Wouldn't that be grand? Divorced, pushing forty, and living at home with her Daddy. Form an orderly queue to the left, gents.

Downstairs, Brad had returned to banging around in the kitchen. It sounded like he was packing up the nonessentials. In another fifteen minutes, Bobby and Gabe returned—soaked but successful. "The trucks are out past the gateposts," Gabe announced. "There's lots of space for cars to pass around them, but we didn't see a single one the whole time we parked and locked them."

Dahlia came downstairs to join them. "Way to go, guys. Now will y'all two *please* get started on the fireplaces? If we get them both out easy, that's half of dad's investment back right there. I'll drag down what's savable from upstairs in the bedrooms, and Hazel's room. Everything I can carry."

"Is any of that furniture worth taking?" Bobby asked.

"Most of it's late Deco or early Nouveau—and it's all in good shape."

"Is that a yes?"

"It's a probably. It's a definitely on Hazel's vanity, though. I think I recognized the manufacturer; or there might be a label inside, we'll see."

"What's Brad doing?" Gabe wanted to know.

"He's breaking down the kitchen. When he's finished packing our stuff and checking for hidden treasure, he can help me carry the big things down." It was momentum, the way she rolled downhill into business mode. The work was something solid and predictable. It was manageable. All she had to do was manage it. "Okay. Fireplaces. This one is a lot smaller than the one in the living area, so take it out first—and do it as fast as you safely can. I'll start piling furniture into the sitting room, and then I'll fill up the space behind you."

"Then what?" asked Gabe, who was already rifling through a tool bag.

"Then . . . lunch—at least, I hope you'll be finished with this one by then. The stone is going to take you longer than you think, trust me on that. But once you've got both surrounds free and taped up in the padding, move on to the other fireplaces.

Their mantels are rosewood, and some of those tiles are in real good shape. People will eat them up."

"After that?" It was Bobby's turn to ask for direction.

"After that, the stained glass, and the gothic windows—except for the rooms where we've stacked tomorrow's load—and the doors and the hardware and the built-ins, and the stair rails, and . . . Jesus H. Christ, we have a lot of work to do."

But it was doable. When in doubt, concentrate on the job.

Abigail couldn't chase them all at once, not while they were working in different rooms and hustling in different directions. Hazel had said she wasn't so strong during the day, so maybe the worst of it was over for now.

Even if it wasn't, there was nothing else to be done about it.

All Dahlia could do was forget the ghosts, or ignore the hell out of them. Remember the payday. Remember Daddy up in Nashville, and the store, and the stock that was getting stale. Forget the eyeless thing in the attic. Forget the woman-shaped shadow in the bathrooms. Remember to be careful with the corner blocks, because those nice ones with the carved patterns are worth more than the simple bull's-eye models.

Her fear and worry didn't magically go away, but she packed them away in a box, taped it up, and put it in the corner. It was just one more thing she could unpack and process when she got back home. It wouldn't do anyone any good right now. It was only in the way.

So remember the tiles, and stack them up neat. If you break them, set them aside, but don't toss 'em. Go for the built-ins if you think you can pull them out of the wall in only a piece or two. Leave them if they have Phillips-head screws. It means they're newer than the 1930s, and they won't be worth the trouble.

Forget the mirrors. Forget the broken glass. Forget the sounds of doors opening and closing when nobody's there.

Remember the cameras—the digital ones have movie mode. You can set them where people are working, like Brad suggested. He aimed one right at himself, like it was casting a spell that would protect him from all evil. For his sake, Dahlia hoped he was right.

If you don't catch anything, you work in peace. If you catch something, you're not crazy, and you're famous on cable TV.

Over the next few hours, they made a dent in the list, but didn't break through it.

Lunch was a hasty affair, cleaning up the last of the lunch meat and cheese, powering through cans of Chef Boyardee, and scarfing down Little Debbies. Better to eat it than to toss it all—or load it up and take it back to Nashville. Maybe if they were feeling especially celebratory or desperate, they'd go get supper someplace before they checked into a hotel.

As lunch wound down, Bobby opened the fridge to reveal a couple of six-packs. "Better finish these up, too."

Dahlia put out her hands and made grabby fingers at the beer. "Ordinarily, I'd yell at you about drinking on the job, but if ever a job required a drink, this is it. Give me one. Hell, give me two—and I'll take one upstairs."

The bottles clinked against each other as she climbed to the second floor. She'd already removed the three small stained glass windows and covered the exposed openings with plastic, though she'd need help with the large one downstairs. She'd gotten the cute pre-war medicine cabinet from the hallway bathroom, but she was leaving the claw-foot tub; it was a five-footer, and you could get those damn near anywhere. She'd toted all the light furniture downstairs and the keep-worthy heavier items, with Brad's help. There was nothing left up there but the big stuff in Hazel's room, which she'd been saving for last.

Brad finished the contents of his beer and set the empty bottle on the floor. "You want a hand with that vanity?"

"Not yet. Give me a few minutes to go through the contents. Could you bring me a box?"

"How big?"

"Big enough to hold a bunch of shit, but not too big for me to carry. Bring me a couple of them, actually. I'd appreciate it."

Only a few of the flat-packed cardboard boxes had made it out of the trucks dry, but they'd have to do. She had a fat roll of packing tape on a handled dispenser to assemble them, and she didn't think Hazel had left so much behind that she'd need more than two boxes to hold it all.

Moths had gotten into the left set of vanity drawers. The grayish-brown fluff in the bottom one might've once been feathers from a fascinator, or wool gloves, or silk handkerchiefs . . . almost anything. Now it was moth shit. She dumped the drawers, one after another, into the plastic trash bag she'd brought for just such a purpose.

Brad soon returned with the flat-packed, corrugated cardboard boxes.

He assembled one for Dahlia while she worked her way through the other drawers, collecting the gloves and hats that remained. Why the moths hit one side and not the other, there was no telling. She picked up one of the dapper little hats and tried it on. It sat jauntily on her head, perched to the side. "I love your style," she said to Hazel, in case the ghost was watching. "I hope you don't mind if I keep one of these. And a clutch or two. Like I ever have any reason to carry a clutch."

Times were changing. Maybe she'd go out of her way to find a clutchworthy occasion.

"A night out," Brad suggested, tugging out another strip of tape and pressing it flat. "Everybody needs one, now and again."

"Sure. A night out."

The wardrobe backing was made of cedar, so the clothes there were in somewhat better shape. Much was gone, but everything that'd been touching the wood was as intact as you could expect, given how long it'd been hanging there.

Brad gasped and dropped the tape dispenser. "Holy shit! What was that?"

"What?" Dahlia turned around. The pushed-aside box with all her fear and worry in it . . . the one she'd left in a corner of her head . . . shook, and rattled, and wobbled for attention. She refused to look at it.

Brad fumbled to retrieve his camera from his shirt pocket, where the lens peeked out for recording's sake. He aimed it at the mirror. He swept it around the room. He pointed it at the mirror again. "I saw something."

"In here? It was probably just Hazel," she said.

When nothing further happened, he sighed and put the camera phone back into his pocket. "Whatever it was, it's gone now. I told you: The cameras are magic for keeping these things away."

"Maybe Hazel just doesn't like having her picture taken."

"That's fine with me. I don't really want to see her. I don't want to see *any* of them."

He went back to the tape, running a long strip down the

bottom edge of the cardboard. It spooled out with a ripping sound, then a loud snip when he cut it off. "Even if I can't prove it, we're working in a real-life haunted house. I don't get why you aren't freaking out and running."

"You don't think I'm freaking out?" She shook her head and tossed the contents of the last vanity drawer into the box. "If I *wasn't* freaking out, we'd be here through Saturday picking up every toothpick, doorknob, and nail. We'd be staying in the house tonight, like brave but stupid sitting ducks. No, sweetheart—I am well and truly freaking out."

"But you could leave. We could all leave."

"*You* could leave," she said flatly. "Pick up your shit and go, if you want—all it'll cost you is your job. But if *I* pick up and leave, it's not just my job; it's the whole business out the window. We're all out on our asses: me and Gabe and Bobby, and my dad. James, and Barry, and everybody else. So, yeah, I'm freaking out. I'm packing up early, and I'm calling my daddy to come help because I'm scared, and then I'm making a run for it. But right now, when there's still daylight burning and work that needs doing . . . no. I'm not leaving."

Brad fiddled with his tape dispenser, looking halfway sheepish and halfway hopeful. "I *could* go, couldn't I?"

"If you're that scared of a ghost in a bathroom, yes. Knock yourself out."

For a minute, she thought he was going to leave a Brad-shaped hole in the door, especially when he said, "Maybe I *am* that scared." But eventually he added, "You put it that way, it sounds like chickening out." Before she could accuse him of exactly that, and demand that he cover up the soldier on his way home, he added, "But I'd have to get a cab, and rent a car, or something like that. And I like my job. Mostly. Except for the ghosts."

"The first one's always the hardest." She closed one of the wardrobe's doors and opened the other, to see if the moths had left anything good behind.

"What was your first worksite ghost?" he asked.

She paused, momentarily distracted by a long knit dress that was last worn circa 1960. She pulled it off the hanger and examined it. The fabric had stretched a little, but not too badly. She folded it gently and put it in the box.

"Dahlia?"

She cleared her throat. "It was a teenage boy. He'd killed himself in the basement of this old farmhouse, probably back in the 1950s. He was still down there, in spirit. He liked to unplug things, and short out the equipment when no one was looking."

"Did you see him?"

"Only once. And once was enough."

They worked together in silence for a few moments more. "Hey Dahlia? You don't think there's any chance that the . . . the thing up there, in the attic . . . the one that followed you into the hall . . . or the thing in the bathroom . . ."

"Same thing. It's Abigail."

"Are you sure she can't hurt us?"

There were drawers inside the wardrobe, on the bottom level. She pulled one open, and thought about lying. "Just because she hasn't hurt anyone yet, doesn't mean she's not capable of it. That's why we're leaving at sundown."

"That's the sanest thing I've ever heard you say."

She nearly smiled, but didn't. "I'm not sure I can take that as a compliment, but you have to be practical about these things."

"Practical about the undead?"

"What else would you suggest? When in trouble, when in doubt—run in circles, scream and shout? The fuck would that accomplish?"

"It beats pretending that everything's fine, and nothing's going on."

Fast as lightning and twice as hot, she snapped, "I'm not pretending anything!" Her heart pounded and she clutched the fragile clothes, then unclenched her fists. It didn't do much to calm her. She hadn't packed up the fear quite well enough, and it was leaking back into her head, her hands, and her voice. "I'm just keeping my shit together, because someone has to! Jesus, Brad. You're a Georgia boy, ghosts shouldn't be news to you. All of us down here, we're not just living on battlefields. We're living on *graveyards*. Even the fake ones have bodies in them, don't you know?"

His voice shook when he said, "Only because I dug one up."

She flung a capelet into the box and yanked out another dress, this one the color of ferns. She mostly left it folded, and hurled that in there, too. She collected everything she'd chosen so far and rose to her feet, wiping her hands on the seat of her jeans. "Goddammit, just *go,* if this is too much for you."

But he rose to his feet, too—and dug in his heels. "I only have to make it until dark, right?"

Exhausted by this entire line of conversation, she sighed. "Yes."

"Then how long is it, 'til dark?" He clutched at the shirt pocket with the camera phone, reassuring himself that it was still running.

"Another six or seven hours, so you might want to put the phone away for a while. It'll start *feeling* dark before that—when the sun falls behind the mountain, but the sun won't really set until eightish."

"And come eight, we're out of here?"

"More like seven thirty," she vowed. "Can you stick it out that long?"

"Without having a nervous breakdown? I make no promises." The quiver in his eyes said he was halfway there already, so a promise wouldn't mean much anyway.

"Let's hold off on the nervous breakdowns. If you have a nervous breakdown, you might drop this vanity when we walk it down the stairs, and then I'd have to kill you, and then I'd go to jail, and no one would be very happy. I'd rather just get Bobby or Gabe to help me, if you're going to run around squeaking like a girl every time you hear a footstep you can't explain."

"Footsteps, I can ignore. Dead soldiers who stand there and look sad . . . fine, that guy wasn't bothering anybody."

"How about apparitions in mirrors?"

He thought about it. "You said Hazel was a nice lady."

"She seems to be. I think she wants to help. Now, do me a favor, dear—put the last box together, and start going through the bureau drawers. Anything that's in one piece, add it to the stash."

Downstairs, the sound of chisels and pry bars gave way to power tools and high fives, as the first fireplace was pulled free of the wall, and then packed up for shipping. Gabe and Bobby relocated the sleeping bags and duffel bags and messenger bags and the last of the personal items to the far side of the room in the main living area, up against the staircase, and got to work on the larger fireplace, a delicate mission in marble.

Meanwhile, Dahlia and Brad finished up the last of the upstairs furniture—grunting and swearing the big pieces down the stairs and stashing them in the parlor, which was filling up fast.

Then, on to the top-floor windows. Not everything was coming with them, but in Brad and Bobby's former rooms there were matching frames with leaded glass in traditional patterns, with a sprinkle of green and yellow squares for pop. They came out easy, in one piece. Only one crack, and that little part could be replaced.

Fuck the tragic pink bathroom tiles. Even Bobby had come to agree. The bathrooms were a waste.

Dahlia and Brad took the hardware off the doors next, wrapping each set in newspaper to keep it all together, then boxing it all up. Next came the doors themselves, along with what decorative hinges remained. Anything modern went into the scrap pile.

Pry bars and saws came out, and the heart-of-pine upstairs was extracted one plank at a time. What couldn't be saved was left behind, leaving islands of wood surrounded by subflooring and joists. The second floor was as stripped as it was going to get, right around the time Bobby and Gabe announced that they needed a hand with the big marble surround. There was one big crack, and a couple of small ones—no big deal, but it took a lot of love and duct tape and padding to get the massive thing ready for the truck and out into the parlor.

On to the rest of the first floor. Two more stained-glass panels, one in amazing shape, one in iffy condition. Bubble wrapped and set aside, with plastic tarp over the holes left behind, since the rain was still drumming, and they were still planning to take the floors. More gorgeous trim, with carved blocks and filigree. All of it oak. The pry bars picked it all down, and Dahlia stacked it all up.

The afternoon wore on, and the rain kept coming.

The thunder and lightning quit, and it wasn't yet freezing, but she thought she heard the intermittent patter of ice mixed in with the droplets. She wouldn't swear to it, but she wouldn't doubt it, either. Everyone ditched their hoodies and jackets, but kept the flannels and long sleeves. Even manual labor couldn't keep them perfectly warm.

Around five thirty, Gabe and Bobby successfully removed the ornate built-in cabinet in the dining area, and, with Dahlia and Brad's help, got it wrapped in moving blankets and duct tape. With all hands on deck and the help of a pair of dollies, they relocated it to the sitting room in two pieces. They had to leave it lying by the entrance, for there was nowhere else to put it. The sitting room was stuffed to the gills, and there wasn't any space left in the parlor, either.

"But we still have the big stained-glass window in the dining room—that's easily worth a couple grand, so we have to take extra care. And then there's the room dividers, the parlor built-ins, and the stair rails," Dahlia noted, mentally trying to imagine the jigsaw puzzle of overnight storage.

"Nah, we can skip the parlor built-ins." Brad took off his gloves and emptied them one at a time, spilling dust, splinters, and plaster bits onto the floor. "The screws were wrong. Phillips, from top to bottom."

"Right. Thank you for remembering." She frowned in that direction anyway, spying the shelving through the stacks of loot, waiting to be loaded up. "Someone did a real nice job of making it look original, damn him. But it's just as well, because we're running out of time for today. I am happy to scratch something off the list guilt-free. We *do* have to grab those room dividers, though. I already checked them, and they're in real good shape. You'll have to cut them out from the wall, but they'll make great bookcases or cabinets."

Gabe cleared his throat. "Um . . . room dividers?"

"Those things that look like waist-high, built-in bookcases on either side of the wall between the parlor and the foyer. There used to be another set in front of the sitting room, but someone pulled them out years ago. There's nothing left but a couple of shadows on the floor."

"So now we're down to the big window and the room dividers . . . ," Bobby counted off.

"And the transom with the roses. Can't leave without that, but it ought to be an easy grab, even if it's painted shut—and I think it might be. So. Big window first, then I'll get the transom. You boys get the last two mantels removed and secured, then move on to the stairs if you have time."

"What about the rest of these floors?" Gabe asked, tapping one foot on the wood for emphasis.

"Fuck 'em," she said. "They'll wait for Daddy tomorrow. We've got about ninety minutes before we pack ourselves up and head out for the nearest Motel 6. If we finish up sooner, we leave sooner. I don't know about you guys, but I'm *done* with this place for today."

"I'm done with it forever," Brad concluded.

"Forever it is," she agreed. "Or until tomorrow, whichever comes first. So let's go, final push. We can do this, but we'll have to hurry."

In thirty minutes, she had the rose glass transom removed

and wrapped, and the ladder moved to the dining room to help address the oversized window with its lovely stained scenery.

In another fifteen minutes, the boys had finished with the room dividers, and they'd been moved to the foyer. Not even Dahlia's Tetris powers could fit them anywhere else.

Five minutes more, and they'd positioned the other two ladders beneath the window, and formulated a plan—who would stand where, who would use which tools, and who would stand beneath.

Twenty minutes more, and the marvelously solid window was loose, and ready to come out. Bobby was outside on the porch, bracing the window from that side. Dahlia was on one ladder, and Brad was on the other. Gabe stood below, working the straps and pulley that would support the heavy old piece as it descended.

One, two, three, and the great window came down intact, thank God. They taped it and wrapped it, and wrapped it again—then let it join the room dividers in the foyer.

"We've got . . ." Brad checked his phone, then slipped it back into his front pocket with the camera lens peeking out. "Another hour before seven thirty. You said we could hit the road at seven thirty, right?"

"Right," Dahlia confirmed.

Gabe looked pained by the whole thing. "But there's still so much to *do.*"

He wasn't wrong, but the itch to go and the need to stay went to war, and the staircase was right there in the middle. It wouldn't be a big deal. If the rails came apart easy enough, they could pop the whole thing into pieces in . . . oh, half an hour between them.

Bobby saw her critically appraising the stairs, and didn't wait for the order. "Okay, fine—one last thing. But only if it comes out easy. If it don't come apart like LEGOs, we can skip it, and leave it for tomorrow."

Dahlia was either relieved to see him take the initiative, or annoyed that he was right—she couldn't tell which. As it was, her dad was going to give her an earful when he arrived and saw how much work was left to be done. But he wasn't here, was he? He hadn't seen the yellow dress, the dead boy, the shadow with knives in its hands and blackness in whatever was left of its heart.

However, the stair rail was big, and obvious, and chestnut, and relatively easy to break down. It'd be stupid to walk away from it when the sun was still technically up. "Okay, the stair rail and spindles," she relented. "And then we're out of here, because we can pull up the steps tomorrow—after Dad takes a look around upstairs. Hey, could someone turn on the rest of the lights? It's getting dark in here."

Brad flinched. "You're sure it's not *dark* dark until eight-something?"

"Yes, I'm sure. It's the clouds and the mountain's shadow, just like it's been all day. Flip every last switch, get yourself a Sawzall, and let's see if we can pull this thing apart on the fly."

But goddamn, it was gloomy in there—even with the over-sized pendant light hissing and popping above, brightening the room with the smell of burning dust and old bulbs. And even when the rails lifted up and off as easy as pie, hardly any sawing required, it was so very dark, for what ought to be late afternoon. Everything was the color of not-quite-dawn, or just-past-dusk, blue-gray and orange from the incandescent lights.

The crew worked fast, pausing now and again to flip another

switch. Turn on the hall light. Turn on the foyer light. Turn on the light in the dining room—yes, it's far away, but it felt like nothing could cut through this grim and dismal atmosphere. If they didn't press every button and spark every lamp, it was like they weren't even trying.

So they tried, and they cut, and they popped out the spindles one by one, stacking them like cordwood by the faceless fireplace in the living area, until the stairs were open and naked with nothing to hold on to, should anybody go up or down them.

"Talk about your open concept," Dahlia observed. The ceilings were so high and the stairs so tall, it was almost enough to give her vertigo. But it was only a little trick of the mind, now that the bannister was gone. Rationally, she knew this. Regardless, she surreptitiously hugged the wall near where she was standing at the top.

Gabe stood beside her, his hands on his hips. "Damn," he said. "We should've done that sooner. It would've made moving the big stuff down a lot easier."

"I know." Dahlia sighed. "I wasn't thinking."

"You were thinking about other things," Brad said.

"Or that. So, is this everything? Do we have it all out of the way? Are we ready to run?"

She was answered by a whistling rumble from outside, as the storm coiled tight around the mountain. The wind shrieked through the chimneys and screeched around the house's corners, pulling at the slices of plastic tarp she'd used to patch the broken glass and other empty places. It was cold, and it was wet, and the air tasted like a tomb.

"Fuck this," Gabe declared. "Let's pack it up, and move it out."

As if in response, the tarp at the end of the hall—the one covering the window there, and strapped into place with duct tape, so it shouldn't have moved at all—ripped free.

It wasn't possible, Dahlia didn't think. She'd used enough tape to silence a choir. All this time, it'd kept out the water, and the wind, too, but now it was flapping toward them, animated by the storm and by something else. Not just the blustery air, not just the swirling rain pushing inside the house.

There was something beneath it, swelling and flailing—the ragged edges of plastic and tape rising and falling, sticking temporarily to the walls and ripping free again.

The sheet whipped about, up and down, left and right, bouncing around in the hallway, but there was more beneath it than the frothy air. A face pressed against it, and a hand. A mouth. A scream.

Gabe froze, his mouth open—sucking on a gasp that wouldn't come out.

Dahlia grabbed his arm. "Down—get down. Now!"

But he was big and heavy and rooted to the spot. "You first!" he squeaked, pushing her past him, setting her on the steps and almost shoving her along them. The helpful motion broke whatever spell held him trapped in place, but not fast enough.

Not before the plastic, moving like a child in a bedsheet at Halloween . . . no, not a child, but something bigger; something that moved as if it was all limbs, and no body . . . not before that plastic swept down upon the spot where Dahlia had stood, and where Gabe was standing now, on top of the stairs where there were no more rails.

Then the sheet hit him, and for a split second Dahlia saw arms pushing through it, reaching for him, hands grasping at him. No, they were trying to push past him. The hands were reaching for her, but she was long gone. Halfway to the bottom, by then.

The thing from the window hit him harder than a flap of wet plastic and stringy tape ever could. It pushed him, and he stumbled.

Dahlia had time to climb back up one step—almost two steps. She had time to graze his hand as he tripped, tangled and confused. He could feel those other hands, the hands that weren't human. She could see it on his face. He could see that gaping, shrieking mouth that spoke with the sound of a storm on a mountain.

He saw it as he reached out and almost touched the pendant lamp—not that it would have held him more than a moment, even if he'd caught it. He watched as the thing charged him, his eyes fixed upon it, all the way to the oak floor a story and a half below.

The plastic fluttered and sank, light as a garbage bag, empty as the house itself.

But not Gabe. Gabe crashed.

14

I T COULD HAVE been worse, or so Dahlia told herself as she staggered down the steps to join Bobby and Brad, who were already circling Gabe. It could've been worse, because Gabe was yelling his head off and writhing, even as his father tried to tell him to "Be still! Hold still, goddammit!" That meant he was alive, and his neck wasn't broken, and he was mostly just pissed off and righteously scared and probably hurt, but not in a life-threatening fashion—or so she hoped and prayed with every rushed, tumbled, stumbled step.

She tripped at the bottom, and caught herself on her hands. She got up fast and scrambled toward Gabe, who had finished hollering and moved on to shrieking in a pitch high enough to scare off rodents.

"My legs!"

"Your ankles!" Brad corrected him. She guessed it sounded like the thing to do, like maybe an ankle didn't seem as big as a leg; maybe this was his dumb-ass way of trying to help, to offer a little perspective, convince him that things weren't as bad as they seemed.

But things sure as shit weren't good.

Dahlia flung herself into the living area, falling to her knees. "Gabe, baby . . . you landed on your feet."

"Like a motherfucking *cat* I did! Oh God, oh God, oh God . . ."

Yes, but he'd landed heavy, on his feet or his ankles or legs or whatever. One was definitely broken, and one might or might not be, but it'd seen better days. His right hand was turning purple too, where he'd caught himself upon the landing. Apparently his legs hurt so bad that he hadn't noticed the problem with his hand yet. Dahlia wasn't about to point it out, not while one of his feet was aiming in the wrong direction entirely. If he wanted to dedicate all his pain attention to his feet, that was fine. Keep it localized. Give him something to focus on.

"What happened?" Brad asked, his own voice an octave higher than usual. "What the hell was that? Something came right at him. You saw it—you all saw it!"

"The plastic, it was just the plastic from the window . . . ," Gabe gasped. He alternated between wanting to clutch and hold his ankles and not wanting to touch them—or let anyone else touch them, either. "Oh God, what did I do?"

"You fell, that's all. It's like you said," Dahlia rambled as she pulled out her cell phone. "The plastic came off the window, that's all it was, and I'm going to . . . hang on. I'm calling 911. You've broken at least one thing, baby. I'm going to get some help."

The bit about 911 was meant to help, but it sent him into a panic. "No, don't do that—it's not that bad," Gabe screeched.

Dahlia had known the boy all his life, and she knew he was panicking because 911 meant this was a real emergency, not just a piece of plastic or a shadow or a cold spot in a house where the ghosts play games with the doors. 911 meant the kind of danger nobody can ignore, or make excuses for, or pretend isn't happening. It didn't matter. They needed help, and she was going to get it.

"It *is* that bad. It's *at least* that bad," Brad said, helping absolutely no one's level of alarm.

Bobby had gotten Gabe sitting up. Gabe leaned against him, alternately moaning and complaining to high heaven, and squealing when the pain spikes drove down deep. His dad clutched him around the chest. "Hang on, bud. Dolly's going to get you an ambulance."

Dahlia's first call dropped.

The second was picked up by an operator asking, "911, what is your emergency?"

She tried to keep herself calm, since she couldn't keep anyone else that way. "There's been an accident—we need an ambulance."

"What kind of accident?"

"An . . . it was a work accident. We're a salvage crew, working on a house. My cousin has at least one broken leg, maybe two. He needs help, right now. Sooner than that, if you can swing it."

The patter of typing continued in the background. "Where are you located?"

"I'm . . . we're . . . we're near the bottom of Lookout Mountain, just above Saint Elmo." She gave the street address, though she hadn't seen any indicator of it anyplace on the house and she had no idea if it'd actually appear on anybody's GPS. "What about you? Where are *you* located?" she asked the operator.

"I'm at the regional call center. Please give me your phone number, in case we're disconnected."

Dahlia complied, keeping one eye on Gabe, who was going pale and starting to sweat. "You have to hurry. He's going into shock."

"I'm in the process of contacting local emergency support services; please stay on the line."

"Listen, lady? Is there any chance you could let me talk to the local support guys myself? The house we're at . . . it's tricky to find, but a local might know which one I'm talking about."

The call promptly beeped, and dropped—right as another hard, billowing gust made the house shudder and lean, unless that part was all in her imagination. Dahlia was about to swear, but the operator called back immediately. "Ma'am?"

"I'm here! I'm still here! You have to send somebody . . . it might be tricky. We'll have to . . . um . . . we have to get my cousin out to the main road. You'll never get an ambulance up here, not with the rain. There's no paved road up to the house."

"Ma'am, due to the storms, your local first responders are experiencing a high volume of calls." The operator dropped a tiny bit of the forced, professional tone. "Power's out to half the county, and there are reports of tornados on the ground."

"You're *shitting* me. They get tornados here?"

"Once in a blue moon, so don't look up. We're doing the best we can, I assure you. Please be patient and we'll have someone out there as soon—"

The call dropped again, and this time, so did everything else.

The world went dark with a pop so loud it made Dahlia's ears ring—a fizzing, electrical bang, and then there was nothing. The lights were gone. The refrigerator stopped running. The weird background static of weather and electricity buzzed through the air, and evaporated. The Withrow house was quiet and dark, except for the shocked breathing and low groaning of its occupants, blinking against the dim and fading light— for it wasn't yet sundown, but there wasn't any daylight to speak of, and the storm leeched the last of the glow from the sky.

Except for what Dahlia's phone said about the time, it might as well have been full-on night.

She broke the uneasy, uneven quiet. "Everyone stay cool. 911 is sending somebody, okay?"

Her phone rang again, displaying the emergency services designation. She answered, only to be greeted with silence, and a dropped call notice.

"Are you sure?" Bobby asked. "Did they tell you for sure that someone's on the way?"

"Yes, I'm sure, but it might take them a while. Hang on, I've got another idea." She rose to her feet and walked away from them, her footsteps ringing god-awful loud on the wood. She pulled up a Web browser on her phone, looked up the Chattanooga Police Department, and called them directly instead.

It took forever for anyone to answer. Dahlia could feel her neck flushing and her pulse rising, but someone had to keep control. Bobby was about to lose it, Brad had lost it already, and Gabe had too much on his plate as it was.

"Chattanooga Police Department."

Her voice shaking, she explained the situation as fast as she could, but the cop who answered the phone cut her off after the bit about Saint Elmo. "To be clear, ma'am—there aren't any life-threatening injuries, is that correct?"

She lost her battle with inner peace. "How the fuck should I know? I'm not a doctor! At the very least, his legs are broken, and the power is out!"

"I could give a *shit* about the power," the cop responded in testy, frayed-nerve kind. "You're in about the same boat as everybody else, all right? Broken legs aren't a death sentence, now are they?"

"But he fell a long way . . . he could have *other* injuries," she said, not because she necessarily believed it, but because it might bring help around sooner.

The cop sighed. "If 911 says you're in the queue, then you're in the queue—but I can't make you any promises, you hear me? Tell me again where you are. Saint Elmo?"

"Kind of . . ." She took a crack at giving directions, then stopped. "Hey, is there any chance you were born and raised here?"

"Close enough. What for?"

"Then maybe you know the old Withrow house near the foot of Lookout Mountain. And before you tell me you can't reach it," she added quickly, "I've got two strong men here with me, and we can get the kid to the paved road at the edge of the property."

"That old compound? I'll be damned, they finally found someone to clear it out." He was mumbling, like he was doing something else at the same time he was talking. Dahlia thought she heard the scratch of a pen on paper. "I'll make a note of it. Give me your number so I can call you back if I need to, or so someone else can, if it comes to that."

She obliged. She looked over her shoulder to where Bobby and Brad were doing their best to be comforting, and Gabe was doing his best to keep breathing, and not pass out cold. She could barely see them, except in outline. She wondered where the lanterns and flashlights were. That would be her next problem. "How long do you think it'll be?"

"Best-case scenario? Half an hour. Worst-case? I honestly can't tell you. We've got every man on deck tonight, and we're doing the best we can. Somebody will call you when help is on the way, so you can start carrying the kid to the road. If there's any chance you can get him to an ER yourself, you may want

to give it a shot—but if you do, call back and let me know, so
I can take you off the list."

She thanked him and hung up, holding the phone with
shaking fingers. She turned on the flashlight app to give them
all a little more illumination. "It's a mess out there," she repeated
what the cop had said. "911 won't make any promises, and the
cops can't have anyone here sooner than half an hour, and it
may take a whole lot longer. He didn't say so, but I heard it between the lines. We're going to have to take Gabe to the road—
we can put him in one of the trucks to stay dry until they get
here."

No one was less thrilled about this plan than Gabe, who
wheezed and moaned at the same time. "I don't know if I can
make it to the trucks, Dahl."

"You can, and you *will*. Your daddy and Brad and me, we'll
get you out there between us. But first we need to wrap up
those legs, to keep them stable."

"I can do it," Brad declared shakily.

Dahlia flashed him a dubious frown. Ten seconds ago he'd
been on the verge of hyperventilating, and now he wanted to
do something useful? "Do you have any first-aid experience?"

"The Boy Scout kind. And I used to be a life guard—so I
was certified and everything. I can do it, so just . . . let me do
it, if neither of y'all knows how."

So he wanted a job to calm him down. It'd worked before,
and Dahlia could relate. "Fine, what do you need?"

"A lantern. Then get me some more of that plastic tarp. Not
the possessed piece of shit that jumped him," Brad specified.
"Rustle up something else, and the duct tape. Bring me one of
those spindles from the decorative rail in the kitchen—they're
little enough, and they'll work fine as a splint." He looked down

at Gabe's other leg, which was starting to swell, but didn't look half so bad as the one that was well and truly wrecked. "Bring me two, to be on the safe side."

A shock of lightning brightened the sky for half a second, then a great crack of thunder shook the house and everyone in it. Dahlia spotted one of the LED lanterns at the foot of the stairs, so she grabbed it and passed it over to Brad and Bobby.

"It's too cold for a thunderstorm," Bobby protested, his teeth chattering—from fear or chill, Dahlia didn't know, and probably, neither did he. "It's *got* to be too cold."

"Ever hear of snow thunder?" Brad asked, accepting spindles and duct tape from Dahlia. His hands were quivering as hard as his voice, but he got to work, ignoring Gabe's groans and squeaks. "Hold him still, Bobby," he directed. "But yeah . . . snow thunder. It's a thing."

Dahlia couldn't watch Gabe squirm, or Bobby do his best to keep from rocking his son back and forth, holding him steady by brute force or nervous tension. She stepped away to the edge of the stairs and looked up, half expecting to see Hazel standing there, or Buddy, or even the miserable phantom of Abigail taking some dismal pride in her work. She halfway *wanted* to see Abigail, if only to throw something at her, flip her the bird, or scream about what a bitch she was—for all the good it'd do them.

"You were aiming for me, weren't you?" she asked the vacant space where no ghosts bothered to materialize. Her words were as tight as a guitar string. "Why? Why won't you leave me alone?"

Through gritted teeth, Gabe joked, "Stop talking to yourself, Dahl."

"She wanted me, and you got in the way."

"You think she wants . . ." Gabe gasped when Brad wrapped

his broken leg with the first strip of tape. "She wants . . . to kill you?"

"I don't know. She wants *something*. You three . . . we have to get you out of here, before she gets any bigger ideas."

"But you have to get out of here, too," Bobby protested. "Especially if you're right."

"I can take it. I can take *her*. I want a word with that bitch."

"Like you want another hole in the head," Brad muttered, his elbows rising and falling as he maneuvered the duct tape around Gabe's heavy shin and ankle. "She's beat you up worse than anyone, until now."

She snorted. "I'm still standing here, aren't I?" She caught herself. "Gabe, I'm sorry, I didn't mean it like that."

"Don't worry 'bout it, Dahl. Not your fault." He gasped more shallowly, not so much breathing as crying.

"Doesn't matter whose fault . . . mine, or Daddy's, or Augusta Withrow's, or anybody's. All that matters is, we're getting you out of here and to a hospital."

Brad rose to his knees, then stood over Gabe. "There—that's about as good as it's going to get. How does it feel?"

"Feels like hell, sir," the boy replied.

"Too bad, because we have to get you upright, anyhow," Bobby declared. He scooted out from his position, half beneath Gabe, and worked his hands under his son's armpits. "Come on. Brad, you take the right, I've got the left."

Gabe shrieked, but did his best to prop himself between the two men on the one foot that wasn't utterly shattered. "Keys," he wheezed.

"Keys!" Dahlia repeated. "Here's the keys to my truck. Bobby? Where are yours?"

"Pocket," he grunted.

Brad strained beneath Gabe's shoulder. "It's pouring out there."

"We won't wash away," Dahlia said grimly. "We can't run, but we ought to hurry as best we can. The sun's almost completely down. I'll get the light, you boys get moving, and I'll catch up in a second."

The guys shuffled slowly, struggling to find a rhythm that would work for all three. Gabe did his best not to wail with every half-step; Brad and Bobby leaned, lunged, and worked against the sheer size of the boy. They swayed from side to side, teetering and seeking balance.

They got him to the front door, and they got the door open.

"Lock it behind us, Dahl," Gabe called.

"Why?" she asked, running up behind them with one of the big lanterns. "Anyone dumb enough to go inside gets what he deserves. Come on, let's go."

She followed them onto the porch, worrying every inch of the way. Gabe was maybe six foot four, and 280 pounds if he was an ounce. His father was a couple inches shorter and a couple stones lighter. Brad was not a great deal larger than Dahlia herself.

By the time they'd reached the top of the porch steps—standing at the edge, where sheets of rain cascaded down around them—everyone had reached the same conclusion, but no one wanted to say it out loud. Brad surrendered, and said it first: "This isn't going to work. We'll never get him all the way to the truck."

"Shut your mouth!" Bobby hollered over the downpour.

But Gabe shook his head. "No. He's right. I can't do this. *Y'all* can't do this. Sit me down, for chrissake. My feet won't hold me. My ankles. My . . . whatever."

Brad was all too happy to comply, and even Bobby lowered Gabe reluctantly, but without complaint. Brad's arms were quivering. They hadn't gone thirty feet, and there was at least a quarter mile left to go.

"What about a wheelbarrow? A dolly?" Dahlia suggested desperately. "We could strap you in, and roll you down to the trucks like Hannibal Lecter."

"Through this weather?" Bobby asked, waving at the curtain of water, then down at the flooded lawn. He was right, and she knew it. The yard wasn't just covered in puddles; it was submerged in ponds.

"We *have* to get him to the truck! We have to try. It's only water."

"It's a swamp out there," Brad argued, "and it's getting worse." He rubbed at his upper arms to loosen them up, or warm them.

Dahlia refused to accept it. "Gabe, what if I get your legs— and the guys get your head and chest?"

Gabe's pupils were huge with the dim, wet light, and with abject agony. He answered her with a question. "What do you weigh, Dahl? A buck thirty?"

"I'm stronger than I look, and the trucks are only on the far side of the stone pillars."

"Only?" Brad squeaked.

"You got any better ideas?" she snapped.

He snapped back, "No, I don't!"

"Then we can't stay here," she insisted. "The ambulance will meet us at the road."

Bobby held up his hands, signaling an idea—for good or ill. "Wait, what if I go first and flag it down? Maybe they have a wheelchair, and they can come get him . . ."

"You think they could get a wheelchair through this mess?" Brad asked, half incredulous, and half hopeful.

Dahlia squinted out through the rain. Another flash of lightning showed the ruts that they'd been using for a driveway. There was gravel under that water, and she could see the grass and stones peeking through. "No, but they'll have a stretcher, or a backboard, or something—and extra hands to help. If they ever get here."

Brad ran his hands through his hair, smearing it back from his forehead. "They can't just *not come*. It's 911. That's not how it works."

She handed him the lantern. "The whole county is in an uproar, and we're in the queue. That's all they would promise. Bobby? Go ahead and make a run for it. You can wave them down and it'll save us time, if they're having trouble finding the place. The cop knew where we are, but God only knows about the EMTs. You got your phone?"

"Yeah."

"Go get a Ziploc bag for it. If your cell gets waterlogged, it won't do you any good." Dahlia went back and pushed the front door open with her foot, then bobbed her head toward the kitchen. "You'll find some baggies in the blue cooler."

While Bobby ran inside, Dahlia and Brad did their best to make Gabe comfortable, not that it was really possible anymore. At best, they could prop him up against the side of the house, make sure he wasn't sitting on any rocks or acorns, and put a couple of bags under his feet. He said it felt a little better. Dahlia couldn't imagine how it made a difference, and wondered if he was only saying so because everyone was trying so hard to help. It would be just like him, to say whatever he thought would make people happy.

Bobby emerged with his cell phone sealed in a clear plastic bag. He crammed it into his back pocket. "All right, I'm out of here."

"Don't you want an umbrella?" Brad asked.

He said no with a jerk of his chin. "It won't do much to keep me dry, and it'll slow me down, to boot."

"Call us when you get to the truck," Dahlia begged. "Even if there's no ambulance, call and let us know you got there okay."

He nodded, zipped his jacket up, and popped his collar. He jammed his favorite trucker hat on his head, hunkered down, and dashed down the stairs, and out into the rain.

Bobby didn't exactly vanish into the storm. His retreating silhouette shuffled back and forth as he sprinted around the deeper puddles, over the mounds of monkey grass, and past the rivulets that were turning into gullies before their eyes. He was still visible, if Dahlia squinted, until he rounded the bend that would lead to the gravel ruts and the stone pillars and then the road—where the trucks were parked off to the side. As she watched the yard fill with water and runoff from the mountain behind them, she silently thanked God that they'd moved the trucks before it got this bad. The guys had been right. The vehicles would've been stuck up to their axles by now.

Brad wrapped his arms around himself and shivered. "Now what?"

"Now we wait, and see what Bobby says when he gets there."

"Dahlia?" Gabe asked from his reclined position beside the steps.

"Yes, baby? How you doing? Hanging in there?"

"Yeah, but . . . do you have any . . . I don't know. Tylenol or something? We have a regular old first-aid kit, right?"

She nodded vigorously. "Yes, we do. But the kit's all packed up, so I'm not sure where it is right now. Let me pull my purse out from under your foot, and I'll give you some of my own." She always kept a little pouch full of tampons, Band-Aids, antibiotic cream, and generic painkillers on hand.

Gently, she raised his less-battered ankle and retrieved her bag, then fished around until she'd located a white bottle of pills. The label said to take two at a time, but the label wasn't talking about anyone Gabe's size, and in Gabe's kind of pain. She dumped four into her palm and handed them over.

"Can I have . . . something to . . . swallow them with?" His words were coming softer, and weren't stringing together very tightly. Either the pain was wearing him out, or this was what shock looked like. Dahlia didn't really know. Like she'd told the cop on the phone, she wasn't a nurse. She couldn't tell the difference between shock and exhaustion, or internal injuries and ordinary terror.

She badly wanted a drink. Gabe could probably use one, too. She didn't know if it'd help or hurt in the long run, but in the short run a swig of booze would make everyone feel better. "Gabe, I'll get you the last of the bourbon, would you like that?"

"I would seriously love you forever," he promised.

"You were gonna love me forever anyway, but I'll be right back. Whatever's left ought to be in my duffel, if your daddy didn't help himself while I wasn't looking. Brad, keep an eye on him?"

"Sure."

Gabe made an effort to smile. "I'm not going anyplace."

"You're also not passing out, falling over, or making any inappropriate effort to rise and shine, do you hear me?" She said this to both of them. Then to Brad, "Don't let him overexert himself."

The guys nodded, and she ducked back inside the house, leaving the door open behind her.

But even with the rain drumming into the clogged gutters and weathered shingles, it was quieter inside the house, and quieter still once she got past the foyer into the main living area, where they'd all slept the night before. The bags were all rolled up, and the crew's personal effects were packed and ready to go—ready for someone to load them up, in the event that the rain ever stopped, and the trucks were ever able to come up close to the house again.

Or, failing that, when her dad arrived with the Bobcat.

The Bobcat wasn't exactly an ATV, but it had a lot of power, and if the water went down a little, the machine could make the journey back and forth between the house and the road. It'd be faster and easier than playing two-legged pack mule, even if it did burn a lot of gas, take extra time, and piss off her dad. He was going to be pissed off enough as it was, unless Abigail put in an appearance and sufficiently scared him half to death—and then maybe he'd have a little sympathy for his beleaguered crew.

She halfway wanted him to see her. It didn't make her feel good, but there it was. She wanted him to *know*.

Now where the hell was the bourbon?

She fished around in her duffel bag, but she'd accidentally lied to Gabe, because it wasn't in there after all. She moved on to Bobby's stuff. No, wait. Last time she saw the bottle, it'd been in the kitchen. Brad had probably packed it up while he was getting the galley in order. Isn't that where she'd seen it last? She couldn't remember. There was too much to remember, and too much going on. And it was getting really, truly dark.

Out of reflex, she flicked the light switch. She knew it wouldn't work, because the power was out in half the county, right? So she wasn't surprised when nothing happened—she just felt dumb for giving it a go in the first place.

"Stupid," she muttered. "But I *do* need a light."

One of the lanterns had been abandoned on a mid-level built-in shelf. She grabbed it and twisted the knob to turn it on. It hurt her eyes, even though she hadn't cranked it all the way up. She looked away, and let her eyes adjust. It still wasn't completely black inside, and the lantern didn't make it all the way bright. It hardly made any difference at all, except to sharpen the shadows, and color them blue and white.

The never-ending dusk lingered, and stretched, and stalled, while the sun dropped behind the mountain.

Dahlia's phone rang.

"Bobby, give me good news."

"I made it to the trucks alive, is that good enough for you?" His voice echoed thickly in the narrow, closed space of the cab, and the rain was a background buzz. "No ambulance, though. I keep hearing sirens, but nothing's come close, not yet. All the emergency vehicles are going up or down the mountain, or past it."

"Shit. So now what do we do? We both know we can't really move Gabe. You bred him too big."

He halfway laughed. "Yeah, you can make this my fault, if you want."

"It's nobody's fault." She sighed.

His fault.

The words flickered like static through the cell's microphone.

Dahlia wasn't even positive she'd heard them. Then she heard the voice again, slashing through the connection. *His fault. You should understand.*

Her cousin said something too, but she couldn't catch it. The words were garbled and faint.

"Bobby?" she whispered. She wasn't sure if she was asking for clarification, or making sure he was still there. She *needed* for him to be there, and she was somewhat unreasonably glad that he was still so close, and that he hadn't just driven off into the sunset. Not that he'd do that to Gabe. But would he do it to her? She didn't want to think so.

Bobby might've been a thousand miles away on a tin can, when he replied, "I *said*, I'll hang out here and keep my eyes open!"

"That's all you can do, I guess . . ."

You were supposed to understand.

"Bobby?" She couldn't hear him anymore, not the hollow timbre of his words inside the truck's cab, and not the low hum of rain on the windshield outside it. She didn't know if he could hear her, either. "Don't leave us here. Don't leave me."

"I—"

The line went dead, but the cell rang again immediately, right on the heels of Bobby's call. Dahlia checked the display and didn't recognize the number, but it started with 423, so it was local. Maybe that meant that an ambulance was coming after all.

Her fingers shook and her throat was dry, but she pressed the green icon and said, "Hello?"

"Ms. Dutton?"

"Speaking."

"This is Susan Hardwick with Hamilton County dispatch—I understand you have an emergency on Lookout Mountain?"

The lights flickered. The lights *shouldn't* flicker. There shouldn't be any power.

Dahlia looked around, and up at the chandelier and pendant overhead. She stepped out from underneath the one, and eyed the other warily. "Yes ma'am . . . that's right. I'm sorry, it's almost right—we're not on the mountain, we're right at the foot, just above Saint Elmo."

"Do you have any power?"

She eyeballed the lights, which shuddered, but remained dark this time. The lantern in her free hand swayed back and forth, and the old house's bones swayed with it. "No, no power. We have a young man with a badly broken leg—maybe two of them."

"Have you been able to move him?"

"No ma'am. He's a big boy, and we're just about flooded in. We'll need a stretcher . . . or an ATV gurney, if you've got anything like that."

"Lord, but I wish there were any such thing," Susan said heavily.

I could make *you understand.*

Dahlia was cold, but she was sweating through her clothes. Her flannel was tacky against her skin, and her palm was so slick she had to squeeze the phone to keep from dropping it. "What about search and rescue?"

"They're occupied for the moment. Now, let me explain the situation, Ms. Dutton: There's a tree down across Ochs Highway, and that's why your power's out. The highway's out too, for now. Nothing coming, nothing going."

"But there are other ways to get to the house, right?"

"If you're talking about Alabama Avenue, you're half right. I know the house you're working at," Susan said. "I saw the note on the report. We used to tell stories about it, back when I was a kid. It's a bad place . . ." She paused, recognizing that she'd gone off script. "So believe me, I understand why you want to be away from it."

"So what do you mean, I'm half right about Alabama?"

I could show you.

"There's storm damage that way, too. We got half a dozen reports of a tornado down toward the Georgia end of that street—and cleanup crews will be slow in coming. Right now, it's not clear when we'll be able to reach you with an ambulance. We have someone on the way, but that neighborhood's a game of chutes and ladders, except with downed trees and power lines."

"There's *actually* a tornado?"

"Weather Service hasn't confirmed, but—"

"But someone's on the way, that's what you said?"

The sound of Susan's reply retreated into the distance, until it was barely a muffled patter of syllables. Did the lights flicker again, or was it lightning? Dahlia looked from window to window, but if there was light outside, it matched the reflections cast by her lantern, resulting in a bleak zero sum.

Her phone drooped away from her ear. She would have pressed the disconnect button, but the dropped call beep told her it wasn't necessary. Slowly, she tucked it into her back pocket. Carefully, she took a step toward the front door.

Nothing happened, so she took another one.

The big pendulum overhead twitched and rocked.

Dahlia didn't wait around for anything to flash, shiver, or

fall. She took a leap forward and ran toward the door. She'd left it open—that's right. It beckoned and whistled as the air slipped around the cutout where the rose transom used to be.

She could make it in a dozen long, fast steps, if she sprinted fast enough. She could make it in a few seconds.

No, you have to stay.

The front door jiggled. With a swipe like an angry slap across a face, it slammed shut before Dahlia reached the foyer.

She drew up to a halt, skidding on the damp wood floor and nearly falling—flinging the lantern up so it shined against the ceiling. It fell back on her wrist to dangle by its wire handle. It knocked against her elbow and her forearm, sending fractured shards of light and shadow wildly through the room.

She steadied the light. She held it up and out, and listened for tornadoes, or ghosts, or anything else that shouldn't be hanging about the Withrow estate.

An electric pop smacked across the house. It wasn't lightning, not quite; it was more like the thrilling punch of a transformer frying a squirrel. There was light, and there was a crack too loud to be thunder. There was a ringing in Dahlia's ears. There was static in front of her eyes.

When it cleared, all the lights were on. The house was bright as day, but somehow, that wasn't any better than when it was nighttime dark and illuminated only by the LED lantern swinging from Dahlia's left arm. Somehow, this was worse.

She looked back to the front door. Still shut.

Gabe and Brad were on the other side—waiting on the porch for an ambulance to bring a stretcher, and for her to bring the bourbon. She still hadn't found it, and now she'd completely given up looking for it. Did they know what had happened? Were they knocking? Would she hear them, if they did?

The leaded glass transom with the Victorian roses glinted in the lamplight.

But that wasn't right. It couldn't glint. It couldn't do anything. It wasn't there anymore. The pendant lamp dripped with crystals; but that wasn't right either. It didn't have crystals—it was an ugly mid-century thing. But the ugly lamp was gone, and above her head there was a bigger, grander model—strung with glittering teardrops of glass. Dahlia wondered when it'd been removed. She wondered what had happened to it, since it must have been gone for years before she arrived.

"Abigail? Abigail, what are you doing?" she breathed. The lantern was useless to her, but she couldn't stand to drop it. She clung to it, in case it was a lifeline back to her real, terrible life, where Gabe was hurt and the mountain was scarred with falling trees, and tornadoes scraped along the ridge like a knife across a wrist.

She heard, almost in answer, but not quite: *Abigail, Abigail, what have you done?*

The words fell in a singsong tone, coming from somewhere upstairs.

The stairs were intact again, and polished recently. The chestnut and fir looked warm and rich and clean. And the mantel, with two marble ladies, but no cracks between them. And the floor, gleaming and newly swept, accented with rugs that were freshly beaten and free of dust.

She climbed up the staircase—where Gabe had just fallen, hadn't he? The spindles were all in place, not a single one chipped, splintered, or broken. The rail was sturdy and thick, and it didn't wobble when she held it as she rose. From the landing, she could see the whole first floor, alight and sparkling;

and she could see the second-floor hallway, with doors open, and tinny music coming from the master bedroom.

The doors were open.

All of them. Even Aunt Hazel's.

She stumbled up the last few stairs and onto the carpet runner, untouched by moths or sun fading. Two doors down on the left. The door with the classic hardware, now undulled by rust or tarnish. She ran for it, and the door crashed shut, nearly knocking out her teeth. It only struck her nose, but it struck her hard. In a moment, she felt blood falling hot and wet, pooling and spilling down over her lip.

"Hazel!" she called. She beat hard on the door. "Hazel, let me in, please! Hazel!"

Through the solid oak came a whisper, soft and sad: *I'm sorry dear, but I can't. She's got you already.*

"What do you mean, she's . . ." Dahlia slowed.

Everything slowed.

A cold drowsiness overcame her, and she almost closed her eyes—almost buckled at the knees. She leaned forward, and a warm, wet drool of blood rolled out of her nose, but she remained upright, one hand pressed against the door to Hazel's room, still praying for help from the other side.

"Hazel," she tried one last time. The word was mud in her mouth, thicker than peanut butter.

She took a step back and lowered her hand. She looked toward the hallway's end, where the window wasn't broken anymore, and there was no flapping bit of plastic to fly loose and menace the crew. The window was whole, and original—the panes were a tidy six over one, with a wood frame on a pulley system.

The little details anchored her. She cataloged them.

No. I can show you.

She turned on her heel, but not on purpose. She strolled down the long hallway, past the other doors: all open, all solid wood, some six-panels and some four-panels, with brass knobs and hardware. It all looked new.

No.

"Stop it," Dahlia tried to command, but it didn't come out. Her tongue was fat and slow. A soft hiss was all she could manage. She kept walking, entirely against her will—an unwilling pilot in a crippled plane. The radio was out. None of the controls were working. She struggled to stop. She strained to fall to the ground.

But Abigail said, *No.*

So Dahlia kept walking, on feet that didn't feel like her own, at a pace that wasn't familiar, and with a gait that felt unbalanced. She reached the stairs to the attic and tried again to stop herself—catch herself on the wall and hold fast, rather than go up there and see whatever Abigail wanted her to see. Her hands didn't work any better than her feet. They stayed at her sides, and with all her strength, all her effort, she could do little more than flutter her fingers.

She would've cried, but her eyes didn't belong to her either. The time for crying had passed, years ago. Decades ago. Longer ago than that.

Stair by stair she climbed, past the sconces that hummed and hissed, because they worked just fine and weren't the rusted-out or missing hunks of metal she'd seen before. Nook by nook, the gas lit them up, and the corridor was brighter than Dahlia had ever seen it, and the wallpaper was pristine—not yet faded or stained, discolored or ripped. It was a light shade of blue that was nearly green, with silver vines and peach-colored flowers running in vertical rows from floor to ceiling.

No. To hell with the house.

The attic trapdoor had a metal handle screwed into place. She grasped it, turned it, and pushed when the small latch clicked. The hinges squeaked. The door lifted away, and she let herself inside the vaulted, skeletal space beneath the roof.

Abigail was there, living and breathing, standing beside the window in a yellow dress. She had one hand on the rough sill, and a worried look on her face. She was very young, and so was the man who stood beside her—the soldier, wearing his khaki uniform with squared-off shoulders and a narrow waist.

"Did you mean what you said?" Abigail asked him.

He did not look at her. He was staring out over the yard, toward the garage and the graveyard that wasn't yet a real graveyard. "Yes, I did. Now you've got to stop this," he told her firmly.

"That's not what you told me before. That's not what you told me, when you said you loved me and we ought to get married."

"You're awful young for that."

"Too young for what?" Surely she wasn't more than fifteen or sixteen. Still a child.

Gregory didn't look much older. He must be eighteen, at least, if he was wearing the uniform, but he might have been as old as twenty. "You're too young to understand, I made a mistake—that's all."

"You made a promise."

"It was a dumb promise, and I shouldn't have done it. Now, listen, Abby. I came back one last time, like you asked—because you said you had to tell me something. But I think it was all for show, and you don't have anything new to say at all. So now

I'm leaving, and I won't come around again. Or, if I ever do, it won't matter any. I liked you just fine, but I'm not looking for a wife."

She swallowed and nodded like she understood. There was something resting on the windowsill, or on the exposed beams that made up the frame. She picked it up and held it low, by her thigh. Her fingers flexed, tightening and adjusting her grip.

"You're not even going to say you're sorry, are you?"

Now he paused, his back half turned to her. "Sorry for what?"

Her hand whipped up, and there was a flash of something sharp and bright rising behind the soldier boy. It came at him from the side. It sliced across his neck. There should've been blood, but Dahlia saw only sparks—that same electric fizzle and pop as if she'd been hit on the head, or as if lightning had struck right beside her.

Dahlia heard the knife clatter to the floor. She heard screaming, and she heard footsteps heavy on the stairs. She was sitting down, and she didn't know when that had happened—when Abigail had let her fall.

She scrambled back from the trapdoor opening, kicking away in a feeble crawl, because her legs weren't working quite right. That awful coldness poured through her limbs and she stopped moving, except to sit up, then stand up, and breathe. Her vision cleared and the young couple was gone, but there was a spray of blood all the way to the ceiling, and a puddle on the floor that must've held a gallon or more, and there was so much screaming, and the sound of heavy things falling, and being dragged.

This way.

Dahlia stepped down onto the stairs and began to descend.

Her eyes were not her own, but in one corner she saw Buddy, young and alive. He'd found the knife, still slick with gore. He was carving a message. The scratch, scratch, scrape of the blade cut down into the naked subflooring.

I was wrong about that, Dahlia thought, since she could not speak. *It was Buddy who left the message. He meant it for her.*

Abigail guided Dahlia down the stairs, and back to the hall, where a rug had been folded around a long, lumpy shape that oozed a dark stain through the fabric, and onto the floor.

Judson Withrow was shouting and dragging one end of the bundle, while his wife screamed like she'd never stop, because there was nothing else left for her to do. Abigail crouched against Hazel's closed door, her yellow dress splashed with blood. She wrapped her arms around her knees and glared at her father, who wasn't having it.

"You get yourself up! You take the other end! *You* did this, Abigail. You did this, and God help me, but you're going to lend a hand in fixing it!"

Her eyes radiated hatred. She shook her head. "I don't *care* if you fix it!"

"You'll care when they take you away for murder, when they lock you up or hang you for it!"

"I don't care about that, either!"

Judson, tall and lean but very strong, dropped his end of the bundle and paused to slap his wife across the face. "You stop that! You stop it now!"

The openhanded blow surprised her enough that she swallowed the next round of wails.

"Thank you," he said roughly. Then, because it was clear that his daughter wasn't interested in lifting a finger, much less a hand, he wrangled the bundle onto his shoulder. It hung there awkwardly, and he balanced the weight on the top of the stair rail with one of his arms.

"Judson." His wife coughed out his name.

He barked at her, "Do you want to help carry this?"

Shocked by the suggestion, her mouth drooped open.

"Then not another word from you! Not another sound, either! I'm going to fix this," he said, changing his grip on the corpse wrapped in a rug. He pointed one accusing finger at Abigail, who refused to budge. "Not for you. But I'll do it for them. I'll do it for everyone else."

He began a slow, measured stomp down the steps. Over his shoulder he said, "Come along behind me and clean up. Get Hazel to help you, if Abigail won't."

From behind the closed door, Dahlia heard a muffled, "No . . . please . . ."

Even then, Hazel had known to hide.

Judson trudged on down, the hem of the rug trailing behind him, leaving a spotty streak of blood in his wake. And somewhere above, at the very edge of her hearing, Dahlia heard the scrape, scrape, scratch of Buddy's knife on the subfloors. How long would it take to leave that message? How many times would he cut it, again and again, for his father or his sisters to sand it away?

No.

Down the hall and past the stairs Dahlia stumbled, fighting just enough to throw off her pace—Abigail could work for control, if she wanted it so badly. Her vision swam, and that incessant knife-scratching noise grated in her ears. She felt herself falling forward, and her eyes cleared in time to see the bathroom door. She threw up her hands—or did Abigail throw up her hands?—and shoved the door away, then toppled inside.

This wasn't the Mamie pink horror. There were no badly dated tiles, no fixtures left over from an awkward mid-century remodel. This was a washroom with a graceful cast-iron tub and a pedestal sink, with a toilet that was capped by a wooden seat and lid, with a pull chain to flush it. There was Abigail, lying on the floor, her shoulders pushed up against the far wall and her feet braced against the bathtub. It was heavy enough to stand against her as she pushed.

Dahlia wanted to retch, and she wanted to leave. There was so much blood—more blood than the young soldier had spilled. Gallons and gallons of it, far too much for one young woman to hold. Or maybe it only looked that way on the tile floor, which was slick with water and mucus and bits of tissue. Abigail wasn't wearing the yellow dress, not now. She wore a robe that started out light green, and by now was so covered with gore that it looked brown and wet as it clung to her legs.

"Abigail, *don't*," Dahlia begged, only barely realizing that she was actually speaking. "Please, I don't want to see your baby."

Abigail stopped pushing and drew herself up to a seated position against the wall. Her hair was soaked with sweat, and it hung down stringy across her face. Blood collected beneath her, spilling out from between her legs to cover the floor in a creeping smudge; it threaded through the grout lines, swamping the tiles, and inching toward Dahlia—who made herself as small as possible between the sink and the tub.

The girl sighed. "It wasn't a baby." She pulled her knees up underneath herself, sitting cross-legged, while the blood still ran. "It came too early, by a couple of months. It came out dead. It was never alive." She leaned her head back against the wall and closed her eyes.

Dahlia looked toward the door. It was open. The blood

would flood her boots in another few seconds. It would pour out into the hallway, before long. Abigail wasn't looking. Dahlia's arms and legs were working. She could run.

Couldn't she?

"If you wanted to," Abigail answered without opening her eyes. "But I don't know where you'd go, or why you'd go there."

"Gabe's hurt. He needs help."

"Help's coming. He'll be all right." She shifted and leaned forward, fixing Dahlia with a pair of enormous and lovely brown eyes with thick black lashes. "Not sure about you, though."

"What? Why? Abigail . . ." She looked again at the door, but did not rise. "Abigail, what have you done?"

"I haven't done anything. All I ever did was trust a boy."

"And kill him."

Abigail waved her hand, like this was true, but a trifle. "But you understand. You wanted to hurt yours. You *still* want to hurt him." She nodded confidently.

Blood licked at the edge of Dahlia's boots. "But I *didn't* hurt Andy. I hardly even fought him. I let him have what he wanted, 'cause he was going to take it anyhow. His daddy has money, and mine has debt. I know how the world works."

"You loved him, and you loved the house. He wouldn't let you keep it."

Slowly, Dahlia pushed against the wall, using the leverage of her own weight to rise. "How do you know about the house?"

"You loved that house, and he didn't even care about it. It was just spiteful, what he did."

"There were reasons," Dahlia protested weakly. She was standing now. Shaky and uncertain, as if all the blood on the bathroom floor was hers—and not just the bit still dripping intermittently from her right nostril. But she was moving under her own power, and that was something. "I couldn't afford it, not by myself. Andy was stupid sometimes, but he wasn't ever spiteful, I don't think."

"You knew him your whole life, almost, and he walked off like it didn't mean a thing. He was done with you before you were done with him. He had someone waiting for him before the ink was dry. She's living with him now, in a house he picked because you gave him a taste for old places. It's a nice house. You'd like it."

"She's moved in? Already? Naw, I don't think he'd . . ."

"Men don't care. Even when they know what they've done, and what it means—they don't care. They just leave us behind to clean up their messes . . . like they never had no part in making them."

"Like *they* left you behind?" While Dahlia spoke, her right hand reached into her back pocket. Was she going for her phone? Was Abigail? "Everybody else is buried over the ridge, in the big cemetery. But not you." She pulled out her cell. The screen had a brand-new crack from corner to corner, but the phone lit up when she pressed the button to activate it.

Abigail didn't answer, and Dahlia was cold again, so very cold. The bathroom was filling up with a chilly fog that caught in her throat and left it raw.

She unlocked the screen. Andy's contact listing was long since deleted, but she knew the number by heart—and she even had a voice mail from a couple of weeks ago, confirming that he'd gotten the last of the papers filed, and she'd hear from the lawyer soon. She pulled up her call history, selected that entry, and looked up.

She didn't see Abigail anymore, but that didn't mean she

wasn't there. The bathroom was an icebox, and the blood on the floor was freezing to an awful slush. It crunched and squished at the same time when Dahlia took a single step toward the door. The next step was more brittle, less juicy. She slipped on the third step, for it was as slick as ice.

The doorknob was so cold, it stuck to her skin.

She turned it anyway, holding the phone with her free hand, and looking down at the screen. Out in the hallway she left red boot prints on the runner, which wouldn't be eaten by moths for another eighty years. Abigail was nowhere to be seen, but the frosted air drifted from the washroom like someone'd left a freezer open.

Dahlia paused and leaned against the wall, feeling the tickle of icy air lift the little hairs on her arms. She tapped the screen, telling the phone to return that call—but she didn't hold the phone to her ear. She held it in her hand, and listened while it rang.

On the last ring, before Andy's voice mail would've picked up, she heard a click, and a thunk as someone on the other end dropped the phone—then a scraping noise as something ran across the microphone. Then a woman spoke.

"Andy's phone. Who's this, and what do you want?"

Dahlia's mouth went dry. If the woman who answered didn't see her name on the incoming call display, then Andy had removed her from his contacts, too.

"Hello?"

She coughed, and said "Hello" softly in return. "Where's Andy gotten off to?"

"Nowhere far. He's in the shower. Who is this? Can I take a message?" When Dahlia didn't say anything, she asked again, "Is there anything you'd like to tell him?"

Was there anything Dahlia wanted to say to Andy? What a ridiculous question. She had no answer for it, so she hung up. The phone fell from her hand, but she picked it up again, and put it back in her pocket.

15

OWN THE HALL, someone was crying. The sobs came wet and heavy, and the girlish squeak between deep, sad breaths only made it sound all the more pitiful. Dahlia's heart ached, or she thought it did.

Was that Abigail, crying in the master bedroom? Was it her, squeezing Dahlia's chest until it hurt?

At the end of the hall, the window was broken again. Wind and rain came driving through the dark corridor—for it was dark again, too: not the half-dark of late afternoon, but the true dark that follows a sunset. Dahlia couldn't remember the last place she'd left the lantern. There was lightning outside—and a roaring sound rising and falling, like a train coming hard and fast around the mountain. But this was no locomotive, she knew. There were trains in the vicinity, yes, but not so close. This was the wind. This was the sound of air moving so fast that it beats, cuts, and hammers everything in its path. No wonder the folks down the street called it a tornado.

The splintering crack of tree limbs rattled her ears, and when the branches fell, they scraped down the house like nails on a chalkboard. They echoed and scratched like a blade on the brittle, cheap wood of the attic's subflooring—cutting letter after letter in an accusation that wouldn't die.

She did not hear any sirens. She did not hear Gabe or Brad talking down below on the front porch. There was nothing but the rain, and the wind, and the widow-makers falling around the house in hard, heavy thumps.

And the crying.

It rose and fell. It trickled through the house, with a lilting quality that was almost musical. Almost real.

"Abigail?" Dahlia called softly.

She heard a hitch in the sobbing, but nothing else.

She knew the hallway, knew the doors. Hazel's room was open because they'd removed the door, and now the spirit couldn't shut it if she wanted to. *So there,* thought Dahlia. *And thanks for nothing, anyway.*

To the left was the open door to the bathroom, and inside it, a spirit shaped like a boy. He looked down into the bathtub, shook his head, then met Abigail's eyes.

The boy wept like his heart was broken.

"Buddy?"

Whatever she told you, I was there. I saw her. She held it in the water, and the devil took them both.

She would've stopped, if she could. She would've hung back and questioned him about the baby, about the bathtub. About the water, because it all came back to the water, didn't it? It tied it all together: the sanitarium, the rain, the plumbing. The bathtub and a baby, and the crying dead boy who'd lived for another thirty years.

But she glided, on a rail.

The third door on the right, as she headed toward the broken window at the end of the hall, that bedroom was hers. She'd dibbed it for her own, on that first morning they'd arrived. Their trucks had been empty. She had loved the house on sight. She'd apologized to it, and made it promises.

She'd had no idea.

The crying behind her faded as she left it, and Abigail's cold hands drew her along, luring her back into that room. She stopped in the doorway, and clung to the frame. She didn't want to go inside. She didn't want the light to flash, or the fierce, weird memory of another time to show her a goddamned thing.

She looked anyway.

Water smashed against the glass of the big bay window, with its huge seat that had briefly worked for a bed. The broken pane let it all spray inside, but the shadow seated on the dusty old cushion didn't care. It shuddered in time with that unearthly weeping. It didn't look like a girl in a yellow dress. It looked like a dead thing that haunted bathrooms because the devil had taken it, and made it stay where it least wanted to be.

Dahlia breathed, "Abigail?"

I thought you might stay.

"I can't stay. You know that as well as I do."

You promised. When you first came, you said you'd never leave.

She frowned, trying to remember when on earth she might've said such a thing. "I think I said that I'd never forget."

No.

"You heard what you wanted to hear. That doesn't make it true." She took a few small steps into the dark bedroom, entirely against her will. Each footfall echoed dully in the mostly empty space. Each raindrop on the glass sounded like a gunshot. She raised her voice, to make herself heard over the stormy riot outside. "Please, whatever you're doing—stop it. I can help you. I can . . . I can call somebody about you . . . about your body. You're buried in the little cemetery here, aren't you? Beside Gregory, I bet. Under someone else's stone. But . . . but . . . before we leave . . ." She was blubbering, and she couldn't stop. "I'll get you a real grave, a proper one—with the rest of the Withrows, where you belong. That boy wronged you, and what happened after wasn't your fault. Not all your fault. I understand why you're mad, but . . . but let me help, let me see if I can put you to rest. Reunite you with your family, better late than never."

The shape on the window seat was blacker than the rest of the shadows in the desolate, cavernous room, so when it rose up and rushed at Dahlia, she could see it screaming toward her. She could feel it, that cold flash that was horribly familiar now. It whistled along with the wind and the rain.

I don't want to be with them—they sent me away, and when I came back, they left me behind. I want to stay here without them. I want you to stay with me.

Dahlia fell back against the wall, but she didn't crash there—she leaned there, and she wiped her aching, leaking nose with her sleeve. "I can't stay. You have to let me go. You have to let us *all* go."

When I came back, they didn't want me. I should stay "out of sight and out of mind," that's how Daddy put it. They wanted to send me away again. I didn't let them. I won't let you send me away, either.

"Nobody's trying to send you away." The spirit was so close, so thick. Dahlia was breathing her in, and it hurt. It was liquid nitrogen pouring down her throat and up into her sinuses, powering through the stuffiness left behind by her bloody nose. "I was only trying to set you *free*. You can stay here forever, for all I care."

Abigail breathed so softly, and it was January frost in Dahlia's lungs. *I did it in here, you know. Momma hid all the knives, so I broke the window and did all my cutting with a piece of glass. It worked faster and made a bigger mess. It felt good to lie down and stop. It felt good to stay here and watch them scream. And when it was over, Daddy wrapped me in a blanket from the hope chest and put me down there in the plot. Not beside Gregory, though. He didn't want us touching ever again, even in death.*

Dahlia couldn't see anything through the thick, viscous form that hovered before her, around her, and maybe even threaded itself down inside her chest to coil in the pit of her stomach. When lightning flashed, she only sensed it like an aura in the room—bright and then gone. It showed her nothing, not anymore.

Then she was moving forward again, foot over foot, dragging and falling and rising. She tried to protest, but Abigail had taken her voice again. Blind and afraid. Step by step toward the window and the soaked, dirty cushion she'd used for a mattress.

She put out her hand, or Abigail did. She needed to catch herself, to feel her way across the floor, but her knees knocked against the window seat and she toppled forward—hand extended—and hit the window hard enough to push panels of glass out into the night, falling to the ground in pieces.

She gasped—even Abigail couldn't keep her from gasping—and leaned back hard, but the shadow pushed again, and now she was flailing, both hands raised and both hands crashing into the frame.

It shattered this time. Her hands pushed out into the night, shoved across the shards that clung stubbornly to the rotting wood. They sliced so fine, so sharp on the old leaded glass, that at first she didn't even feel the cuts. Dahlia flung herself backward, away from the window seat and the window and the sprinkles of glass, wrenching out of Abigail's grip and into the middle of the room.

Then came the heat, and from the blood or surprise or simple pain, Dahlia found her voice.

She took her strength back from the icy shadow and yelped an objection that came out harsh and weak. But her second try worked better, and it was more like a yell. The third time was the charm, as she toppled backward onto the floor, flinging glass and gushing blood.

Finally, she screamed.

Now you have *to stay.*

She screamed again, and kicked at the shadow girl—not harming her, no, and not even pushing her away.

But she was on her hands and knees, and Abigail had either let her go, or she'd run out of energy to keep her, because Dahlia managed to scramble forward on bleeding arms, leaving terrible streaks of blood behind. The hot liquid pulsed and spit, from the right side worse than the left, but both arms were gushing in tandem with her pulse. She felt the blood throbbing out of her. She remembered a leak in a brake line on one of the old trucks, before her dad had bought the new ones. She remembered the way it'd spit and jerked with each twitch of the brake pedal, and she'd thought it looked like a fat, gruesome vein.

Thank God she couldn't see her own arms. Thank God it was too dark, and thank God Abigail didn't have her by the throat anymore. The ghost had let her go, maybe just to watch

Dahlia suffer like she'd watched her family suffer through the years.

"Fucking brat," she spit. Blood was everywhere, all over everything, but it was drying now—so it didn't trip her up with slippery puddles beneath her elbows and knees as she crawled. It didn't hurt. It didn't flow. It only tasted like pocket change.

She staggered to her feet, trying to hold herself up on the doorframe, but her hands weren't working right, and when she rose, sparkling silver static filled her head.

"This is bad," she said, partly to see if she was able to speak at all, and partly to remind herself that she was still alive. "But Brad's downstairs. Boy Scout," she blabbered. "I need a Boy Scout. Can't tourniquet both arms myself, now can I?"

She almost laughed, but it wasn't worth the trouble. It was much more useful to scream with all the air she had left.

"Brad! Bobby!" she added her cousin's name, in case he'd come back from the trucks with the ambulance crew. Was he back yet? How long had he been gone? She didn't know. She couldn't tell. She couldn't see. She couldn't remember if she'd been in the house for an hour or a year or a lifetime.

Dahlia was weak, but she was moving, and Abigail watched cruelly, like Abigail did best. Dahlia could feel those empty, frigid eyes somewhere above and behind her. She looked back and saw only more darkness, but she knew Abigail now. She knew what a monster . . . No: "What a brat," she mumbled again, as she fell down the hall, and to the top of the stairs.

Hands and knees were easier. No, hands hurt too badly: they were too cut up, along with the light, pale skin of her forearms and wrists. The slashes were long and deep, by the ghost's design; Dahlia was losing too much blood, too fast, to keep moving like this.

"Brad!" she tried again.

Headfirst, on her belly more than her hands or knees, she slid roughly forward, catching herself on her shoulder, on that platform where the staircase turned. She slithered, slipping in her own fluids, trying to arrange herself for less of a bumpy slide down the rest of the way.

Feetfirst, how about that? Better than headfirst, or hands first, when there was nothing left to hold on to, and everything past her elbows was on fire, or going numb. Or . . . both? Everything was supposed to go black, when you lost a lot of blood and passed out; but everything was already black in the ruined house, so everything went gray and fuzzy, instead. Everything was speckled with silver and white as the stars filled her eyes, but she wasn't all the way down the stairs yet.

"Brad . . . Bobby . . ."

The door was open. It had to be. She'd left it open, but something might have shut it behind her.

She laughed, because the front door was the last door remaining. They hadn't cut it out yet, so it was the only thing left to slam in her face—here in the real world, right now, where she was bleeding to death on the stairs.

No, she was sliding down the stairs feetfirst, on her butt and on her back. She could bleed to death on the first floor, if it came to that.

Her head banged hard on the edge of every step, but she was moving, and it wasn't Abigail puppeting her through the house like a doll. She was doing this her own damn self, Abigail be damned.

Damn it all.

Damn her wobbly ankles when her feet hit the first floor, because she couldn't stand any better than Gabe. Damn the red and blue flashing in the distance, and the sharp, cutting noise of something electric. Damn Bobby too, because he was yelling at her—and it ought to be the other way around. If anyone needed yelling at, it was probably Bobby. Bobby'd left her for Andy. That's not how family was supposed to work.

But, Jesus, she needed him now.

If there'd been any rail left to follow the stairs, she would've pulled herself up on it. If there'd been anything to lean on, she would've grabbed for it. She struggled to her knees, thinking she'd give crawling another try, but fell over as soon as she got herself upright. Her elbows slipped out from under her.

Now you have to stay.

"Shut *up*," she said. Or she thought she said it. It might've just been a tumble of vowels and bloody saliva, for all she knew—but who cared, when she could see the front door ahead. It was at the end of a tunnel. No. Everything was at the end of a tunnel, even the chandelier and the hole where the fireplace mantel used to be, and the space on the floor between her shredded hands. She saw it all in fits and starts, in the punctuation of lightning and of blue and red, and a pale bit of ambient glow from the lantern she'd lost downstairs, which was lying on the floor, on its side. She didn't know how it'd gotten there. She couldn't remember the last place she'd had it.

All sensation was bleeding out of her body. The gray fog was filling her up, taking the place of everything else, even the pain. Her hands didn't hurt. Her arms only felt uncomfortably warm. Her knees ached, and so did the back of her head; but like everything else, that was something far away—at the end of a tunnel, or in someone else's body.

In someone else's dream, or afterlife. Whatever this was.

"If I die here," she vowed with a thick slur. "Oh, I'll stay, all right. I'll remind you every day . . . ," she said, "every night . . . every hour . . . every minute . . . how you were wrong, and . . . your father was right. Except . . . except he shouldn't have . . . fixed anything. He should've . . . sent you away for good. He never . . . should've . . . let you come back."

When nothing hurt, it was all right to crawl again. If she could find the energy. She rocked back and forth like a baby learning to crawl, building up momentum. Forward. One hand, one knee. One foot, then the other.

Where the hell was Brad? Where the hell was Gabe? What happened to Bobby? He was there, wasn't he? She'd just seen him, she was pretty sure. She wanted to yell at him.

"You . . . want some company, Abigail?" A long strand of red spittle dangled from her bottom lip, then dropped to the floor. "I'll give you . . . some company. I'll haunt the fuck out of *you,* and I'll dedicate . . . eternity . . . to making you miserable."

Her elbows buckled, and she dropped to the floor, face-down. She had a dim idea that she'd cracked a tooth, but couldn't bring herself to care. Her eyes wouldn't open. Or they were already open, but she couldn't see anything except that tunnel—except when she turned her head, and saw the open front door, and the storm beyond it.

"You'd better pray—you'd better hope and pray, that when I leave this place . . . when I leave this life . . . I'm gone forever."

The last thing she remembered was a gust of leaves that billowed, and spiraled, and settled into her hair, and stuck to the floor, where her blood was already drying. Her ankles were chilled, like icy hands were touching them. Holding them. Feeling their way up her legs.

The last thing she felt was the cold, wet wind blowing inside.

The last thing she knew, everything was quiet. Everything was dark.

And the next thing she felt was pressure, cinched around her upper arms; both of them. Tighter than Abigail's awful hands had ever held her. When she wiggled her feet, she didn't feel that icy grip, not anymore. She smelled rubber, or latex. She heard voices, and didn't recognize most of them.

But Bobby's she knew. He was babbling nearby, making up explanations that only halfway made sense—but then again, she could only halfway hear them. "There's a broken window . . . there's a lot of broken glass . . . no, she didn't do it herself . . . I think she fell in the dark . . ."

Someone lifted her. Someone set her on a board that was hard and uncomfortable; it rubbed on all her bruises, and made them ache. She didn't open her eyes all the way because she didn't have the energy, but through the slits where her eyelashes blocked the narrow view, she saw the glint of light on metal, and thought maybe it was a badge on someone's uniform. Not a policeman. Not a man at all. A woman with a medical uniform, a jacket with an emblem on it.

Dahlia couldn't read it.

The trip across the Withrow house's swamped front yard

wasn't fun for anyone. She was strapped down and jostled as her porters stumbled, and their boots tangled in the wet grass and stuck in thick mud. Her head was braced so it couldn't roll, but each thump and heave brought a swell of blood into her mouth.

Her arms ached, and she couldn't feel her fingers.

Bobby shuffled beside her, holding up that big blue-and-white umbrella—shielding her with it, to the best of his ability. He was doing a shit job of it, in her opinion, but he got an "E" for effort. He was talking to her all the while, telling her to hang in there, that Gabe was in the ambulance; and they were going to get her to the hospital, too; and why did she call Andy? He'd called Bobby to ask what was going on, and he didn't know what to tell him . . .

. . . his voice droned on, and she wanted to tell him to shut up, but it was better background noise than the rain, or the wind, or the radio static from the dispatchers calling back and forth to one another, talking in a code of numbers and commands.

Inside the ambulance. Closed doors. Quieter, and drier.

Someone was daubing at her face and neck with a towel.

To the left, she heard Gabe. She opened her eyes just far enough to see him through that fringe of damp eyelashes. He was bundled up, but he was looking at her—saying her name—asking her something. Like he wasn't concerned about his legs at all, because it's not like he was bleeding to death or anything.

There were needles, and there was a clear fluid in a plastic bag. She didn't feel the prick of it, and didn't feel any improvement. She only felt sleepy, and the rolling motion of the ambulance crawling along the asphalt was enough to lure her to sleep.

She dreamed of a carnival with spinning lights and chiming sirens.

She dreamed of coldness, and fog, and blood.

16

"H OSPITALS ARE FUCKING tedious," Dahlia declared.

Gabe, who'd wheeled himself into her room in a chair, could only agree. "There's not a damn thing to do, and it's too noisy to sleep. I feel sorry for people who get stuck here for weeks at a time."

"Ugh, don't talk that way. Two days has already been long enough." She sank back into her pillows, which were propped behind her back to let her sit up. "But they're supposed to let me go tomorrow. Since I'm going to live, and all."

"Supposed to?"

"Yeah, I have to take . . . it's like . . . an exit interview. The guy ought to be here any minute. When he signs off on it, I can check out in the morning. How long did they keep you?" she asked.

"Not even overnight. Broken ankles aren't do-or-die. They sent me home ASAP, with this sweet-ass ride," he said, popping half a wheelie and setting the chair back down again.

"Are they both broken?"

He shook his head. "Naw, it just sounds cooler that way. The left one is busted in a couple of places, but the right one's only sprained. *Badly* sprained," he emphasized. "It ain't a sexy new scar for chicks to dig, but it's a good story. *And* I've got a scrip for some *serious* painkillers, so things are looking up."

"I'm glad you're making lemonade out of all this. Beats sitting around feeling sorry for yourself."

"I kind of like the chair," he said brightly. Then he quickly added, in case that was in bad taste, "You know, since it's not forever. *That* would suck."

"I'm very glad it's only temporary."

"The joystick is fun; I can pretend I'm in my own video game. But Dad says my cast is already starting to stink, and I think he's right. In another five weeks . . . who knows what it'll smell like."

"Ass. It'll smell like ass," she assured him.

A knock on the open door announced a man wearing navy and gray business casual. Dahlia figured he was a little younger than her, maybe thirty. He looked clean and friendly. "Hello? I hope I'm not interrupting."

"Nope. We were just discussing sexy scars and smelly casts. Are you Dr. Jacks?"

"Yep, that's me."

Gabe introduced himself, and said politely, "I was just leaving. But Dahl, Uncle Chuck says he'll be here first thing in the morning with all your stuff, to drive you home."

"Did he . . . is the house . . . ?" She wasn't sure what to ask, not exactly.

Her cousin piloted himself in a little semicircle, trying to navigate back around the bed. "Dad and Uncle Chuck hired a couple of local guys, and between them and Brad, they got the copper roof squared away this morning. I'm not sure how much else they mean to take . . . but it was quiet in there." He glanced over at the doctor. "That's what Dad said. You know what I mean."

"Sure, it's quiet—now that I'm gone." She rolled her eyes. "Well, whatever. I'm glad they're getting it finished up."

"Me too. So I'll see you tomorrow, all right? My butt is buzzing, so that's probably Dad texting to say he's here to get me. Nice to meet you, Dr. Jacks."

"Likewise," he replied.

With a good-bye wave, Gabe puttered out into the hallway, and was gone.

The doctor closed the door behind him, and pulled up a chair beside Dahlia's bed. He adjusted himself on the seat, and fiddled with a satchel full of paperwork, withdrawing a recorder, and setting it on the bedside tray. He pressed a button to turn it on. "So . . . you know what this is about."

"Yeah, the surgeon warned me, when he came in to check his work." She wiggled her arms. They were bandaged from her thumbs to her elbows. "He says it's not as bad as it could have been. I won't lose any sensation, not permanently. And my fingers are all still working, so none of the tendons got sliced too bad."

He rested a clipboard on his leg, and pulled the cap off a pen. "You were lucky."

"If you say so."

"You wouldn't?" He raised an eyebrow.

"Lucky to be alive? Yes. Lucky to have face-planted through an old single-pane window? Not so much."

"But you understand there's been some concern. Do you want to tell me what happened?" he asked, his eyes all wide and friendly. He was young, but he'd perfected his therapist's air of "trust me, I'm here to help." It was too polished. It made her trust him even less.

Even if the compassionate show wasn't bullshit, Dahlia didn't particularly want to talk to the guy. What could she say that wouldn't sound completely insane? She'd been thinking about it ever since yesterday, when the surgeon had mentioned this little visit. Standard procedure, she'd told Dahlia. Oblig-atory, for a case like this one.

She didn't take a deep breath. It would look too much like she was setting something up, or giving something away. Instead, she shrugged. "There's not much to tell."

"Tell it anyway, if you're feeling well enough."

"Gabe got hurt, and we were trying to keep him calm, and immobile. He wanted some painkillers, and I offered him a bourbon chaser—but I couldn't find the bottle. I know he's a minor, but man, you should've seen his ankles. I was trying to help."

"Of course, I understand."

"But the power was out, and it was dark in there, what with the storm and all."

"Mm-hm."

"While I was looking around, I heard a window break up-stairs. I thought maybe a tree branch had come through it, or something like that—and we need those windows, and those old floors. Those kinds of things are the bread and butter of the family business. So I guess I thought maybe I could cover it up with plastic or something, if it wasn't too bad. That way, the rain wouldn't soak the floors."

"But what about Gabe?"

"Brad was out there with him on the porch, and neither one of them was going anywhere. Bobby had gone to the trucks, to wait for the ambulance. There wasn't much I could do except turn up that bottle of bourbon . . . and cover up the broken window, if I could find it." She paused, remembering the truth, and building her lie along its framework. "I picked up some plastic sheeting and duct tape, and went hunting for the prob-lem. I found it in the master bedroom. Water was getting all inside the place, and since the ambulance still hadn't arrived, I tried taping up the holes. And you know how well that worked out."

He scribbled something on the form that was attached to his clipboard. "But you've left out the most important part: How you actually cut yourself."

She glared at him. "I *didn't* cut myself. I *got* cut, when I fell."

"Poor phrasing on my part. I'm sorry. Please go on."

"The rest is a little blurry. It happened real fast, and then I lost a shit-ton of blood, as you may note from my records," she said, sounding huffier than she meant to. "There was a window seat, you see—and I stood up on it, to reach the window. But I was doing all that in the dark, and I lost my balance. I started going backwards, and tried to catch myself forwards, out of reflex. My hands went through the glass, tearing them all to hell. I dragged myself back downstairs, and that's where Brad and the medics found me. The end."

Dr. Jacks performed another brief round of scribbling. "But there was a phone call. You called your ex-husband moments before the accident occurred," he said carefully.

"You've never butt-dialed anyone before? Never in your life?"

"Is that what happened?"

She nodded. "Yes, that's what happened. I was falling down a flight of stairs with my phone in my pocket. Believe me, I felt stupid about it when I found out."

Dr. Jacks sat forward, and fiddled with his pen. "All right, that's . . . possible. But you spoke to Carrie, and asked about Andy."

"I have no recollection of that, whatsoever. Look . . ." Dahlia sighed heavily, and adjusted herself on the pillows. She wanted

to push the button for more meds, but she restrained herself—
even though her arms ached like mad. "I've seen my arms—
I was watching, when the surgeon took off the wraps to get a
look at them. I know it looks like I took a razor to them, up
and down. But if I were going to slit my own wrists, why
would I carve up my fingers, too?"

"Working with a piece of wet glass, in the dark . . . the cuts
on your fingers could've been accidental."

"If I really wanted to die upstairs, why would I try so hard
to get downstairs, and to get Brad's attention?"

"Second thoughts? It happens all the time."

"Honey, if I wanted to die, I'd use one of my guns, and do
it quick—without any fanfare. And without all this goddamn
pain," she added through her teeth, when a sharp flare of agony
shot up and down her right hand. "I sure as hell wouldn't do it
when Gabe was in desperate need of help, and there was an
ambulance on the way."

"But suicide attempts are rarely logical or well planned.
You'd been under a lot of stress at work—"

"No more than usual."

"You were the boss on this operation, far from home—"

"It's Nashville, not Nevada."

"You'd recently signed off on a divorce."

"You've got me there."

"And, I am led to believe," he said, gently but firmly, "that
you lost a house in this divorce. An old one, like the one you
were working on in Saint Elmo."

She snorted. "Ha! It wasn't a third the size of the Withrow
place, and it needed almost as much work. It was a beautiful
house, and I loved it, and I hated to lose it. But you know what
I do for a living? I fart around in nice old houses, taking pieces

of them with me. For fuck's sake." She leaned back and winced. "It wasn't the end of the world."

He was quiet for a moment. "No, I suppose it wasn't."

"So would you please sign off on me, or whatever it is you have to do? I just want to go home."

"Even though you're going home alone, to an empty apartment?"

"Even so, yes. I've got a good GP in Nashville who can look after me from here on out, and . . . and . . . what do I have to promise you? That I'll seek therapy if I find myself depressed, or having dire thoughts? I can do that. Do you want me to promise I'll talk to someone before I do anything drastic? That's fine. For that matter, if you want me to leave my guns with Daddy, so he can keep them locked out of reach—that's fine too. Just tell me what you want from me. What do I have to say to convince you that this wasn't my own doing?"

"It's not a matter of making promises," he said in his most soothing voice. It made him sound like a liar. "This is a formality. We can't really keep you here against your will, unless there is demonstrable proof that you are a danger to yourself or others. You can leave in the morning," he said with another click of his pen. "No one will stop you. The hospital has to cover its bases from a legal standpoint, you understand. I'm only doing my job."

She was relieved enough to melt right into her pillow fort, but she couldn't allow herself that cautious joy quite yet. Not until she was actually free and clear, and on the road back to Music City Salvage.

But when Dr. Jacks left, she relaxed enough to nap. The hospital wasn't so bad. The food was shit, but what could you do? The drugs were good, and that more than made up for it.

She had her own TV remote, and her cell phone. Even with the cracked screen, she could entertain herself for one more night.

It was really rather peaceful, except for the beeping machines and the intercom, and the weird guy down the hall who kept waking up yelling for someone named Brenda.

But it wasn't a poltergeist-plagued work site.

Her father called from a hotel, and gave her the rundown on the day's work. They'd gotten the last of the windows and floors, and the chestnut barn had been taken down to splinters. In another few days, the whole shebang would be razed to the ground, and then it'd be over. Did she still want some of the furniture that'd been left behind? She could have it, if she did.

She told him "no thanks," and that she'd buy her own later. Take it for the shop. Maybe one of the guys could upcycle it into something cool . . . for someone else.

That was all right with Chuck. He understood. Anyway, he'd see her in the morning, bright and early, with bells on. All right. Good-bye.

Dahlia napped some more. There wasn't much else to do, and even surfing the Net on her phone was more than her ragged fingers felt like doing for very long. Drugs and sleep were a better way to pass the time. When she woke up again, she found some flowers and a card. According to one of the nurses, Bobby had brought them by, but he didn't want to wake her.

She was touched, until she read the card. The flowers were from Andy, so now she didn't want them. She didn't need his stupid, guilty gesture because he'd heard through the grapevine that maybe Dahl had tried to kill herself in a grand old house . . . and you know what? Fuck him.

"Give them to somebody else," she told the nurse. "Someone who will appreciate them better than I do. They're pretty enough, but I don't want them. Find an old person, or a little kid, or something."

She didn't know where they ended up, and didn't care.

It was twenty minutes until visiting hours were over, and that was a good thing. Once the visitors quit coming and going, the hospital got quieter. There were fewer kids tramping down the halls, and fewer people asking doctors too many questions, and giving nurses too many demands.

But there was still a quarter hour left on the clock when a quietly cleared throat announced that Augusta Withrow had arrived. Dahlia smelled the older woman before she opened her eyes—that fancy perfume that suited her perfectly, with an afternote of tobacco and expensive hand lotion.

"Hello there."

"Ms. Dutton, I hear they're sending you home in the morning."

She wriggled herself back to a mostly seated position. "Yes ma'am, that is correct."

Augusta let herself inside the room, and took the chair that Dr. Jacks had left beside the bed. "That's good to hear. I heard what happened, and . . ." She hesitated. "And I'm sorry," she concluded.

"Everyone got out alive; that's the important thing."

"Yes, yes it is," she nodded. "But I suppose you feel that I wasn't honest with you, or your father."

"What good would honesty have done?" Dahlia asked.

"I could've warned you about . . . her. I could've told you about Aunt Hazel's room, at least. I might've sounded like a madwoman for it, but it would've given you some measure of sanctuary."

"I figured it out." She corrected herself. "Well, Hazel told me."

Augusta raised one thin eyebrow. "You saw her?"

"She seemed like a nice lady. Where will she go, when the house is gone?"

"I'm sure she'll come up with something. Always an innovator, that one." She squeezed her hands around a small purse, then opened it with a pinch of the clasp. "I brought you something."

"That wasn't necessary . . ."

She withdrew something small and rectangular, and fiddled with it. "I went back to the house, while your father and his men were working on the carriage house roof. You left this behind—or someone did, I'm not sure who."

"What is it?"

"A camera," she said as she handed it over. "It was running . . . I don't know how long . . . before the battery went out. I wasn't sure if I should give it to you or not, but I thought . . . there might be something on there, something you could share with your father, if you needed to. The place is empty now; I felt it myself—not a hint of anyone, even Aunt Hazel. He might not believe you."

"He doesn't need to believe me. He can believe Bobby, or Brad, or Gabe. They all saw things; they all had stuff happen that they couldn't explain."

"They didn't receive the worst of it, though." Augusta gazed thoughtfully at Dahlia's hands.

"Gabe might argue."

"Gabe didn't almost die. You were the one she wanted. Maybe because you're a woman—it might be that simple. Or maybe because you were alone and angry." She used those words like she'd heard them before.

"What made you think that?" Dahlia asked.

"Dear, you wore it like a suit. But she picked you, that's my point. The time may come when you want someone, some-where, to understand. So, here, take the camera. I don't know much about these things, with their little memory chips and whatnot, but it was recording the night . . . the night that every-thing happened. Someday, you may want to see what it caught."

Then she rose from her seat, and closed her purse.

"Ms. Withrow?"

"Yes?"

"You knew they were buried there, didn't you? In the little family plot that wasn't supposed to be a plot at all."

She frowned, and for a second Dahlia thought she'd guessed incorrectly. "They? What do you mean, *they*?"

"Abigail and her boyfriend, the one she killed. Your grand-father buried them there, and he never said a thing."

Either Augusta Withrow was a world-class actress, or she was genuinely confused, and more than a touch appalled. "Good God, no. So that's where she went? Right down into the ground, next to the house?" She shuddered, and Dahlia caught a whiff of her hair spray. "No, darling. I only knew about the baby. She threw it in a ravine in the woods, but my father went and got it. He buried it in the fake cemetery, beneath a rosebush."

"I thought you said . . ."

"I know what I said. You didn't need to know every damn thing."

Dahlia turned that image over and over in her head after Augusta was gone. A boy who'd seen something terrible—and tried to do the right thing. Part of the right thing? Well, he did *some*thing. The overgrown plot was where everything secret went to disappear, so why not the poor little corpse. Why not his sister. Why not her lover.

Put them all in the ground. Plant the seeds, and harvest the ghosts.

In the morning, her father arrived as promised—with open arms and a big bouquet from everyone at Music City. She accepted the flowers and then the hug, and she returned it gently. She sniffed the flowers deeply, declaring them perfect.

Bobby and Gabe had already headed north to start sorting the inventory, and Brad was driving the other truck—so it was just Dahlia and Chuck on the way back to Nashville. They talked about safe things: the loot they'd acquired, and what the price tags would look like.

"My insurance premiums will surely rise like Easter morning, but this was still a good pick." Chuck's head bobbed heartily. "The copper on that roof alone, and the chestnut, and those mantels . . . and I saw the rose transom you pulled out. That thing'll go for a fortune!"

"It ought to. It hasn't got a crack, and that's a miracle."

"The big scene from the dining area, the one with the orchard, and the birds, and all that . . . it's got some damage— but it shouldn't cost more than a few hundred bucks to repair. Once it's fixed, I'm going to list it for about thirty-five hundred. We can get that easy, I think."

"List it for four," she suggested. "It's right up Teddy Milson's avenue, and he always tries to jack you down a few bucks."

"Good call, good call. I'll drop him an e-mail with a picture when we get it off the truck."

He said that like it'd happen with a click of ruby heels, or a snap of fingers. But back in Nashville, it took almost as long to unload the trucks and catalog the haul as it had to collect it from the estate. Dahlia insisted on participating, and her dad insisted that she stay home for at least another day or two—but when she came back, she still had a leisurely week of labeling boxes, calling some of their usual clients, and taking pictures for the Internet.

But not with Brad's old camera.

She kept that in her messenger bag, untouched. She didn't want to watch whatever it'd caught—not yet—but she couldn't bring herself to throw it away, either, and Brad had never asked about it. Maybe he'd assumed it was lost. Maybe he was glad it was gone.

Hard to blame him. Hard to blame anyone.

"Now, I don't know what happened back there," Chuck told her, as they sat in his office and finished off a pair of sandwiches from a nearby takeout place. "I don't expect you all to tell me, if you don't want to go into it."

"Good, then I won't. One of us needs to sleep at night, and you're the boss, so it'd better be you." She popped a potato chip into her mouth and chewed it slowly. She swallowed, and asked, "The um . . . the cemetery, though."

"What about it?"

"Daddy, come on. You saw the tarp. Brad or Bobby would've told you, I'm sure."

"About the soldier?" He took a big bite of his BLT and almost killed it off. "They told me."

"So what did you do about it? Did you report it to anybody?"

"Nope!" He shook his head. "Not our problem. Leave it for the wrecking crew, or the park service. We got the truck in past the closest grave—it was a squeak, but we didn't run anything over. Or anybody. I told Bobby to go throw some dirt down there, cover the hole back up again, but that was the full extent of my involvement. As far as you know, we never found a thing in that fake cemetery, or in the house, either."

"Just rats and bugs and bats."

"That's right, Dolly-girl, my Snow White child. Plausible deniability."

She toasted him with another chip. "To plausible deniability."

He toasted back with a bit of bacon. "I'm just sorry it got so crazy for you, so fast. In all seriousness, Dahl—if I'd known, I never would've taken the offer. I'd have sent that old lady packing so fast . . ."

No, he wouldn't have. He was too happy to assume the best, and ignore the worst. But hindsight is 20/20, and it's a goddamn liar.

"Then it's just as well you didn't know." She held up a tablet and showed him their eBay page. "Because Teddy's loss is some other dude's gain. A couple of guys got bidding on the orchard glass. It went for almost five grand."

Chuck whistled. "It hasn't been a week, and we're already on the verge of breaking even—with a third of the stock still sitting on the floor, and another third waiting in the storeroom. I'd list it now, but we don't have anyplace to put it! You know," he said, more quietly, less joyfully. "We really needed this. The way Nashville Erections screwed the pooch, if the Withrow place hadn't come through . . . I don't know."

"Yeah, Daddy. You *do* know." She scratched at the edge of her left-hand bandage, and stopped herself. "It doesn't matter, now. It may have been the worst job ever, but Gabe will be back on his feet in another few weeks, and once these wraps come off, I'll have some sexy-ass scars. Chicks dig scars."

"Are you switching teams?"

She laughed. "Hey, if the right girl came along and wanted to settle down, I'm sure we could work something out. If she's willing to look past my stitches, and she's handy with power tools, it might just be true love. For real, Daddy—next time I clean these cuts, I'm going to show you. It's gross as hell, but the swelling's gone down, and I've got some motion back already."

"You're doing all right with that tablet and stylus. With your sleeves pulled down, no one would ever know you did a slice-and-dice through a window."

"I'm just lucky that my left hand got the worst of it. The right one only got a couple dozen stitches. So long as I'm using those super-fat markers you keep around for labels, my handwriting looks just about normal . . . but the wraps do make for slow typing. Eh." She shrugged. "I was never very fast, anyhow."

"Atta girl. Look on the bright side." Chuck's phone chimed with a message. He checked it, and beamed. "Scars, broken bones, and all—the Withrows are the gift that keeps on giving!"

"What now?"

"Mountain Town Construction has put in for the chestnut!"

"I thought Graystone Building was taking it . . . ?"

Chuck vibrated with glee. "They made an offer. It was a good offer. But I wondered if Mountain Town wanted to make a better one."

"You're a greedy old man," she said with love. She got to her feet, wadded up her lunch trash, and tossed it into the can beside his desk. "And I'm a busy girl, so I'd better get back to it."

"Back to what? You're not overexerting, are you? You aren't supposed to overexert. I thought we made that clear. If you're going to overexert, you can just go home."

"I'm doing inventory, and stop saying 'overexert.' I'm just counting up and measuring the windows that Bobby sorted in the back, and I've got my handy-dandy screen here to do all the hard stuff for me, I promise."

"All right then. Hop to it."

She returned to the inventory corner and called out, "Hey, Bobby? You back from lunch yet?"

"In body, or spirit?"

"Whichever one is more likely to move those doors for me, because we're almost done with the windows—at long last, praise Jesus—and the doors are next."

He finished a bottle of beer with one long, drawn-out swallow and belched to punctuate the end. "Then my spirit is fucking useless, and my body will have to do. Gabe says it's not worth much—but he's one to talk right now."

"Is he here? I thought he wasn't coming back until tomorrow."

Bobby cocked his head toward the retail end of the warehouse. "He's manning the register, and playing Mr. Customer Service. So . . . mostly he's talking to girls and showing off his crutches. You should hear him." He chuckled around another burp, and reached for the last of the windows. Paint flaked away under his gloves, dusting the floor as he moved them to the far wall. "Making up stories about how it happened. To hear him tell it, he's practically Indiana Jones."

She grinned, and booted up the inventory program. "Yeah, I bet."

They finished up the first round of doors, sorting the interior six-panels from the eight-panels and the four-panels, and measuring up the exterior doors, except for the big front jobbie with the sidelights. The rose transom hadn't been original to the set, so she didn't mind splitting it up.

When all the door management was done, Bobby declared yet another beer break. Dahlia thought about arguing, but she was tired. It turned out that when you lose a lot of blood, it doesn't all just magically come back. Sure, they give you some in the hospital, but beyond a certain point, your body is expected to pitch in and help.

She needed a little rest, but she didn't want to admit it. "Fine, take your beer—and I'll take a bathroom break. I could stand to disinfect anyway, after handling all that old shit."

"*I* was the one doing most of the handling."

"You know what I meant."

"Whatever. See you in ten."

Chuck Dutton pawed through one of the Withrow boxes, wondering where its contents ought to go. It looked like a bunch of vintage women's wear, and God knew he had no clue how to price it or where to sell it. Perhaps Dahlia had planned to list it all online. More likely she wanted to keep it for herself. His daughter had a vintage clothing collection that grew by the year, though she almost never wore a stitch of it. He didn't judge. He collected ridiculous shit of his own. It ran in the family.

"Bobby?" he called out. His nephew was on the other side of a shelving unit full of windows, doors, and stray panes of glass.

"Uncle Chuck?" came the reply.

"Where's Dolly at?"

"Bathroom, I think. Greasing up her stitches. "

"All right." So he'd ask her about it when she got out.

While he waited, he shoved his fingers through the hats, feathers, and gloves, picking up a beaded bag and putting it down again. There was another one in there, more like a clutch. It was black and green, and the beads were good-quality glass— even a manly fashion know-nothing like him could see that at a glance, and feel it by the fabric's weight.

Something was inside it. Something stiff and crinkly.

He unfastened the clasp and found paper, folded over until it fit into the small hand purse. The paper was old . . . probably older than Chuck. It was brown at the edges, and along the seams.

"The hell is this?" he asked quietly, unfolding it with gentle fingers.

It was a set of sheet music, missing the cover. There were only three pages, printed front and back.

Chuck couldn't read music, but he knew a murder ballad when he saw one.

"THE FAMILY PLOT"

B. D. WITHROW

(1934)

Come all you wicked women,

And listen to this tale,
It's of a dreadful murder,
The truth I will reveal,
Near Lookout Mount in Tennessee,
A shocking deed I know,
It happened one September night
Not many years ago.

There was a young man, Greg'ry M.,
A soldier brisk and gay,
Likewise one Abby W.,
Fair as the rose of May.
This fighting lad and his fair maid,
Did close together dwell,
And soon in lust with this bright girl
Unwary Greg'ry fell.

It was the young man's folly,
He toyed with a heart so wild,
And soon, to her misfortune,
He got her quick with child.
Tongues wagged and people whispered,
Wondering if they ought to marry,
So she told her Greg'ry darling,
"They will soon know what I carry!"

It was one early autumn night,
When he to her did say,
"I like you true but love you not,
And soon, I'm on my way."
But at the bottom of the mountain

She did ask to say good-bye,
He told her he would meet her once,
If she promised not to cry.

Then in an attic room they met,
Where many an hour they'd passed,
But little did poor Greg'ry think,
That night would be his last.
Abby drew forth a jagged knife,
It was both long and sharp.
She seized his neck and plunged it
So deep into his heart.

Loud she heard her mother cry,
And then her father said,
"Oh God, my girl, look what you've done!
You've killed the young man dead!
We'll bury him in uniform,
Within our family plot,
We'll stash his bloody body
In the safest place we've got."

Father took the corpse outside
And wrapped it in a rug.
He found a place 'neath no man's stone
And there he dug and dug.
He buried him in uniform
Within the family plot.
He stashed the bloody body
In the safest place they'd got.

Though New Year came around and went,
No baby e'er was seen.
Abby birthed and drowned it on
The eve of Halloween.
Now the baby's buried too,
Within the family plot,
The little body's hidden
In the safest place she'd got.

Years went by and Abby snared
Another young man's eye,
They made a plan to marry
On the fourth of next July.
But when they met to celebrate
The secret was revealed!
When her brother told the guests
About the infant she had killed.

"Every word of that's a lie!"
Did Abby say out loud,
She swore an oath of innocence
Before the gathered crowd.
"There's never been a newborn child,
No murder did I do,
You should go and ask the Devil,
He can take me if it's true."

The Devil heard her offer,
He listened to her lies,
And up from hell he did appear

To seize his pretty prize.
Now Abby's buried right there, too,
Within the family plot.
Her mortal coil rests inside
The safest place he's got.

So if you are a young man
With a bonny maid to woo,
Be careful with the vows you make
And who you make them to.
For wicked girls will weave a web.
Be sure you don't get caught,
Lest you find yourself one day
Beneath a family plot.

Epilogue

D AHLIA TOOK HER bag into the bathroom, because she'd been toting around all the things she needed to care for her injuries. The special antiseptic, the antibiotic, the anti-whatever-else, and so forth, and so on. She hated changing the bandages, but she was getting to where she could clean things up fairly quickly and fairly neatly all by herself.

Bobby'd said ten minutes, but they both knew it'd be more like fifteen or twenty. It'd take her most of that time to sort her arms out anyway, which was the other reason she didn't complain about him taking advantage of their post-Withrow detente.

She closed the bathroom door and flipped on the light—a retro number scavenged from some old factory someplace that was just barely too new to call vintage, and entirely too ugly to charge money for, which is what it was doing in the employee bathroom. Outside, someone was running a forklift, moving those long chestnut boards into secured storage. When it rumbled up close to the bathroom wall, the fixture vibrated, and the yellow incandescent glow wobbled around the little room.

The bathroom was a single seater, which was fine when you only had half a dozen people on hand at any given time. It wasn't a big room, but it had a toilet and a sink, and a broken-down hutch that held cleaning supplies and toilet paper. Dahlia dropped her bag on top of it and pulled out the necessities. She lined them up on the hutch's lid, and glanced down into her bag.

And there was Brad's digital camera, in its black casing with its gray lanyard.

She still hadn't played whatever footage it'd captured, and now wasn't a good time to get curious. Twenty minutes at most, that's all she had—and she needed to spend it all cringing and dabbing at pink, puffy skin around black stitches. Besides, the battery was surely dead by now.

It wasn't even hers. She should give it back to Brad.

She *would* have given it back to him, but he'd quit the day she came home from the hospital. He just . . . handed in the keys to the truck, thanked her dad for the opportunity, and vanished back to grad school, or wherever that kind of guy goes when he's lost track of himself. She wished him well . . . and she halfway wished he'd taken his camera, so it wouldn't hang around tempting her like this.

The bathroom was cold, and her hands were cold—despite the bandages, and the sock-like covering she wore beneath her sleeves. The warehouse was always drafty, and this chill was ordinary and familiar. It wasn't fingers. It wasn't a shadow without any eyes.

She turned on the water. The pipe rattled, and the faucet handle shook.

While she waited for the cold stuff to turn warm, she pressed the camera's power button. She wasn't sure why.

The display lit up. The low-battery light flickered, but there was still enough juice to run it.

She shouldn't do this. She should turn it off and drop it into the waste bin beside the toilet. That would be the smart thing to do. It'd be the easy thing to do, for her fingers were stiff with healing, and with the washroom chill. It was always cold in there, wasn't it? Yes, but was it always *this* cold?

She pressed the back arrows to view the most recent file. It was forty minutes long, but the time and date stamp showed that yes, the video had been captured on *that* night. But Brad hadn't been wearing the camera, had he? He must've set it down someplace, or dropped it.

Dahlia pressed play.

She didn't plan to watch the whole thing. She wasn't going to sit through forty minutes of listening to herself scream. She only wanted to know where the camera had been—what room it had been watching. No way in hell she was going to torment herself with the rest.

With her mummy-wrapped left hand, she shielded the screen from the glare of the bulb overhead. She turned up the volume.

Mostly, she saw darkness. Mostly, she heard the rain and thunder, and the hiss of digital static from the speaker. But as she squinted at the display, broad strokes appeared: a straight line that turned out to be a windowsill, and the back of a chair. Brad had either dropped the camera or left it in the dining room.

She held it up to her ear, and heard the storm rage. She checked the screen. Still nothing but darkness, brightened for a second at a time when the lightning flashed it away.

She pushed the fast-forward button and saw nothing, until her own shadow came bursting in, looking for that bourbon. She recognized herself mostly by her posture and her gait, for the image was so dim it was heavily pixelated. Whatever camera model this was, its low-light recording was positively awful.

Dahlia knew what came next. She already knew there would

be screaming, and blood, and her own ungainly slither down the stairs. Suddenly, she wondered what her dad had done with all the bloody wood. He must've left it behind. She hadn't seen any of it in the batches so far.

He must've seen the blood. He must've known it was hers. The thought made her queasy.

She leaned back against the hutch and rested her weight beside her bag. The thought of her dad walking into that house and finding what looked like a murder scene . . . it must've been awful. No wonder he was so happy to avoid any discussion of what had happened there.

She fast-forwarded until she saw herself lying in a dark lump near the edge of the foyer. She knew it was her—that dying thing on the bare floor. The recording was low on details, and that was a mercy. She didn't really want to watch it, and when Bobby came yelling into the picture with a lantern, the screen went almost white before it adjusted.

And then it flashed, and the camera's green light went red. The screen went dark again, and it stayed that way.

Dahlia exhaled a quivery breath. She popped out the memory card, threw it into the toilet, and flushed, then chucked the camera itself into the waste bin beside the sink.

The "hot" water had finally kicked in, but the sink drained slowly, so it was a third full with steaming water, with more pouring in.

"Enough of that. Arms, me and you need a few minutes of quality time with some antiseptic." Her voice shook, and she didn't like that. She was only cold, and only recovering from something that almost killed her. She planted her hands on the sink, but didn't lean down. "And when we're done, we're talking to Daddy about throwing a space heater in here, I swear."

There was a flicker behind her, half-spotted in the mirror. A hint of movement, from something very close to her in that too-small space.

Dahlia smelled autumn leaves and rain. She heard wind, and tasted blood, and she glimpsed a figure in the mirror. It stood behind her, barely an impression of a young woman, a spill of dark hair, a yellow dress.

The lightbulb burst, and the room went white.

And the room went dark.